RISK WORTH TAKING

MUSIC FOR THE HEART - BOOK THREE

FAITH STARR

Music For the Heart 3: Risk Worth Taking

Copyright © 2017 by Faith Starr

All rights reserved. This copy is intended for the original purchaser of this e-book ONLY. No part of this e-book may be reproduced, scanned, or distributed in any printed or electronic form without prior written permission from Faith Starr. Please do not participate in or encourage piracy of copyrighted materials in violation of the author's rights. Purchase only authorized editions.

Image/art disclaimer: Licensed material is being used for illustrative purposes only. Any person depicted in the licensed material is a model.

E-Book ISBN:

Paperback ISBN:

Editors: Ann Curtis, Rebecca Fairfax, Faith Starr

Cover Artist: Kelly Martin

Published in the United States of America

This e-book is a work of fiction. While reference might be made to actual historical events or existing locations, the names, characters, places and incidents are either the product of the author's imagination or are used fictitiously, and any resemblance to actual persons, living or dead, business establishments, events, or locales is entirely coincidental.

Warning

This e-book contains sexually explicit scenes and adult language and may be considered offensive to some readers. This book is intended for sale to adults ONLY, as defined by the laws of the country in which you made your purchase. Please store your files wisely, where they cannot be accessed by under-aged readers.

∼

DISCLAIMER: Please do not try any new sexual practice without the guidance of an experienced practitioner. Faith Starr will not be responsible for any loss, harm, injury or death resulting from use of the information contained in any of her titles.

There is no love without forgiveness, and there is no forgiveness without love.

Bryant H. McGill

1

LOGAN

My heart pounded so hard vibrations sounded in my ears. I fucking loved it.

Stepping toward the edge of the stage, high on adrenaline, I flung my guitar pick into the sold-out crowd. They screamed and cheered because one lucky son of a bitch would now have a souvenir from the band to take home.

Trevor did the same with his drum sticks. Poor Joey, our keyboardist, had nothing to give. He blew air kisses. *Pussy.*

Joey, Trevor, and I made our final bows then headed off to the wing. Our roadies handed us towels to dry off.

"Fucking great show!" I fist bumped the air and jumped up and down, my thoughts and movements still on overdrive, the fuel igniting me burning me up inside. A mind-blowing feeling.

"Fantastic show." Trevor clapped his hands, feeling my vibe, shifting from foot to foot.

"Time for a well-deserved break." Joey nodded.

A mini-vacation had been on Joey's mind for quite a while. It had actually been on all our minds. This would be our last show for this leg of the tour. We now had a three-week break until we had to hit the road again, and I couldn't wait to take full advantage of every second of our time off.

Our band, Steam, had become über popular over the past year. We steadily climbed the charts with several of our songs. Things were changing for the better, but with that came a lot more responsibility and a lot less privacy. I'm not going to lie, I took full advantage of the celebrity lifestyle with the abundance of women that came along with it, but I also missed the ability to do ordinary things. And that was why I had a vacation planned starting the following morning at the Addison Family Ranch located in the middle of nowhere in the California mountains. Away from civilized life as I knew it. My family had taken me there every summer during my childhood years, so I continued the tradition as an adult, minus the folks.

The guys and I cruised over to the sitting area where Teva, Joey's girlfriend, and Dani, Joey's twin sister, cowriter for the band, and assistant, who also happened to be Trevor's girlfriend, anxiously waited to celebrate with their men. I couldn't wait to get out of Dodge. The guys had gone from groupies to double dates. I needed a breather from my lovesick bandmates.

"Before you all rush off and celebrate, I wanted to have a quick briefing, since I know you will be heading in different directions tomorrow. But trust me, that doesn't mean you won't be hearing from me." Camilla, our feisty manager, smirked, and gestured for us to come together.

The guys, their girlfriends, and I gathered on the small sofas. We mashed together like sardines since the room was so small. And fuck sitting on the floor. By the looks of it, the carpet probably hadn't been cleaned in years.

"First of all, don't forget we have the video shoot in New York in two weeks. While there, we'll promote our next single on the alternative satellite radio station. I already have an interview lined up for you guys. We'll also be doing a charity visit to a local hospital. The story will be mentioned on a nightly entertainment show. You know me. I'm all about publicity, boys. I've also been contacted by a producer interested in your sound. He wants to speak with Joey and Dani about possibly writing something for a film project he's working on.

There's lots of good stuff in the works. Let's keep the train moving forward."

Guess my break wouldn't be much of one after all.

"Teva and I are leaving town tomorrow for ten days," Joey reminded her.

"I know. Have fun. Just be in New York when you're supposed to be. All your flight-arrangement itineraries have been e-mailed to you. Please review the information prior to heading out so that there are no surprises. Most importantly, enjoy yourselves on your break. You've all worked extremely hard. But be ready to come back and kill the rest of the tour."

Trevor nodded along with Dani. They had no plans of leaving town, deciding to stay local and chill.

"Excellent. I'll also send you an e-mail summing up what we spoke about in case some of you weren't listening. The next item on my agenda concerns one of Logan's fans."

All eyes went to me with Camilla's carrying the most intensity. I shifted uncomfortably in my seat, feeling as though I had done something wrong when I knew I hadn't. At least I didn't think I had.

Camilla had a passion for busting my balls. I immediately went on the defensive and crossed my arms, figuring the poor guys huddled under my dick were about to get crushed again.

"We've been receiving a lot of mail from the same fan. It usually doesn't faze me when we get repeated letters, but this person is reaching out more frequently, saying she's followed the band around to several cities and knows you personally on a first-name basis. She claims you mean a lot to her. I don't know whether anything will come of it, if she's a mere teenager with a celebrity crush, or if she's the stalker type. But either way, I'm keeping abreast of the situation and will keep you up-to-date if anything changes. Right now, our media team isn't responding to her. But we've made a file for her mail in case this turns into something bigger."

I shrugged, blowing off her warning, relieved she hadn't cornered me on something that actually held some weight. Not that I wouldn't stand up to her, but my mind and body had shifted gears into vacation mode. I wanted up and out.

The girl was probably just another fan who wanted to get up close and personal to the band, me in particular. Interesting that the girl said she knew me, though. Then again, fans claimed to know us on a regular basis because we were pasted all over the Internet. Therefore, I brushed it off as nothing.

"Please don't blow this off, Logan."

Son of a bitch if Camilla didn't constantly read my thoughts.

"I'm simply putting it out there so you're aware of it."

Fine, I'm aware of it. Now please move on.

Hurray! She shifted her attention toward the others. "I'm sure you're all cognizant of the fact that not all fans have good intentions. I'm keeping a close eye on this situation for now, so you have nothing to worry about. But keep it in mind."

Christ. And here I thought she had finished with me.

"That's pretty much all I have for you, unless any of you have anything on your minds you want to bring up or discuss?"

She surveyed us, all of us silent, shaking our heads to her question.

"Oh yeah, one more thing. In case I didn't mention it previously, enjoy your holiday, relax, and do whatever it is you want *without getting into trouble or making headlines.*" She flashed me a hard grin. "Although in this business, any press is good press."

Why did she zero in on me and not the others when she made that specific request? Sure, I took top honors as the manwhore of the bunch, but still, I took insult to her comment. Fucking Joey and Trevor didn't do a good job of hiding their snickers either.

"Don't look so disappointed, Logan. I only speak the truth."

Again with the mind reading.

I hoped she could hear the big *fuck you* I currently said to her in my mind.

This time the girls chucked along with Joey and Trevor. They obviously knew the thoughts going on in my head.

2

DREW

The fluffy white clouds were an arm's length distance away. I wanted to reach through the small oval window and touch them. Sure, I knew they were basically water vapor and ice crystals, but I allowed my imagination to run wild, especially when I had never been this close to them, other than when I had walked through fog, which didn't count.

Crap! I grabbed my sister's hand, squeezing the life out of it.

"Ouch," she huffed, trying to shake me loose. She gaped at me.

"What was that?" My heart picked up speed. I tapped my foot nervously on the dirty carpet.

A *ding* in the aircraft caused me to peer up at the fasten seatbelt image, now brightly lit.

Focus on your breath.

Closing my eyes and placing my free hand over my chest helped me do just that. I didn't want my panic to escalate to the point of hyperventilation. The worst part about being in this plane was that I had no means of escape. I was confined in a flying vehicle, riding ten-thousand feet above the ground for the next hour or two, thanks to my sister, Kate. Something I'd had no forethought into. It had kind of been thrust upon me.

Did I say yet how much I hated to fly? Now would be a good time to do so.

So here I sat in the narrow confines of my seat on my very first plane ride, getting tossed up and down like we were on a carnival ride. Did I mention I also detested rides with lots of movement?

My purse had multiple pockets in it. I dug through all of them in search of the travel-sickness medication I had brought along with me 'just in case'. The turbulence wreaked havoc on my equilibrium.

"You'll be fine, Drew. You need to chill out. You're stressing me out, and I have enough on my mind. I can't worry about you as well."

Why did I agree to go on this trip with her?

"Gee, thanks for the love." My sarcasm couldn't have been any more obvious.

"Don't mention the word *love* to me. I just got my heart stomped on, and here you are, thinking about yourself." She reached for a tissue inside her pocketbook.

Oh man, here we go again.

And for the record, I was thinking about myself right now, mostly about how I'd be able to tolerate getting through an entire week with my crabby sister.

"Give it some time. It's still an open wound. Be in the mindset that this trip will provide you with a breather to relax and come to terms with what happened."

She gawked. "Open wound? More like a heart ripped in two. Do you have a needle and thread?"

Blankly, I stared at her.

"I didn't think so. If you did, I'd ask you to sew it back together for me."

Jeez, what a drama queen.

"Kate, I get it. But if it was going to happen, isn't a small part of you glad it happened before the wedding rather than after? I mean, if Joe was so uncertain, at least he didn't go through with it, which would've hurt a hell of a lot worse."

"That's where you're wrong. I don't think you get it at all. You've never been in love. You've never had someone dote all over you."

Excuse me? Maybe she didn't consider the long-term relationship

I'd had back in high school love, but I had. My heart never got over it, either. Probably because I caught the jerk cheating on me. Yup, you want to talk about devastation. He had been my first everything, including my best friend and confidant. All of it lost in a heartbeat.

Crock.

Of.

Shit.

All these years later I was still on the mend, completely closed off to other men as a result. So in this instance – come to think of it, most every instance – I disagreed with my sister. I got the hurting part firsthand, and it angered me that she negated my feelings and my one and only experience in the love department, pretending my relationship had little to no significance.

"It is what it is. It's horrible what he did to you, but you can't change it." Did my annoyance slip through in my tone? Eh, I didn't care. She had put me on edge.

"Don't you think I know that?"

She needed a shrink to tag along with her on this honeymoon, not me.

Yeah, her honeymoon. Her fiancé, Joe, should have been sitting in my seat. The jerk walked down the aisle at their wedding and decided he couldn't go through with it. What a good time had by all. I say that with a scowl on my face and sarcasm in my tone.

The best part was she had planned her honeymoon at the very same ranch my ex used to visit year after year with his family.

"Hello?" She nudged my arm.

Lord help me.

"Yes, Kate. I know that."

"Then please be a little sympathetic about my situation."

"Am I not on your honeymoon with you?"

I'd tried talking her out of leaving town, informing her that running away wouldn't solve anything, but she wanted no part of my logical thinking. She claimed she needed out, the sooner the better, so she wouldn't have to face the humiliation and questioning from friends and family in her heartbroken state.

"I couldn't very well let the trip go to waste, and I sure as shit wasn't letting Joe go. Let him stay home and explain his horrific behavior to our family and friends. Besides, you know we paid for the trip in advance and the ranch has a no-refund policy."

"Which is why I'm here with you, right?"

That was me, forever the good daughter who stepped up to the plate when necessary. Unlike my sister who only thought about herself and gave both of my parents plenty of heartache with her wild ways.

"Thank you, Drew." She dried her damp cheeks.

The plane bumped up and down. I clenched my muscles.

Screw this. I popped the pill out of the silver sleeve and swallowed the medicine whole without a drink, only to realize afterward it was a chewable. Oh well. Hopefully swallowing it wouldn't minimize its effectiveness. And with any luck it would kick in soon. The dizziness from the motion was getting worse by the minute. I also hoped the pill would put me to sleep. The box stated drowsiness *may* occur. I prayed I'd get that side effect. Anything but to have to endure this bumpy flight and Kate's constant replay of her wedding ceremony that had gone to hell in a handbag.

3

LOGAN

The flight flew by at record speed. Not literally. A funny thought, though. Perhaps it felt as such because I'd slept during most of it. I also couldn't wait to reach my destination, counting the minutes until I would be in the great outdoors instead of cooped up in a tour bus for hours on end, weeks upon weeks, months upon months.

Susanna and Jack, the owners of the ranch, made it a habit to send their private van to the airport to collect the new batch of guests. They ran the ranch like a camp with a start and end day. A person couldn't just show up during the week. Reservations had to be made months in advance. There were planned activities, some structured, some not. Most, if not all, of which I didn't attend.

They kept the groups intimate, only allowing at most fifteen guests to visit during a session. They loved to personally get to know every visitor. Susanna and Jack were awesome.

With guitar in hand, I exited the plane and zipped through the crowd to baggage claim. That's where I saw Brian, Susanna and Jack's son and ranch hand.

"Hey bro." He pulled me in for a semi-hug, both of us patting each other on the back.

"Good to see you. Where's Layla?"

"She's out front with the van. Some of the other guests arrived earlier."

"Excellent. I've got my duffel and my guitar. I'm good to go."

"How's the tour going?"

"Great. No complaints on my end. But I'm definitely ready for a little R and R."

"Good luck getting my parents to give you some." He chuckled. "They have a busy week planned for you guys."

"They know I'm not one to follow the rules."

He smirked. "I know that all too well."

We chatted for a good fifteen minutes while waiting for a family of four, the last of the guests to arrive, before going outside to board the bus.

"Why don't you all climb aboard and make yourself comfortable? I'll go ahead and load the baggage in back." Brian got right to it.

Layla exited from the driver's side to assist him.

"Logan, it's so good to see you." She gave me a loving hug, in a sisterly fashion. "You look great as always."

The three of us had known each other since we first started walking. I viewed the Addisons as family.

"As do you. You're as beautiful as ever."

She blushed and slapped my arm.

"You better not let Eddie hear you speak to her like that, even though you mean no harm by it," Brian warned in his Southern drawl.

"Who's Eddie?" I stood behind the van and assisted with the luggage. My guitar stayed firmly in my grasp. I would never let my baby get thrown on top of a pile of suitcases.

"My fiancé." She flashed me her sparkly engagement ring.

"Well, I'll be damned. Eddie's a lucky guy." I nodded in agreement with my sentiment.

Risk Worth Taking

We finished loading the suitcases and closed the back doors. Since I was the last guest to get in the van, I got the shit seat next to two teenagers. At least I had my headphones to tune them out if and when they began arguing with each other. We had about an hour and a half trek to the ranch.

The teen girl's eyes lit up when I sat next to her, her mouth falling open.

"You're Logan Trimble of Steam, aren't you?" She slapped her hand over her mouth.

"In the flesh. And you are?" I offered my hand to shake hers.

She shook mine straightaway. "Jordana. I'm a *huge* fan." She blinked rapidly.

"It's nice to meet you, Jordana."

"You too." She squirmed in her seat and accidently hit her brother. He shoved her.

"Stop moving. I don't have much room as it is."

"Don't mind him." She brushed him off with her hand. "He's my obnoxious brother, Camden." She elbowed him in the ribs and gave him a dirty look.

"Keep your hands to yourself." He pushed her again.

"Both of you, enough. It's been a long trip, and I'm already tired of your arguing." The father intervened.

Jordana's cheeks flushed in embarrassment. She crossed her hands on her lap and bowed her head.

That was fun. I retrieved my headphones from my backpack and tuned in to music on my phone. I had officially ended the meet-and-greet portion of the ride. Susanna would make introductions between the guests later at the welcome dinner, but she made it a point every year to respect my privacy by not mentioning my celebrity status directly. She kept it on the down low as much as possible and asked guests to refrain from taking photos of other guests unless given permission to do so. That rule she enacted on my behalf.

My stomach gurgled, which reminding me of Susanna's cooking. She made everything from scratch. Her meals were better than any five-star restaurant I'd ever eaten at. I couldn't wait to get there and eat up.

It was a long-ass, bumpy ride. Thank goodness by the time we arrived at the ranch the afternoon heat had begun to dissipate, bringing in some cooler air. Nights in the California mountains required a sweatshirt, days T-shirts and shorts, the perfect balance of hot and cold.

Layla gave us a brief rundown of the schedule for the evening, then dropped each group off at their respective cabins, a schedule I had no intention of following other than the welcome dinner. S'mores at a bonfire with a bunch of families? Uh-uh. So not my thing. I pretty much kept to myself at the ranch, regrouping and playing music on the rocking chair in front of my cabin. It was something I cherished every year, along with participating in other solitary activities that helped ground me and keep me humble in a less chaotic world, one free from the paparazzi and chaotic lifestyle I had become so accustomed to.

My duffle got placed on the luggage stand inside my cabin. Sure, there were dressers and a closet, but I preferred to live out of a suitcase, something I did often and did well. Besides, I didn't want to waste any more time.

With guitar in hand, I stepped outside onto the deck, where I sat my ass on the hardwood rocking chair. I lifted my baby out of its case and began to strum, tapping my foot and breathing in the fresh air.

Ah, it didn't get better than this, the fucking life.

4

DREW

Talk about feeling grateful. Kate and I had a two-bedroom cabin. I didn't understand why, since she and Joe were supposed to be honeymooning, but I had no complaints whatsoever. Hey, I was all for sharing, but sleeping next to my sister in a bed for a week? No thank you. That was where I drew the line.

"Let's go explore the grounds." Kate stood in the doorway to my room, her excitement evident in her gestures and tone.

"I want to get settled first." I unpacked my shorts and placed them in a dresser drawer; my mind zoning out and wondering if *he'd* ever stayed in this cabin with his parents.

Stop thinking about him.

How could I not, especially knowing my ex had slept in these very cabins during his many visits to the ranch.

Deeply, I exhaled, that all too familiar pain in my chest making its presence known.

"Get settled later. This place is gorgeous. Let's go take a walk. Besides, dinner's in an hour."

"You go on ahead. I'm going to stay here and unpack. I'll meet up with you at dinner."

The words *vital*, *crucial*, and *critical* didn't do a good job of describing my mind's urgent longing for a break from Kate. She made me absolutely crazy. More importantly, my emotions were out of whack. I needed to get them in check.

She sighed in an obnoxious manner. "I hope you're not going to isolate yourself in this room for the entire week."

To reiterate, Kate made me crazy. Still, I bit my tongue. She knew damn well my ex used to vacation at this ranch and that it had to be difficult for me to be here. But then again, I had to keep in mind it was Kate I was dealing with, so she probably had no clue, and if she did, wouldn't care less. I clenched my jaw, the condescending tone in her voice like nails scratching across a blackboard. Ugh. Both of them were horrible sounds to have to endure.

"We just got here. I want to unpack and get myself situated. Please, go take a walk and explore the grounds." *I beg of you.* I shooed her away.

She huffed. "Fine. I'll see you in an hour."

She stormed down the hall. The screen door slammed behind her. Good riddance.

Finally, some peace and quiet. I plopped on the bed in relief. The plane ride had been anything but relaxing. I didn't mean to sound unsympathetic to Kate's situation. I honestly felt horrible about it, but my sister's defense mechanism since birth had been to belittle me when she became upset, something I wanted no part of. Especially since I was currently dealing with my own troubled feelings. She had no concept of the word boundaries, knew nothing of them or how to respect them; therefore, my words of rebuttal when she spoke to me in a harsh tone went in one ear and out the other. *Adios. Bye-bye.*

After resting for a few minutes, I finished putting my clothes away. In the bathroom, I washed up and applied a touch of lip gloss and eyeliner. I had only packed a few essentials from my makeup stash because I had no intention of wearing much of it, figuring most of the activities I planned to participate in over the course of the week would be spent outdoors in the presence of families and couples. Need I say more?

Ah, the great outdoors. I kicked rocks along the dirt road that led to the dining hall.

The soft sounds of a guitar being played caught my attention.

A guy sat on a rocking chair, strumming a beautiful melody. I closed my eyes, relishing the sound.

Wait a second.

The playing and chord building sounded awfully familiar.

No way. It couldn't be. What were the odds?

The shock at the likelihood hit me like a ton of bricks, the anticipation killing me. My heart now raced at the possibility of such a freakish coincidence. I wiped the back of my neck with my sweaty palm and tried to sneak a peek at the master musician, but the damn wooden columns which led from the railing to the overhang in front of his cabin hid his face.

The insanity taking place inside my brain was wreaking havoc on my nervous system. I sighed at the absurdity of my thoughts. My ex had come here years ago as a teen with his family. Sure, he had probably returned for visits now and again, but with fifty-two weeks in a year, I couldn't imagine the probability of running into him during my stay.

But then again, anything could happen, right?

I shivered at the mere thought.

The guy played magnificently, with brilliant precision. The soothing rhythm flooded me with memories of my ex. He had adored his guitar too, possibly more than life itself.

Shit!

I stumbled, too wrapped up in my head to concentrate on the uneven path beneath me. At least I didn't fall. Nor did I get the guy's attention.

Thank God. I didn't want a stranger seeing me topple over on my ass.

Upon arriving at the dining hall, I spotted Kate chatting with two women. I approached and politely waited for her to finish speaking before introducing myself.

She acknowledged me, smiling. "Drew, this is Erin and Jan."

"It's nice to meet you two."

"They're celebrating their five-year anniversary." Kate beamed.

"Happy anniversary."

"Do you two want to join us for dinner?" Jan asked.

I wondered whether Kate had informed them we were sisters or if the women thought me and Kate were *involved*.

"Sure."

My sister agreed on my behalf without giving me the opportunity to speak for myself. Not that I cared. If anything, with any luck, chatting with these ladies would distract her from her depressing thoughts about Joe and me from my nagging thoughts about my ex.

The four of us sat around a table as others gathered inside the open space. There were several tables set up, which could hold about eight diners each. I scanned the room, feeling curious about who we would be spending the next week with.

That was when *he* walked in.

And by he, I was referring to the most gorgeous man I had ever laid my eyes on, that being my ex, Logan Trimble, in the flesh.

Air. I was desperate for more of it. The extra oxygen from deep breathing did nothing to satisfy my lungs. It felt like I was dying a slow death. I sucked in another mouthful of air. What the fuck?

Shit! Shit! Shit!

With my elbows leaning on the table, I buried my face in my hands. I had to get the hell out of the room. A feeling of suffocation overtook me, the walls closing in on me.

When I took a sneak peek around me, I discovered Kate staring at me, her brows furrowed.

Think. Think. Think.

. . .

"I have to use the restroom." A good excuse. Albeit, the total understatement of the century. "Please excuse me." I eased my chair back and rose, making sure not to face him. I dashed to the exit at lightning speed.

Once outside on the deck, I tried to calm myself but quickly discovered slow breathing wasn't helping. Nor did watching the Addisons' dogs, who waited by the exit to the dining hall, in the hopes of getting leftovers from guests. My stomach understood their desire for food.

My hands—and my body—trembled out of control. This couldn't be happening. I wasn't in the right mindset for the showdown which would invariable take place between me and Logan. I'd given that man my heart, for years, and in return, he cheated on me, the asshole.

The disgusting image of the event, the one when I walked in on him and that bimbo getting hot and heavy at his friend and bandmate, Joey Fine's house, caused me to scowl.

Jerk!

Back and forth, I paced on the deck, thinking maybe moving would help stop the jitters. If only.

Of all the places Logan could be, he had to visit the ranch now? While Kate and I were here? I wanted to slap myself just to convince myself I was truly awake, at the total irony of it all.

Switching things up, I stopped the pacing and rocked instead, almost like a psych patient would, trying to bring some sense of inner calm. For all intents and purposes, my present situation could almost be described as sheer insanity.

Ooh, a rocking chair.

I contemplated sitting on the old wooden thing, maybe adding a bit of eerie music in the background to go along with the lunacy taking place in my mind and body. Yup. I could definitely pass as certifiable.

My stomach grumbled, hungry. I made small circles over it. *Yeah, that will really satisfy the emptiness in it.* But I couldn't go back inside, not ready to face him yet. No way, no how. If I could at all. *Ugh!* I buried my face in my hands. This royally sucked.

Maybe the ranch offered room service. *Nah, probably not.* The place wasn't a resort in any sense of the word. It housed private cabins with full kitchens. Great, right? No, because I had no food to prepare in mine.

Wait *a second*.

The owners had left a small basket of treats on our kitchen table. That could work in my favor. Hmm, how many granola bars would it take to provide me with enough nutrition to sustain me for the next few days, so I could remain in *isolation*? Kate's stupid reprimand, not mine. Now I had a justifiable reason to not spend every waking moment with her on this trip. Woohoo! Let's hear it for positive thinking.

Anxiety fueled me as I grasped the full impact of my situation. Logan Trimble was here. *He was here!* And so was I. *Fuck!*

Hold on. This was absurd. I mean, come on. I couldn't hide from him all week. Sooner or later, he would see me. So why postpone the inevitable? Besides, why should I be the one in hiding? *He* should. Mr. Guilty Party.

My heart racing, I put my big girl pants on and walked over to the screen door. The problem was I didn't feel so big right now, self-consciousness consumed me.

How do I look?
Is my make up still in place?
Let him eat his heart out!
Wait, is my hair a mess?

More importantly, did this ranch have medics in case I suffered heart failure? With my heart's current state of overdrive, there was an actual possibility for some myocardial mayhem.

Anger suddenly filled me. How could he still affect me so profusely? And why did I continue to give him power over me?

Like I have a choice in the matter, a small voice said.

Shit, now my own thoughts betrayed me too.

On a five count, I inhaled and exhaled, trying to regain my focus.

. . .

Maybe he won't recognize me.

Yes! The thought totally uplifted my spirits. My hair had been shorter back in the day.

Who was I kidding? I rolled my eyes at my brain's poor attempt at trying to come up with an excuse to save me from this hell.

With one final deep breath, I opened the door and stepped inside. *Whew.*

I couldn't have picked a better time to enter. Susanna rang a small bell in front of the room to gather the group's attention. Her husband, Jack, stood by her side. Everyone focused on them which gave me the opportunity to slide in unnoticed and grab a chair in the back of the room. The buffet, though, being located behind Susanna, meant I couldn't get to it from here. *Darn it!* Eating would have to wait. My stomach growled in protest.

"Welcome to the Addison Family Ranch. We're so happy to have you here with us for the next week. I hope everyone's had a chance to meet one other. And if not, don't worry. After dinner we're hosting a bonfire, where we'll make introductions. There will be plenty of opportunities to make new and hopefully lifelong friends during the course of your stay. As an aside, we encourage you to capture as many memories as you can on your cameras and on video, but we ask that you please respect the privacy of other guests and not take pictures or videos of others without prior consent."

Her gaze flicked to Logan.

Yup, he had certainly made something of himself over the years. Had I?

"Every night we will post the schedule for the next day's activities right here." She pointed to a large white dry-erase board mounted on a wall. I didn't bother to read it. My interest remained fixed on the back of Logan's head, his hair still shaggy and yes, still beautiful.

I wonder if it's still as soft.

With that thought ringing in my head, I forced myself to check out the itinerary on the dry-erase board because staring at Logan wasn't doing me any good. My thoughts kept wandering back to when we were together.

I sighed and rested my elbow on the table, chin in fist.

Damn Logan Trimble!

"We'll be dividing you into groups for all the activities," Susanna continued, "which will happen on a rotation basis. After dinner our son, Brian, will organize you into groups by name and number. Please take note of which group you'll be in prior to going to bed tonight, so you'll know where you have to meet up in the morning for your first activity. We'll keep you plenty busy with lots of fun outdoor adventures, but if you find you want to take a break, please let one of our staffers know beforehand. We'd hate for other guests to miss out on their scheduled activity if a staffer has to wait for you to show up. If you find you're running late for whatever reason, please come to the dining hall. I'm usually in here prepping meals. I can either escort you to your group or have you join another group, depending on what the activity is and its location on the ranch."

It would probably be beneficial for me to let the staffers know tonight I'd be holed up with my e-reader. That way they wouldn't be expecting me to show up for any of the scheduled activities. I had downloaded a few good books at the airport prior to departing, so I had more than enough to keep me occupied while here.

"Brian, Layla, Andrea, Kyle, Bruce, Stephen, Patty, and Taylor will be leading the groups and assisting around the ranch. Feel free to ask them for assistance as well as me and Jack. We're here to make this vacation as relaxing and carefree for you as possible. I don't expect you to have all their names memorized by the morning, but by week's end, trust me, you'll know each and every one of them by heart. They're going to give you a vacation to cherish. So, with that being said, I'm not going to take up any more of your time because I'm sure you're all starving. Please come up and help yourself to our delicious buffet. Everything's fresh and home-cooked daily by me, Patty, and Andrea. For those of you who informed me in advance that you follow a vegetarian diet, those dishes are on the left side of the buffet. Bon appétit."

She waved her hand over the buffet and stepped behind it to help serve with some of the other employees. Jack assisted in keeping the line of guests flowing smoothly, joking around and talking with each person who passed by him.

So far, I found the place to be extremely welcoming. The smell of the food alone put me in a semi-hypnotic state. Too bad I couldn't eat any of it. I wanted to wait for the mad rush to dissipate, especially for the tall, well-built hunk of a man named Logan Trimble to get his meal and perhaps take it to go. Yeah, I know—wishful thinking on my part.

Kate spotted me and approached.

"Why're you sitting back here?"

"Because when I came back from the restroom, Susanna was talking to the group. I didn't want to interrupt." God willing, she'd buy my rationale.

"Well, now she's finished and dinner's ready. Come on. Let's go get something to eat. It smells fantastic in here. I'm starving." She licked her lips.

For once I agreed with her, my stomach begging for whatever Susanna served that intoxicated my sense of smell. Unfortunately, Kate would be the only one tasting that decadent food. The small amount of confidence I thought I had gained walking back into the dining hall must have decided to chill outside with the fresh air and the Addisons' dogs.

My hands still trembled with fear of the unknown. Pretty pathetic, I know. But that was how deeply Logan had hurt me, and my heart had never recovered because of the pain he had inflicted on it.

There was no way around it—I'd simply have to wait until he finished eating and left the building.

"Are you okay?" Kate gave me a thorough inspection from head to toe.

Wow, how touching that she'd actually detected my unusual behavior. For the most part, she remained too consumed in her own thoughts to take notice of others around her.

"My stomach's a little upset." I rubbed it and scrunched my nose to make my lie sound more plausible. "It's probably from all the traveling. You go on ahead. I think I'll go sit outside and get some fresh air. I'll come back inside when I'm feeling better."

She shrugged and left for the buffet line. She evidently hadn't caught sight of Logan yet, because if she had, she would've been chewing his ear off and pointing in my direction.

I stepped out onto the deck again and sat on the wooden rocking chair, using my feet to push me back and forth at a slow and steady pace. I didn't understand why I continued to torture myself. In the big picture, the situation regarding me and Logan was no big deal. People ran into their exes every day, and the world didn't come to an end. Except in my case: did those people carry around as much baggage as I did over my failed relationship?

My stomach gurgled so loud one of the dog's ears perked up and he looked over at me. *Shit.* I couldn't go much longer without nourishment. I didn't want to pass out from low blood sugar.

On the bright side, maybe the guests would be finishing up soon and leaving the dining hall to head over to the bonfire.

Okay, Drew, you can do this. It's time to walk the plank. I certainly didn't want or need an audience witnessing the dreadful occurrence.

The three or four steps to the dining hall entrance felt more like three or four miles as I trudged to the door. Peeking through the screen door, I saw guests beginning to shuffle out on the other side of the building. *Yes!* What a relief. Perchance I'd be lucky and get to ride solo in my quest for food.

The dining hall hummed with the few remaining guests when I entered, most of them bringing their empty dishes to the counter for washing.

I hightailed it over to the buffet line, where staff members had already removed most of the food. Damn. It was slim pickings by this point, but I didn't care. Beggars couldn't be choosers. So I gathered what scarce food remained and sat at an empty table. I scanned the room, noticing a couple of stragglers chatting over tea and coffee. Fortunately for me, Logan had never been the chitchatting type. He wasn't one of them.

With closed eyes, I made a silent prayer of thanks for his absence, then opened them and dug in to my food. The macaroni and cheese tasted as scrumptious as it smelled and even after all this time, was still hot.

Too hot.

Ouch!

I burned my tongue. I fanned my mouth and went to take a drink when I realized I had forgotten to get myself one.

Shit. I hurried over to the beverage bar, poured myself a glass of ice water, and took huge gulps.

Mmm. It felt so good, washing the remnants of scalding-hot food down. I drank some more for good measure. That was when I felt *his* presence, his *all-consuming* presence.

"Excuse me." He reached in front of me to get a glass.

Great! He didn't recognize me.

For added insurance, I admired the wall opposite us.

So far so good.

My glass could use a refill, but I waited for him to finish filling his cup with lemonade first.

When I turned around, his gaze caught mine and my eyes widened.

"Drew?"

He stepped back, staring at me.

I could tell he had the same amount of awe going on as I did. At least I'd had a breather to prepare myself for our chance meeting. Not that it helped calm me down in any way, shape, or form.

Shit! Shit! Shit!

My palms had begun to sweat so profusely I thought I'd drop my glass. I set it on the counter next to us.

"Hi, Logan. Fancy meeting you here." I hated my nervous giggle. It always showed up at the most opportune times, like now.

The corners of his lips rose. I'd seen the gesture on multiple occasions. He was amused. *Jerk.* His smile got my heart beating faster every damn time.

"What're you doing at Addison Ranch?"

Was that delight in his voice? Say what? I hadn't expected him to be so thrilled to see me yet my psyche welcomed it.

"I guess I could ask you the same question."

"I'm here for some R and R." He swiped his hand through his hair. "Wow, I can't believe you're here. You look fantastic."

It didn't get missed that he gave my body a once-over. Let's hear it for the minimal amount of makeup I'd put on. I guess some of it remained on my face after all.

I dried my hands on my shorts and picked up my glass. I took a few sips of water, hoping that would help my overly dry throat and numb tongue. The darn liquid didn't want to go down, though. Swallowing became a struggle.

"I'm here with Kate, my sister. Do you remember her?"

"Of course I remember Kate. I guess things must be better between the two of you if you're vacationing together."

His eyes narrowed; suspicion in them. He knew there had to be more to the story. He and I had been together long enough that he knew all about Kate. In fact, he'd never been fond of her mean-girl style of dealing with people.

"No, things aren't better. We're here on her honeymoon."

His brow went down. "Her honeymoon?"

"Yeah. The groom changed his mind at the altar, so here I am." I put my hand up to emphasize my pretend enthusiasm, spilling water out of my cup in the process. I ignored the mess. Logan glanced at the small puddle on the floor but didn't say anything.

"That's fucked-up. Guess her loss is my gain."

Huh? My confusion must've given me away, because he clarified.

"We're both here together." He pointed between the two of us.

"I wouldn't quite say we're here *together*."

Shut up, mouth!

He chuckled at my comment.

"I was just about to eat dinner." I didn't know why I'd said that. He hadn't asked. My nerves had me saying stupid shit in an attempt to fill the awkward silence.

"Mind if I join you?"

Say what?

I blinked so much, I probably resembled someone with a nervous twitch disorder.

"Sure, why not?" I forced my lips to smile without quivering and took some deep, calming breaths as I traipsed to the table. The deep breaths didn't do shit to help calm me down, and with Logan following so close behind me, I caught a whiff of his cologne.

Ugh! He still wore my favorite scent.

Stupid jerk.

And why did the few short steps to the table feel more like a two-mile jog?

5

LOGAN

Well, I'll be damned. And to think, I'd wanted to bolt after dinner. Bumping into Drew? Shit, the last thing I ever expected to happen, especially out here in the boondocks. I found it to be almost surreal. And yet here she was, as beautiful as I remembered but sporting longer hair. Her sparkling green eyes still brightened up her entire face. And her smile? Fuck, it could light up the sky on the darkest of nights.

I wondered if she still hated me. Not that I'd blame her if she did. I'd royally fucked things up between the two of us. And despite the fact that I took full responsibility for my actions, it still felt like she'd ripped my heart out when she broke up with me.

Drew saw through all the bullshit and knew me as Logan Trimble, a regular guy who loved to play guitar, not the well-known guitarist for Steam. Hell, for all I knew, she was a follower of our band and viewed me differently now that the guys and I had become famous.

Nah. Somehow I knew that when it came to Drew, that would never be the case. She used to come watch me and the guys play local gigs, cheering us on and beaming with pride even if our audiences only had five people in them. Back in the day before we'd made it.

Hmm, how things changed. These days our audiences and paychecks were a lot bigger. We didn't get mobbed every place we went, especially when we rode solo, but our faces became more recognizable on a daily basis as our popularity grew. And along with that fame for me were the nightly fucks with nameless women who didn't mean shit to me. The best part about sending them off on their merry way afterward—they couldn't hurt an already broken heart. To this day, I still winced when I thought about the look on Drew's face when she had walked in on me and that slut making out on the couch.

Christ, what a fucking painful memory. I released a heavy sigh, my usual when rehashing the past.

At the table, I sat opposite Drew and watched her take a small bite of her food, subsequently wiping her mouth.

Fuck, I couldn't believe she sat in front of me. I consciously blinked to make sure my mind hadn't taken off to dreamland because the chances of bumping into her at the ranch had been slim to none.

"You used to come here with your family every year."

She remembered. How touching.

"Yes, ma'am. This very one."

"It's ironic that Kate wanted to come here on her honeymoon, huh?"

"I'd say. What a coincidence." Or possibly a sign? I preferred the latter.

She shrugged and took another bite of her macaroni.

I felt somewhat relieved she had taken the lead in the conversation because I suddenly had difficultly stringing coherent thoughts together, something that never happened when I spoke to a woman. But Drew wasn't just any woman. She was *the* woman.

"I'm impressed with your memory. My parents used to bring me up here every summer for a week. I'm keeping the tradition alive, or at least I'm trying to." Whew, luckily my brain got on board and worked properly, giving my mouth intelligent words to say.

Her eyes took on a somewhat dreamy haze. "I know this may sound crazy, but I can still remember you going on and on about your experiences here as if they happened yesterday."

"Now you too will get to see what I bragged about. This place is still as beautiful."

"I haven't seen much of it other than my cabin, which I must say is quite cozy and comfortable. It also helps that Kate and I have a two bedroom."

Drew had her own room. That meant she'd have privacy. Great.

Shit. I needed to stop this train of thought pronto. She probably only acted friendly toward me because of the situation we currently found ourselves in, when in reality, I'd bet my life on the fact she despised me. My smile abruptly faded.

"Maybe I can give you a tour? I know this ranch inside and out." The words kind of slipped out without any forethought on my part. I waited anxiously for her reply, hoping and praying I hadn't jumped the gun.

She took another bite of her mac and cheese, her free hand twirling a piece of loose hair. I watched her intently, thinking about how I used to slide that wavy brown hair behind her ear. And the scent of it? Mmm, she had always used a shampoo I loved the smell of. I inhaled deeply, the divine scent quickly coming back to me.

Fuck.

I couldn't help but stare at her, yet I didn't want to make her feel uncomfortable. I noticed by the way she shoveled food into her mouth without responding that I was doing exactly that.

Rejection sucked and I had a feeling it would greet me again in the very near future.

"So tell me how things are with you?" I swallowed the lump in my throat. I didn't want to hear her blow me off so figured I'd postpone the inevitable with a bit of distraction. Where the fuck had my self-confidence gone? I pressed my lips together, disappointed in myself.

Her gaze met mine. "I work at my dad's veterinary clinic, and I'm also taking a few classes. I know you're still doing the rock 'n' roll thing with Joey and Trevor. That's amazing."

. . .

"Yup, it is."

Seems she knew about us. Then again, how could she not? I mean, not to boast, but the guys and I were plastered on T-shirts, posters, YouTube, the entire social medial gamut. You name it, we were on it. I had no clue if or how much she followed the band, though.

"You guys always did have something special." She raised her glass and took a drink.

She and I did too but because of me, had lost it. Could that change while at the ranch?

"You should come hear us play sometime."

She shook her head. "I don't think that would be such a good idea. Besides, these days I only listen to country."

I grabbed my chest in mock pain. "Country? You used to hate that shit." I still did.

"My taste in music has since changed," she stated all too matter-of-factly. Her eyes met mine, defiant.

Point taken. I got her drift. Her taste in music changed because I'd ruined the genre for her that I played in.

"Listen, Drew, what happened between us happened years ago." She had never given me the opportunity to properly apologize. I figured why not jump at the chance. I had no idea if or when I'd get another one.

I tapped my foot nervously on the wooden floor, my knee bobbing up and down in anticipation of her response.

"Why don't you tell my heart that?"

Ouch!

I leaned back in my chair, the blow she gave me fierce.

"You know what, I think I'm done. If you'll please excuse me, it's been a long day of traveling. I think I'm going to head back to my cabin." She stood, picked up her plate, deposited it with the others, and headed for the exit.

Oh no, she didn't.

"Drew." I sprinted after her, catching her before she made it out the door.

She spun around, and a single tear slid down her cheek. Fucking déjà vu, if my heart wasn't crushed all over again. The pain inside me hurt more now than it had back in the day. To see her crying over a stupid mistake I'd made years ago.

I reached out and wiped the wetness off her cheek.

"I have to go." She focused her attention everywhere but at me.

"Can I walk you to your cabin?" I wanted to kick myself. My plea sounded more like a last-ditch effort to keep the conversation going.

"Why?" Her bottom lip jutted out.

"Because I want to." Try desperately wanted too.

She swallowed hard. "I don't think that's such a good idea."

Seems nothing I said to her counted as a good idea.

"Come on, Drew. If you won't let me walk you to your cabin, at least let me give you a tour of the ranch tomorrow morning. It's a gorgeous place, and I'd love to show it to you."

"We have activities in the morning." She still wouldn't look at me.

"I'll show you a much better time." I raised my brows, trying to lighten the mood.

It worked too because a hint of amusement overtook her.

She could take my comment however she saw fit because I meant it in every way imaginable.

"Fine. I'm in Cabin Two." She peered down at the ground.

Fuck, yes!

It was a plus she couldn't see my relief, especially when I fist bumped the air in front of me.

"How 'bout I treat you to the free breakfast beforehand?" My confidence had come back with a vengeance. I felt pumped and ready to proceed.

She smiled warmly and nodded. "Sure. Sounds like fun." She gave me a slight wave and exited the dining hall without glancing back.

Yes, it does. I let my disappointment slide because she had agreed to a date the following morning.

I wouldn't necessarily call it a date.

Buzzkill.

We were off to a good start. A great start, actually. I was a man on a mission to make things right, effective immediately. I had this week, which would give me the perfect opportunity to do so.

With Drew gone for the evening, I trekked back to my cabin. I had no interest in having s'mores with families and couples nor did I have the desire to socialize with anyone at the ranch. Well, other than Drew, now that I had discovered her here.

Me and my guitar resumed our positions on the porch. I played for what felt like hours. Jordana and her brother showed up at some point and sat in front of my cabin, where they watched my impromptu performance. I didn't mind. I kind of dug playing for an audience of two. It was both intimate and thrilling.

She left with her brother. I continued to strum well into the night. I knew if I went inside my cabin, my thoughts would drift back to Drew. Not that they had drifted off her.

When I couldn't keep my eyes open any longer, I trudged inside and collapsed on the bed.

∼

I blinked a few times, then squinted, letting my eyes adjust to the bright light filling the cabin. I had forgotten to close the blinds last night. My body seriously argued it required more shut-eye.

My phone informed me of the time. It also revealed it only had one bar of battery life left to it. Yeah. Recharging the thing became a high priority. I did just that.

Not that I needed the device so far out in the mountains, pretty much cut off from the modern world—the main reason why I loved the place so much—but still, I enjoyed using the other functions it offered, especially being able to listen to music.

The only contact to everyday life as I knew it was the emergency phone in the dining hall. The Addison family provided poor, basic Internet service in there as well for those who couldn't live without it—usually the teenage crowd. I loved more than anything to unplug from society for a week.

. . .

Being I still had on the same clothes I had traveled in, I figured a shower would do me some good. Kind of gross. The guys and I had a habit of washing the day's grime off after each show, and that included days off as well.

The minutes couldn't tick by fast enough. My thoughts were on one thing and one thing only: Drew. I couldn't wait to spend the morning with her. I dressed at hyperspeed. I hadn't felt this excited about something other than music in forever.

I advanced down the rocky path to the dining hall, another family strolling nearby. So far so good. Other than Jordana and her brother, nobody else seemed to recognize me, another reason I loved hanging out at the ranch. A place which treated me like everyone else.

Drew and Kate were sitting at a table in the back of the large room. Guess even with all my rushing, I still ran late. Most of the guests were already clearing their dishes.

Drew caught sight of me, and our gazes locked. My heart picked up speed from the intensity of her stare, the power in it penetrating and affecting me as much now as it had years ago.

Kate looked up, outwardly taken aback, when I pulled a chair out at the head of their table and sat.

"Logan Trimble. What the hell are you doing here?"

Drew must not have mentioned our run-in the night prior. I didn't know whether to process that as a good or bad thing. My gut told my optimistic self to take a hike because otherwise Drew would've said something to her sister.

Drew frowned at her sister's rudeness. "Kate, please. Good morning, Logan." She greeted me brightly, causing my heart to beat a smidgen faster.

"You knew he was here?" Kate all but scolded.

Drew nodded, playing it off as nothing. "We ran into each other last night."

Kate's mouth opened slightly, and she glared at her sister with wide eyes. "Why didn't you tell me?"

She shrugged. "I didn't think it was a big deal."

Ouch. Talk about a knife wound to the gut.

"No offense." She gave me another stab.

"None taken." Well, a little taken but I kept it quiet.

"Damn, it's been years." Kate's personality changed gears for the better. She dug in to her blueberry pancakes.

"It certainly has." Too long, in my opinion. Not about seeing Kate. That I could care less about. I was referring to seeing Drew.

Drew gazed at the empty space in front of me. "Aren't you hungry?"

"Not really. I think I'll grab some coffee, though."

"Is it too early for you?"

Her radiant smile had sucking in air.

"For me? Nah. Late to bed, early to rise. If you two will please excuse me, I'm going to get some caffeine into my system. Do either of you want anything while I'm up?"

They both shook their heads.

At the coffee bar, I decided to go for half caff instead, my body not requiring caffeine in its already jittery and overstimulated state.

Brian fixed himself a cup of joe next to me. "I hope you're not bailing out on activities this morning." He spoke with playful sarcasm.

"Sorry, bro. You know me well enough not to bother to ask. I'm going hiking."

"You disappoint, my man." He smirked, one of teasing.

"How about we shoot some pool later this afternoon or tomorrow?"

"Sounds good." He dropped his stirrer into the small wastebasket, patted my shoulder, and took off. I added a touch of cream and sugar to my cup, then moseyed back over to Kate and Drew, stopping for a mini bran muffin first. I sat at the table with them.

Kate leaned back in her chair and rubbed her stomach. Drew's food had hardly been touched. Maybe she experienced the same butterflies swirling around in her stomach as I did, as prissy as it sounded.

"I'm stuffed. I hope we do something active this morning, so I can burn off all the pancakes I just ate." Kate shoved her plate to the side and tossed her napkin on it.

"You're on vacation. Live it up." Drew clearly wasn't, using her fork to play with the food on her plate rather than eating it.

Kate peered at the activity board. "Oh goody, we start with horseback riding. I've never been on a horse before."

Maybe she had never been horseback riding, but if I remembered correctly, she had quite the reputation back in the day for straddling her legs and taking the reins. Sure, it was only hearsay, but multiple guys confirmed it, so I took it as the truth. Drew and her sister were total and utter opposites.

Drew and I had been each other's firsts. I had no clue about her current state of affairs in the bedroom, but if she hadn't changed and still held on to her strong values, she'd kept a tight leash on her body.

"Shall we head out?" Kate disregarded me with her question. "We're supposed to meet at the stalls in ten minutes. It'll take us some time to walk over there."

Drew paused. "Um...Logan and I are going to go hiking instead. But I'll catch up with you later."

Kate rose and stood behind her chair, her hands going on her hips. "We're supposed to be on this trip together. That means participating in activities together as well." She sounded somewhat juvenile.

"I agree we're on this trip together, but that doesn't mean we have to remain joined at the hip."

Kate scowled. "Really? Let me guess, you're going on a walk with *him*." She pointed at me, disgust overtaking her.

Yeah, I got it. She still despised me for what I did to Drew. Her body language got her message across loud and clear. I remained silent, not about to get involved in an argument between the two of them.

"He has a name. It's Logan. And yes, I'm going hiking with *him*. I'll catch up with you later." Drew stood as well. She pushed her chair in and picked up her plate. "Are you ready, Logan?" Her attention shifted toward me. She sounded frustrated as hell, her tone curt, and the glower she gave Kate? Wow, what a doozy.

I would've preferred to have had a tad more coffee in my system before taking off, but I had no intention of informing Drew about that. I didn't want to give her a chance to change her mind about going hiking with me.

She brought her leftovers to the trash and disposed of them, the food she'd hardly touched. Kate bolted for the exit, not a happy camper if my gut guided me correctly, which for the most part it did.

In the kitchen area where guests weren't permitted, me excluded from that rule, I retrieved two bottles of water from the fridge.

Drew waited for me on the other side of the buffet. The staff had explained to everyone that guests were forbidden from entering the kitchen area due to liability concerns.

I stepped around the corner and handed her a bottle. "Ready?"

"VIP treatment?"

"Huh?" Her remark didn't make sense to me.

She gestured to the kitchen area. "You're allowed to go back there, but we peons aren't?"

Chuckling, I replied to her smartass comment. "The Addisons consider me part of the family, which means I have free reign to do as I please while here."

"Aren't you special?" she joked.

She was to me.

A cool breeze blew against us when we exited the dining hall. I hoped it would stick around for our hike.

"Shouldn't I let one of the staffers know I won't be attending the horseback-riding activity? Susanna said last night we were supposed to inform them if we weren't going to participate, so they wouldn't wait for us."

Drew had always been the responsible party in our relationship.

Relationship.

I seriously needed to stop thinking about the two of us in those terms. That was then, this was now.

"Wait right here. I'll let someone know." I skipped down the three steps of the deck and caught sight of Layla. The staff members all had walkie-talkies. I let her know Drew and I had different plans, so she could tell the person in charge of horseback riding that Drew wouldn't be in attendance.

Drew stayed put until I returned.

"All set."

"Great. So, which direction are we headed in?" She looked left then right.

"Follow me, babe. I'll be your guide for the next few hours."

She took a firm stance and crossed her arms over her chest, her bottle hanging from her grip. "*Babe?*"

Shrugging, I put my hand out in surrender. "What can I say? Old habits die hard."

She rolled her eyes but followed me down the stairs. We made a left turn and passed other guests gathered together in various groups as we strolled down the path. None of them gave us a second glance. They were too busy chatting.

Once we passed the stables, the rocky road got narrower and it became woodsier.

Drew paused. "You're not going to get us lost, are you?"

"'O ye, of little faith. You must trust."

"You're asking me to trust you?" She might've been giggling, but her comment stung.

"Yes. I'm asking you to trust me." I caught her gaze when I said this, so she'd know I had no plans of fucking this up again, whatever *this* was.

She took a deep breath, we continued walking.

"Is this path intended for guests to walk on, or is it something you discovered while exploring one day?"

"Brian and I like to go to the lake and fish. This is one path that gets you there. Guests are taken on an easier route."

"And we're not taking the easier route?" She kept a steady stride next to me.

"Nope. I'm all about challenges." I raised my brows in a flirtatious manner, peering over at her. Her cheeks had a nice shade of pink highlighting them. Her rapid breaths didn't go unnoticed either. It couldn't have been due to our hike because we'd just begun and were far from moving at an aerobic pace.

"I remember that about you." She flashed me a half-smile.

"Do you?" I wanted to hear exactly what she remembered. I hoped she had kept some good memories of us to go along with the main one that ended our relationship.

"Yes, I do. I remember you being the type of person who never gave up on what you believed in, that you fought for what you wanted."

Except for her. Drew was the one thing I'd never fought for. It had been my biggest mistake to date, other than betraying her.

It was my turn to take a deep breath.

"How about you? I seem to remember you doing the same."

She shrugged and scoped out the rocks on the path that lay ahead of us. "Not for everything." She pouted, making me feel like shit again. It made me think about how much damage I'd done to her and how unfair and cruel it had been of me to treat her so poorly, with such disrespect.

"Do you still enjoy writing?" I tried to lighten the mood. Drew wrote the most magnificent poems. I still had the ones she wrote for me tucked in a shoebox, hidden in my closet. Nobody knew about my secret treasure.

Her eyes lit up, providing me with some relief. "Yeah, I still love to write, although I don't write poems anymore."

"Really? Then what do you write?" She'd piqued my curiosity.

"Songs."

Say what? This was news to me. I never remembered Drew playing an instrument. Sure, she would sing along to our songs and could carry a tune, but this surprised the shit out of me.

"What kind of songs?"

"Back in the day, I used to watch you play the guitar. I desperately wanted to be able to play like that. So after we broke up, I bought myself an old guitar at a pawnshop and started taking YouTube lessons and tutorials, as crazy as it sounds. I spent every waking hour when I wasn't working or studying, practicing. Obviously, I don't play as well as you do. But I can play well enough to put basic melodies to my lyrics."

My mouth dropped open in surprise. She fucking played the guitar? And she wrote tunes? This I had to see and hear for myself.

"That's awesome, Drew." The excitement in my voice came across sincere and enthusiastic, as I had intended it to.

She shrugged, kind of blowing off the topic. "It's a hobby. I get no joy out of playing for others. I prefer to play in solitude. I find it cathartic and healing."

"Would you consider playing something for me?"

"Are you kidding me? You want a novice to play the guitar for you? Absolutely not."

"I would never judge you. I'm excited for you, and I'd love to hear some of your music."

She looked at me. "I don't think you'd be entertained by the type of music I play." Sadness clouded her features. It killed me inside.

"And why's that?"

"Because it's country."

I grabbed my chest, same as I had done before when she told me she listened to it, as if in pain. "Ah, you wound me."

She giggled. That sight was much better than the gloominess that had filled the green of her eyes, a shade that matched the trees surrounding us perfectly.

"Seriously, will you play something for me?"

"I don't know." She glanced down at the rocks again. "As I said, I only play for myself. I've never played for anyone else."

"You've never played for Kate, your parents, or a boyfriend?" I threw that one in there for information-gathering purposes.

"No. I'd rather not get criticism or feedback from others."

"Not all criticism is bad. Joey and Dani make it a point to be open to receiving input from me and Trevor regarding new music they write. It brings more creative energy to the table, and the songs usually end up better as a result."

"But I don't write songs for the public."

"Songwriting can be a lucrative career."

"I'm sure it can. Taylor Swift got her start as a songwriter before she took over the charts herself."

"See? You could become the next Taylor Swift."

Not that I listened to Taylor's music but knew how popular and successful she had become over the years.

"No, thanks. Remember I just said I don't enjoy playing for an audience? Now you, on the other hand, do it for a living."

"I have no complaints. The guys and I do pretty well for ourselves. Hey, how about this, I'll play for you if you'll play for me."

"That's not a fair compromise. You're used to playing for people. I'm not."

I'd get her to play for me by week's end, guaranteed.

"It's kind of steep over here. Give me your hand." I stuck mine out toward her to assist her in climbing up the rough terrain.

Her skin felt silky to the touch as I enveloped her delicate hand in mine. *Shit.* I didn't expect to have such an overwhelming reaction from merely touching her, my cock semihard as a result. I adjusted my baggy shorts, hoping she wouldn't notice.

She kept her gaze on mine while I assisted her up. She fell against my chest once level with me, her free hand resting against it for support until she steadied herself.

We stared at each other in the stillness surrounding us. Her breath hitched from our close proximity. Mine did too.

I didn't want her feeling my hard-on, so I took a step backward when every fiber of my being wanted to throw her down on the ground and have my way with her.

"This next area is extremely rocky," I warned, needing to move, the intensity of the moment too strong for my liking. "Please be extra careful." I kept her hand in mine and continued to lead us to our destination.

"I think there's a method to your madness, Logan Trimble. Now I know why you didn't want us to take the easy path."

What could I say? She had caught me. I winked at her
.

She smiled at my cockiness but kept her hand in mine. It felt so strange to be with her, as if years hadn't passed since we'd last been together intimately. And oddly enough, I felt as comfortable with her now as I had back then. Her hand still fit perfectly in mine too, the same way it always had.

The terrain got rough. There were several stretches where I had to put my arm around her to prevent her from slipping or tripping over loose branches low to the ground.

"I feel like I'm on "Survivor," she huffed, panting, and out of breath. "Do you mind if we take a water break?"

"Of course not. If it's any consolation, the lake is only about three minutes ahead. It's beautiful. I think you're going to love it."

She swallowed a few gulps and recapped her water bottle. I found her to be so adorable.

"Okay, then let's move forward, so I can see this beautiful lake you speak so fondly of." She clapped her hands together with a sudden burst of energy.

With her hand in mine again, we followed the guided trail, her eyes widening when she caught sight of the magnificent scene. I had to admit, it was truly breathtaking. There wasn't a cloud in the sky. The sun shining down over the still lake and tranquil landscape made the water sparkle like diamonds.

"Wow. This is gorgeous, Logan. Do other guests get to see this?"

"Not this view. The lake's big. Guests get to see the lower portion. Only the Addison family and the staffers get to witness its natural beauty from this angle."

"It's amazing. What a great place to come and think, huh?" She continued to survey the area.

"It is. That's why I brought you here. We can take our shoes off and put our feet in, if you'd like? The water's usually pretty cold, but it's refreshing."

She nodded excitedly.

"Come." I led her to the large rocks where I always sat when I came for visits.

She dropped down next to me, already unlacing her sneakers and pulling her socks off. I wondered how she would feel if I requested we go skinny-dipping.

In my best interest, I decided against doing so.

She tiptoed over the small rocks on shore until she hit the lake. She toddled into it until knee-deep.

Mmm, I knew how to heat up those shivers of hers. My arms would do a much better job than the ones she wrapped around herself. Yep, plenty of items on that checklist.

With an overdose of enthusiasm, I tossed off my sneakers and socks and joined her.

"It feels so clean and invigorating. I love it." She cupped some water in her hands and splashed it on her face. Some of it fell on her white T-shirt.

Damn, talk about impulse control. I couldn't take my eyes off her hard nipples peeking through her bra underneath her damp shirt which now clung to her skin. She had no idea either, frolicking and playing in the water without a care in the world. Well, my cock most definitely had a clue, its hardness visible.

I bent my knees so my bottom half hid beneath the water. I was surprised my dick stayed so erect, the temperature of the water fucking cold as ice.

She moved about. I kept my secret to myself, getting a kick out of her relaxed and carefree nature, watching her splash about, thoroughly reveling in the goings-on.

She suddenly faced me, her eyes narrowing suspiciously.

Fuck. Maybe she had caught me staring at her chest. *No.* I didn't think that was the reason, even though I had no clue what went on in that intelligent mind of hers. But I learned quickly when a devious smile appeared and she splashed me.

Oh, I could totally play her game, and much better. I reciprocated, my splashes more aggressive, getting her nice and wet, two words I loved together when it came to women.

She gasped. "So unfair!" She took in her wet attire and crossed her arms over her chest to cover herself.

"I never did play fair." I was more than pleased with her T-shirt situation.

"Paybacks are a bitch, you know." She smirked and stepped closer, doing her best irritated impression.

She bent forward, placed both hands under the water, undoubtedly plotting her revenge, when she lost her balance and fell in. I rushed over and pulled her upright. Sure, we stood in the shallow and I knew she could swim, but I jumped at the opportunity to have her in my arms again, with this being a perfect excuse.

. . .

Drew broke out into a fit of hysterics. "I can't believe I just fell into the lake."

She laughed so hard tears fell from her eyes. I loved seeing her so comfortable and lighthearted. I also loved how close our bodies meshed together. I wondered whether she too felt the heat rising between us in the chilly water.

She rested her hands on my shoulders, her amusement ceasing when she caught sight of the seriousness of my expression. Hers became unreadable, but her eyes said it all. I took a giant leap of faith and brought my lips to hers.

At first she hesitated.

I snaked my arms around her waist, bringing her closer and holding her snuggly in my grasp. I couldn't hide my erection from her any longer. She'd easily feel it pressing into her.

Her lips softened, opening to mine, allowing my tongue to slip inside and swirl around hers. One of her hands went into my hair, the other around my neck. She tasted as good as I remembered, actually better.

My hand brushed over her hip. I rested it on her ass. Too bad she had denim shorts on. It made it difficult to get a good feel, but my mind had no problem filling in all the adjectives to describe it: firm, tight, meaty. Mmm, I could go on and on. Bottom line, I wanted her ass bare, as well as the rest of her body.

Our tongues devoured each other. We gyrated our hips in synchronized movements. She moaned slightly and hooked her leg around my waist. I reached for her other leg and wrapped it around me as well, her body weight now supported by mine.

She broke the kiss. "Logan, why're you doing this?"

"Because I haven't been able to think of anything else since bumping into you last night."

"Me neither."

Her back arched, she tipped her pelvis into my cock, rotating it in slow circles. We stared at each other, our eyes locked tight. The back of her hand caressed my cheek. "

I've missed you."

Really? I had no clue if she intentionally said the words, but I was so glad she had.

"I've missed you too, babe." I hadn't realized how much until now that I had her back in my arms. All the nameless and faceless women I had fucked over the years meant nothing because I felt nothing. My heart had remained empty, locked tight so nobody could penetrate and fill it again only to destroy it.

Here Drew and I fucked with our clothes on, and it had more fervor and earnestness to it than all the women I'd been with combined. Fuck, deep shit didn't do justice to describe my current situation.

6

DREW

My head screamed at me to stop. My body told it to fuck off, to go along with the ride for as long as it lasted. It felt like I hadn't been touched by a man in forever.

What I should've been doing was

telling Logan to leave me alone. But I couldn't. And the reason why? Because I held the same amount of love for him now as I did the first day I'd met him in the cafeteria line during our freshman year in high school. He'd cut in front of me, his hair shaggier back then, his jeans and t-shirt ripped and faded. I told him to move to the back of the line. He offered to buy me lunch. Fast forward four years to me catching him with another woman. So, as much as I loved him, I also hated him. Talk about polar opposites when it came to my feelings regarding Logan Trimble.

As long as I remained in the mind-set that while vacationing at this ranch it was no-holds-barred, I'd be okay. *Hopefully.* I would merely go with the flow and see where things led. A rather challenging feat for my fragile heart.

Did I honestly have a choice? Logan's presence in my life all those years ago had kept my heartlight aglow, whereas when he left, he'd sucked all the brightness out of it, causing darkness to fill it instead. I knew the flutters I felt being in his arms again were indicators he was reigniting it, his existence light enough to reincarnate feelings I never thought I'd be capable of experiencing again.

Here we were, standing in a lake, going at it like a couple of horny teenagers. I wasn't sure if it was a one-time deal but I very much wanted to find out, especially since he said he'd missed me.

Insecurity quickly set in. Had he only said those words because we were in the heat of passion, because I said them first, or did he mean them?

My thoughts became too scattered to give them any more attention. My body had other ideas, writhing in ecstasy against him topping the list.

He deepened our kiss, his tongue taking charge of mine. He loved control and acted mighty confident with those skillful hands of his too.

When he raised my shirt, I shivered from his touch and the coldness of the water. He followed a direct path to my breasts hidden beneath my bra. He tweaked my hard nipple between two fingers.

"Ah." I had forgotten how good it felt to be pleasured by someone other than myself. It had been quite a while for me. I'd engaged in a few one-night stands in the hopes they would help me get over him quicker. Nope. I felt worse after each encounter, not better, especially when none of them compared to Logan in the sack, in conversation, in my comfortableness with them, in everything.

He graced my neck with a trail of kisses, only to come back up and seize control of my lips again.

His messy brown hair got messier. I raked my hand through it.

The feel of his erection rocking against me leaving me breathless, drowning in bliss.

"Fuck, Drew. I want you so bad." He groaned against my cheek.

Yeah, I could relate. I wanted him too, but I also couldn't get lost in this sexcapade and say things I would later regret, words such as *"I never stopped loving you"* and *"I'll never stop loving you."*

Every part of me felt deprived. I snaked my hand down between us, fumbling with the elastic band and tie of his shorts. He assisted, lifting the fabric a few inches off his hips so I could get to his boxers. I moved them out of the way and hallelujah, I had found my salvation.

Wow, he seemed much bigger than I remembered. Either that or my vibrator and the other men I'd been with were pint-size in comparison to him.

He gently bit my lower lip. I wrapped my hand around his hardness, getting a nice, full grip. I continued to grind against him and, with the slightest amount of pressure, pumped my hand up and down over his erection, teasing the mushroom tip, the water making him smooth and slick to the touch. It was so easy to get lost in him, to him.

I better watch myself.

He released my lips and moved to my neck, where he planted sweet kisses across it.

Onward to my chest where he fisted my shirt, bringing it up over my breasts. I arched my back in offering.

He unclasped my bra with ease. I tilted my head back, my vision already getting hazy.

"You're so beautiful, Drew. And these fucking breasts... My God, they're as exquisite as I remember."

He kissed a circle around one, then the other. He always did make me feel like the most beautiful woman in the world. And here he did so once again.

I brought my hand lower and cupped his sac, kneading his delicate flesh.

Being mindful of the texture of his rigid length, I explored his shaft again with swift movements. I felt somewhat out of practice. It had been a while. But from his rapid breaths against my bare skin, I assumed he fancied my technique.

He placed his mouth over my nipple, flicking it with his tongue, sucking on the soft flesh surrounding it. I couldn't have squeezed my eyes tighter if I tried, the sensations rising inside me driving me mad with desire.

He released my breast and drove straight to the other one.

I became more vigorous with my hand, which in turn made him tug harder on my nipple with his teeth. Painful pleasure shot through me.

I mewled.

He groaned.

I rubbed myself against him with more force.

He thrust himself deeper into my palm.

The haziness intensified, a wave of ecstasy slowly rising in my pelvis only to rapidly spread itself outward to every part of my body. I shattered against him, trembling, convulsing in his arms.

"That's it, babe. I love to see you come."

My eyes flicked open to find his boring intently into mine. A concrete barricade wouldn't have been able to hold back the shockwaves of pent-up sexual energy rippling through me, my body shaking, taking me back to a fantasyland where he'd kept me housed in his loving arms. Well, maybe the loving part was a fairyland my mind had conjured up, but I still went with it, loving the thought.

"Logan!" My eyelids snapped shut, too heavy to remain open.

"Yes. Scream my name, Drew," he encouraged.

"Logan!" I cried out again without the need for further prompting.

His body stilled against mine, tensing as he emptied himself into my hand.

Shit.

Both of us were out of breath. I rested my forehead against his, neither one of us saying a word.

Alrighty then, let the uncomfortable aftermath begin. Yippee, I couldn't wait.

He cupped my cheek. "See? I told you you'd love the lake."

The lake? How about the man holding me?

At least he had broken the silence and did it so lightheartedly.

"You were right."

"I usually am."

Playfully, I slapped his arm.

"Where are you going?" His smile died when I left for the shore.

"I'm freezing my ass off."

"And here I thought I warmed you up!"

Ever the egomaniac.

Once on land, I checked out my see-through shirt and soaking-wet jean shorts. Questions were 99 if not 100 percent going to be asked back at the ranch.

My hair was sopping wet. I flipped it over to squeeze some of the excess water out. It would be an uncomfortable hike back, for a variety of reasons.

He joined me by the rocks, the underlying muscle tone and definition of his pecs underneath his wet T-shirt heating me up again. I breathed deeply and focused elsewhere.

Get control of yourself!

"Like what you see?"

My cheeks warmed. They were probably as red as they felt too.

"Maybe I do. Maybe I don't." I fastened my bra and fluffed my shirt. It did nothing to shield my hard nipples.

"I like what I see."

Naturally he stared at my breasts, my very cold ones.

I swallowed hard and sat on a rock to steady myself. He made me feel so off balance.

He stepped toward me. My heart picked up speed. I had no clue what he planned to do. He sat next to me and put his socks and shoes back on. I couldn't help but pout as I did the same.

After he finished, he got up and extended his hand toward me. "Ready to finish the tour?"

"You mean there's more?"

"Depends what you mean by *more*." He spoke flirtatiously.

"Are you always this smooth?" I took hold of his hand and stood.

"I don't get many complaints from the ladies."

"I'm sure you don't." I hoped he didn't hear the sarcasm in my tone. Then again, I hoped he did.

He brushed his lips against mine, causing my heart to melt a tiny bit more. So much emotion filled the air around us.

"Come on." He tugged me forward to get moving. "There are fresh berry trees up ahead. We can pick some if you want."

"What kind of berries?"

We strolled lazily along the trail.

"Blackberries. They're so ripe and delicious up here."

"Yum. I love blackberries."

He lit up at my comment. "You're so adorable, Drew."

Even though I loved hearing the words fall from his lips, I blew off his compliment. I needed to remain levelheaded.

My clothes stuck to me as we walked. I kept pulling them off my skin. I prayed the warm sun would help dry out our garments. I'd hate for others to see the two of us soaking wet in our clothing when we hiked back to the land of the living.

"Take off your shirt." He undoubtedly noticed my constant attempt at separating my top from my bra.

My jaw dropped. "What? I'm not taking my shirt off."

"Why not? It's not like I haven't seen the girls before," he replied way too seriously.

Is he kidding me?

With a mock scowl, I regarded him. "The girls?"

"Beautiful ones too." He winked.

Such a cutie. Seriously though, he had become a player over the years, tabloids shouting out about him and his sexcapades on a regular basis. "I prefer to keep it on."

"Suit yourself."

We strode about a half mile until we reached the berry bushes. There were tons of them filled with plump, ripe blackberries.

"Shouldn't we wash them first?" I removed one from a stem and inspected it.

"Nope. No pesticides are used on these bushes. It's nature at its finest. Go ahead and eat it."

I popped the berry into my mouth, its juices squirting out as I bit down. "Mmm. It's so sweet."

He chuckled at my enthusiasm. "Have as many as you want." He picked a few and ate them as well.

"I wish we could take some back to the ranch with us."

"Susanna grows fresh produce, herbs, and vegetables behind the house. I'll take you there. You can pick whatever you want to your heart's content."

Damn, I felt as though I'd scored the VIP treatment on this trip, not Logan. Let's hear it for Kate's honeymoon, especially since I was probably having a ton more fun than my sister. Speaking of which. "I wonder what time it is."

I didn't have my phone with me so had no clue how long we'd been gone.

He shrugged, which meant he didn't have his with him either.

"Do you have to be somewhere?" He ate another berry.

"No."

"Good. Neither do I."

"I am a little hungry, though. I didn't eat much at breakfast."

"I noticed. Not a morning eater?"

"I wasn't hungry. But now I'm starving."

"Then I must feed you. What do you say we head back to the ranch?"

"Sounds like a plan."

We continued holding hands but followed a different route back to camp, the return trip much shorter.

Guests were huddled in front of the dining hall when we approached. Kate caught sight of me and stormed over. *Christ.* Too bad I didn't have earplugs because I knew an earful was about to come my way.

"Where've you been? You missed all the morning activities. Lunch too. You worried me." She shifted her attention to Logan, taking in his damp attire.

"We were on a hike. Did you have fun horseback riding?" I wouldn't feed into her maternal reprimand and questioning routine.

"It would've been more fun if you were there with me."

Ugh, enough with the guilt and snide comments.

"Maybe next time." I shrugged, not apologizing for my disappearance. "I'm going to head back to the cabin and change. Then I'm going to eat."

"Hello? If you'd listened to what I just said, you'd know lunch is over. And at this rate, you're probably going to miss the next activity too." She stood firm, her arms crossed, causing me to feel a tinge of remorse. Here she mourned her lost relationship with Joe while I gallivanted around the ranch with Logan.

"I'm sure I could get us something to eat." Logan joined in on the conversation, ignoring the part about missing the activity. "I should probably change too. Come, I'll walk you to your cabin."

Kate narrowed her eyes at me, the warning sign I had stepped into dark and dangerous territory by getting involved with Logan again. I couldn't and wouldn't argue with her over this topic, but I also didn't see myself as hurling my fragile heart into the scary wild. Rather, I viewed the situation as me making a sound decision to cautiously dip my baby toe into it ever so slightly.

She huffed and rejoined Erin and Jen. They welcomed her with open arms, which made me feel somewhat relieved even though guilt still pulled at my heartstrings.

Logan didn't hold my hand during our walk. I considered it a good thing. It gave me some breathing space. He seemed to suck up all the oxygen in the air whenever he came within five feet of me, causing me to lose all rational thought.

"I'm fine getting myself to my cabin. Yours is right here." I stopped and pointed toward his porch on the left.

He eyed me quizzically, probably wondering how I knew it belonged to him. I didn't say anything about hearing him play his guitar on the porch the night before.

"I know you'll be fine, but I want to walk you."

We continued along the trail.

Good. He didn't mention anything about my knowledge of his housing situation.

"Such a gentleman." I grinned.

"I've been called worse."

Ah. He truly was a sight to be seen, especially when he smiled the way he did now. His gorgeous blue eyes sparkled brighter, if that was even possible.

We said nothing about the fun we'd had back at the lake. I could only speak for myself, unsure about him, but my thoughts remained in a tailspin. The last thing I wanted—another one-night stand, especially with Logan.

"I wonder if we were on the same flight." I initiated a change of thought process. "But I think I would've noticed if you were on my van to the ranch."

"I would've definitely noticed you." He looked at me with warmth in his eyes.

My cheeks suddenly burned again. They probably resembled the color of raspberries.

"I know Layla and Brian make two trips to the airport to pick up guests. What time did you ride in the van?" He kept his attention on the landscape surrounding us.

"Um, I think around two."

"Then we were on the same bus. I got on last."

"Oh, that explains it. Kate and I got to the van first, since we carried our luggage on board. Brian asked us to sit in the back to leave room for others still arriving. I still felt groggy from the antinausea medication I had taken on the plane, so I pretty much passed out as soon as my butt hit the seat."

He nodded in acknowledgment and stopped, pointing to the left. "Here's your cabin."

My gaze followed the direction of his finger, surprised to discover we were already there. Guess I had zoned out.

"Why don't you stop by my cabin when you're ready? Then we can go get something to eat."

"Okay." I twisted my hands together in front of me. I didn't understand why I suddenly felt so vulnerable.

Hello, you just let him bring you to orgasm at the lake!
There was that.

Breathing deeply, I dared to look up at him. When I did, I found him staring intently at me.

"I enjoyed the hike."

Yeah, so did I. Too much for my own good.

My heart raced a dab faster. I tapped my foot against the gravel with a touch more vigor. "Me too." All movement on my behalf then ceased. I didn't know what to do with myself.

He took me into his arms, placed his hands on my cheeks and brushed his lips over mine ever so gently.

My eyes remained closed after he released me. I wanted more. When I realized I wasn't going to get it, I opened them. He had the same amount of desire going as I did.

"Okay, I'll see you in a bit."

Off I went, sprinting

to my porch, taking the stairs in twos and running inside the cabin. I hustled to my bedroom and collapsed on the bed. What in the hell had I done?

7

LOGAN

*W*hat the hell was I doing? And why did she take off like she couldn't get away from me fast enough after I'd kissed her? In all actuality, could I blame her? I mean, we hadn't spoken in years and out of nowhere she appeared in my life again, an out-of-this-world surprise. I still couldn't believe she'd actually given me the time of day, especially with my past sinful behavior toward her. I'd never planned for things to turn out as horribly as they did. I had put myself into a bad situation that went further than intended, and one I should've nipped in the bud but stupidly didn't.

Joey, Trevor, and I *had never been* the partying types. We loved playing music and being present while doing so. But on that night, we'd played a fantastic gig and got plastered, drinking a lot more than intended.

We always knew where to find booze if we wanted it—Joey's place. A raging alcoholic, his father kept liquor bottles stashed all over the house.

There we were, three horny teenagers, acting goofy and having fun when Dani unexpectedly showed up with a few of her girlfriends. Hot ones, I might add. The other guys had been single, but me? Drew and I had a great thing going, but that didn't mean I couldn't look.

The girls joined us in the living room for drinks. One got chummy with Joey, another tried to get chummy with me. I kept pushing her off me, telling her I had a girlfriend, but she didn't care. She continued to run her hands over my chest and thighs. In the end I became so blitzed, I stopped caring too.

Dani and the fourth girl went to her bedroom, but not before Dani made a point of showing her disgust with me, her eyes taking in her friend straddling me on the couch. By that time, the girl's hands were in my hair and underneath my shirt. And I didn't stop her from doing it. My bad.

"I hope you know what you're doing, Logan." Dani's glare shot daggers at me.

Joey and his girl had made tracks to his bedroom. Trevor had taken off solo. In retrospect, I should've tagged along with him. It would've rerouted the path my life had taken in the relationship department.

"I'd think twice if I were you, because you're about to make a huge mistake," she warned. "And I won't back up whatever story you feed Drew. Please keep that in mind before you do whatever it is you plan on doing." She whipped around and stormed off with her friend in tow.

"Don't listen to her. She's just jealous."

Dani? Nah, she wouldn't let a guy get close to her for a multitude of reasons, her scumbag abusive father the major one.

The no-name bimbo ground her hips against me. By that point I was so bombed, I didn't know my right from my left. Not being much of a drinker, a few shots had me down for the count, and I more than paid for my foolishness in a number of ways.

I had forgotten I'd told Drew earlier in the day that I planned on heading over to Joey's place after our gig. She had made plans with her family and couldn't attend, otherwise she would've been straddling me, and none of the stupid shit that went down would've transpired.

The chick on my lap slid her tongue down my throat. My cock took it upon itself to join her in the grinding action. My hands held her full ass, shifting it on top of me to appease my aching dick.

. . .

A knock came at the door.

Screw it. I didn't give two shits about the visitor. It wasn't my house. Dani or Joey could answer the door if they wanted to. I was heavily involved in my make-out session.

Stupid, stupid, stupid.

I closed my eyes, replaying the scene and reliving my ignorance.

Drew opened the door to find the girl on top of me, top off, bra still on.

"Logan, how could you!"

She ran outside.

I shoved the bimbo to the side, on the couch. She gasped. It wasn't like I gave a shit. I had to get to Drew.

She was backing out of the driveway. I dashed toward her car, screaming for her to stop, but she wouldn't.

Those were the last words she'd said to me up until the night prior when I saw her in the dining hall. I'd tried to speak with her post incident, but she'd refused to hear me out. I went to her house not once, not twice, but a handful of visits over the course of several weeks. Her parents never failed to tell me to leave.

The sad reality was nothing I said would pacify her or fix the mess I'd caused. I figured I'd give her time and space to simmer down. She didn't. She never spoke to me again until now. I'd only kissed that skanky girl at the party and felt her up but, well, no buts. My behavior had been wrong in every sense of the word. No rationalization could justify my despicable actions. Talk about one of life's major fuckups. That had probably been my biggest one to date.

My head throbbed from strolling down memory lane. I moped back to my cabin to get changed for lunch, my mood somewhat somber even though I should've been high as a kite after the fantastic experience Drew and I had shared at the lake. Except I wasn't, and my stomach had twisted itself up into knots. It hurt like a son of a bitch.

Maybe a shower would wash off the tension pooling in my muscles.

Nope.

Toweling dry and dressing didn't leave me feeling any better either. My muscles still felt tight. I knew of one thing and one thing only that would help clear my mind and no, jacking off wasn't it.

With guitar in hand, I stepped onto the porch and planted my ass on the rocking chair.

I played one of our newer songs, a ballad. I lost myself to the rhythm, becoming intently focused on strumming the cords. I tapped my foot and bobbed my head to the soft melody.

When the song ended, I took a deep breath to find Drew standing in front of the porch, her hands resting on the ledge.

"That was beautiful."

People told me on a nightly basis I played great, usually fans wanting to get up close and personal to Logan Trimble, the guitarist of Steam—not Logan, the guy who loved to kick back, relax, and play his guitar for fun. The way Drew's eyes beamed with pride, I knew she saw the real me, the Logan who used to chill in his garage and play his guitar for hours on end, day after day.

Smiling, I set my guitar down next to me.

"Is that song new to your set list?" She walked up the steps and stopped a few feet in front of me.

"Yeah."

"I love the melody."

And I loved how her eyes regarded mine, not full of lust like the women I fucked who couldn't care less about me. Nor did they give me the impression that they viewed me as the man whore who screwed different women on a regular basis without giving a crap about any of them. What touched me the most was that Drew had an entirely different image of me, and my gut told me it most definitely wasn't one of hate.

"Are you ready to go eat?"

Her question snapped me out of my deep thoughts.

"Sure." Not that my stomach could tolerate food, the knots inside tightening again, but she required food, and I wanted to spend more time with her. "Let me just put my guitar inside my cabin. You can come in if you want."

Her smile vanished, and she placed her hand on the railing. She chewed on her bottom lip. I didn't understand her nervousness around me.

Maybe it's because you screwed her over and she doesn't want a repeat.

Fuck.

My own bout of anxiety kicked in, my palms a tad sweaty and bile rising toward the base of my throat.

"I'll wait out here for you."

Imagine that.

Inside my cabin, I tucked my guitar safely in its case on the couch.

Taking a deep breath, I went back outside.

Drew had left the porch and was kicking rocks on the dirt path in front of my cabin. She spun around when she heard the door snap shut. I skipped down the few steps to where she stood.

"I hope the Addisons don't get mad that we're not following the schedule they have set for us."

We journeyed to the dining hall.

"I've never followed their schedules, so I can assure you this comes as no surprise to them. But now I have an accomplice to do it with." I winked at her. She smiled and showed off her beautiful white teeth.

It reminded me of the day she got her braces off back in ninth grade. Talk about excitement on her part. The first thing she'd done when we left school was drag me along with her to a local candy shop, so she could eat as many gummy candies as her heart desired. The two of us had gone crazy eating Swedish fish, with the stomachaches afterward to prove it. As expected, her mother blamed me for getting Drew home late, which then made her late for her orthodontist appointment to get her retainer.

"Don't be getting me into trouble, Mr. Trimble." She raised her finger.

"I can't promise you that. It all depends on what kind of trouble you're referring to." I raised my brows.

She opened her mouth to say something but stopped herself. I took her silence as a good sign because I had a knack for reading Drew pretty well, and right then, I picked up the vibe she was on board for whatever I had up my sleeve. At least I hoped she did. How about desperately prayed she did.

We entered the dining hall to find Patty and Susanna in the kitchen prepping for dinner. Susanna's eyes opened wide when she caught sight of us.

"Logan Trimble, how many times do I have to tell you to eat during serving hours?" She spoke to me like one of her own. "This isn't your kitchen, my dear, where you can come and go as you please." She spoke seriously, but her lips curled up into a smile.

"We had so much fun, we lost track of the time."

Her eyes narrowed at my superb excuse. "Go on and get yourself something from the fridge. You know where it is. There are still a few sandwiches from lunch wrapped up as well as a fruit salad. Help yourself. Are you enjoying your stay so far, Drew?" Her attention shifted toward Drew, who stood next to me.

"Yes, I'm having a wonderful time. Your ranch is beautiful."

"Why don't you go grab us some seats, and I'll get us some grub."

Drew nodded and sat at the closest table, watching me do my thing in the kitchen.

I put a few sandwiches on a plate and scooped some fruit salad into a bowl. I remembered Drew being a big fruit lover.

With the skill of a waiter, kind of, I brought the plates to the table and set them down in front of her, sitting next to her so we could share.

"We've got a smorgasbord of tuna salad, egg salad, and turkey and Swiss." I gestured to the plate, indicating she could dig in first.

She reached over and picked up half an egg salad sandwich.

Now with food in front of me, my stomach grumbled. Maybe the pain in it earlier had been from hunger. Not.

Yum. Fresh baked bread with turkey and Swiss. I took a hefty bite, and realized we had no drinks. I remedied that situation, getting us two cups of Susanna's homemade lemonade from the counter.

"You have to taste this. It's to die for. Susanna squeezes the lemons herself." I placed a cup in front of Drew and took a hearty sip from mine.

Drew's eyes opened wide as she drank. "Oh my God, this is the best lemonade I've ever had."

"Right?"

"And the fruit's so fresh." She scooped more fruit salad onto her spoon. I leaned back in my chair.

"Maybe after lunch I'll take you to her garden, so you can pick apples, pears, and whatever else she has growing."

"That would be awesome. Thank you."

"Anytime. I know how much you love eating fruit."

She paused between bites, eyeing me suspiciously.

"What? You used to eat all the apples, peaches, and pretty much anything else with seeds or pits in it at my house whenever you came over."

"Yeah, I remember your mom saying something about it too." Amused, she resumed eating.

"She was just happy because she thought it was me eating all that healthy shit. I didn't have the heart to tell her it was you."

"Whatever happened with Joey and Dani's father? I remember hearing stuff about him."

"I'm not going to get into specifics because it's their story to tell." I took another bite of my sandwich.

"I would never ask you to betray their trust."

"What I can tell you is their father passed away." I never gossiped or talked shit about others. All secrets tossed at me remained safely tucked inside, right where they belonged.

She frowned. "I'm sorry to hear that."

"Don't be."

Her eyes were questioning. "How're your parents doing?"

At least she got the message I didn't want to talk about Joey and Dani. But now she'd asked about my parents. To be honest, I didn't want to discuss them either.

"I wouldn't know. We don't speak often. They never agreed with my career choice." I washed down a bite of my sandwich with some lemonade.

She nodded in understanding. "I remember back in the day they weren't so keen on the idea of you pursuing music as a profession."

"Yup. They wanted me to go to college to learn a profession and play guitar as a hobby. I took a few classes at the local college to pacify them, but little did they know, I spent most of my focus and energy on my music with the guys. Once we started making enough cash to the point I could support myself, I stopped attending school. That didn't sit well with the folks. They basically cut me off, telling me they'd love to see how far the few bucks I earned on a weekly basis would get me."

The thought that my parents lacked faith in my guitar-playing ability still put me on edge and angered me. Hence, I hated talking about them.

"That must've been a difficult period for you. Music's a hard business to break into and earn a steady income from."

"At the beginning, things were rough. There were many nights I slept in my car. I didn't feel right bunking with Joey or Trevor for nights on end. They got pissed, telling me I could live with them for free, but I knew they didn't have a pot to piss in either and didn't want to add to their own burdens. I firmly held on to the belief that things would get better, and fortunately, they did. I have no complaints."

"It hurts me to know you had to sleep in your car."

Her frown made me feel uneasy. I didn't play the self-pity card, had no rhyme or reason to. As shitty as those days had been, they made me more grateful and appreciative of what I had now.

"It is what it is. Luckily, those days are behind me." Thank God.

"I'm glad. So what's the story with your current schedule?"

"We travel *a lot*."

She bit her lip.

"It's part of the job."

"I'm sure it is. I'm so curious about how the process works. Do you travel by plane, bus? Do your instruments travel with you? How do you transport them? How do you choose which cities you'll visit?"

The questions were flying.

"Slow down." I chuckled, putting my hand up to stop her from continuing.

"I'm sorry. Similar to you, I guess bad habits die hard."

"First off, we have a manager who schedules all our performances. Secondly, the guys and I travel together when we're on the road. And thirdly, our equipment comes with us wherever we go."

"That's so cool. I'm happy for you. It's what you always wanted." The sincerity in her smile told me she spoke the truth. Not that Drew ever engaged in the lying-type role.

She had no inkling how much I wanted her. Sadly, I didn't know how things would pan out between us, what would happen. No guarantees.

Stop the fucking sappy relationship thoughts.

I snapped myself out of whatever place my mind kept drifting to when it came to Drew. These were the facts: she and I would both be at the ranch for the next week, I had an obligation to make amends to her for my past wrongdoings, and finally, closure would provide me with the ability to move forward without my strong feelings for her holding me back any longer.

. . .

Yeah, right. Keep dreaming.

At least my first two points were factual. Not too sure about my last one.

"It is. As I said before, I have no complaints. I'm beyond thankful for the ability to play my guitar and earn money doing it."

"So I take it the band is on a break this week?"

"Yup. I'm taking full advantage that we have a few weeks off."

"A few weeks?"

I had more fucking money in the bank and in investments than I knew what to do with. I, being a realist who had no clue how long my fame would last, chose not to piss my savings away on fancy cars and lavish vacations. I banked my dough, spending it how I saw fit while also planning ahead so I could maintain my current lifestyle if things with the band ever took a nosedive south.

"Things have been good for us, and because of that, I'm able to take extended breaks. How about you? You said you work for your father and are taking classes."

I wanted to shift the attention off me and on to her.

"I'm only working for my dad until I graduate. I hate living at home."

She grimaced. I couldn't blame her. Her mother and father were helicopter parents to the nth degree. They never did approve of me, my independent nature being too intimidating and possibly threatening for their taste. They didn't agree with my career choice either, another major strike against me. I didn't give a shit. Drew supported me, and that's all that counted.

"You still live with your parents?" That sucked big time.

"Thanks for making me feel so good about it." She spoke teasingly and took another drink of her lemonade. "Trust me, if I earned enough money to live on my own, I would. I think my dad purposely keeps my salary fixed, so I can't afford to leave his house, but I don't think any other employer would be as flexible with my schedule in regard to my schooling as he is. I can honestly attest to the fact that there is such a thing as too much togetherness." She set her glass down.

"What about Kate? Is she at home too?"

She shook her head. "No. She lives with Joe, her fiancé. Her stuff's still at his place, which will be an interesting situation after we leave the ranch. If she moves home, it'll really stink for me. I can't imagine the two of us living under the same roof again. She's a royal pain in my ass."

Her sister was a piece of work. "So what is it you do for your father?"

"Schedule patients, well, the animals, because they're our patients."

Her explanation was cute but unnecessary. I knew the animals were the patients. She was such a lovable and sweet person.

Stop thinking about her this way. She's out of here in a week.

"My parents don't trust anyone to take care of the finances so my mom does the payroll and other accounting stuff in back while I run the front."

"Sounds like a lot of responsibility, especially when you're going to school as well. I'm sure they're not looking forward to the day you leave."

"You know my parents. They'd be happy to keep me under lock and key until the day I get married."

Yes, I know.

She gave me the perfect opening to dig deeper again. "Speaking of which, any fiancés in your past?"

"No. You?" She focused on me.

I sensed her apprehension about hearing my response.

"No. It would be kind of difficult to have one with my current lifestyle. I pretty much live on the road."

Not that our hectic schedule stopped Trevor and Joey from moving forward with their loves. They were the epitome of role models when it came to combining their passion for music with maintaining steady relationships. I often wondered whether I could do the same.

Where the fuck did that thought even come from, especially with me being the bandmate who bragged about every fuck I engaged in?

My thoughts were in a perpetual state of contradiction. It drove me crazy.

"Hmm, it sounds like you're living the typical rock 'n' roll lifestyle. Is it safe to say you have groupies located in various cities across the globe?"

Her attempt at refraining from wincing as she spoke the words wasn't successful.

"It makes things convenient for now without all the emotional baggage that comes along with a relationship." *Excuses, excuses.* "How about you? You're in one place. No steady boyfriends you thought would lead to more?"

She used her spoon to scatter her left-over fruit around the plate. I knew exactly where her mind had drifted to. Shit, I was such an ass for bringing up the subject. We might have been kids when we dated, but one thing we'd always agreed upon was our forever future together.

A small piece of turkey must've fallen out of my sandwich and onto the table. I zeroed in on it.

She sighed heavily. "No. None that I'd write home about."

Did that include me. "So are you saying there have been some?"

"I did date after you, Logan."

She made her frustration with my assumption that I had been her one and only loud and clear in both her tone and the tight line of her lips.

"I didn't mean it that way."

"Do you want me to tell you there were no others?"

Yeah, I would.

An inevitable attack would face me shortly.

"I didn't mean that either. Tell me whatever you want." Talk about being at a loss for words.

She closed her eyes and breathed deep. Hmm, I had apparently hit a nerve. She had something on her mind she didn't want to discuss. I felt it.

"If you don't mind, can we go and pick that fruit now?"

She balled up her napkin, tossed it on her plate, and brought it over to the garbage can, where she dumped the leftovers into the large black bag.

Well, that conversation had gone well.

8

DREW

While tossing my trash, I tried to collect myself. I knew Logan wanted nothing more than for me to tell him I'd been celibate all these years while he gallivanted around with one-night stands night after night, as if my life had had no purpose without him. Well, unfortunately for him, I'd never allow anything like that to happen since I was the type of person who got up and dusted myself off when I fell. Sure, in certain situations the task proved more difficult, with Logan being one of them.

He sat waiting for me at the table, the light in his eyes a bit dimmer. Something went on in that mind of his, but it wasn't my place to probe. We weren't in that type of a relationship anymore.

He led me out of the dining hall and up the rocky trail to Susanna and Jack's house, a lovely two-story log cabin. A hammock was strung up in the front yard and there were some rocking chairs on the front porch, all very welcoming and homey. I paused at the edge of the landscape, not proceeding any farther. "Are you sure they won't mind that we're on their personal property?"

"Not at all. They want their guests to feel at home during their stay, and if that includes picking fruit from their garden, respectfully that is, they're all for it."

Behind the house was a greenhouse along with several fenced-off areas filled with herbs and produce. Peach trees stopped me in my tracks. Fruit filled them. Yum, I couldn't wait to taste a juicy peach.

"May I pick a few?" I knew he had said Susanna wouldn't care, but I still didn't want to overstep any boundaries.

"Of course. Feel free to pick to your heart's content. I can attest that they taste even better than they look."

My mouth watered simply admiring the plump peach just out of reach. I got on my tiptoes and stretched my arm as far as possible but couldn't grab it. Logan came to my rescue and wiggled it off the branch. He handed me the fruit.

I rotated it in my palm, inspecting it. I couldn't wait to sink my teeth into it.

"Are you going to eat it now, or would you rather wait?"

"Why don't we share it?" The thing was the size of an orange. "It's too large for me alone, and I'd hate to waste it."

He nodded in agreement. I bit into the skin, juice immediately dripping down my chin. I closed my eyes. What orgasmic deliciousness!

"Oh my God, you have to try this." I held it in front of his mouth. He cupped my hand and brought the fruit to his mouth.

Using the back of my free hand, I wiped my chin. Was that still peach juice or drool? Damn, how was it every move Logan made had seduction written all over it? Or could it be due to my skewed vision?

Either way, I stared intently as his lips parted and he bit into the fruit. His tongue skimmed his bottom lip to clean the juice off.

Lord help me.

I wanted to lick that juice off his lips.

Mesmerized, my heart speeding up, I stared at him in admiration. How pathetic was I? It made me realize

how sexually deprived I felt.

"Your turn." His brows rose slightly. Hunger filled his eyes. It most likely matched mine.

He again cupped my hand but this time brought the peach toward my mouth. I sank my teeth into the fruit, this bite tasting even better than the last one.

"My turn." He spoke in a hushed voice.

Our joined hands brought the peach toward his mouth. To my surprise, he released my hand and kissed me instead, tongue and all. The peach dropped from our hands, thumping when it hit the ground. Or perchance it was the sound of my heart beating against my chest.

My lids were already too heavy to keep open. I snaked my arm around his neck and slid my fingers into his hair. His tongue danced with mine, soft but aggressive, a perfect balance, a perfect kiss.

I tasted residual peach flavor in his mouth. Mmm, more divine than the fruit we'd dropped on the grass.

Logan swung his arm around my waist and drew me closer until our bodies meshed together. His erection didn't go unnoticed, especially with the manner in which he circled it against my pelvic area. I breathed into his mouth and moaned ever so slightly.

He tilted his head to the right, then the left, his tongue never breaking contact with mine, his hand fisting my hair. I fancied this rough side of him. I had never experienced it before. What else did he have up his sleeve. Inquiring minds wanted to know. Mine included.

He broke the seal between us and leaned his forehead against mine. "Fuck, Drew. I can't seem to get enough of you or keep my hands to myself when I'm near you."

Sadly, my gut reaction was to question every word he said due to the mistrust I still held inside me. I also didn't want to be viewed as one of his groupie women located in various cities that he spoke about earlier. Sure, I had taken part in a few one-night encounters myself, but that type of behavior went against the values I held true to my heart. I only acted upon them in an effort to try and relieve some of the pain in my heart, hoping that being in the arms of another man would help me do so, when in reality all those hookups did was make me long for Logan more.

Pulling back, I released myself from his arms. "Guess your concept of sharing is different than mine." I spoke lightheartedly in an attempt to break the intensity between us. If the butterflies in my stomach and the trembling of my hands had anything to say about it, things moved way too fast between us.

"Guess so." He studied me. "You okay?"

He cocked his head to the side, curiosity and a touch of concern written all over his face.

No. I wasn't okay. Try a frickin' basket case inside.

I played it cool, though. "Yeah, why wouldn't I be?"

"I hope you'd tell me if you weren't."

His gaze penetrating into mine had me biting my bottom lip. He had caught me. Guilty as charged.

"Hey guys, what're you up to?"

Layla's voice came out of nowhere, scaring the hell out of me. I grabbed my chest in surprise. I also took two steps backward, creating a good amount of distance between me and Logan.

"Picking peaches." Logan clearly wasn't fazed by her sudden appearance.

She lit up with excitement. "That's exactly what I'm about to do. My mom's making peach cobbler tonight."

Retreating inside my mind, I contemplated whether she'd seen me and Logan kissing and waited until our moment ended prior to approaching us. Not that she'd care, but my cheeks still burned at the thought.

"She makes the best cakes and pies." Logan's eyes fixed on me when he spoke.

"Why don't the two of you help me pick some?"

"Sure." I agreed to Layla's request without any forethought, somewhat relieved at the interruption. It provided me with some distance. I kept getting sucked into Logan's web and had to consciously remind myself to take a step back.

"Great. I only pick the red ones. The green ones aren't ripe yet. You can place your pickings in this basket. Also, feel free to take some back to your cabin if you want to."

Easy enough.

I got busy picking peaches within my reach. Logan got the ones higher up. Layla went to a different tree altogether and gathered her own.

What fun. I fully immersed myself in the activity, such a different one than I'd engage in in my everyday life. Here I was in the middle of nowhere, up in the mountains, at a ranch, picking fresh fruit off a tree. Who would've thought I'd find this adventure of Kate's so relaxing and enjoyable? What an awesome place to unwind. Too bad Logan had me so twisted up in knots it was difficult to fully do so.

After gathering peaches, I helped myself to a few pears. They weren't as ripe, but I savored the experience nonetheless.

Layla said her good-byes and left for the dining hall, carting two full baskets of fresh peaches. I had two peaches and a pear in my hand to bring to my cabin.

Logan and I wandered to the main area in front of the dining hall. Guests were scattered about, talking animatedly about the activities they'd engaged in earlier in the day.

Kate stood with two women, different than the ones she'd been with earlier. I wanted to speak with her, since I had pretty much abandoned ship since meeting up with Logan.

"There you are. Where did you get those?"

She referred to the fruit in my hands.

"Want one?" I handed her a juicy peach. "Logan and I just picked them off the fruit trees."

The mere mention of Logan's name had her all but cringing, but it didn't stop her from taking the peach.

"Oh, I almost forgot. This is Lena and Marcy." She gestured to the two women standing next to her. "And this is my sister, Drew, and her *friend*, Logan."

"We're about to go shooting. Do you want to come?" Kate spoke with a plea of desperation. I suddenly realized why. Joe owned a handgun and loved going to the shooting range. Empathy kicked in for my poor sister.

"You don't have to go if you don't want too, Kate."

"No. It's important for me to keep busy."

Even though I understood her rationale, at some point she would have to stop and feel her feelings. I gave her credit, though. She could've been isolating in our cabin, crying, but instead she was out and about, participating in all the goings-on. That deserved props on her part.

"Sure, I'll go with you. Logan, do you want to come shooting with us?" I didn't want him to feel left out.

"Why don't you go on ahead with Kate, and I'll catch up with you later?" I could swear a pout took shape on his gorgeous face. But still, he had to understand I had come to the ranch with Kate, even though I wanted to spend every waking and sleeping minute of my visit with him.

Wait. I didn't just say that, did I?

"Okay." Ouch. Defensiveness took over. I had no clue why. I consciously tried to restrain myself from giving off the feeling overtaking me. It drove me crazy that I didn't know what went on in his mind.

"Have fun with your sister."

"You look familiar to me." One of the women Kate had introduced us to studied Logan, her eyes bright with recognition. And here I thought she was gay. Obviously not, with her ogling him so blatantly.

Maybe she's bisexual and has been one of his many partners.

Humph!

Jealousy reared its ugly face and took over my defensiveness. I quickly reeled it in so others wouldn't notice.

"Aren't you the guitarist for Steam?" She smiled wide, suddenly realizing the connection.

"Yup. That would be me."

She lit up, her gestures becoming animated like a crazed fan would behave. I watched in awe at the scene taking place in front of me.

"I absolutely *love* you guys! I've been to a couple of your shows." She bounced up and down with glee.

Imaginary neon warning signs flashed in front of my eyes. I didn't think I could deal with Logan's budding popularity, especially where women were concerned.

He shifted uneasily, his eyes darting back and forth between me and the fan. "Thanks."

"I know this probably isn't the time or place, but would you mind if I took a selfie with you?"

Typical celebrity crush behavior.

He stepped closer to her, his body stiff. I knew he couldn't possibly behave so awkwardly with all his fans. It had to be the predicament he now found himself in.

Logan wrapped his arm around her waist and smiled, a forced one, if my observations were correct. Maybe it was the one he used for media coverage and band photos. If so, it needed work, because his real one blew me across the ballpark. This one, not so much.

The girl's friend held the phone and snapped a few pictures. Fan girl then asked Logan for a hug. He stepped out of her reach immediately afterward. How moving. He always did have a soft heart, except when he broke mine. During that time in his life, the damn thing had turned cold as ice.

Kate's eyes narrowed, her lips tightened. Her negative attitude really started to piss me off. She had to let the Logan thing rest.

One of the staffers signaled for everyone's attention.

"We would appreciate if you could all head over to your meeting places for your next activity."

"Ready?"

No.

"Sure." I agreed against my mind's wishes, having lost all motivation to go shooting with Kate.

"Have fun." Logan spoke without much gusto.

Damn, between him and my sister, I didn't know which one of them to comfort first. Some serious therapy would help them both.

Kate won first prize as the recipient of my interest.

I followed her since she already knew the other members in our group.

We climbed onto the back of a pickup truck along with a few other guests. Jack drove us to a shooting and archery range located about a mile away on the ranch premises. The place looked cool as shit. I had never shot a gun or an arrow. My adrenaline kicked in at the anticipation. I couldn't wait to play with the firearms, as awful as that sounded.

The staffer named Kyle assisted Jack in giving us basic instructions on handling and loading the rifles. They gave us a short lesson on target practice, then called us up individually, with Kyle and Jack providing additional instruction and feedback. I didn't want to stop once I got the rifle in my hands, aiming for the bull's-eye so much more fun than I'd thought it would be. I got pretty darn close to the center circle too, impressing myself.

The forty-five minutes flew by and we were again on the pickup truck, now heading back to the main area of the ranch. Kate remained quiet and to herself during the short drive.

We climbed out of the truck.

"You okay?"

Her eyes were heavy, ready to cry. "I have my ups and downs. Right now, I'm in a downswing."

"Do you want to talk?" I offered a listening ear.

She shook her head. "I appreciate you asking, but there's really nothing you can do or say to change how I feel. It's something I have to work through. I think I'll get my reader and hang out on the porch."

"Maybe I'll get mine and read too."

We strode back to our cabin. The sound of Logan's guitar stopped us in our tracks. He sat on his rocking chair on his porch, strumming away.

"I can't believe he's so famous. Crazy."

She too preferred country music. Steam songs would never show up on her playlist. Joe was a good ole southern boy who drove a Ford pickup, hunted and fished, and loved going to country bars. Kate easily converted to his lifestyle, minus the hunting and fishing.

"Yeah, crazy." I knew his band had gained fame but didn't realize how much. I chose not to follow them on social media for obvious reasons.

Logan noticed us and ceased playing, interrupting our private conversation.

"How was shooting?"

"Amazing. I'm ready to go back again tomorrow."

He smiled at my reply. "Maybe I'll have to tag along with you. Sounds like I missed out on a lot of fun."

"I'll meet you back at the cabin." Kate interjected rudely and shuffled off.

"Sorry about her bad manners." I stepped onto Logan's porch. "So, what were you playing? It sounded great."

"One of our newer songs. I'm messing around with it."

"Can I hear it again?"

"On one condition."

Knowing exactly what his condition would be, I narrowed my gaze.

"You play one of your songs for me after I'm finished."

"I already told you, I prefer to play for myself rather than an audience."

"I'm not an audience."

His rebuttal did nothing to change my mind. "An audience can be one or ten thousand."

"Come on, Drew. I'm excited to hear you play."

He did a great job of being persuasive, his adorable grin getting underneath my skin.

My shoulders slouched in defeat. "Fine."

His eyes lit up. "Really? Great. Let me go inside and grab you a chair." He sprang into action. He brought me a wooden chair and set it next to his rocking chair. "Have a seat."

Why had I agreed to play him one of my songs?

He picked up his guitar, adjusting it comfortably on his lap, and began playing the same beautiful melody again. As much as I tried to concentrate on his flawless technique, my nerves intensified as the song progressed. When he finished, my hands were trembling and my heart thudded against my chest. I had also broken out into a sweat. What a sight to behold.

He studied me. "You look flushed. Do you want a drink?"

Yeah. How about a shot of vodka? Too bad I knew he meant water.

"I have bottles of water. Let me get you one."

See. I knew him so well, yet he had absolutely no clue why I was such a wreck.

He handed me a cold bottle when he returned. I rubbed it against my forehead and across the back of my neck. I twisted the cap off and took a sip.

"Don't tell me you're this nervous because you're about to play a song for me."

Guess he did have a clue. "I told you I prefer to play for myself."

"Hey, just so you know, I'd never judge you."

The bottle resting between my hands got ample attention. I played with the wrapper around it.

"I'm not going to force you. I'd love to hear some of your music, but not if it's going to make you feel this uncomfortable. Don't sweat it."

It wasn't that. I was more scared about him hearing my lyrics than playing a song for him.

"What's the verdict?"

"Would you mind if I took a rain check?"

Disappointment filled his blue eyes, but I couldn't do it. Not yet.

9

LOGAN

Drew must've felt relieved about her decision to forgo playing me one of her songs because her natural color returned to her cheeks.

"Being you love animals and all, if you want, I can take you to the rabbit and chicken pens tomorrow morning, and you can help feed them with Layla."

She smiled brightly. "I'd love that."

"I figured as much, which is why I offered."

"Let me ask you something. You say you don't usually participate in the planned activities when you're here. So then what do you usually do over the course of the week?"

"Well, as I told you, I come here to relax. I'll tag along with Brian and some of the others when they go out at night. There's a town not far from here. It's small and quaint. It has a bar or two, where we'll shoot pool and throw darts. But I'm perfectly content sitting in this very spot, playing my guitar, and doing nothing else."

"So I'm assuming you always get the same cabin when you visit?"

"I do."

"I think I'd get bored if I lived this far out. It's so isolated from the rest of civilization." She scanned the forest surrounding us.

"Which is exactly why I come here. There's something about the fresh air, Susanna's homemade cooking, and the quietness that I enjoy immensely. It's a reprieve from the chaotic world we live in."

"I see your point, especially in your situation, where you say you travel a lot. I envy you a bit."

"Why's that?"

"Because you've seen so much, whereas I've hardly seen anything."

How I would love to show her the world. But in a sense, I envied *her*. She had the stability of being in one place. Not that I regretted my career choice for one second, but the job more than took its toll after a while.

"I definitely can't complain. I've been very fortunate."

She raised her brows as if about to ask me another question but refrained.

"You've still got your whole life ahead of you, Drew."

"I know. But I often feel stuck in a situation I'm not happy to be in."

Good, she started to open up to me. That meant she felt some sort of trust building between us again.

"Would you care to elaborate?"

She shrugged. "I don't know." She shifted sideways on her chair. "You knew what you wanted to do from a young age. And you remained steadfast and determined to follow that path. I admire your ambition and fortitude. I guess I never really had a passion toward anything other than writing, but that doesn't count. It's a hobby, not a career choice."

"Don't pooh-pooh it. People could say the same thing about playing guitar. I chose to make it my career."

"But you were born to perform. It's in your blood."

"Who knows? Maybe you were born to be a writer."

"A songwriter who's afraid to play her music for others and let it be heard? I don't think so." She sighed. "I've taken a variety of classes, hoping to be inspired or find my calling, but it still hasn't happened yet. I'm afraid it never will."

She was too beautiful to pout.

"So take a risk. Right now. Take my guitar, and play me a song."

She crossed her legs and folded her hands on her lap. "I can't."

"Who says?"

Her eyes flicked to mine, then down at her hands again.

"Forget I said anything."

"I don't want to forget you said anything. This is obviously something that weighs heavily on your mind. If you don't want to play for me, at least tell me about your writing. Tell me how it makes you feel. If it makes you feel as good as playing the guitar makes me feel, you might have already found your calling."

"Having a passion for something and being able to support yourself while doing it are two different things."

"You have a job and you go to school. Why can't you fit what you love into the equation as well?"

"Because like I said, I feel stuck. I'm having trouble figuring things out. Besides, you know I suck at math."

She gave me a poor excuse of a smile. I dug her pun, though, a cute one.

"The only way you'll ever know if it's what you're meant to do is by taking a risk. If you don't, trust me, you'll regret it forever."

"Are you speaking from experience?"

It's too bad that experience sat by my side. To this day, I still regretted never taking the risk to try and win her back.

"We all have things we regret." I didn't give her direct eye contact with my reply.

"Tell me one of yours."

Did she refer to our break up or something else?

"We all have our demons." I glanced at her, not ready to go there yet.

The sadness and disappointment in her eyes killed me. I knew an inevitable conversation would take place in the near future if we continued to hang out together. I wanted to postpone it, though. She wasn't in the mindset to play her music for me, and similarly, I wasn't in the mindset to rehash the past. I delighted in being with her in the present. Unfortunately, the early days kept creeping themselves into the picture.

"We certainly do." She twirled a few strands of hair in her ponytail.

There were a few moments of silence until some crunching on gravel caught our attention. Kate frantically ran along the path in front of the cabins.

Drew jumped off her chair and ran down the stairs to meet her sister.

I couldn't hear their conversation but watched them chat. Kate gestured animatedly while speaking. Drew nodded in agreement with whatever the hell her sister said to her.

A few minutes later, Kate dashed off again, toward the dining hall. Drew shuffled up the stairs to my porch in a slower manner. She sat on her chair.

"Is everything all right?"

"I'm not sure. One of the staffers went to our cabin to inform Kate she'd received a phone call from Joe, her fiancé, or ex-fiancé. I'm curious to see why he called."

"Maybe he regrets walking away?" I sure did.

"Yeah, I think he might. If you saw the two of them together, you'd agree they seem very much in love. When he bolted from the ceremony, it came as a shock to everyone. His parents ran after him, along with mine. Kate ran to the bride's dressing room in hysterics. The other bridesmaids and I attended to her."

"Did she speak to him after he ran off?"

"No. There was so much chaos and confusion at the venue. The band stood by, ready to play. The caterer stood by, ready to serve. It was a disaster."

She exhaled.

"Both sets of parents agreed to tell the guests to go inside the banquet room and enjoy the party, minus the bride and groom, I might add. Sheer insanity. A lot of guests remained, mostly family members. I think they thought Joe had cold feet and would have a change of heart. I did. It was heartbreaking for my sister. She wanted *out*, pleading for me to take her home. She didn't want to see or talk to anyone. We snuck out of the building through a back door. I texted my mom during our drive home to fill her in. She told me I should have kept Kate there, so she and Joe could talk things out."

"Fuck." I had nothing else to add.

"Fuck is right. Kate cried the entire ride home, not that I blamed her. I cried too. When we got home, she told me she wanted to leave. She said she was embarrassed by the entire situation. She also said she couldn't bear to face anyone. She pretty much demanded that I go with her, telling me the ranch would be the perfect place for her to get her thoughts together. I tried to convince her to speak with Joe first, arguing against skipping town because she'd have to face him sooner or later. She tuned me out. She called the airline, had them cancel Joe's ticket and issue a credit in his name, telling them an emergency had come up and he couldn't make it. She then purchased me a round trip flight without getting my permission first."

My lips formed an O in response to the story.

"Kate dragged an empty suitcase out of the storage closet and wheeled it in front of me, telling me to pack up for a week. I told her our parents would flip out if the two of us got up and left town without saying anything. Kate couldn't give two shits whether they cared or not. She said we were both adults and could make our own decisions, reiterating how she needed to escape but didn't want to go alone. It just so happened I was on break from school, but my parents would miss me at the clinic. They depend on me to be there."

"Wow, this story keeps getting better and better." I sat forward on my rocking chair in anticipation of hearing the rest of it.

"I called my mom to fill her in on Kate's decision, which included me. She screamed, begging me to convince Kate to change her mind. I couldn't. Not that I blamed her for wanting to leave. I'm sure I would've felt the same way. With all the arguing going on between me and my mom, Kate said she couldn't take anymore. She booked us a cheap room at a hotel near the airport so nobody would be able to find us. She insisted we shut off our phones to avoid any more contact with the family. So, here we are, two days into Kate's honeymoon and Joe's calling her."

"Holy shit." That's pretty much all I could come up with.

"Yup. I called my parents after we landed. They blamed me for a change, saying I could've talked her out of coming. Whatever."

She brushed the thought off with a flip of her wrist, her expression hardening, showing her displeasure.

"I tried. There was nothing more I could do other than tell her I wouldn't come with her. I knew she'd go alone if I didn't because she's stubborn that way. And I didn't want her to be by herself when she felt so depressed."

"You're a good sister." As much as I loathed Kate, a part of me now rooted for her, hoping her fiancé had called to work things out. She had also brought Drew back into my life so I for one was Team Kate.

"Thanks. Although I haven't been by her side too much, thanks to you."

Her grumpiness made me smile.

"Hey, none of that. The fact you're here with her speaks for itself. I'm sure her seeing the two of us together isn't helping matters either." I almost hated to admit it.

"Yeah. It must be hard for her to be alone with her thoughts, but she's going to have to face them at some point. As cruel as this may sound, I can only tolerate her in measured doses. Does that make me a horrible person?"

"Absolutely not. Like I just said, you're a fantastic sister. You comforted her after the asshole ditched her. You took her home, so she wouldn't have to see anyone. And then you came with her on her honeymoon against your will. That says a lot about your character. You're a dedicated and loyal person. And trust me, if I had to spend a week with Kate, I'd lose my mind."

She giggled. It made me feel good to know I had lightened her mood.

"I appreciate you saying that. Kate loves to reiterate what a selfish person I am."
"Fuck Kate."
She broke out into a fit of laughter.
"You're right. Fuck Kate." She nodded in solidarity.
"Hey, do you want to see something?" The thought of where I wanted to take her came to me out of nowhere.
"Sure, I'd love to."
"Great. Let me put this away first."
I took care of my guitar by putting it in its case inside the cabin, then rushed back out to the porch, grabbing Drew's hand, and leading her down the stairs.
"Where're we going?"
I dragged her along at a rapid pace.
"You'll see." I felt a surge of adrenaline the closer we got to our destination.
We stopped in front of a cabin.

She grimaced at it. "This is what you wanted to show me?"

"No. There's more. Come with me." I led her up the stairs.

She tugged on my hand to stop me. "We can't go up there. It's someone's cabin." She scanned the area to make sure nobody was in sight.

"It's fine. Whoever's staying in it is probably at an activity. Besides, we're not going inside. I just want to show you something on the porch."

She shook her head in rebuttal, not giving in to my strategy to get her up the stairs. I released her hand and went to my intended target. I squatted and pointed to a wood plank on the railing.

She eyed me inquisitively from the edge of the stairs. "What're you looking at?" Her feet remained fixed in place.

"Come see for yourself."

She checked out the path again to make sure no guests were strolling along it. She approached and kneeled next to me.

I pointed to a small heart engraved on the plank. It had the letters *L* and *D* and the word *forever* inscribed underneath them inside the heart.

She reached forward and traced the outline of the image with her finger. "My gosh, when did you do this?"

"The summer after we graduated. The last time I came here with my folks."

"I can't believe it's still here." She retraced the engraved letters and heart shape around them.

"Yeah, I couldn't either. I found it a few years back. Susanna and Jack maintain these cabins no a regular basis, painting them and changing wood where necessary. I guess this piece never needed changing, and new paint didn't effectively cover my engraving. Odd, huh?" *Or a message from above, perhaps?*

She rubbed her finger over the word "forever."

"Yeah. Odd. What made you decide to show this to me?" Her eyes remained glued to the heart, her tone sincere, not at all accusatory.

. . .

"I guess I wanted you to know you weren't the only one in pain after we broke up." I had trouble keeping my emotions in check.

"Thanks for sharing that with me. It means a lot."

"It's true. I never intended to hurt you." Here I tried to postpone the inevitable yet kept bringing up the damn topic.

She nodded in understanding but didn't give a verbal response.

"Come. We better get out of here before someone accuses us of breaking and entering."

I stood, extending my hand. She took hold of it.

She paused at the bottom of the stairs.

"You did hurt me, though, Logan. More than you can ever imagine." A few tears escaped. I cupped her cheeks and used my thumbs to dry the wetness underneath her eyes.

The pain in my heart was overflowing. "I know, and I'm sorry." I leaned forward and planted a soft kiss on her lips. I didn't know what else to do.

Kids screaming and gravel being shifted around broke the shared intensity of the moment. A family of four emerged, the kids running toward the cabin with their parents following behind.

"That was a close one. Let's get out of here." A wave of relief crashed through me.

The two of us nodded our hellos to the family when we passed by them. They didn't say a word about our secret visit.

10

DREW

"I wonder if Kate finished her phone call yet." Now that we were in front of my cabin, I became curious about the outcome of her conversation with Joe.

"Why don't you go inside and see if she's in there?"

"I think I will. You can come with me if you want."

"I would hate to make her feel out of sorts with me in there."

"That's sweet of you, but you don't have to wait outside. Come on."

He followed me inside the cabin. Music played in the back bedroom.

"Hang tight out here for a minute. I'd offer you something to drink, but there's nothing except tap water."

He put his hand out to pacify me. "I'm good. I'll wait here on the couch."

Logan got comfy on the sofa and I went to find my sister. Her suitcase rested on the bed, and she stuffed clothing inside it.

Her cheeks were red-stained from crying.

"Kate? What's going on?"

"Joe wants to make things right." She forced a smile and placed her hand over her heart.

I sat on the bed next to her suitcase. "What did he say?"

"He couldn't apologize enough. He admitted he got cold feet. He said the reality of marriage hit him while standing at the altar and he became paralyzed with fear, since his parents' divorce royally fucked him up. I thought he had worked through his shit. Apparently not." She sighed heavily, continuing to pack.

"So..." I gestured for her to elaborate.

"So when he heard I left town, he became frantic at the huge mistake he'd made. He assured me I'm the only woman for him, and that there'll never be anyone else."

She smiled through her tears.

A small part of me still held a grudge against Joe for the pain he inflicted on my sister, but his screw up had brought Logan into my life again. And for that, I was eternally grateful, as selfish as it sounded.

"He also told me he apologized to all the guests, telling them to hang tight because a wedding would take place. That's when mom and dad informed him you and I left. He said he tried calling us nonstop, but the calls kept going to voice mail. You shouldn't have agreed to shut off your phone."

What? I only did what she'd asked.

"So once again, he had to apologize to our friends and family."

"I take offense to you blaming me for shutting off my phone. You were crying hysterically. I merely did what you suggested. And might I remind you, I'm the one who told you not to leave town, to speak to Joe first."

She rolled her eyes. "What's done is done."

Of course, when it came to Kate taking responsibility for herself, she blew it off. She always had.

What gall of him. "Don't you think he should've faced the reality of his situation prior to walking down an aisle in front of a hundred and fifty people?"

She gaped at me. "Why aren't you being supportive?" She crossed her arms.

"You should be happy for me."

Happy for her? The guy ditched her at the altar and now begged for forgiveness? I was *concerned* for her. I'd seen the aftermath. I didn't want to see a repeat.

"You know what I think? That you're jealous things are working out for me in spite of everything that happened." She resumed packing as if she hadn't voiced such horrible words to me.

My gaze fixed on her, I clenched my jaw tight. She had to be kidding me. I'd had it with her, all her years of verbal insults and abuse…this was the final straw. I rose, the tension in my muscles making it difficult to stand.

"I can't believe you just said that. For once in your life, give me a break and stop turning shit on me. I'm getting tired of it. Scratch that. I *am* tired of it, sick of it if I'm being totally honest. If I didn't support or care about your happiness, I wouldn't have traveled across the country to be here with you. So cut the bullshit. As opposed to you, who is holding on to Joe's every word, I guess I'm skeptical about his intentions. To me, actions speak louder than words. But you're a grown woman who can think for herself. I'm certainly not going to try and stop you or try to change your mind."

Her body softened. She packed the last of her clothing and zipped the suitcase closed.

"I am a grown woman, and I want to be with Joe."

She wrapped her hand around the handle of the suitcase and hoisted it off the bed, setting it on the floor between us.

"So you're leaving without finishing out the week?"

"Yes. I have no reason to be here. This was supposed to be my honeymoon with Joe. We had both arranged our work schedules around it. I don't want to waste what's left of it with you, no offense. I want to spend it with Joe instead."

No offense?

Why it bothered me so much, I didn't understand, yet I shouldn't have expected anything less from Kate.

"We're in the middle of the mountains. How do you plan to get to the airport? And more importantly, how did you arrange a flight out on such short notice? There are only so many flights coming in and out of that small airport we flew into."

She pulled the handle release, so she could wheel her suitcase.

"Joe took care of most of the arrangements online during our phone conversation. Brian agreed to drive me back to the city. He's picking me up in a few minutes. My flight doesn't leave until tomorrow, but Susanna said she needs him here, so tonight I'll stay at a hotel near the airport, and tomorrow morning I'll leave for Vegas. Joe will meet up with me later in the day at the hotel he booked us into. We'll get dressed, pick a fun place, and get hitched. Then we'll spend the remainder of our stay touring and seeing the sights."

She beamed.

"This mess has set me and Joe back quite a bit financially, but I'm hopeful in the end everything will work out the way it's supposed to."

The enormity of the situation had me dumbfounded.

"I can't believe you're leaving me here. You're the one who begged me to come with you."

She shrugged. My sister could care less about leaving the ranch without me.

"You're free to leave, but you'll have change your ticket yourself. I paid for your trip out here. Between mine and Joe's last-minute flights to Vegas, it's costing us a fortune. Thank goodness our tickets were transferable, but it's still costing us a shitload of cash. Let's hear it for Joe's Visa card."

"I'm still stuck on the fact you dragged me up here, and now you're leaving without considering my feelings. And now you want me to pay or make arrangements if I want to leave early. What the hell, Kate?"

She twisted her lips up on one side. "Get off your high horse, and be real. You want me to leave. Think about it. Now you'll have Logan all to yourself without me bothering you. So give *me* a break when you say I don't consider your feelings. Enjoy the rest of your vacation. It's on me and Joe."

She waltzed toward the door, dragging her suitcase behind her.

Jeez, talk about being full of shit, because even if Logan wasn't at the ranch, she still would've left me high and dry. It had nothing to do with him and everything to do with her and her selfishness.

I had so much to say but found myself at a loss for words, all my emotions stuck at the base of my throat. I blocked the exit to her room.

"What?" She stopped in front of me.

"My God, Kate. You know what? I'm done. I've tried to be patient, but you're so damn impulsive. You don't think before you act." I gestured in an effort to get my point across and release some of my pent-up agitation.

"What's that supposed to mean?"

"The entire wedding fiasco. You didn't want to hear anything anyone had to say, nor did you want to speak with anyone. Instead, you chose to run off to the mountains, out of touch from society. Great coping mechanism. Now Joe calls, claiming he made a mistake, asking you to forgive him and marry him in Vegas. Don't you think a conversation or two should take place beforehand? You're agreeing to walk down the aisle with him so soon without talking about what took place? I'm sorry, but I find this to be a bit fucked-up. I get people make mistakes and get nervous, but to walk out on your bride? Uh-uh." I shook my head. "Maybe it's just me and the way I rationalize things. All I'm saying is, maybe you should take a step back and consider the situation from an outsider's point of view."

She put her hand out, palm up.

Come on, did she really not understand my point, or did she play stupid?

"Any *rational* outsider would view this as a beautiful love story. The groom got cold feet only to realize he lost the love of his life, so he chased her down, and married her."

She smiled in her dreamy state, her expression darkening to one of anger when she saw the disbelief on my face. "Let me tell you what I think. I think you're taking my situation to heart, wishing Logan Trimble had chased you down all those years ago, declaring his undying love for you. But he didn't. He fucking bolted. So don't try to make Joe sound like the bad guy here. If you should be mad at anyone, it should be the asshole, wherever he is right now."

Try down the hall, big mouth! And w
hat a horrible thing to say.

"Fuck you, Kate!" I stormed through the cabin, past Logan, and out the front door. I took off running. I didn't know where I headed, but my feet kept moving at a steady pace. Now all I needed was for my mind to shut the hell up and leave me alone.

"Drew! Drew!" Logan's calls got louder the closer he got to me.

I ran faster.

And faster.

But not fast enough.

Maybe for once in her life, Kate was right. Maybe I did feel jealous of her and Joe's relationship. Here the love of her life wanted her back, whereas mine had cheated on me, never to be heard from again until now, an unplanned meeting—maybe an attempt—to make things right.

My legs ached. My heart ached. My thoughts ran on overdrive. I didn't know how much farther my feet could take me.

My lungs required oxygen. I panted heavily, trying to inhale as much air as I could.

Stopping, I rested my hands on my thighs. I bent over and tried to catch my breath.

Logan caught up to me and mimicked my pose.

"What the hell, Drew? Why did you take off so fast?"

"I wanted fresh air." In this case, I really did, in more ways than one.

"Air you could've gotten on the porch. Why did you feel the urge to run?"

"Please don't psychoanalyze me right now." I put my hand out to stop him in his tracks. "I'm sure you heard what Kate said. None of it has to be repeated. Nor should it."

How mortifying that he had been there to witness her outburst about him. I exhaled, trying to release the tension in my body. Sadly, it did nothing to calm me down. Neither had my sprint across the rocky path from my cabin.

"Do you mind if I ask you a question?" I stood upright, still trying to get a steady breathing pattern going again.

He did the same, taking slow, deep breaths, his height a few good inches taller than mine.

"Sure. Ask away."

He licked his lips, causing me to lose my concentration, especially when his tongue glided across his bottom lip. It caused my female parts to wake up and take notice.

Jerk. I exhaled again because his hotness pissed me off. Why couldn't he look like shit right now?

Focus. Get back on track.

Right. I put my hands on my hips. I hated being confrontational, but I had to know the truth.

"Back at the cabin where you showed me the engraving, you said you wanted me to know I wasn't the only one who'd gotten hurt after our breakup. If you truly felt so much pain, why didn't you ever reach out to me?"

He started breathing harder again.

"I did. You rejected all my calls and refused to see me whenever I came to your house. What did you expect me to do?"

Shit.

He spoke the truth. I had shut him out. It amazed me how we only remembered what we choose to.

Of all times for Kate to be right, it had to be this one, the lightbulb bright in my head now, a high-wattage, powerful-as-shit one too. I *had* expected Logan to chase me down.

Tears flowed in a continuous stream down my cheeks. I couldn't hold them back any longer. All these years I'd held on to a pipe dream. How desperate could I have been, when it was clear Logan had moved on, admitting to having sex with groupies? Why hadn't I moved on? Had he scarred me for life?

And therein lay my answer. He not only scarred me for life, he'd also scarred me for all other men. Logan had stolen my heart and never bothered to give it back. I now realized why I hadn't been able to move forward, I had nothing left to give. Logan had already sucked all the love out of me.

This newfound awareness hit me hard. I sat on the rocky path with my knees bent in front of me and wrapped my arms around them, resting my forehead on top. The darkness when I closed my eyes was such a metaphor for my shit mood.

"Hey, talk to me. I hate seeing you like this."

For a minute I'd forgotten he was there. He'd sat next to me, mere inches separating our bodies from touching. He tried to caress my back, but I retreated.

"What're we doing?" I lifted my head and wiped the tears from my eyes.

. . .

He shrugged. "I don't know, but whatever it is, I like it."

The tenderness in his features warmed the coldness building inside me.

"I do too. That's the problem." I bit my lower lip and focused downward, using my foot to play with the rocks.

"I don't see a problem."

"Of course you don't. What happens at the end of the week? Do we part and pretend our time together on this trip never happened?"

"I honestly don't know what's going to happen after we leave. What I do know is I want to spend every waking moment I'm here with you. Fuck that, every sleeping moment too."

Closing my eyes, I rubbed my forehead. "I don't know that I can do what you're suggesting."

"And what is it you think I'm suggesting?"

My eyes blinked open. He brushed my wet hair from my face and dried my tears with the back of his hand.

Come on. I couldn't be that naive.

"I know exactly what you're suggesting. For the two of us to spend the week screwing around, taking hikes, dining together, exploring, and playing music. In all conscience, I don't know if I'm capable of doing those things with you of all people, especially the first part."

"Are you willing to give it a try? I am."

"Hello? You're a man." I didn't try to hide my sarcasm.

"Hey, that's not fair. Just because I'm a man doesn't mean I don't have feelings. I hurt the same way you do. I may show it differently, but it doesn't mean your pain is any worse or less than mine."

He was right. We both had the same amount to lose.

"Think about it, at least now you won't have to worry about babysitting your sister. We'll have the rest of the week to do with as we please. Let's agree to take it one day at a time. Are you okay with that?" He again tried to caress my back. I allowed him to.

"My mind and heart are telling me two different things."

. . .

He brushed more hair off my face, his fingers gliding up and down my cheek. "Go with what your heart says."

Maybe I was a glutton for punishment, because I wanted more than anything to spend the next few days with him. The challenge I foresaw was the need to remain in the present. I couldn't allow myself to project about what would happen after we left the ranch. For all I knew, we would hate each other by week's end. Though I highly doubted it, believing the total opposite, actually.

11

LOGAN

At least she'd stopped crying. "Do you want to head back to your cabin to say good-bye to Kate?"

She sighed. "I don't want to, but I know it's the right thing to do."

I stood and assisted her up. I kept her hand in mine during our stroll back to see her sister off.

Kate wheeled her suitcase into the living room right as Drew and I stepped inside the cabin. Drew's hand remained protectively in mine. I squeezed it for encouragement to indicate she should go and say something to her sister.

She did.

She rubbed her free hand against her thigh. "I'm sorry. I didn't mean to attack you. I want you to know I'm on your side no matter what decision you make in regard to Joe." Her words came out hushed.

Kate smiled and a few tears rolled down her cheeks. She embraced Drew.

. . .

When the two of them parted, Kate pointed her finger at me.

"You better be good to her, Logan Trimble. Don't break her heart again, or you'll have me to deal with."

She spoke with conviction.

She winked at Drew and rubbed her sister's arm.

"I'll do my best not to." My assurance was mostly for Drew.

A horn out front startled us. Kate peered out of the window. "Brian's here."

He parked the van. I grabbed Kate's luggage, and we escorted her outside.

"We're sorry to see you go, but it sounds like you're leaving for all the right reasons." Brian put Kate's suitcase in the back of the van.

"The best reason." Her entire face lit up.

She ran over to Drew and hugged her tightly. "I'm sorry I acted so bitchy." She pointed at me again. "Remember what I said, Logan." She winked at Drew again and climbed inside the van.

Drew and I watched Brian back up and drive off.

Drew wore a proud smile.

"What're you thinking?"

"I'm happy for her. I really am." She continued to watch the van until it was out of sight.

"You know who I'm happy for?"

She shook her head.

"I'm happy we have two cabins all to ourselves. Now if I remember correctly, you mentioned screwing around, playing music, and a bunch of other shit that doesn't stand out. I'm game for starting with the first item on your list." I prayed she would be on board.

She laughed. "I also said you're a typical male, not in those exact words, but you get my drift."

"Damn right. I bet I can beat you to the bedroom. I'll even give you a head start."

"Slow down, Mr. Trimble. I didn't agree to sleep with you yet."

Really?

I frowned. Maybe I had read her cues and body language incorrectly. *Damn.*

"But that doesn't mean we can't do other things." She raised her brows suggestively. She

bolted for the stairs, skipping every other one, and dashed inside the cabin.

Fuck yes!

I was right there with her.

She stood in front of her bed, shifting her bodyweight from foot to foot. I sensed her nervousness. She had absolutely no reason to feel it.

"Hi." I stepped toward her.

"Hi." She tucked loose hair behind her ear.

Another step forward and her body was mere inches in front of mine. "Just to make sure we're both on the same page, what kind of *other things* were you referring to?"

Her cheeks flushed pink. Always one to be on the shy side when it came to verbalizing her desires in the bedroom. Still, we'd been teenagers then. For all I knew, she could've mutated into a wild beast in the sack, but I seriously doubted it.

She shrugged, vulnerability filling her.

Nope. Things hadn't changed. She still had the shy thing going.

"How about this?" I nibbled on her earlobe.

"That's good." She angled her head to the side.

"What about this?" I planted a trail of light kisses down her neck.

"That's good too." Her voice got quieter.

Two for two. I took things a step further, heading lower, toward the rim of her shirt. Her chest rose and fell. The shirt covering her luscious breasts needed to say good-bye, and fast, because I'd been fantasizing nonstop about seeing her beauties again.

While raising the bottom of the pink cotton material, I relished the velvety feel of her soft skin. The shirt got tossed on the floor.

She placed her hand on my chest, her fingers splayed against it, her eyes hungry.

With the green light I presumed she gave me, I unclasped her bra, removed both straps off her shoulders in unison, and slid the thin lacy material down and off her arms. The undergarment joined the shirt on the floor.

Bashfulness overtook her. She brought her hands forward to cover her breasts.

That wouldn't do. I removed them and placed them on my shoulders instead.

Much better.

My mind agreed with the visual in front of me. I breathed deeply, taking her in. Fuck, a glorious sight, her breasts larger than I remembered, each one a perfect handful.

Palming her bare flesh, I covered her rose-colored areola with my lips, my tongue flicking her erect nipple.

Her fingers dug into my hair, fisting it.

"You're so beautiful, Drew." The words of truth slipped out without any forethought.

I stroked her other nipple with my thumb, cherishing it, rolling it between two fingers.

Her tight abdomen was grazed with kisses. I headed lower, to the faint trail of light hair below her belly button. Unfortunately, the barricade called the waistband of her shorts stopped me. I didn't consider it a problem whatsoever. They got unbuttoned promptly.

She stopped me with her hand before I got to the zipper and bit her lower lip, hesitating.

Red light. I wouldn't move forward unless she wanted me to. I waited patiently for her to decide.

She stepped closer to the bed, pulling me with her.

She took it upon herself to lie down, her eyes immediately closing.

Green light.

Her body tensed when I climbed over her and rested my body weight on my forearms.

I stepped on the breaks. Not an easy feat with Drew half naked underneath me.

My lips found hers. Our mouths opened. My tongue dove inside. It wanted company. Our joined tongues danced wildly, the connection intense.

She softened against the mattress. I took a risk, rocking my cock into her. She raised her pelvis to meet it, welcoming it.

Her action surprised me, causing me to look at her. She did the same to me and

draped her arms around me, hugging my chest tightly against hers, our gazes locked on one another.

It was too much intensity for me to wrap my head around, so I changed positions. I journeyed south to her breasts, sucking on one then the other. Right now, I needed her like oxygen. I enveloped her supple flesh with my mouth, my hand cupping her fullness.

"Please."

Her wish was my command.

I kissed my way down to the waistband of her shorts. She didn't stop me when I reached for the zipper. I breathed a sigh of relief.

Zip.

With the shorts now free, I nudged her to lift her hips so I could get the bottoms off easier.

First I had to ditch her sneakers, though. Adios Converse. The shorts came off next.

Fuck me.

A morsel of a white G-string with lace edging presented itself. I did a double take to make sure my brain wasn't fucking around with me.

While gliding my hands up her smooth legs, the nerve endings in my fingers became hypersensitive due to the sexual energy she emanated. I teased by running my finger underneath the elastic band of the triangle fabric covering an area of her body she had me salivating over.

She raised her hips in offering.

Entering the speed zone, I scooched down and off the bed, kissing her luscious body as I did so, resting my knees on the low pile carpet.

She watched me tug on her legs, causing her body to drift down the mattress toward my hungry mouth, her pussy mere inches in front of it yet too far for my ravenous appetite.

Fuck, she smelled good.

She blinked, shielding her breasts again with her hands.

"Don't cover yourself. I love seeing your body like this, wanting for more."

Her cheeks flushed darker. She closed her eyes and took a deep breath, her modesty evident. I would go with it for now.

"These aren't needed right now. Lift up for me, baby, so I can get them off." Goodbye tiny strip of satin and lace covering her small patch of hair.

She didn't respond verbally but did as instructed.

Her scent drove me fucking wild. I had to taste her.

I dragged her down another inch or two toward the edge of the mattress, closer to me, and wrapped her legs around my shoulders before diving in, not giving her a chance to rebut.

She tasted better than I remembered if that was even a possibility. And so fucking wet too. My cock twitched in my boxers, dying to get inside her.

Not yet.

She'd made that point perfectly clear.

Parting her folds gave me better access to her opening. I probed her channel with my tongue, circling my thumb over her swollen clit.

She reached out for me. I held one of her hands, our fingers now intertwined.

I buried myself in her glorious pussy, lapping at her sweet spot, kissing, delving my tongue inside her. I wanted all of it.

She squeezed her thighs against my head, her breath picking up speed.

"Logan..."

The way she said my name penetrated deep into my soul.

I sucked on her clit, my thumb now probing her, my actions and her reactions creating a beautiful and steady rhythm.

Shit. I hadn't eaten a girl out in forever, safe sex being a top priority and all. Fucking with condoms was about as far as I agreed to go. I barely kissed the women I fucked either. My dick and fingers took excellent care of their needs with no complaints from the ladies afterward, but lots of coming if I did say so myself.

Crazy, but in this moment, I didn't think twice about the repercussions of my actions with Drew. I hadn't even asked her about her past activities in the sack. But deep down, I knew I didn't have to. I knew she had a moral compass like that of the Pope. Okay, maybe not that pure, but it got my point across. And I got as much pleasure seeing her squirm in delight as she got from the pleasure engulfing her.

Her body trembled and shook, fully allowing the sensations to overtake her. Our hands remained locked together, her free hand gripping the comforter for dear life, her thighs pressing tighter against me.

"Logan...Logan..."

Hearing my name spill from her lips while I drove her mad with ecstasy—possibly the best damn thing I'd heard her say all day.

I continued to suck on her clit until she pushed my head off her.

"It's too much."

Too much? Ha, she couldn't have been more wrong. It was never too much, at least not from my perspective. I wanted as much of her as I could get, as much as she would give to me.

All good things came to an end, this experience being one of them. I unwrapped her legs from around my neck and set them on the mattress, her calves, ankles, and feet hanging over the edge of the bed like dead weight.

Her eyes flicked open, catching mine. She smiled.

"That felt great." Her heavy eyelids closed.

It did for me too.

"I'll be right back. I'm going to go rinse my mouth."

I left for the bathroom, where I cleaned myself up. I rested my palm against the countertop, glancing in the mirror and scratching the back of my neck, my thoughts racing a mile a minute.

Whew. I let out a deep breath. I had jumped into the deep end with Drew without a life vest. She kicked up old feelings I hadn't felt in years, and it scared the living crap out of me.

12

DREW

*O*h. My. God. Best oral sex *ever*.

My body remained limp on the mattress, my limbs too heavy and exhausted to move.

Logan entered the room and laid beside me, me flat on my back, him on his side, his hand immediately going to my breasts, caressing and playing with them.

Not usually the bold type to take charge in the bedroom, I felt a sudden urge to do so. I also felt it only fair to reciprocate his generosity. I flipped onto my side and leaned my palm against his chest. He studied me warily.

Yup, that's right, buddy. It's your turn. I pushed him over so he lay flat on the bed. Hope shone in his baby blues. What a lucky day for him. And his erection tented his shorts, so hard for me. What a morale boost.

A fit of giggles broke out. I covered my mouth.

"Laughing at a guy with a hard-on isn't so good for his ego, babe."

"I'm laughing because here I am, butt naked, and you're still completely dressed."

"Exactly how I like it, but I'm game for stripping down with you."

He jumped into a seated position and began his strip tease. He made me crazy with his boyishness, so carefree and full of life. I loved that about him. I always had.

Wow, he had bulked up over the years. I studied the definition of his chest, muscles galore. I licked my lips. The other guys I had been with didn't hold a candle to Logan.

He grinned, removing his shorts without an ounce of self-consciousness. And why should he? With a body like his he could be a nude model.

Come to think of it, I probably should've been removing the garments for him, but I preferred watching him do it. So sexy.

His eyes remained fixed on mine, famine in them. One would think he was about to receive his very first blowjob. I knew different because I had given him his first one.

When his boxers came flying off, my breath hitched. Fuck, he looked good. I mean *really* good, good enough to eat. *Ha-ha.*

I smiled at my inside joke. He eyed me suspiciously.

Distraction worked wonders to satisfy his curiosity. I climbed on top of him and straddled him. The poor guy probably thought we were about to have sex. Sorry, Charlie. Not yet. My heart hadn't prepared itself for that kind of an intimate connection with him yet.

Leaning forward, I outlined his lips with my tongue.

He closed his eyes and brushed his fingers over my back ever so gently. I thought he might be aggressive, but no. He acted tender and loving in his touch. My heart became a pile of mush, all of it belonging to him.

Our lips met, our tongues desperate to find the other.

He slid his hand into my hair and removed the ponytail holder, allowing my hair to fall loose, onto his face. He brushed it aside.

My hands rested against his chest. I ended the kiss and nipped my way across his neck, up to the delicate skin of his earlobe.

He grunted in satisfaction, stroking every part of me, sending bolts of electricity to my core. And here I thought I was already past the point of exhilaration. What a headrush to feel so cherished. Even if only temporarily.

Moving down his chest, I kissed one nipple, then the other, exploring his six-pack with my hands and tongue. Another inch lower had my mouth at the hair slightly above his erection.

He gathered my hair, fisting it.

He had the agony of desire in his steady eye contact. I had to put him out of his misery. And mine.

Licking my lips to lubricate them started the fun. I brought them over his tip, relishing every drop of salty fluid oozing out with the knowledge I made him feel this aroused. He tasted divine, delicious, every square inch of him a delicacy in itself.

Hollowing my cheeks, I took in as much of him as I could, wrapping my hand around his width, pumping up and down in synchronized movements with my mouth.

Logan pressed my head lower, indicating he wanted me to take him deeper. My hands and lips worked together in unison, his girth and length huge. *Gosh.* I couldn't wait to feel him inside me. The thought alone had me gyrating against his legs.

He released his death grip on my head.

"Bring your ass up here." It wasn't a request. Rather, a command.

As much as I had shared of myself with him in the past, it had been years, causing me to feel reluctant.

"Come on. I want your ass up here." He gestured with his hand for me to get a move on it.

Getting myself situated over him was a challenge. This compromising position magnified all of my insecurities.

With swift motion, he lowered my pelvis toward his mouth, his tongue flicking my clit.

Holy shit! Forget all previous self-doubting thoughts, with this being the epitome of experiencing all things good. I honestly didn't think I had it in me for another round after the mind-blowing orgasm he'd just graced me with. Boy, I couldn't have been more wrong.

"Suck me, baby."

Oh yeah.

I had forgotten my purpose, his tongue distracting me to no end.

I lowered my mouth over his rigid length. At the same time, his tongue entered me, sliding in and out as my head bobbed up and down over him.

The faster he probed me, the faster I took him in. When he slowed the pace, I did the same. I read his cues, following his every move.

He squeezed my ass, one of his fingers getting a little too close for comfort. I paused, wondering where the hell that appendage of his intended to go.

When his pinky nudged lower, teasing the tight flesh in back, I tensed. I had never done anything I considered so taboo before.

"I won't put it inside. I promise. But let me play. You'll love it."

Love it? I'm not too sure about that.

He resumed sucking on me, his tongue doing its thing against my overly sensitized flesh. My body relaxed, sinking lower, getting caught up in the delightful sensations filling me

He probed my back entrance again, keeping true to his word by not inserting anything, merely taunting.

Instinctively, I tensed again.

"Relax, baby."

I tried, I really did.

Lo and behold, as much as I hated to admit it, when I finally let go of my anxiety about the experience, my pleasure meter hiked up another notch.

. . .

Logan had been right. Between his fingers and mouth playing up front and the slight pressure in back, he had me suffocating him, my pelvis collapsing on top of his face as lightness filled me, my thoughts becoming fuzzy in the process.

He raised my hips, the poor guy longing for air.

Time to focus on him again. I took him deeper into my mouth, exploring the ridges of his shaft, so lost in ecstasy I stopped thinking about my gag reflex. And wouldn't you know it? He almost fit in his entirety. Who would've thought?

"That's it, baby."

My lips tightened around him. I swirled my tongue around his tip. I kissed my way down his length, continuing my exploration. My hand continued to stroke him while I cradled his sac in my mouth.

Mmm, so soft and delicious, comparable to the rest of him.

"Fuck, Drew," he growled from underneath me.

Using my tongue, I drew a line up his shaft.

Back at the head, I circled my tongue around and over it.

He tensed, stilling, his cock twitching in my mouth. He tugged on my hair, removed his dick from my mouth, right as he came and shot out onto his stomach. He always was the considerate type. Except, of course, when he'd cheated on me.

Not wanting to ruin the moment, I let the thought slide.

His cock softened yet he remained steadfast on his feeding frenzy between my thighs, my vision going hazy as a result, my toes curling. I released him and grabbed on to the comforter instead.

My surroundings became somewhat out of touch, the echoes of my moan far off in the distance as my body combusted over and around him, shaking as yet another orgasm ripped through me.

Holy shit!

What a ride.

I collapsed on top of him, my cheek getting messy with his wetness. I didn't care. I would've swallowed every last drop if he hadn't pulled out of my mouth. Only Logan, though. No other man could or would ever satisfy my taste buds the way he did.

He lifted my head, laughing when he witnessed the sight.

"Oh really?" I leaned forward and licked him clean.

Damn straight. I had showed him.

His jaw hung slightly open in response. "Fuck, Drew. That's hot as shit."

"You're hot as shit."

So much for feeling vulnerable and insecure. I currently stood on the edge of the *Titanic* with Leo DiCaprio holding on to me, the queen of the world, flying high and proud along with him.

"Christ. It's too bad my cock needs a breather or else you'd be in big trouble." He chuckled.

"Similar to you, Mr. Trimble, I too don't mind getting into trouble when the situation calls for it." I winked at him and crawled off the bed, flipped my hair over my shoulder, and strutted to the bathroom, where I prepared myself for a shower.

Logan joined me not a minute later, almost out of breath. It made me happy. Like a cute and cuddly puppy, he had followed me.

He wrapped his arms around me, the two of us staring at each other in the mirror mounted over the vanity. He rested his chin on top of my head, and a sweet smile broke out on his beautiful face.

I spun around and draped my arms snuggly around his waist, hugging him, all my emotions suddenly overtaking me. My breath picked up speed and I tensed.

"Hey, what's wrong?"

Shit, he'd noticed.

He raised my chin.

I focused on the muscles of his chest, anything to not have to look into his eyes. Mine always did speak for me, revealing things I didn't want known to others.

"Nothing." My tone had no conviction in it whatsoever.

"You never were a good liar."

No, I wasn't. Still, I shrugged, blowing off his comment.

"Come. Let's shower." I withdrew from him and moved toward the running water. He took hold of my arm, stopping me. *Ugh!* What did he want?

"Promise me you'll talk to me if you need to."

Smiling, I released myself from his hold, and stepped under the hot water.

My inner turmoil baffled me. I should've been floating on cloud nine. Logan had blessed me with two phenomenal orgasms with those big, strong hands of his. And his mouth? Oh dear Lord, don't even get me started on the skillset he had going with that tongue of his. I got hot and bothered merely thinking about it and him. He oozed sexuality. So then why did my heart ache so much?

Probably because he'd told me we should take this thing going on between us day by day, something I didn't think I could do. My head had jumped into fast forward mode, months ahead to the part where I cried myself to sleep at night with a broken heart again because of him.

13

LOGAN

*H*ot. And by that I didn't refer to the water raining down over me and Drew. She had gained a hefty portion of confidence with that mouth of hers over the years, and it drove me all kinds of wild.

And her physique? There weren't enough words in the dictionary to describe it. She had the entire package going on, flawless breasts to fill my hands, small, perky nipples to suck on, and soft pink areolas to wrap my mouth around. *Mmm.* So exquisite.

Great. Now my cock stiffened, thoughts of her creamy pale skin and erect peaks being the culprit for its sudden rise. And the visual—the shower pouring down over her nakedness as she tipped her head back, closed her eyes, and rinsed the shampoo out of her hair—fucking unbelievable, every man's wet dream.

Then there was her tiny waist, the one I currently stared at in admiration as she squeezed excess water out of her long, flowing locks.

. . .

I never realized hair washing could be such a sensual experience. She indeed made it one.

While rinsing herself she gave me an up-close-and-personal view of her tight ass, which had the ideal amount of meat on it, perfect for squeezing and grabbing on to when I fucked her senseless.

When.

A key word rattling repeatedly in my mind.

She washed her face, bringing my attention to her finer points, like her freshly manicured nails.

And last but certainly not least, her pussy. The taste of her still fresh in my mouth, my mind; her flavor as succulent and delicious as the rest of her. The thought of sampling her juices again had me practically drooling and my cock aching for more.

Her eyes met mine.

Shit, I had to catch my breath. She had the most gorgeous shade of green known to mankind, flecks of gold highlighting them.

Patience was no longer in my vocabulary. I pushed her flush against the tile wall and took hold of her hands, fisting them above her head. She didn't argue.

Leaning forward, I crushed my lips against hers.

Our tongues danced with each other from our dire need to get closer. At least I felt the insane urge, but by the way she licked my lips and swirled her tongue around mine, I could swear we were on the same page. I nibbled on her bottom lip. She followed the outline of mine with her tongue.

My free hand skirted across her chest, to her nipples, firm and supple. I took one between two fingers and rolled it between them.

She moaned into my mouth, the vibrations of her desire only heating me up more. More being the key word. I needed and wanted it from her.

I reached behind her and cupped her ass, bringing her pussy forward to meet my begging cock. But I had no intention of breaking and entering. I respected her wishes to wait, against my dick's request.

She lifted her leg and wrapped it around my waist.

Struggling to break her hands free from my tight grip wouldn't work to her benefit. She'd have to wait. I wanted them out of the picture.

She grunted in protest, causing me to smile against her lips. She mimicked my gesture.

Two fingers on my left hand stretched her tight channel, my cock green with envy. I could hardly wait until she removed the *DO NOT ENTER* sign on her pussy, so I could bury myself balls-deep inside her. My wishful thinking and impatience would have to remain on hiatus.

She arched her back, pressing her head against the wall. I got my thumb involved, using it to stroke her clit, her hips dancing to the rhythm of my fingers.

Unlocking my lips from hers, I brought mine to her scrumptious nipple instead, swirling my tongue around it.

Again, she jiggled her hands, trying to release them. This time I allowed her to. She immediately brought one down to my cock and wrapped her small hand around it, slowly running it up and down over my rigid length.

Now I grunted, but mine most definitely wasn't in disapproval.

I fucked her hand, my fingers fucked her, the two of us moving our bodies to get in the best possible position for liftoff.

"I can't wait to be inside you, baby." The thought alone almost had me blowing my load in her palm.

"I can't wait either, but not yet."

"I know. I won't push. I'll wait until you're ready, but I have to admit, every part of me is dying to be inside this tight pussy of yours." Which only made me that much harder. Her tightness around my fingers had to mean it had been a while for her, making me feel like a million bucks.

Her gaze penetrated mine, she stroked my cheek with the back of her finger then down underneath my chin. Wow. Talk about a moment. This without a doubt one of them.

Sucking in a gulp of air helped me to slow things down. I brushed my lips against hers, slipping my fingers out of her and instead wrapping my arms around her, cradling her body tightly against mine.

She released my cock and snaked her arms around my neck.

For some reason, the lust consuming me had somehow left the building without giving me a heads-up and something tingly replaced it. I couldn't describe it. More of a feeling, a fucking sensational one to boot.

This time when I kissed her, I did so in a more controlled manner with precision, focus, and intent.

She slid her hand into my hair. I did the same to hers, then cupped her cheek.

Drew broke the kiss, resting her forehead against my chin. We were both out of breath but not out of need, rather, out of neediness.

Fuck. Fuck. Fuck.

Her slim fingers glided up my chest. We stared at each other for what felt like an eternity but in reality, probably only lasted a minute or two, if that.

Her eyes twinkled.

"Kind of feels like old times, huh?" A sense of comfort and familiarity filled me.

She skimmed her hand up my neck and into my hair. She nudged my head down so she could kiss me again but with a tad more vigor. She let my tongue know hers meant business.

Unsure of what she wanted, I let her take the lead. And she did so without hesitation, using her pointer finger to draw a straight line from my neck down to my erection. She wrapped her hand around the base and began moving her palm in an up-and down-motion, swiping her thumb across the tip for added stimulation and lubrication. Not that my dick required it. She had me juiced and ready to go.

Following her cue, my thumb leisurely trailed down her neck but stopped to take a detour to play with her erect nipples first.

Delicately, I brushed my lips over her ears. She tipped her head to the side. I continued to kiss her neck, up to her chin, finishing off by again taking possession of her lips.

Her clamped thighs needed an intervention. I nudged them apart to give me easier access to her still swollen clit, where I teased by making deliberate circles over it, just above and below. She cooed in delight, spiking my adrenaline.

Our lips parted. Little pecks here and there, tongue action in between.

She became more forceful in her grip, using steady pressure along my shaft only to soften when she slid her hand underneath to my sac, rolling my balls in the cup of her palm.

"Fuck, Drew." I wanted those suckers in her mouth.

With a sinful glare, she licked a trail down my chin, gracing it with kisses during her decent. She followed a steady path down my neck and chest, where she flicked my nipple.

The anticipation of what she'd do next became too difficult to bear.

She removed my hand from her body and continued to lick me, now at my abdomen. She skipped over my cock and got on her knees.

Fuck. How could she be so close yet so far?

Drew hovered slightly over my raging hard-on. Desire filled her emerald eyes when they caught mine.

I sank my hands into her hair, encouraging her to get on with the show.

She kissed the tip, bringing her luscious lips forward and placing them over my cock, her hand joining forces. She moaned in delight, swirling her tongue around my shaft, taking me inside her mouth, bobbing up and down over my length, her hand in sync with her head movements. If I hadn't come during our first episode, I would've already exploded, but the second time around it usually took me a bit longer. I hoped she'd be up for the challenge.

She reached up and skimmed my abs. She brought her hand around to my ass, squeezing it.

The sight of her mouth enveloping me? Shit, the ultimate aphrodisiac.

To get a better view of her face without her hair obstructing my view, I gathered it in my fist and bunched it on top of her head. She peered up at me from under her lashes.

"Mmm," she purred.

What the hell had I done in my life to deserve this? *She* was moaning in pleasure from sucking me off?

I whimpered.

I also felt selfish. She deserved to feel good too. I wanted my fingers stroking her, but my cock wanted no part of that thought. I thrust my hips forward, pushing myself deeper into her mouth.

To my surprise, the wave inside began to rise.

Her hands became slippery in their ministrations, her mouth the culprit for that along with the water still raining down over us. She moved at a steady pace.

It baffled me how the water hadn't turned cold yet. Maybe it had, but she had so eloquently caused my body heat to rise, it would've made it difficult for me to notice the temperature anyway.

The magnitude of goodness filling me rapidly escalated, the all-too-familiar sensations in my dick building to gargantuan proportions.

And more.

I tugged on her hair, trying not to be rough, but I couldn't hold back any longer.

My muscles clenched, my cock contracted, and a sense of numbness possessed me. All thoughts ceased, all the hoopla taking place throughout my body now focused on my cum being released into her mouth, my body stilling, my dick twitching, jerking. All the while, she continued to lave, dart, and flick her tongue over me. I moved her head, the intensity too much. I growled along with my release.

Fuckin' A.

Best blowjob ever.

She stood, rinsing her mouth with water at the same time. She snaked her arms around my waist and rested her head against my chest. I caressed the silky smoothness of her hair.

She peered up at me, beaming, with her chin still comfortably leaning against my chest.

I brushed loose hair off her face.

"Logan Trimble, I haven't had this much action in one night in forever." She hummed in satisfaction.

Her statement rang like music to my ears. Unfortunately, I couldn't say the same, even though tonight's activities put all other experiences to shame, except the ones including Drew all those years ago.

"Drew Scarlett Sanders, you amaze me."

She bit back a response to my compliment. I had to give it to her. She did a marvelous job of keeping her emotions sealed. I would have to change that.

"You've tired me out, but I'm hungry."

"Can I take you to dinner? I know a great place close by that should still be open. And if it's not, I'll make it so it is."

She nodded, grinning. "Sounds great. I've worked up quite an appetite."

Too bad the more I got of Drew, the hungrier I felt for her.

"But first, I think I owe you something." She cocked her head to the side. "Fortunately for you, I'm the type of guy who believes in giving as much as receiving."

She smiled again.

"Turn around and bend over."

Apprehension registered on her face.

"Don't worry. I totally respect your wishes. I would never force you to do anything you're not ready for. Now go ahead, turn around, lean forward, and hold on to the wall."

She took a deep breath but did as I requested.

"Good girl." I zigzagged my finger down her back. She shivered at my touch.

I got on my knees. The surface underneath me wasn't forgiving, the tile cold and hard. I didn't care. I wanted her warm and soft pussy inside my hungry mouth again.

I inched forward and swiped my tongue between her folds and up to her hooded clit.

She bit back a sound. Oh, I would get her to verbalize more of them very soon.

Spreading her lips gave my tongue better access. I lapped and kissed her sensitive flesh.

She bore down, wanting, needing more. I could easily take care of that for her.

The angle posed a challenge, so I got my hand involved, a finger entering her while my tongue danced across her and up to her clit.

I held on to her outer thigh to keep her body where I wanted it, encouraging her to widen her stance, because my tongue wanted to get more involved.

I rhythmically slid my finger in and out, cradling it deep in her channel, my mouth feasting on the outside. I wiggled my tongue around, making circles and figure-eights, and gently sucked the tip, having the time of my fucking life. Her body shook.

"Yes, right there! Keep doing what you're doing." She held my head.

Enough said.

Her pussy swallowed my finger, drawing it in as much as it could. She ground herself against it, sporadic moans making their presence known, coming steadier, louder.

I continued to kiss, suck, and finish her off by paying ample attention to her clit, and fuck, did I ever. She clamped down on my finger and her knees buckled. I assisted in keeping her upright.

Her body pulsed, my tongue remaining steadfast, my lips kissing her sweetness. I wanted her to go as long as she could.

"Yes, Logan... Please!"

Being she asked so politely, I continued to feast on her, causing her body to convulse for minutes on end. Did this woman have any clue how fucking sexy she was? I certainly did.

Her legs wobbled. I kept a firm grasp on her so she wouldn't fall.

. . .

She lifted her upper torso into an upright position, her head angled down with eyes closed. She giggled. "I'm so dizzy."

Me too, but not from the sex.

After rising, I wrapped my arms around her until she got her bearings.

"Wow." She sighed.

Wow.

I had to repeat it to myself.

Once she was stable, I stepped out of the shower, grabbed two towels off the shelf, and wrapped one around my waist before assisting her out and drying her off.

She flipped her head over and towel dried her hair. She tied the towel up on her head. And when she bent down to do this simple act? Shit. I had to swallow my tongue and restrain myself.

While moseying back into the bedroom to retrieve my clothes, I wondered whether I should have my testosterone level checked, because whenever I saw Drew bend over, walk, cross her legs, or anything else, my cock stood at attention. What the fuck? Something had to be wrong with me medically. I didn't lack pussy. I had women throwing themselves at me left and right. But my body never reacted to them with such fervor as it did to Drew. I felt somewhat humiliated by my dick's newfound unpredictability. If she thought me fucking her topped my priority list, she couldn't have been more wrong. Like I'd said, sure, she had the entire package going on, but that was only a small part of what I wanted from her.

I selfishly wanted the entire fucking thing.

14

DREW

Ooh, I shivered when I stepped out of the bathroom, the air chilly.

Logan already had his clothes on in the bedroom. He sat on the edge of the bed, studying me, while I gathered something to wear from out of the dresser drawers.

"Susanna's going to be so mad at us. We keep showing up to the dining hall during off-hours."

"Don't worry about Susanna. I've known her since I was a kid. She runs a tight ship with the guests, but I'm not considered one of them. Since you're with me, you get to bend the rules along with me."

His eyes ate me up watching me dress, which made me feel somewhat self-conscious. I shielded myself as best I could with my towel and stood with my back to him. I slid on my undies and slipped my arms through my bra straps.

His warm breath against my neck surprised me.

"Please allow me to assist you with that." He clasped the hook closed.

Feeling more comfortable now that I had my privates covered, I didn't care if he watched me put on the rest of my clothing.

Inside the bathroom, I brushed out my hair, adding a smidgen of eyeliner and lip gloss to finish off.

He observed from the doorway. "You don't need makeup. You're prettier without it."

"How would you know? You haven't seen me in full makeup in forever."

"I have a good memory. Besides, I don't think you could be any more beautiful than you already are."

This man threw me off balance when he made those types of comments. He made me believe he wanted more. I couldn't allow myself to get sucked into the fantasy of us being alone together at the ranch, something so easy to do so when I didn't have everyday life getting in my way.

"Thank you. That's kind of you to say." My gaze met his in the mirror.

"There's no need to thank me. It's the truth. And furthermore, I should be the one thanking you for giving me the opportunity to spend time with you after how things ended between us."

"Please don't remind me."

My stomach grumbled loudly. We both looked down at it and laughed.

"Come, I must feed you." He put his hand out.

We left the cabin and leisurely strolled to the dining hall in the dark. I had no clue of the time. It had to late, though, because the sun had set long ago.

Guests were sitting around a fire. One of the staffers played a guitar and hosted a sing-along.

Brian caught sight of us and signaled for Logan to come say hello. He rose from his chair and greeted us.

"How about playing a few tunes for the guests?"

"I'd love to, but Drew and I are starving. We're going to get something to eat."

"Okay, bro, another time."

. . .

He patted Logan on the back and gave me a slight wave. He returned to the guests.

I wasn't sure if I had read the situation correctly, but it seemed to me Logan felt uncomfortable with Brian's request.

Logan placed his palm against my back and led me inside the dining hall. Two kids were sitting on the couch playing on their tablets. Kids these days and their electronics. Crazy. Even out here in the woods, they couldn't part with them.

"Have a seat, my lady." Logan gestured, pulling out a chair for me. "I'll go check out what's left from dinner. I'll be right back."

I sat tight and waited. My stomach's gurgling reminded me about feeding it.

The two girls from the couch excitedly rushed over to where I sat.

"Are you dating Logan Trimble?" one of them asked, full of enthusiasm.

"Logan and I are old friends," I replied graciously.

"You're so lucky. Did you know him before he became famous? What was he like? Did you know he has lots of girlfriends?" The other girl tossed questions at me, her eyes just as wide with interest as her friend's.

Lots of girlfriends?

Fangirl one nudged her friend's arm. "Don't speak about other girls in front of her. She might get upset."

She spoke as if I didn't exit, as if I wasn't sitting right in front of them.

"Upset about what?" Logan had come out of nowhere. He set a few plates of food in front of me and considered the two girls standing next to the table.

"Your fans over here have been asking me questions about your fame, your *girlfriends*, you know, celebrity stuff."

His eyes locked on mine. He had to see my disappointment.

The two girls hooked their arms together and stared at him in awe, gawking, clueless about the tension rising between me and Logan.

I should've handed them napkins to wipe up the drool spilling from their mouths.

Stop it! I shook my head at my horrible thought. I couldn't be angry at his fans. These girls were mere teenagers with an obvious celebrity crush.

"Girls, if you don't mind, I appreciate your interest, but I'm here on vacation and would prefer to hang low."

"Sorry, Logan." Fangirl one pouted.

"How about later I take a picture with both of you, so you can show your friends when you get home?"

Her frown reversed. "That would be great. Thank you so much."

Fangirl two jumped up and down, clapping her hands.

The two of them hurried back to the couch, bubbly and giggling.

"I wasn't sure what you wanted, so I brought a variety of samples of what I could scrounge up in the fridge. I'm sure it tasted better fresh instead of microwaved, but beggars can't be choosers. Besides, everything Susanna cooks is delicious, no matter how it's heated up."

He sat next to me and dove in to his food. Did he really think I'd ignore the scene that had just taken place?

"I'm more interested to hear about all these girlfriends you seem to have."

Ugh! I hated to sound so jealous. But h
ere we were, trying to rebuild something that had ended due to a lack of trust, and I had the feeling he wasn't being completely honest with me.

He placed his elbows on the table, steepled his fingers, and rested his chin on top of them.

"First of all, let me start by saying I do not have lots of girlfriends.

They're one-night stands, never to be seen or contacted again. There's a huge difference between the two."

My eyes widened. "You must be very proud of that accomplishment." I had to make an effort to tone down my bitch level, but I couldn't help it. Anger filled me. Did he consider me the same as these one-night stands he spoke about?

"Hey, it is what it is. I told you before I have fun with groupies. I didn't lie or keep it from you. I don't understand why you're putting me on the defensive or why I feel the need to explain my behavior to you. We're not in a relationship."

Bam!

What a blow to my heart.

His words hit so damn hard. A huge part of me wanted to run out of the room, tears pooling in my eyes, but I didn't. Being an adult meant I had to communicate my feelings. And I planned to do exactly that.

"I'm not asking you to explain anything. I guess there are a lot of things we don't know about each other anymore."

"You want the deal on my life? Okay. Here it is. The guys and I got picked up by a label. Fast forward a year or two, and our songs are steadily climbing the charts. We sell out stadiums, we require security when we travel together as a band, girls hang posters of me and the guys in their bedrooms, fans wear T-shirts, hats, and pins with Steam photos on them, and our social-media channels are exploding."

Sure, I knew he had become famous, but maybe hadn't realized precisely how much. I had made an active attempt over the years to avoid anything Logan Trimble, including his band's music and newfound popularity.

"That's amazing. I'm happy for you." I'm sure my countenance said the complete opposite of my words. But I was happy his dreams had come true for him, unlike mine. Then again, I had no idea what my dreams were. Two things I did know: I loved to write, and I loved Logan Trimble.

"Spill it, Drew."

Between Logan and Kate, I'd had about all the drama I could handle for one day. I pushed my dinner plate away, my appetite all but gone.

"I have nothing to spill. If all you expected was for us to hang out and fool around this week, I'm sorry to say you can go fuck yourself. Actually, I'm not sorry at all. I should've known this week together wouldn't mean or amount to anything with you. My bad for having unrealistic expectations."

I stood and stormed out of the dining hall, running back to my cabin as fast as my legs would take me. Not an easy task in the dark.

Once inside, I locked the door, a first since arriving at the ranch. I felt like pulling a Kate, packing up my shit, and getting the hell out of this place, not dealing with the situation at hand or the aftermath.

A loud banging at the door had me shutting myself in my bedroom. But even with my door closed, I still heard Logan yelling my name, continuing to pound on the thin door. He banged so hard, he'd probably make a hole in it. I didn't know whether to cry or scream, wanting to do both.

His voice got louder. I didn't understand how. I had locked the door. He couldn't get inside. But his voice sounded awfully close.

Shit, he knocked on the frickin' window in my bedroom.

"Please open up! Don't shut me out again! Let me explain!"

Grrr. I shuffled out of my room, unlocked, and opened the front door. I sat on the couch, placing a throw pillow next to me to create distance if he decided to sit as well.

"Christ, what the hell, Drew?"

His clenched jaw and harsh tone only made me angrier.

"Back at you. What the hell, Logan?"

He sat on the other side of the couch, his body facing me. He brushed his hand through his hair.

"As I was saying, the band has become well-known. We can still ride solo without mobs chasing us, but when all of us are together, it's a totally different story."

"Your life is so different from mine now. Swarms of women must trail after you. It's hard to process."

"I'm still the same person. Just because strangers know who I am doesn't mean I've changed. Sure, they only see the part of me I show them, and I don't act like myself for the camera, but inside, my core values are the same."

Values? Hello, cheater!

He brushed his hand through his hair again. "Please don't look at me with such disgust. You know deep down I have good morals. I fucked up with you. I get it. I'm sorry. I can't rewrite the past. Let me clarify by saying that other than the guys, you're the only other person who knows the real me. The women I sleep around with couldn't give two shits about me. All they care about is fucking a rock star or trying to gain some sense of fame."

The reality of his present lifestyle was overwhelming. I rubbed my forehead, tension filling it.

"I get approached by fans a lot these days which is why I love coming to the ranch. I savor being a regular guy here, especially with you, without the need to try and impress anyone, other than you, of course." He swallowed hard, his shoulders hunched.

My heart hurt. "You've never had to try to impress me. You always have."

He sighed heavily. "It means a lot to hear you say that. I know you've never judged me, something hard to find in people the guys and I meet these days. Which is why being here with you has been so fantastic. Do you know how crazy it is to have strangers taking pictures of you everywhere you go, posting shit online for the entire world to see?"

I shook my head. I had no clue about living that type of a lifestyle.

"Eventually, I started hamming up my negative behaviors. It became my method of telling everyone to fuck off, that Logan Trimble could do whatever the hell he wanted. The worst part is our label encourages my deviant behavior because it gets us more views."

His attention drifted elsewhere. I watched him, keenly interested in hearing what he had to say.

"I'm considered the bad boy of the band. I'm the guy everyone points at whenever there's trouble or when shit goes down."

His gaze met mine again.

"It gets old real fast. As far as the band goes, the guys know I would never do anything to jeopardize or compromise their integrity. As far as the public goes, I give my fans what they want, a cocky son of a bitch who doesn't give a shit about anyone or anything. The fucked-up part is that my asshole behavior only makes me more popular. So when you originally asked me why I come to the ranch, it's to get a mental break from all that shit. It can really wear on you if you let it."

He rubbed his chin, the sadness in his eyes breaking my heart. I wanted to reach out and touch him, offer him comfort, but couldn't. I still had my own internal shit to deal with.

"Being out here in the quiet helps me get back in touch with who I am at heart. It grounds me, keeps me humble. The Addison family treats me no differently than they did when I visited as a kid, the only difference being requests for tickets and autographs for their family and friends."

"Hmm. The rock and roll lifestyle doesn't sound as good as it's cracked up to be."

I couldn't imagine living my life that way, not being true to myself. But when push came to shove, was I? I attended classes I had no interest in, I still worked for my father, and I lived at home. Those were not lifelong aspirations.

"Listen, I'm not complaining. I'm more than grateful for how far we've come. There's nothing else I could see myself doing other than performing, playing for thousands of fans. It's the greatest fucking feeling in the world. And the paychecks aren't bad either."

He smiled. Finally some lightheartedness entering the conversation.

"I didn't get into discussing band stuff with you because I wanted to hold on to the normalcy with you for as long as I could."

"The only Logan I know is the guy sitting across from me, the one being honest with me about his feelings right now." I angled my body toward him and hiked my knee up on the couch, tucking my foot underneath my other leg.

He sighed, probably because I hadn't kicked him to the curb.

"That goes for you too. You're very good at pulling back. If I agree to be open with you, please do the same with me."

Sure, I nodded, but agreeing to his terms would be easier said than done.

"So let me get this straight. When I get home, if I search your name, you're going to burn out my computer screen?"

He put his hand out, smirking. "I have to say, I'm a little hurt you never did."

"Now that I know the truth, I probably would've felt worse if I had, seeing the 'bad boy' you speak about portraying, because I'd think it's who you have become instead of it being an act."

"You're right." He nodded in agreement. "Okay, I take it back. I'm glad you never researched me. But please, so you know, unless it's our social media team posting pictures of the band, most of the shit you see and read about online about me and the guys isn't true."

"When do you go back on tour?" My fragile heart already missed him, feeling lonely at the thought.

"In a few weeks. I'd love to spend a huge chunk of my break with you if you'll let me."

The desperation on his face tore me apart.

. . .

"Oh Logan." I couldn't hold back from not touching him any longer. I crawled across the couch and onto his lap, where I straddled him. "I would want nothing more than to spend more time with you."

He smiled. "Good. I'm glad."

We kissed, his tongue making its presence known but not in a lustful manner. Rather, the kiss had a great deal of feeling in it. I might even go out on a limb and say it tasted like a promise as well.

Logan wrapped his arms around my waist. I wrapped mine around his neck. We continued to kiss. Then we kissed some more, as if were our first time together. In a sense, I considered it to be a new beginning for us. I prayed this new chapter would have a happier ending.

15

LOGAN

Drew's stomach made a loud noise. She covered it with her hand. A faint blush spread across her cheeks.

"Miss Sanders, in all the excitement you didn't eat your dinner."

She sighed. "I lost my appetite, but it's obviously come back with a vengeance. I'm starving." She circled her hand over her belly.

"Me too. What do you say we try dinner again but with a table for two and no surprise guests?"

"I don't mind surprise guests and yes, I'd love to get something to eat with you."

I wasn't sure how much I believed her about the surprise-guests part. The eating part, yes, her stomach had made her hunger evident to probably half the ranch it gurgled so loud.

She eased off me. I stood, took her hand in mine, and faced her. "Thanks for hearing me out. It means a lot to me."

"It means a lot to me that you opened up." She smiled warmly.

Hand in hand, we walked back to the dining hall. And by good fortune, we discovered no guests inside. *Thank God.*

Our dirty dishes remained on the table, right where we'd left them. I hated wasting food. I suddenly remembered Susanna and

Jack's dogs loved eating leftovers. Maybe Drew and I could feed ours to them after we finished with our meals.

Fresh food got reheated and I brought the goodies I'd hunted down in the kitchen to the table, setting them in front of Drew. "Help yourself."

She did without any hesitation whatsoever.

"Mmm, this fish is delicious. I think my stomach will agree. I'm so hungry, anything would be delicious by this point."

Feeling hungry myself, I tasted the fish, agreeing with her opinion of it.

"You're right. It is good."

"Let me get us drinks."

Her sweet ass shook side to side during her waltz to the counter to get two glasses of ice water. I studied her face when she returned. Contentment filled her features. Filled mine too.

She set my drink in front of me.

"Thanks." I took a sip.

She dug into her food again.

"Ah, my stomach thanks you." She continued to feast on her dinner, pretty much clearing the plate. I loved seeing a girl with a hearty appetite.

"Thank Susanna. She cooked it. I'll have to keep better track of time in the future to make sure to feed you properly."

"Yes, you will. You've worked me to the bone today, Mr. Trimble."

"A little hard work never hurt anyone."

"So true. Speaking of hard work, tell me about your days on the road."

"Typically, after our shows we travel through the night to our next destination. I'll usually wake up early to workout because once my day officially begins, there's not much time left over for anything other than prepping for the next show. The guys and I meet up with our manager when we arrive at the venue, do a sound check, review procedures for meet and greets, and any other business or tasks our manager wants us to take care of. On a good day, we'll have a few hours to kill, depending on the venue and how late rehearsals and preparations take beforehand. Other days it's one task after another with no breaks in between. For the most part, meet and greets take place prior to performances. That frees us up later on."

"Like for groupies?"

Wow, sarcasm at its best.

A shrug gave her my reply because she spoke the truth. After-parties used to happen more frequently, less now that the guys were tied up with their girls, figuratively speaking of course. And if they were into kinky shit, they never spilled details to me about it. Not that I wanted any.

"I know this may sound odd, but where and how do you meet them?"

Say what? I scrunched my face up, the topic not one I wanted to discuss with her.

"Come on, I want to know."

She saw right through me. She always could.

"Well, a lot of our hard-core fans come to sound check. And they definitely dress for the occasion—low-cut tops and high-rise shorts. You get my drift." I backhanded the air, not wanting to give her any more food for thought. "When the guys and I finish playing, we head down to where they're sitting to sign autographs, take pictures, and other shit."

She didn't require a play-by-play.

"Other shit?"

Fuck. I sighed at her question, feeling slightly on edge discussing this with her.

"Please continue."

Hold your horses, partner. I put my hand up to pacify her, mostly to give me a pause to figure out how to word it properly without making her feel bad or jealous. Drew had the sensitivity gene locked down tight.

"If we like a girl in particular, we'll make sure she's seated up front at the show. We'll then have someone on our security team bring her backstage following the performance. Fans seated in the front tend to make their presence known. If we want to see more of them, we'll have security escort them backstage."

"And these strange women agree to sleep with you just because of who you are?"

"You wouldn't believe what women do to get with us. But again, I'd rather not delve deeper into this with you. It's not something I'm proud of."

"I'm sure your ego is." She flashed me a half-smile, but her eyes had pain in them.

"It is what it is." I flashed her a lopsided grin.

"How do you live with yourself?"

"You mean to tell me you've never fucked a guy just because you wanted to?"

Say what? Her body language answered the question for me. *No way.*

"I'm not thrilled admitting to you I have, but in my defense, I did know the guys' names and also knew a thing or two about them."

Them?

My jaw dropped. I couldn't believe the words she'd spoken. Talk about a double standard. Yes, I'd confess I had no issue with me fucking countless women in my past but had a serious problem with her fucking *any* other man.

"You've had one-night stands?"

. . .

"It's not something I'd like to write home and brag about. If I'm being totally honest, since we both agreed to be open with each another, I thought acting out would help me get over you faster."

Double what the fuck? She could have drawn a stake into my heart, it ached so much.

"And did it?"

She shook her head.

Thank God for small miracles.

Not that I wanted her to suffer but because I didn't want her finding comfort in the arms of another man. I always did hold the selfish bastard card firmly in my grasp.

"So what did you do?"

Please say you abstained in an attempt to overcome heartbreak.

"I tried it again, maxing out at three guys. I felt worse with each one I spent time with. It really sucked."

Three? I swallowed hard at her answer, not expecting it whatsoever. I couldn't hold back my displeasure.

"Fuck, Drew."

"Don't look so disappointed. My total can still be counted on one hand." She raised one and wiggled her fingers in front of me. "I'm sure you can't say the same."

She had me there.

"I'm not disappointed *in* you. I'm disappointed you felt the need to behave a certain way because of me."

She shrugged. She set her fork on the plate, and slid it toward me. Guess she had finished eating.

"Like you said, it is what it is."

"So what did it take to finally get over me?" Not that I wanted to hear her answer because if she asked me the same question, I'd have to confess I never truly got over her.

"Are you trying to feed that big ego of yours?"

I wanted her to see the seriousness in my expression, so I looked directly at her. "Not in this particular case."

"I don't know how to answer your question... Time maybe... And I'll admit the pain lessened, but it never fully left. It stuck with me as did the rest of my feelings."

Did she mean the feelings of love she had toward me as well? My heart raced at the possibility.

"Christ, Logan. Why are you bringing all this up?" She crumpled up her napkin and tossed it on the table in front of her.

"You're the one who started it by asking questions about groupies." I defended myself, even though groupies had nothing to do with where our conversation had drifted.

"Yeah, I did. But I didn't bring up how I dealt with the aftermath of our failed relationship. You did."

"The topic was bound to come up sooner or later, so we may as well bite the bullet and discuss it now."

She eyed me, not saying a word. *Okay, I'll go first.* "I have to say, you seem to still be carrying around a lot of anger toward me." It emanated from her being.

"In all seriousness, do you blame me?"

"Not for a second. I just wish I knew how to break the wall down, so I can get close to you again."

"Trust builds with time. You know that as well as I do, especially rebuilding it. Right now, we have a few days ahead of us to spend together as we please. But it doesn't mean I'm willing to put my all into something I'm not sure will turn out in my favor."

"No one ever knows how things will turn out. And I already told you, I want to spend more time with you back home before I hit the road again."

"Then it's back to your groupies, right?" She glared at me. "I know we're not in a committed relationship anymore, but I'm not okay with that nor should you expect me to be."

"First of all, if we're together, we're together."

"I remember you telling me the same thing years back, and it didn't have such a happy ending." Her jaw tightened, her body stiffened.

"Fuck, Drew. This is exactly what I'm talking about with your walls. Didn't you specifically tell your sister people make mistakes? I fucked up. I made one, a huge one. But there's nothing I can do to change the past. What's done is done."

She buried her face in her hands. "Oh my God. I'm completely mortified right now."

"Hey, if it makes you feel any better, I fuck strange women because they don't mean anything to me. I don't have to feel anything toward them."

She raised her head, her gaze fixed on mine. "And that's supposed to make me feel better *how*?"

"It means you're the only one I ever attached feelings to it with." I scooted closer to her.

"That was years ago. We're older now. We've grown up, changed. It doesn't mean we can pick up where we left off."

"I know, but I'd like to try." I lifted her hand to my lips and kissed it.

"You say that now because we're stuck up here in isolation world. Once you get back to reality, things will be different. It's not fair to me."

My nostrils flared, my irritation meter rising rapidly. "So are you saying you're not willing to at least give it a try?"

"I don't know what I'm saying anymore." Tears spilled down her cheeks. It destroyed me. I wanted to console her, but feared touching her. What if she rejected me? No thanks. But I also wanted her to remain open and keep talking because soon enough, she'd shut down again.

"You were the love of my life, but you broke my heart. It's not an easy thing to recover from. Trust has been a major issue for me ever since because of it."

Her tear flow increased as did my pent-up guilt.

I directed the anger fueling me at myself for fucking her up emotionally the way I evidently had. But I couldn't do anything about it now. I couldn't rewrite the past. It was history.

"I'm confused too. But the one thing I am sure about is how I feel when I'm with you." I had to hold back my own tears by this point.

. . .

"Please give me some time." She spoke in a hushed voice.

"I'll give you all the time you need, baby."

I sure hoped the time we had left together at the ranch would be enough for her because the suspense of what her response would be was killing me.

16

DREW

*L*ogan suggested we feed the dogs outside the dining hall after we ate, offering to give them the leftovers we hadn't eaten earlier. He gave me a quick rundown on what the ranch dogs were permitted to eat, showing me a posted sign next to the exit door.

Hanging out with friendly dogs elevated our moods from the intense conversation we'd engaged in during dinner, both of us coming down and relaxing while feeding and giving the dogs love. It also showed me another side of Logan I had forgotten about. He became so spirited around animals, overly mushy toward them. His kindhearted nature brought a smile to my face.

The dogs chowed down every last morsel we offered. They whined and begged for more. We promised we'd visit again soon with more treats for them, not that they understood us, but it made me feel better.

Back on the main trail, others were still gathered around the campfire. Brian waved us over. I tried to read Logan's thoughts. I wanted to join the fun. I could tell Logan didn't, but the sweetie pie agreed to come with me.

I thought engaging in activities with others might be a good distraction from the heaviness surrounding us.

The group sat around, sharing favorite stories about the happenings at the ranch. I had nothing to share, since I had only participated in one shooting session.

We listened as mostly the teens spoke animatedly about the fun they were having. One of the fangirls who had approached us earlier in the dining hall interrupted her friend's incessant chatting and directed her attention at Logan.

"Excuse me, Mr. Trimble, would you mind playing a song for us? Brian has a guitar. He played it for us earlier."

Brian and Logan exchanged knowing glances. I had no clue about their secret, but I found the girl's question to be adorable and heartwarming. She beamed, staring at him, along with the rest of the teenyboppers sitting in the circle, waiting for his reply. Logan eyed me questioningly. He certainly didn't need my permission. I loved hearing him play.

"Your fans want to hear a song, me being one of them."

His entire face lit up at my response. He retrieved the guitar from Brian. Everyone watched Logan adjust the guitar on his lap.

"I'll play under one condition." He posed his stipulation to the entire group, making sure they listened closely.

"What?" They spoke in unison.

"That we do this together. You guys request a song. I'll play it. You sing along. Agreed?" He acted so carefree and in his element being center stage. I envied his ability to not be affected.

"Please play '*Pray for the Best in Times of the Worst!*'" another teen girl yelled out, giddy with excitement.

I had no knowledge of the song, but the kids surely did. As soon as Logan strummed the melody, all of them started singing, not missing a beat.

It surprised me that some of the moms in the group knew the lyrics as well. I'd have to ask him about the tune later, even if I did feel somewhat ignorant about having to do so.

What a phenomenal show he gave the audience. The group swayed to the music, and some of the parents danced to the choral singing. The counselors clapped to the beat. It was exactly what Logan and I needed to relieve some of the tension from dinner. At least for me it was. I couldn't speak for Logan, but by the gleam in his eyes, I knew he felt damn good, as did I.

He kept his focus primarily on me, winking and smiling at me while playing for the others. My heart went pitterpatter because of it.

When the song came to an end, a few of the girls rushed over to him and asked if they could take selfies with him. He kindly agreed. The girls became somewhat starstruck when he stood next to them. I completely understood their captivation. I too became enthralled and entranced by his charm when I got close to him.

After he finished taking pictures, Brian took him aside.

"Sorry, Logan. I hope I didn't put you on the spot."

"It's all good. Just please don't do it again unless we speak about it first. You know I like to remain on the down low during my stays at the ranch."

"You betcha." Brian patted Logan's arm and returned to the group.

Logan clasped my hand in his and we took off for our cabins.

We stopped in front of his, reaching it first.

"Do you want to come in?" He had a glimmer of hope in his voice and expression.

And here came my dilemma. Did I stay with him, or did I go back to my cabin all by my lonesome?

"I think I'm going to call it a night. Would you mind walking me to my cabin?"

What?

I frowned along with him at the words that came out of my mouth.

"Really?" His response had less than an ounce of cheerfulness in it.

. . .

"Really. Trust me. It's not that I don't want to."

"Then say you'll come inside."

I shook my head. "Not tonight." The words practically had to be ripped out of my mouth because my heart argued against them.

He sighed and glanced down at the rocky path. Poor guy apparently wasn't used to women saying no to him. My pathetic reality. But I had said no for my good, not his.

Our hands swung between us as we strolled along. A family of four passed us.

"Good night, Logan." The teenage daughter in the family waved at him. "Thanks for playing. It was amazing."

He acknowledged her with a nod and a slight wave.

"Your fans love you, Mr. Trimble."

"All of them?" He raised a brow at me.

Wouldn't he like to know?

Unsure of what to say or do, I giggled at his question. It had caught me off guard.

"You didn't say no," he teased.

"Damn. You really have become an egomaniac."

In response to my comment, he picked me up and swung me around. I held on to him, laughing along with him.

"Do I hear you complaining about my current state of mind, Miss Sanders?"

"Not at all." I chuckled

"Good."

His lips came crashing down on mine, the kiss desperate, ravenous with yearning. I inched down his body until my feet hit the ground. The rest of me still felt light, as if floating above us. He had a gift for making me feel weightless.

He nudged his growing erection against me and gripped my ass, tugging me closer until we gyrated against each other.

Our tongues went at it as though they couldn't get enough of each other, our hands feeling the same amount of dire need.

"Fuck, Drew. I'm dying to have you."

"In time." I spoke breathlessly.

Our lips went at it again, our heads shifting left, right, any which way to connect our mouths, our tongues.

A whistling sound hummed in the background. I paid it no mind, the sound of Logan's heavy breaths capturing my attention more.

The whistling got louder. Logan retreated.

I blinked, stunned by my public indecency and loss of control to find Brian and some of the other staff guys heading toward us.

"Take it inside, you two. This is a family place, rated G." Brian chuckled.

Holy shit! I rubbed the back of my neck and stared at Logan, too embarrassed to confront the guys chortling a few feet in front of us.

"Fuck you." Logan snaked his arm around my waist and drew me in tight against him. "You're just jealous."

"How do you put up with that cocky asshole, Drew?" Brian let out a hearty laugh.

Incapable of speaking, I smiled instead. At least the darkness would hide the redness I knew filled my cheeks.

"Have fun, you guys. Maybe we'll see you in the morning at breakfast. Unless you're too busy doing *other* things." Brian and the others in his posse snickered, waved good night, and continued on their journey.

"Don't pay him any mind. He's a great guy." Logan's assurance wasn't necessary. I already sensed that about Brian.

"I'm sure he is." I inhaled, requiring oxygen. "I can't believe they saw us behaving so naughty in public." My hand instinctively covered my mouth in shame.

"Naughty? You mean, *kissing*? Ooh, we're such rebels."

"Fine, Mr. Smart-ass. Let's just say it wasn't rated G."

"I wouldn't want it to be, especially with you."

He took hold of my hand after I playfully slapped his arm. We continued toward my cabin. He led me up the steps to my door.

"So..."

Hint. Hint. He wasn't subtle.

"So... Until tomorrow, Logan Trimble."

"You're really going to leave me out here with a hard-on? I never thought you were the cruel type."

"I'm not the easy type either." I feigned innocence.

He cocked his head. "Playing hard to get only makes me want you more."

"Good. Then tomorrow you shall have more of me." I winked and stepped up on my tiptoes to reach his cheek, where I planted a soft kiss. "Good night. Sweet dreams."

His mouth fell open. I understood his disappointment. I felt it too but also relished having the upper hand for a change.

Once inside my cabin, I went straight to the bathroom in high gear. I didn't wait for the shower to heat up either before I tossed my clothes on the floor and stepped inside, the water frigidly cold.

A knocking sound at my front door had me opening one eye. I had no clue of the time, but my body told me it was too early to wake up.

"Who is it?" I dragged my tired butt to the door, still dressed in my pj's.

"Room service."

I'd recognize Logan's sultry voice anywhere. My feet suddenly had more pep in them. I picked up my pace and opened the door, grinning.

"Good morning, gorgeous." He perused my body with a devilish smile. "I love the look."

Bashfully, I covered my chest.

"No, don't do that. Seeing your hard nipples poke through that shirt is fucking hot, babe." He licked his lips.

I slapped his arm. "Come in."

"Sure, I love to *come*."

"Logan," I admonished.

"What? If I'm being totally honest, I'd love to see a lot more than your perky tits, especially with you standing in front of me all sexy. I brought us breakfast, but I'm suddenly feeling hungry for something else."

He set the paper plates on the table and picked me up.

"Wait. I want to brush my teeth first." I giggled as he carried me to my bedroom.

"I don't plan on kissing your mouth, babe."

"You have such a way with words."

"I have a good way with my tongue and fingers too. I'm about to show you just *how* good."

He dropped me on the bed and dragged my legs toward the end. The man almost ripped my boxers off, his demeanor dominant, hot, and sexy as hell. Heat rushed through me. I clenched the muscles in my pelvic region.

"You left me in a bad state last night. I haven't been able to stop thinking about this magnificent pussy of yours since."

Oh my God. I had no words, only panted breaths.

His mouth came down hard against me. My hips bucked, the pleasure already too much, especially with a full bladder.

"Mmm. You're even better than I remembered. Not that I ever forgot how fucking decadent you are."

He did have a way with words, the kind which made me blush. At least he couldn't see my flushed face, since his was buried somewhere spectacular.

One of my hands squeezed the comforter. The other fisted a chunk of his hair, encouraging the pace he had going. My moans did as well.

His tongue worked wonders against my clit, cherishing it, sucking on it, flicking it, doing everything in its power to build me up hard and fast.

Mission accomplished.

"Yes, right there!"

His fingers joined the party between my thighs, one or two of them entering me. I met his hand thrust for thrust.

He removed them, fucking me with his tongue instead.

"Ah," I cried, delicious tension building inside.

"Come for me."

With my back arched, my legs wider apart, I opened my eyes to find his closed, fully immersed in what he was doing.

Seeing his head move as he pleasured me and how he pinned my lower half against the mattress as if he couldn't get enough of me brought me over the edge.

My eyes snapped shut, lightness filled my being, and delightful sensations pulsed underneath his mouth and fingers.

Breathing heavily, my body trembled against the bed. Next thing I knew, something hard and yummy introduced itself to my lips. Like a magician, he had made his shorts vanish and now straddled me, his cock hovering above my face.

"Suck me, baby. I'm so hard for you it hurts."

Yes. Yes. And yes. I brought my hand forward and dragged it up and down his rigid length, using the wetness seeping out from the tip as lubrication.

He stopped my hand. "I want your mouth. Fuck me with your mouth."

His dirty talk had me scorching in flames. My body still tried to come down from the high, and here he tried and succeeded at bringing it up again.

So he wanted me to fuck him with only my mouth. I could do that. I brought my mouth forward, sampling the slit on his tip. It oozed sexuality as did its owner. I had to agree with him, he too tasted better than I had remembered.

"Ah..." He agreed with my sentiments exactly.

Without him noticing, I snuck my hand in. Or maybe he did, but he didn't stop it from helping. I wanted to go with the theory he adored my technique too much to give a shit.

Molding my fingers around his wide girth while my mouth took him in made me hungry for more, more of something I couldn't give him yet, so this would have to suffice.

He watched me suck him off, releasing a heavy breath, his eyelids drifting shut, his head tilting slightly back.

He went deeper inside, slowly withdrawing only to slam into my mouth again. My hand prevented him from hitting my throat even though I wanted all of him.

My free hand drifted up his six-pack abs to his chest. He positioned his hand over mine, keeping it firmly in place. It blew me away how in his rough-and-tough state he still managed to bring sweetness to it, doing my heart in, having it throw in the towel in defeat. He had won me over once again. Not that he had ever lost me.

His body stilled over mine. He went to pull out of my mouth, but I stopped him and nodded slightly in the hopes he'd understood my silent message, his expression now a question. One I didn't bother to respond to.

He shot into my mouth, his warm liquid sliding down my throat. I swallowed, allowing the remnants to go down with the rest.

Logan sighed heavily and vacated my mouth.

"Fuck, Drew."

One of the legs he leaned on met the other, and he collapsed onto the bed next to me.

I flopped on my side and placed my hand on his chest. He took it in his, covering it.

"I think I like your idea of room service."

"I do too." He closed his eyes, his fingers delicately dancing over the back of my hand.

17

LOGAN

We showered and dressed. Drew said she wanted to participate in some of the activities offered at the ranch. I hesitantly agreed, selfishly wanting to be alone with her but understood her desire to try out some new things she wouldn't have the opportunity to do at home.

To my surprise, I had a blast. We ended up following the ranch schedule to a tee. I hadn't done so in forever and hated to admit how much I missed the fun to be had. It probably had more to do with the fact Drew and I did the activities together.

Once again, when it came time to say good night, she left me high and dry, wanting for more. I didn't get her firm decision to hold out. She had let me do almost everything else to her except the act of making love.

When I thought about it in those terms, I understood her rationale completely.

The following day we did much of the same, going with the ranch guests on a rafting excursion, something Drew had never done but wanted to.

I had to say I got more pleasure watching how much she relished the experience than I did seeing her in a sexy two-piece, one I encouraged her to cover. I didn't appreciate the other male staffers, husbands, and lesbians checking out her slim, flawless frame. I wanted it for my eyes only. She blew off my suggestion to put on pants and a shirt, denying others viewed her in that way. She obviously didn't see in herself what the others and I saw.

When we got back to the ranch, we dressed for dinner. Believe it or not, we managed to join the other guests, earning me applause from the entire Addison family and the other staffers in the dining hall. I wanted to tell them all to go fuck themselves, but Susanna and Jack were in the room, so I refrained from doing so.

"You said you occasionally leave the ranch to go into town with Brian and some of the other staff members. Since tonight's our last night here, do you think they'd mind if we tagged along? That is, if they intend to go out later. I'd love to see something new outside the ranch."

Damn. I wanted our last night to be spent alone together, but I agreed to her terms, wanting her to enjoy herself and the limited time we had left in this beautiful place.

"I'm sure they wouldn't mind at all. We can talk to Brian after dinner."

But between those two events — eating and speaking to Brian, I wanted to feed Susanna and Jack's dogs our leftovers, since we had a lot of them. I asked Drew if she wanted to do the same.

"Of course I do."

She picked up both our plates, and I led us outside where three dogs lounged on the dock. They jumped up with wagging tails when they noticed we had treats for them.

Drew and I sat on a bench and fed them. The other dogs scattered around the ranch definitely missed out on a gourmet meal. The three guys in front of us snarfed down the food, licking the plates clean.

We cuddled them and gave them love. They sensed Drew as being a dog person. They wouldn't stop kissing her and begging for her to give them belly rubs, which she did.

Since I too loved dogs, I joined in the fun. It was one of the reasons I fed whichever dogs happened to be at the ranch. Susanna and Jack took in rescues. Every summer when I visited, I had new friends to meet.

"I love this big shaggy guy." Drew giggled, fluffing the hair on his face.
"I think he shares your affection. Maybe I should be jealous."
"Nah. I've got enough attention to give both of you."
A warm sensation filled me, one I hadn't felt in years.
She kissed the top of the dog's head and stood. "The guys are about to start the bonfire. Should we go speak to Brian to see about later?"
Oh yeah.

We brought our dirty dishes inside the dining hall to be washed, then made our way over to Brian. I pulled him aside so the guests gathered around him wouldn't be privy to our conversation.
"Hey man, are you guys going out tonight?"
He nodded. "We are. Want to join us? You're leaving tomorrow, and you still owe me a game of pool. The bar we're heading to has a few tables."
"You're right. I do owe you a game or two, so yes, I'll join you. Drew's going to tag along with us."
He cocked his head to the side. "You know how my parents feel about guests leaving the ranch."
"Consider her my guest. She goes where I go."
He peered at Drew, oddly not making a sarcastic comeback. "Fine. But let's not advertise our brief excursion. Got it?"
"Got it." I understood his point loud and clear. Drew nodded affirmatively to indicate she understood as well.
"We'll head out as soon as we finish with the bonfire. You can either join us or meet up with us at the van after we're done with the guests."
"We'll meet up with you later." I wasn't in the mood for another round of family fun. Sure, the sing-along we had engaged in had

been entertaining and all, but I wanted to take the little time I had left at the ranch to detach myself from the world around me. Drew had more than changed up this visit. I participated in things I hadn't done in forever and had to say, it felt pretty fucking awesome.

She and I sought comfort in a hammock nearby while Brian and the other staffers hosted the bonfire.

The two of us lay vertically, side by side, both of us using our feet to rock the hammock back and forth.

"This is nice." I brought her hand to my lips and kissed it.

"It is. It's so peaceful and relaxing. If we stay here much longer, I might just fall asleep."

"Have I tired you out?"

She smiled ear to ear. "You have. It's been an amazing day. Thanks for taking the rafting trip with me."

A tingling phenomenon took over my heart, the overflow spilling into my other organs. What the fuck?

"The day's not over yet." I had a hint of flirtation in my tone.

"You're insatiable."

"It seems I am. It must be the pheromones you're emitting making me feel that way."

"Yeah, right." She sneered.

"I'm serious. Being around you is giving me a constant hard-on."

She chortled. "You're crazy."

Crazy for her.

"Hey Logan, we're about to head out. Let's go!" Brian called to us, already strolling with the others down the rocky path toward the parked van.

"Are you ready to see how the natives up here party?" I rose from the hammock, making sure to steady it so it wouldn't toss Drew overboard once it became unbalanced.

"I can't wait." She lit up.

We all piled into the van. There were three rows, plenty of room for everybody. Drew and I sat in the middle, her hand in mine during the entire thirty-minute drive. She listened to the animated conversations taking place, me joining in when relevant. I had known most of the guys and gals for years.

The blackness on the road ahead began to light up with signs for the various establishments we passed the closer we got to town.

Brian pulled into a busy parking lot on the outskirts. Drew's mouth fell open. "Don't tell me this is a country bar?"

"Yeah, yeah, you don't have to rub it in." I teased her.

"Now I'm even more excited."

"I bet I could top your enthusiasm for the country-western thing." I whispered so others wouldn't hear me.

She smirked. "I'd love to see you try."

Ooh, she played hard to get again.

"How would you feel about placing a wager?"

She cocked a brow. "That all depends on how you feel about losing?" She didn't plan on giving me an inch.

"You know I'm a sore loser, babe. I usually do whatever I can to win."

"Bring it on."

She raised her shoulder, smiling, giving me a nice view of her dimples.

"You've asked for it now."

"We'll see."

I grinned at her cockiness.

The place hopped for a weeknight. My motto, the more the merrier. And as long as Drew stood or sat next to me, I didn't care how crowded the place became.

We gathered around a large table, the guys ordering a pitcher of beer as soon as the waitress greeted us. Layla's fiancé, Eddie, joined us as well. From the brief conversations we'd had in the van, he seemed decent enough, attentive, doting all over her, kind of the way I behaved toward Drew.

Out of nowhere, Drew clapped her hands with glee, rose from her chair, and dragged me out of mine.

"What the hell?" I followed her lead to the dance floor.

"Dance with me. I love this song."

Fuck me. She actually had me dancing to a country tune, a first and last for me.

At least the paparazzi weren't around to witness this atrocity. The positive was the tune had a slow tempo beat, which meant I could hold her body snugly against mine. The thought alone kicked my breathing and adrenaline up a level.

18

DREW

Logan wrapped his arms around my waist, our bodies merged without an inch of space between them, on the dance floor.

His cologne intoxicated me. By this point I wouldn't doubt if I had alcohol poisoning, my body so drunk on lust for him, way past the point of being publicly acceptable.

Admiring his stunning face, I clasped my hands behind his neck. His gaze went to mine, the intensity in his eyes so thick I almost couldn't breathe. It baffled me how he sucked all the oxygen out of my lungs with a simple glance.

He leaned forward, planting a delicate kiss on my lips, his hand going to the back of my head, encouraging me to deepen the connection between us. He opened his mouth, his tongue finding mine, the two of them intermingling.

My fingers clawed at his hair, underneath, where I gripped a handful.

His lips closed, gently brushing over mine, only to open again, allowing his tongue to glide over my lower lip then inside my mouth.

My area of longing, which became my entire body, clenched in need as I got lost in the kiss, his loving touch, his masculine scent, his warm breath.

"Mmm..." I moaned into his mouth.

He tilted his head in the other direction, his tongue getting more forceful with mine.

Heat emanated from my pelvis area, spreading from my core to my limbs, my fingers, my toes. I felt flushed, high, even though I hadn't sipped any alcohol yet.

My fingers brushed over the five-o'clock shadow on his chin and I rested my palm on his cheek, our tongues wild in their dance to the slow cadence of the ballad playing in the background.

He jabbed his erection into me.

"Logan." His name was whispered into his mouth, my breath somewhat panted.

"I want you so bad." He nibbled on my ear, my neck. It's as if nobody else existed except the two of us with Garth Brooks and Trisha Yearwood singing in the background.

My hips gyrated against his hardness, the part of my brain that controlled my libido on overdrive. The more time I spent with this man, the more difficult it became to not cave in to my body's wishes. I couldn't allow myself to have sex with him yet because once I did, he would have me completely: mind, body, and soul. I didn't feel ready to take that leap of faith. I didn't know if I ever would. I had too much to lose. But that didn't mean I wasn't deriving pleasure from all the other fun we engaged in.

Unbeknownst to me, the song had changed to a faster beat. Logan and I remained joined at the hip, our lips matched up perfectly, our tongues becoming more ferocious in their endeavor.

My heart raced.

I wanted more.

So much more.

Fuck!

I winced in pain, bending over to rub the back of my calf. I glared at the couple next to us, wasted off their asses, dancing like wild chickens. The idiot girl didn't realize she'd just kicked me.

"Are you okay?" Logan spoke with concern.

"Yeah, I'm fine." I inspected the back of my leg to make sure. The girl had on spiked heels too. Damn, that had hurt.

"Why don't we take a break? I could use a drink." Logan's hand possessively held mine.

"Me too. For dancing to such a slow, I sure am overheated." I flirted, giving him a look-see through my lashes, my eyes catching his shining down on me.

He chuckled. "You're killing me." He placed his hand over his heart, patting it. I placed mine over his, clasping his fingers underneath mine. He kissed the back of my hand and winked at me.

Ah. I melted a bit more. I could've too. My body so hot it felt as though I had spiked a temperature. Screw the beer. How about a cup of ice instead? Better yet, an ice bath.

He guided me back to the table where all eyes went to us. I focused elsewhere, somewhat embarrassed the group had seen me and Logan's outward display on the dance floor.

"Hey, you guys started without us." Logan pointed to the empty pitcher of beer, getting the attention off us in a jiffy. I squeezed his hand in thanks.

He pulled my chair out for me and waited for me to sit before doing so himself in the chair next to mine.

"You owe me a game, bro." Brian pointed at Logan from across the table.

"You're right. I do. Let's do it." He took a swig of his untouched beer. "I'll be back in a few. You better watch yourself with these assholes." Logan kissed my cheek.

"Just for that, I'm going to ask Drew to dance with me during the next slow song," one of the guys joked.

"The fuck you will, Kyle. I know where those hands of yours have been. Keep them to yourself and off her." The lightheartedness from a second ago was gone from Logan's voice.

"Yeah, well, I don't want to know where those suckers of yours have been. On second thought, maybe I do." The guy named Kyle chuckled and drank more of his beer.

Logan shot Kyle a bird over his shoulder as he and Brian left for the pool tables.

Here I sat, alone with the rest of the staff. I felt somewhat awkward.

Layla flashed me a warm smile. "Ignore them."

The men at the table moved on to a different topic, saving me from my discomfort. I listened to them share stories about guests past and present, comical tales too. They had some doozies to tell me about. I found it difficult to imagine some of the crazy stuff they spoke about taking place at the calm and serene ranch. I couldn't breathe I laughed so hard, delighting in the break. Logan had my emotions all over the place. It felt nice to experience one feeling, something I hadn't been able to accomplish since arriving at the ranch.

"Wait, I have a good one for Drew since Logan and Brian are out of earshot." Layla's eyes brightened with amusement. "Let's tell her the story about when the two of them played a practical joke on me."

"I remember that!" the guy sitting at the end of the table cheered, tapping his hands on the hardwood table. I still didn't know his name yet. Could that be because I had pretty much ditched all the hosted activities.

"We had this whacko guest who *really* had a thing for Layla. Don't worry, Eddie, this was long before you came into the picture." The yet-to-be named guy took over storytelling duties from Layla.

"Anyway, the guy acted like a leech, following her around everywhere she went." He aimed his attention primarily at me. By this point the others had broken out into hysterics because they obviously knew how the story ended.

"Layla tried trading off with the other counselors so the guy wouldn't be in any of her groups, but somehow, he managed to show up to every single activity she hosted. Well, later that night, all of us here were hanging out in the dining hall. The guests had already gone to sleep for the night. So Logan and Brian come inside, pretending to be all worried and concerned, telling her the guy's outside, peering in the window, freaking the crap out of her."

Layla nodded in agreement with how the guy narrated the story so far, her closed-mouth smile now a permanent fixture on her face.

"Logan and Brian hammed it up, making her a nervous wreck. She got so worked up, she asked Brian if she could sleep in his cabin. Do you remember that, Layla?" He tipped his chin in her direction.

"Like it was yesterday." She spoke with playful sarcasm.

"The following day they told her they saw the guy hiding behind bushes, watching her from afar. Later that night, they put a sticky note on the mirror in her bathroom, scribbling something on it. I don't remember the exact words, 'I want to watch you naked in the shower,' or something like that."

"To be precise, it said, *'I can't stop thinking about how you would look naked in the shower.'* I still have the note hidden for insurance purposes." Layla winked at me.

The yet-to-be named guy telling the story belly laughed, as did the rest of the group.

"Go on and finish the story." Layla put her hand out as if passing the mic back to the speaker.

"Right. Layla became so panicked she went to her parents. They were about to confront the guy when Brian and Logan fessed up." He began to choke, coughing, still cracking up. "Susanna and Jack were so pissed at those two knuckleheads. Needless to say, the guy was harmless, leaving a few days later with his family, never to be seen or heard from again."

"The jerks." Layla smirked. "I got them back, though." She spoke mostly to me. "I snuck inside Logan's cabin and *borrowed* his guitar. I'm sure you're aware he loves that darn thing more than life itself. Boy, did he become a wreck over it too, questioning and interrogating everyone at the ranch about its whereabouts. Oh, he lost his cool *very* quickly." Her grin got wider.

"I played stupid. I told Logan that Brian had mentioned something to me about hiding it from him as a joke. I also told him not to confront Brian, to wait until the following morning. I agreed to help him get back at my brother for playing such a cruel joke on him. Being a typical guy, Logan believed me, thinking I'd really help him after what he had done to me, buying into my ploy at revenge."

She moved animatedly in her chair, a wicked grin on her face. I sat on the edge of mine, dying to hear the outcome.

"Let's see." She stared out into space and reminisced. "Brian was hosting a marshmallow roasting or something, so Logan and I took the opportunity to sneak into my brother's cabin. We started with his dresser, rearranging the clothes in them. We took one shoe from each pair in his closet and hid them underneath his bed, where he wouldn't think to look for them. In the bathroom, things got fun." She bounced up and down.

"We glued the caps to his shampoo bottles so they wouldn't open. I also painted his soap with clear nail polish. Oh my, so much fun."

"The following morning, Brian knew exactly who to blame. I'll give you a hint, it wasn't me. Logan went to his cabin, demanding that Brian give back his guitar. Brian argued he had no clue where it was. I just *happened* to be in the background, laughing hysterically at the two goofballs. That's when they realized I had screwed with both of them. They deserved it."

My belly ached. I hadn't let loose so freely in forever. These guys were a riot, the entire lot of them. And they all got along so well. Now I understood why Logan loved sneaking off with the staff. He got to see a side of the ranch the guests didn't, plus enjoy all the perks it had to offer.

"What's so funny?" Brian studied us, he and Logan now standing next to the table, the group still bursting at the seams with hilarity.

Logan kissed the top of my head again and sat next to me, the gesture making my heart flutter.

"I told Drew about the disappearing guitar prank." Layla slowed her laughter.

"What a riot. I remember it well." Brian grimaced.

"I found it funny." Logan began chuckling along with the rest of the group. "Fuck, you were so pissed." He focused his attention on Brian. "You came to the dining hall wearing one shoe because you said all the left ones had disappeared from your closet. Oh my God." His over-the-top energy and spirit spilled out on to everyone else at the table. "I still remember your hazed and confused expression and how your parents and everyone else in the dining hall thought you had lost your mind. What a great memory."

Brian caved, joining the merriment at the table. "We sure did have some good times together, huh?"

"That we did." Logan eyes were on me when he responded. "Still do." He spoke in a more serious tone.

He winked at me, the warmth in his eyes and touch indicating the meaningfulness of our chance at a do-over.

I squeezed his hand, a warm and giddy sensation filling me. I had to concentrate on my breath to slow it down.

We carried on at the table for another hour. It got late so we decided to call it a night. All of us piled into the van and it was back to the ranch.

During the ride, I rested my head on Logan's shoulder, the gentle bumping of the road beneath us causing my eyes to close. The last thing I remembered before falling asleep—Logan kissing the top of my head.

19

LOGAN

Drew passed out cold during the drive back to the ranch, with the slight sleep twitches to prove it. I hated to wake her, but I had to get her out of the van. I gently shook her.

"Come on, baby. We're back."

She struggled to open her eyes, lifting her head off my shoulder. She glanced around to take in her surroundings.

"Oh, I was in such a deep sleep." She sat upright, a big yawn engulfing her. She sluggishly climbed out of the van with me behind her.

"Have a good night, guys. Thanks for taking us along. We'll see you tomorrow." I gave Brian and the others a nod.

Drew and I strode along the dark path to the cabins. I used the flashlight app on my phone to light the rocky road in front of us.

"Do you want to stay with me tonight?" I didn't want to make assumptions, since she had shot down my request every other night. But I bit the bullet and asked anyway, tonight being a last-ditch effort.

"I'd like that a lot."

Say what?

I almost did a double take but reeled in my enthusiasm so I wouldn't freak her out.

"Me too."

My heart picked up the pace at the mere thought of waking up next to her.

"I need to get some things from my cabin first, though."

I'd agree to anything she asked as long as she didn't change her mind about sleeping in my cabin with me tonight.

We took the short hike to her cabin so she could collect some of her toiletries. I told her not to bother to bring pajamas, informing her sleep attire wasn't necessary. She flashed me a closed-lipped smile and grabbed a pair anyway.

Hey, you couldn't blame a man for trying.

It was good I had left the light on in the small family room of my cabin. It provided enough light for the two of us to see where we were going so we could make it up the stairs to the front door.

Once inside, she surveyed the space. "Huh, it's the same as mine, but the decor is different."

"Susanna put special touches in each cabin. She decorated all of them."

"I think yours is nicer than mine." She studied the art, kitchen table, and small odds and ends scattered around the room that made it feel homey.

"I think so too, now with you here in it."

She snickered. "Are you always such a charmer?"

"That all depends. Are my charms working on you?" I took a step closer to her.

"Do you really have to ask?"

I tucked some loose hair behind her ear. She leaned her head into my hand, yawning again.

"Come on, sleepyhead. Let me get you to bed. You're tired."

"That I am." She followed me to the bathroom, where she set her toiletry bag on the counter. She got busy brushing her teeth. I did the same.

We also took a quick shower, which she demanded, stating she wanted to wash off the sweat from the bar.

Finally, we made it to the bedroom.

Talk about self-control. She sported short hip-hugging boxers with red hearts all over them and a loose-fitted white T-shirt hanging off her shoulder. Sexy as fuck. Too bad I had to keep my dick tucked inside my boxers. Not that it mattered. Drew could hardly keep her eyes open. As disappointed as I felt, I let her rest. I prayed we'd have more opportunities for sexual recreation at a later date.

She stood next to the bed, hesitating, watching me get underneath the plush down comforter and fluff my pillows, leaving ample space for her to do the same.

"What's wrong?"

She bit her bottom lip, a behavior she did often when concerned about something. "Maybe this isn't such a good idea."

And there went the wheels spinning in her head.

"Get in the bed, Drew. You know I'd never disrespect you. I promise the only thing these hands are going to do right now is hold you. I can't speak for how they'll behave in the morning when we wake up, though."

She giggled. And with that, climbed underneath the blanket and sheets, kicking them around to loosen their grip, since they were tucked so securely under the mattress.

She scooted closer to me, resting her head on my chest with her arm draped over it. I stroked her damp hair, my shirt already sporting a wet spot from it.

Before I knew it, she was dead asleep, while I, on the other hand, had trouble getting settled. I think it was the first time we'd gone to sleep together in the same bed. In high school, for obvious reasons, her parents forbid close contact like this, both in public and private. Mine didn't give a shit one way or the other. They knew exactly what Drew and I were up to in my bedroom with the door closed.

Believe it or not, we rarely did much of anything except talk and listen to music. She never wanted my parents to view her in a bad light. And on the few occasions when she did sleep over, she would sleep in the guest room. Of course I would sneak into bed with her in the middle of the night, only to end up back in mine early the following morning so my folks wouldn't catch me. Not that they cared, but Drew did, and I respected her wishes. Always had. Always would.

It felt damn good to have her in my arms, her warm breath blowing gently against me with each exhalation, her body relaxed against mine.

A disappointing thought came to mind. This night was it for us at the ranch. It had been an incredible week, but I knew things would be drastically different when we left. We wouldn't be safe inside our tiny cocoon any longer. I didn't want paparazzi making any negative comments about her. And I knew all too well my insane life would be one hell of a culture shock for her, especially if and when the media got hold of this. They loved portraying me as a man whore, with make-believe stories to go along with the pictures of me and the unknown women they posted. I'd never cared, until now, wanting no bullshit printed or broadcasted about Drew.

Joey and Trevor came to mind. They were going to flip out when they heard Drew and I had spent the week together. They hadn't seen me go gaga over a woman since she and I had been together. No other woman had been capable of capturing my heart. And the reason for that—Drew had never given it back to me. And yet here I lay, twirling her hair around my finger, my mind going in a million different directions about how she and I could make the rebuilding of our relationship work, especially when she still lacked trust in me.

After tossing and turning and losing patience with my body's disinterest in sleep, I quietly slithered out of the bed, tiptoed across the creaky wooden floor, and shut the door behind me. I didn't want to wake her.

My guitar sat waiting for me in the den; playing it the only thing I knew of which would help stop the whirlwind of thoughts spinning out of control in my head.

Closing my eyes, tapping my foot, and bobbing my knee to the rhythm better enabled me to lose myself to the music, melting into its glorious sound. I played and played, my body unwinding, my mind finally clearing.

"Logan."

Drew stood in front of me, snapping me out of my trance. I set the guitar down, leaning it against the wall. I took hold of her hand and she sat on my lap.

"Sorry if I woke you."

"It's okay. You couldn't sleep?" Her eyes showed concern.

"No." I had nothing more to add to the subject.

"I hope it wasn't anything I did."

I wouldn't tell her otherwise. The fucking emotions seizing control of all rational thought in my head scared the living shit out of me. And I knew I couldn't run from them. Not this time. It would hurt too much. I had been there and done that once before. It sucked ass. I didn't want or wish for a repeat.

"No, baby. I'm only sorry I woke you."

"What were you playing? It sounded pretty." She shifted, now sitting angled on my lap, and rested her head on my shoulder. I wrapped my arm around her with our fingers entwined.

"It's the same song you heard the other day. I'm still playing around with the chord structure."

"I always did love to hear you play."

The compliment coming out of her mouth did weird shit inside me, my chest area feeling warm and fuzzy as a result.

Warm and fuzzy?

Christ. Call me royally fucked.

My crazy thoughts came back with a vengeance. So much for my reprieve from their torment.

"What's bothering you?" She lifted her head and gazed into my eyes. I didn't get how she could so easily sense when something was wrong with me. I usually did a pretty good job of hiding my shit.

"I've been thinking about the tour." My statement did speak the truth, but I left out my main worry, us parting again. I didn't want us to.

"What about it?" She showed sincerity and interest.

"Soon I'll be on the road again." The awareness I'd have to leave her a sad reality.

I tried to read her thoughts, all the while praying she couldn't read mine and see how fucked up they were.

"Aren't you used to being on the road?"

Whew. I felt somewhat relieved her psychic abilities had taken a detour. She clearly hadn't picked up on my dilemma.

"Yeah."

"I don't get it. What's the problem, then?"

"It's nothing. My mind goes off on tangents every now and again."

She flashed me a get-real expression. "Come on. I know you better than you think I do. Tell me what's bothering you." Our thumbs rolled over each other, our hands still clasped together.

We had only been together in this place for a few days. I couldn't spring the heaviness of my thoughts on her. I mean, shit, she didn't even trust me enough to have sex with her yet. And part of me didn't trust myself not to screw her over again.

"I don't know." Talk about trust. I had already broken my agreement about being honest and open with her. "I'm also thinking about the video shoot we have scheduled in New York City next weekend."

"And?"

Edginess filled me. Maybe it was because she didn't show any signs of regret or remorse about us having to part once I hit the road again while I kept trying to figure out the many different scenarios to keep us together.

Up and down my emotions went, like a yo-yo. I knew I wanted to be with Drew more than anything. What I didn't know—whether or not I could give her what she deserved, a steady relationship. I had never been committed to anything or anyone other than the guys in the band since gaining fame and constantly being on the road. In many ways, I preferred it, the freedom it gave me to do as I pleased. But in other ways, it sucked. I felt torn. I had a chance for a do-over with Drew but unfortunately, the timing presented a huge challenge.

. . .

"And nothing," I shrugged.

Drew released my hand and climbed off my lap. She stood in front of me, placing her hands on her hips, her eyes full of hurt. "Why won't you talk to me? You keep telling me to trust you. How do you expect me to do that if you won't open up to me?"

Matching her upright stance, I took it up a notch and paced nervously in front of her, swiping my hand through my messy hair. "Do you want to know what I'm really thinking about it?"

She sighed. "Hello? I've only been asking you that question repeatedly for the last several minutes."

"I'm thinking about how things are going to change between us when we leave this place tomorrow." I continued to walk back and forth in front of her.

She pouted and focused on the floor, clasping her hands together in front of her.

Maybe I had been wrong. Maybe she too had fears and doubts about our future together.

"I'm thinking about it too, a lot in fact. But I'm trying not to get ahead of myself. Trying to stay in the moment, you know?" Her tone became softer.

"I do know, but the clock is ticking, and that time is coming sooner rather than later."

"You did say you have a few days before you shoot the video in New York. That means we'll at least be able to spend some time together, right?"

"And then what?" I put my hand out in question, staring at her as if she had all the answers.

"I don't know. I guess we'll have to figure it out. I don't expect you to change your lifestyle for me. I'm trying to be a realist. You're in a famous band touring the country. You admit to hooking up with various women after your shows. I can't compete with that, especially when I'm at home and you have temptation knocking at your door every night."

She always reverted to the same old shit about mistrusting me when it came to me being with other women. I got the feeling she'd never be able to move past the mistake I'd made all those years ago.

"Do you really think I'd screw around if the two of us were in a committed relationship?"

"What're you even talking about? We've been together for what, two or three days. Don't you think you're jumping the gun by talking about the two of us being in a relationship again?" Her growing frustration became apparent in her tone. Smoke would've been blowing out of her ears if it could have, her cheeks red to match the emotions I sensed from her.

"Why does speaking about this make you so upset?"

"As much as I want to, I don't think I can allow myself to go down that road with you again. Your life consists of traveling for weeks on end with various women throwing themselves at you constantly." She closed her eyes and breathed hard. "I...I just can't do it, Logan." A tear slid down her cheek.

I stepped toward her, a foot of distance between us, and wiped it off. "If I could turn back time, I would. But I can't. There's nothing I can do to change the past. Let my actions now speak for the present. We'll never be able to move forward if you don't let go of what happened."

She gazed up at me. "How can I let it go? You broke my heart." More tears trailed down her cheeks.

My level of frustration now rose to match hers. "I know. I live with that guilt every fucking day. Give me the chance to mend it. Please."

She threw herself into my arms, her tears wetting my T-shirt, holding me for several minutes, the two of us seeking the other for comfort.

She gently pulled back. "Please sit on the couch." She wiped her wet cheeks, drying the backs of her hands on her boxers.

I didn't get why she wanted me to do so. I remained standing.

"Please... Sit down, Logan."

Fine. I did as instructed, figuring I'd find out soon enough.

She padded over to the wall and picked up my guitar, sitting in the chair I'd abandoned earlier.

What the fuck? Did she intend to play me one of her songs? *Yes!* I remained quiet, not wanting her to change her mind.

She stared at the thing, strumming a few chords. I watched in silence, smiling in appreciation, astounded by her brilliance.

I'm certain my inner pride and admiration for her was on full display.

Unbelievable. She had learned how to play the guitar on fucking YouTube, of all places. And she played well. Not in my league, of course. I mean, I played professionally, but still. She did great for a novice who did it as a hobby.

She began to sing.

An internal walk
That led nowhere good

Eyes wide open
From where I stood

Is it something I did?
Is it something I said?

Her brow creased as she posed the questions, her voice blowing my mind. I never realized she could sing so beautifully; the melody phenomenal too. Her country ballad kicked ass.

A heart full of love
Now forever broken instead

Tears cascaded down her cheeks, causing me to withhold my own.

Shadows of you
Are all that remain
If only the real you
Could take away all my pain

Vulnerability filled her. In how she swallowed hard, and in how her knee bobbed up and down as her foot rocked against the wooden floor. In the breaths she took between verses and in the softness of her tone.

Her lyrics ripped me to shreds, every word a reminder of how I'd hurt her. I would prove to her I could remove or, at best, lessen her pain.

Did you mean what you said
Did you say what you meant
Why bother to ask

She shrugged.

I came, I saw, I went

Find your truth
I now know mine
We were too young for a love like ours
To stand the test of time

. . .

Untrue. I shook my head because she was wrong.
    She shifted her gaze from me.

> *Moving on*
> *The hardest thing so far to do*
> *Moving forward*
> *My hope is that you did too*

The realization of the century suddenly hit me. I hadn't move on, and now I knew she hadn't either. If she had, she wouldn't be in my cabin right now singing this heartbreaking song to me. She would've taken flight the first night I approached her at the ranch. But she didn't. She had spent every waking moment with me.

> *Shadows of you*
> *Are all that remain*
> *If only the real you*
> *Could erase all my pain*

> *Shadows of you*
> *Are all around me*
> *I'm still trapped in your heart*
> *Please set me free*

This woman was trapped inside my heart and forever would be.

Risk Worth Taking

> *Buried, I can't seem to find my way out*
> *Buried, from a cheatin' heart no doubt*
> *I'm still buried, buried, still buried*

> *Shadows of you*
> *Are all that remain*
> *If only the real you*
> *Could erase all my pain*

Tears streamed down her cheeks at a continuous rate as the last strummed notes came to an end. She carefully set the guitar down and leaned it against the wall, where she'd found it.

My emotions had me so choked up I could barely swallow. I breathed deeply, unsure of what to say. So I acted instead. I took her in my arms and comforted her. Maybe I didn't have the right words to speak, and maybe I couldn't undo the past, but I had faith she would give me a chance to right my wrongs.

She had to.

She just had to.

20

DREW

*B*eing this close to him was heavenly. I cherished his strong arms enveloping me, his head resting on top of mine while he caressed my back.

"Thank you for sharing your beautiful song with me."

His comment had me tilting my head up, so I could see his face, his eyes watery, his touch filled with emotion.

My own thoughts and feelings bubbled to the surface. I blinked away my tears. He wiped them for me.

"I'm so sorry I hurt you. Let me make things right between us. Please give me the chance to." His desperation was evident.

Even though I wasn't sure he could follow through with what he asked, I nodded in agreement. Our lives were different now. The rational part of me argued against the two of us staying together, reiterating all the negative outcomes that could possibly come into play. And deep inside, I knew I'd always carry a tiny bit of mistrust for him, especially knowing if we did agree to any sort of a commitment, we'd be apart for weeks or months on end and he'd have women fawning all over him.

The emotional part of me thought differently. It wanted me to believe he and I could be together. That I couldn't pass up on an opportunity for us to do so, especially one that had come out of the blue, totally unexpected. Fate must've had a hand in it because things didn't work out this perfectly unless they were meant to be.

Weeks, months, or years with him weren't required for me to know the man had been and would always be my forever one and only. I had spent years of my life with him and these past few days only confirmed what my heart already knew.

He tipped my chin up so he could plant a delicate kiss on my lips. One with so much warmth it caught me off guard, causing my breath to hitch and my legs to become weak.

I sensed his hesitancy to move further, so I wrapped my arms around his neck and encouraged him to kiss me again.

Our lips parted, and our tongues met in an unrushed manner. Rather, heartfelt and tender.

As his tongue swirled around mine, my thoughts drifted off to the song I'd played on repeat after our breakup. An old seventies song sung by David Soul, *"Don't Give Up On Us."* If my mother hadn't been so obsessed with that decade's soft rock hits, I probably would've never heard it. That ballad mimicked my thoughts. I would never give up on Logan. As much as I thought I had, I now realized I hadn't.

Tears flowed, I lost myself in his arms, in his breath, in him.

He waited for me to make the first move. I knew he didn't want to pressure me. I also knew tonight would be the night. I wanted more, craving to feel that connection between us again.

"Make love to me, Logan." I didn't know how else to let him know the time had come, the mood ripe for the taking.

"Are you sure?" He wiped my tears again. "We don't have to rush things."

We kind of did. We had tonight. The following day, everything would change. I wanted my special moment with him with no distractions.

"I'm positive."

He didn't jump up and down with joy. He didn't lift me up hurriedly to get me to the bedroom. Instead, he kissed me, his respect and utmost care for my well-being only confirming my decision to take the next step with him.

I broke the kiss, held his hand tightly in mine, and led him to the bedroom where I sat on the edge of the bed. I knew this wasn't the real Logan. He had always been the dominant and confident type in the bedroom, probably more so now with all the experience he claimed to have. Yet he let me set the pace.

He leaned down and placed his hands on my cheeks. My heart raced, my palms got sweaty in anticipation. I knew one of the most memorable chapters of my life lay right in front of me.

The sparkle in his blue eyes staring into mine, his face mere inches above mine, had such extremeness to it for some strange reason. I couldn't tear my gaze from them.

He brought his lips to mine, the sensitivity in them exhilarating, bolts of euphoric energy spreading throughout my body, pooling between my thighs. Years of pent-up feelings ready to be released.

Logan gently guided me until I was lying flat on the mattress, the lingering aroma of his cologne only firing me up more. His masculine scent drove me to insanity, and better yet, his choice of cologne combined with his natural scent drove my sex meter up and off the charts.

His body rested over mine. He leaned on his forearms, both of us regarding the other.

I wrapped my legs securely around his waist.

He kissed my cheek.

My neck.

"You're beautiful. You always were. You always will be, especially to me."

"As are you." I skimmed the back of my hand over his stubbly jawline.

He kissed me again, his tongue tracing my bottom lip, entering my mouth. Mmm, he tasted decadent. I couldn't get enough of him.

I got shivers when he skimmed his hand down to the bottom of my T-shirt and fisted it. He pulled it over my head torturously slow. I raised my arms to assist him in getting it off.

Cold air blew over me but didn't cause my chill. He had with his close proximity.

He inhaled deeply, taking me in, studying me with no judgment whatsoever; on the contrary, quite the opposite.

Vulnerability filled me because of the intensity with which he devoured me with his eyes. I too inhaled deeply.

He cupped my breast, squeezing it, flicking his thumb over my hardened nipple, bringing his tongue closer and swirling it around my pebbled flesh.

The yummy fragrance of his shampoo wafted in the air, his hair still damp from our earlier shower. It tickled me when he moved. I squirmed under him.

My heart raced in eagerness, the electrical energy I'd felt earlier firing my neurons from one to the next at lightning speed, about to cause an outage from overheating. He would have to call in fire rescue soon because his scorching touch would most definitely require first aid. It was too bad we were in the middle of nowhere. I'd no doubt burn up in flames by the time help arrived.

Logan emanated sensuality. He knew it too, which made him that much more attractive. There was nothing like a confident man in the bedroom, especially one equally handsome. My sex clenched at the notion.

He licked a slow path south to my naval, moving at a leisurely pace. My breath picked up speed to match my rapidly beating heart, the suspense killing me.

I reached down and dug my fingers into his wet hair.

He glanced up at me, raising his brows and licking his lips. I bit my lower one in response, anxious for him to get a move on it yet also wanting to take it slow. A paradox.

Untying my boxers and easing them down, Logan splayed his fingers wide. He skimmed them over my knees, my shins, my ankles, my feet, my toes. Delicate kisses followed behind, giving me goose bumps.

My body melted into the mattress. He hovered slightly above my thighs. He kissed one inner thigh, the other. I squeezed my pelvic muscles in the hopes it would slow down my enthusiasm. I didn't want to come across as desperate, but when it came to Logan, I couldn't hide my impatience.

Daring to peek down at him, I discovered his lips and hands still teasing, exploring the entire area around and in between my thighs except where I wanted them the most.

"Humph." A protest was imperative. I ground my foot into the mattress to key him into my displeasure.

He smiled against my skin, peering up at me. "Mighty demanding girl, aren't you?"

"Yes, right now, I am." Maybe my response would encourage him to get the show on the road. The entire area he toyed with throbbed with rapture.

He seemed almost entranced, lowering his mouth, using his hands to spread my legs wider, doing the same to my folds, his tongue so close to making contact.

The pad of it swiped across and in between my area of desperation.

Finally!

"Yes," I moaned, off in the twilight zone, wrapping my leg around his neck, becoming more aggressive with his hair, fisting it. He didn't stop his ravenous attack on me, so it obviously didn't bother him.

"Mmm." This time a soft purr escaped my lips. I would give testimony that this man had a PhD in oral sex. His skills knew no bounds.

Pressure rose, spreading like wildfire when he plunged a finger inside me. I must've been wet because it easily glided in and out while his tongue worked its magic up front, kissing, teasing, licking.

"Logan..."

His eyes sought mine again, my vision becoming blurred.

I tugged him upward, wanting his lips on mine, the ones on my face, that is. See, I could be a dirty girl when I wanted to be. He made me feel so alive.

He obliged, crawling up my body inch by agonizing inch, stopping at my breasts. He sucked on my nipple, releasing it with a *pop*.

My senses heightened in every way, his smell became more mind-altering, his touch more sizzling, his gaze more intense, his grunts more fervid. And the taste of his tongue when it greeted mine, a combination of the two of us, spine-tingling. My heart wanted gentle, make-love sex. The rest of me craved take-me now, fuck-me sex. Was it possible to have both?

My hands explored the muscles of his back, tension filling them as his pelvis worked hard against mine. Shit, at this rate, penetration could be off the table.

He moved over me, our bodies finding a steady rhythm against each other. Sparks ignited quickly and transformed into the most beautiful fireworks ever on display.

To my dismay he shifted, dimming their incandescent light. It went without saying he sensed my impending orgasm.

"I'm being selfish tonight. I want you to explode on my cock. Not beforehand."

He sounded rough, a man on a mission who knew exactly what he wanted and ready to take it, not mindful with his word choice, which only intensified my desire for him to ginormous proportions.

"I want you so bad." The words blurted out breathlessly. I wasn't used to being so forthright with my wishes, especially in the bedroom.

"Fuck, I want you too, babe. Do you want me to use a condom?" He panted by this point as well. "I test myself regularly and I always use protection. I'm clean."

"I'm on the pill to regulate my periods. I've never had unprotected sex. I don't want there to be any more barriers between us, ever again. No condom."

He smiled over my lips. "I've never had unprotected sex either. You better be ready for this, because I'm about to blow your mind."

"You already have."

He paused, the heat between us briefly freezing. "You've blown mine too, in a countless number of ways."

Now I craved the make-love sex. How could I not after hearing such sweet words of praise?

He got busy removing his clothes then climbed on top of me again, skin to skin. I breathed mindfully to remain in the glorious moment.

When he aligned himself with my opening, in all his bareness,
I swallowed hard, my heart racing from a combination of things: eagerness, fear, the magical connection we shared.

In my wildest dreams, I never thought he and I would be in a bed making love again even if I'd pictured it constantly. But this was real. His thickness probing my entrance wasn't a figment of my imagination, a fantasy, a dildo, or my hand. It was Logan, all six-foot one inches of him, a perfect specimen of a man.

My hands rubbed over his damp skin to ground myself, to prove this wasn't make-believe.

His warm breath blew against my cheek, his hand drifted down between us. He fisted his hardness and repositioned it at my entrance.

His tip nuzzled inside, slight apprehension causing me to tense my muscles.

"Relax," he whispered against my lips.

It had been a while for me, and never with this much feeling behind it, other than when it had been with him. My biggest despair —that our act of intimacy could be the last for us to share together— a truly horrifying thought.

Using my hand, I spread myself wider for him, until my body granted him full access with no tension remaining.

Time seemed to stand still, my body somewhat unable to move as he inched deeper inside. My body had forgotten about his large size.

"Please relax, babe. I won't hurt you."

Those infamous last words.

He brushed his lips over mine. I prayed with every fiber in my being he spoke the truth.

I stared into his eyes. He gazed into mine.

A wave of pleasure ripped through me, settling where our bodies connected. A wave of something different settled in my heart, causing it to feel as full as the rest of me.

. . .

My body experienced an "aha" moment, quickly remembering Logan, relaxing into his gentle thrusts.

My hand pinpointed his ass, squeezing it and suddenly feeling the itch for more.

And man did he give it me, going deeper. And deeper. As far as my body would take him.

"Ah." What a glorious ride. I arched my back, the searing sensations having me digging my foot into the comforter, my hand curling into a fist.

"You feel better than I remember." He breathed against my ear.

I pushed him over onto his back. He slipped out during the process. No worries whatsoever on my part. I remedied the situation by straddling him.

He grabbed on to my hips, his satisfaction with my dominance evident in his touch, his eyes.

I wrapped my hand around his length, hovering above it, my legs tucked next to his sides. I closed my eyes and came down on top of him, immediately crying out in a delirious state of bliss.

"Fuck!" The word shot out of my mouth with exuberance. I rested my hands on his bent knees, holding on to them as if my life depended on it. More like it did.

"Fuck is right, baby." He shifted my body over him, the new position hitting that sweet spot inside me.

"Ah!" I cried out, the fervor multiplied by ten. Screw that, a hundred.

He clasped our hands together. I forced them over his head, leaned forward, and kissed him, restraining him while continuing to ride him, my body welcoming him in as though he'd never left.

He pumped into me, lifting his hips to match my rapid pace.

My eyes flicked open, studying his sweaty face, his panted breaths, his slightly parted lips. He must've sensed it because he too opened his eyes.

I smiled.

He smiled back.

My heart became putty, more than usual when it came to Logan.

The three words I felt for him desperately wanted to come out. It took everything I had to keep them tucked away. Way too soon to say it even though my feelings had never changed. They never would either.

My lips remained inches above his for several seconds.

He brought his to mine with more urgency.

I opened my mouth to him, our tongues going at it more aggressively. The sparklers igniting my female anatomy spontaneously combusted into a poeny, the name for the firework which resembles a large ball with no tail, no trails, only a colorful, spherical ball of heavenly bliss. Mine shot off in a deep shade of purple, my favorite color.

"Right there, Logan. Please, keep it there." I couldn't hold back any longer.

He did just that, keeping the momentum going steadily.

Light-headed didn't describe the divine happenings taking place in my head from breathing so rapidly.

I released his hand, grabbing on to the blanket instead, burying him inside me to the point I couldn't see straight. Everything became a haze as heat collected and pooled in my core, spreading throughout my entire body. I would most definitely be in need of that fire extinguisher about now.

Everything faded to black.

"Logan!" I screamed out, giving in to the pleasure ripping through me.

He tensed under me, going still, gripping my hips, locking me in place, grunting, releasing himself into me. His body jerked, his lips parted slightly, the muscles in his face tightened.

"Fuck," he grumbled.

Fuck was right. I fell on top of him, resting my head on his chest. I focused on my breath, trying to catch it.

His caressed the wet skin on my back with featherlight strokes.

My eyes felt too heavy to open, so I kept them closed.

We remained in this position for several minutes. It took me a while to gain enough strength to lift my head so I could see him.

He swiped my hair off my face. "Hi." He smiled brightly, sweetly.

"Hi, back." I returned the gesture, playing with the small patch of hair on his chest.

He had fun with my hair, twirling strands of it around his finger. The emotion in his gaze burned into me, engraving a permanent mark on my heart, the one with the reserved sign in his name on it, now reinforced.

Again, I held back from saying what I felt, instead resting my head on his chest again in fear my mouth would betray me.

I closed my eyes, keeping them shut. That was all I remembered before falling fast asleep.

21

LOGAN

I opened my eyes, my body warm. Drew had remained in the same position she'd fallen asleep in: her head resting on my chest, her image peaceful, her body relaxed, limp over mine. I had to take a leak, but it would have to wait. I didn't want to wake her. I also had no fucking clue of the time.

It amazed me that a week had passed, and we would be boarding the bus soon. Part of me couldn't wait to get the hell away from the mountains and back to city life. The other part cherished the solitude of being alone with Drew.

She shifted. I ran my hand through her silky hair. I loved how long she had let it grow over the years. A sexy-as-hell style, especially now, her locks cascaded around her face. Stunning.

She lifted her head, her eyes barely open. She squinted. "What time is it?"

"I have no idea. Did you sleep well?" Again, I smoothed her hair.

"Like a baby. You?"

My heartwarming caress across her cheek easily answered the question for me, but I still replied. "Fantastic."

An interesting notion because I rarely, if ever, let a woman stay in my bed. Once we both got what we wanted from each other physically, adios amiga. Not only did Drew spend the night with me, she also practically slept on top of me. The craziest part, I had a killer night's sleep. I couldn't remember when I had last slept so peacefully.

Here

I'd come to the ranch for a reprieve from my hectic life, and somehow it had gotten even more chaotic. It blew my mind how something so unbelievable had fallen so easily into my lap, almost too easily, which in my experience meant turbulence lay up ahead.

She stretched then climbed off the bed, my cock taking notice of her ass as she sashayed across the room to check the time on my phone. She smiled when she caught sight of the evidence. I shrugged, grinning with pride, having nothing more to add.

"We should probably go eat breakfast before packing. The van is leaving in about an hour and a half."

Did that mean she wasn't going to take care of my cock situation? I pouted. I'd have to try another tactic.

"What's the rush? I can't go to breakfast with a woody." I pointed to the offender.

"Yeah, I don't think it would be appropriate."

Go ahead and laugh, luscious.

Placing that glorious mouth of hers over my dick, or better yet, burying my cock balls-deep inside her pussy became all I could think about. Let her laugh about that.

"Maybe you can help me out with my *problem*." I extended my hand out toward her.

My urge to pee vanished, not like I'd be able to piss in my current state anyway.

She jumped onto the bed, full of life and carefree. Her eyes glistened.

Wow, someone was a morning person, me included.

She straddled me, exploring my chest with her hands. "You've bulked up a lot." She surveyed the areas she touched, heat emanating from her fingertips, burning into my skin.

"I'll take it you approve."

"Approve? It's fucking hot," she purred.

Fuck me and her hotness. And she spoke differently now. Guess she had grown up, not the young girl I remembered anymore, now a self-assured, sensual woman, the ultimate turn-on. My dick dug it too.

She stared at my erection, skirting her hand down my abs, a bit lower. She held my cock firmly in her grasp, lust filling her. I loved her confidence, but now I wanted to resume control and take charge.

22

DREW

He thought he would control how this went down. *Silly man.* Not if I could help it.

I gathered my hair and twisted it into a knot to get it off my face. *There.* Now I could see him in all his delicious nakedness. I moaned in delight, inching my way down his body until my face and his cock were in perfect alignment. I brought my head forward and kissed the tip of his rigid length, licking the wetness, keeping my eyes on his. Need filled them, famine.

Opening my mouth, I enveloped him, taking in as much of him as possible. I sucked leisurely, only to speed up, then slow down, teasing him to no end.

He fisted my makeshift bun, encouraging me to take him deeper by drawing me forward. His shaft became slippery under my grasp, thanks to my bobbing mouth.

"Fuck, Drew."

Satisfied I brought him so much pleasure, I smiled, glancing up at him. His gaze bore into mine which turned me on to the nth degree. So I continued to watch his gorgeous face, using my tongue to lick a swirly path up to the mushroom tip. Wrapping my mouth around him again was the finisher.

"I'm going to come if you keep that up and I want to be inside you when I do."

Too bad for him. I was having fun. I cupped his balls, sucking with varying grades of tension.

He hardened beneath me and pushed me back, releasing himself from my grasp.

I hoped I hadn't done anything wrong, but if his eyes spoke the truth, I knew I hadn't.

"Lie down." His tone was commanding. I liked it.

As instructed, I rested on my back, opening myself up to him in a myriad of ways.

He climbed over me, using his feet to spread my thighs wider.

"God, I'm jonesing to be inside you, baby."

"What're you waiting for?" My body screamed for its own release.

"Fuck me, Drew."

"I plan on it."

His eyes went wide.

I kind of shocked myself at my own forthright behavior.

He aligned himself, my giddiness fading as he buried himself inside me with more energy than patience.

I gripped his hair. Our tongues danced to their own beat. He drove into me harder, a heavenly concoction of delirium and intoxication building with each thrust forward.

"Logan!" I cried out, the surge rising, too much to contain any longer.

He flipped me over, so I sat on top, right back where I'd started. I rested my hands against his chest, losing myself,

my body controlling the depth and speed of our connection. He must've wanted more because he seized my hips and conducted our symphony instead, moving me with more oomph, his cock buried so deep I couldn't see straight. Between that and his gentle rubbing of my clit, he had me all but shattering into a million pieces.

"Take me with you." He hardened inside me. I continued to buck and rock my hips over his.

My body felt light, tingly, swollen, plus all the other melt-in-your-mouth and succulent sensations women should feel when reaching climax. Yet Logan took me even higher. A tidal wave of ecstasy ripped me apart at the seams, my body combusting over him, tremors of elation bringing me to heights I never thought I'd reach.

Holy shit. I collapsed on top of him, panting heavily. He stroked my back, our skin glistening with perspiration.

"Now that's what I call a good morning." He sounded somewhat muffled, his mouth buried underneath my hair which had come loose. He brushed it off his face.

I leaned up so I could see his beautiful eyes. We observed each other.

He broke the trance by speaking. "We should probably get dressed or else Brian will come bang the door down. I myself don't want him seeing you in your birthday suit."

Bummer. Not the part about Brian seeing me in my birthday suit. I didn't want that either. The part about me and Logan having to get dressed to leave the ranch.

Lethargically,

I crawled off him and went to the bathroom to shower. He followed closely behind and joined me under the spray.

"Ready to go home?" He rinsed his hair.

"No. Kate's honeymoon has been awesome."

He chuckled. "I agree. Let's hear it for Kate."

"In the end, she got married at a shotgun wedding in Vegas, had a mini honeymoon, and I got a free and kick-ass vacation at a beautiful ranch."

He pulled me into his arms. "Do you think you'd feel the same way about the trip if the two of us hadn't run into each other?"

"Are you fishing for a compliment, Mr. Trimble?"

"From you, I'll take any and all I can get."

"Then the answer is, no, I wouldn't have had as much fun. To be honest, I would've probably left when she did if I had to stay here by myself."

"Too much excitement for you?"

"Oh, you've given me plenty of excitement. I've had more action this week than I have in years."

His ears perked up. "Say what?"

I brushed him off. "Wouldn't you like to know?"

"I would, actually."

Things unexpectedly turned serious.

Me and my big, stupid mouth.

"Let's just say things have been quiet between the sheets, unless you count me using my hand or a vibrator action."

His eyes perked up as much as his ears did. "That's fucking hot. Now look what you've gone and done." He pointed to his growing erection.

His insane testosterone level was off the charts.

He guided my chin up to meet his gaze. "All kidding aside, how quiet?"

I sucked in my lower lip, nibbling on it, the topic not one I wanted to have a Q and A session about. I flipped the question in his direction to give me some breathing room from the insecurity taking over me.

"How about you? From what you've told me, you bed-hop on a regular basis."

He shrugged. "I'm not going to lie and say otherwise. The opportunities presented themselves, and I took advantage of them."

Christ. He came clean about his sluttiness as if he'd merely binged on Oreos late at night. My insecurity morphed into self-protectiveness. "Am I another one of those opportunities?" I felt somewhat hesitant of the answer he'd give me but breathed a sigh of relief when he shook his head.

"You've never been an opportunity, Drew. You've always been a privilege."

Could he make me swoon any more? How was I supposed to respond to something so mushy?

I guess I didn't have to because he leaned forward and kissed me.

"You're nothing compared to the women I meet on the road, baby. Far superior. All they're after is money and a story to share with their friends."

"Then why do you play along?" I didn't get it.

"As I said, they offered, I agreed. No strings attached."

I couldn't help but feel disappointed he had become such a playboy. Again, self-doubt made its presence known. In a few short weeks, he'd be right back on tour with the same trashy women propositioning him.

"Your turn. Tell me about the past boyfriends you've had since me."

Shit. Would slinking out of the shower go unnoticed?

A breath of encouragement was mandatory prior to voicing my reply. "There haven't been any."

The admittance felt worse than I thought it would. I washed my face so he couldn't see it, not wanting to admit I had put a steel barrier around my heart to protect it from ever getting broken again.

"Hey, look at me."

Sorry, buddy, not this time. I didn't budge, so he physically spun me around. *Ugh!*

"What?" I was unable to hide my defensive stance.

He held his hand up in surrender. "I'm sorry. We don't have to talk about it if you don't want to."

Dammit. I rolled my eyes because if things progressed between us, he'd find out sooner or later anyway.

"I did date, Logan." I hated to sound so pathetic.

"And?"

"And what?"

"Did you fuck the guys?"

"That sounds cheap. I'm not cheap, and you know it."

"I didn't say you were. In fact, you're far from it, on the opposite spectrum."

His comment appeased me, so I continued to participate in the conversation as an adult would, even though my inner teenager felt pissed and wanted to argue with him.

"Aside from the one-night stands I told you about, I slept with one other guy. I dated him for several months but ended it."

"And why's that?"

"Now I don't want to talk about it anymore."

"Enough said. Can I ask you one more question?" He held his finger up, giving me puppy-dog eyes.

Against my better judgment, I gave in.

"Fine. Shoot." A bit of sass revealed itself in my tone.

"Did you love him?"

"No." I slumped my shoulders in defeat.

Meanwhile, his eyes lit up with all kinds of elation. *Jerk.*

"So that means I've been the only man you've ever loved?"

How cocky could he possibly be?

"I'm glad you're so pleased."

I sighed at the pathetic reality that he'd be the *only* man I'd ever love, period.

"How about you? Have you been in love again?" I couldn't face him because if he answered yes, I'd be crushed. The tile on the wall could use a bit of bleach.

He guided my chin in his direction, forcing me to look at him. "Only you." He planted a soft kiss on my lips. I melted against him.

So with all the women he'd fooled around with, I had been his only love to date.

Risk Worth Taking

Resting my head against his chest, I wore a huge smile, delighting in the feel of his warm, sturdy body holding mine. My mind also delighted in knowing things could possibly work out for us in the end after all.

23

LOGAN

We dressed for breakfast. Drew had forgotten to bring clean clothing, so we made a pit stop at her cabin where she dressed and packed up the few things she'd brought with her to the ranch. We headed back to my cabin with her suitcase in tow. I packed up my stuff, basically throwing dirty clothes into a plastic bag, since I had lived out of my duffel.

Of course breakfast had ended when we reached the dining hall.

Susanna put her hand out when she saw us. "Really?"

She got a heartwarming smile from me, the same one that won her over year after year. She served me and Drew but gave me a loving hug first.

"Be good to this girl, Logan." She peered in Drew's direction. "She's a keeper. Much better than what I see you with online."

Susanna followed me on social media?

"You're like a son to me, so I keep tabs on you, the same as I do with Brian and Layla." She patted my back.

Warmth filled me. Sadly, my own mother didn't feel the same way.

Her words were acknowledged with a nod. Drew and I sat at an abandoned table. I ate all the hearty food Susanna had piled on our plates—omelets, pancakes, fresh fruit from her garden, and potatoes with onions. Well, I ate mine. Drew didn't eat much. In fact, she hardly touched anything on her plate.

"You okay?" I shoveled another bite of pancake into my mouth.

"Yeah. I'm not much of a breakfast eater. You sure seem to be." She watched as I continued to dig in to my scrumptious food.

"Actually, I usually have a cup of coffee and a protein bar or something else light in the mornings because I can't work out on a full stomach. It makes me nauseous. But Susanna's breakfast looks and smells too good to pass up. Besides, I don't plan on working out any time soon unless it's with you in a bed." I winked.

She chuckled. "Enjoy your breakfast, stud muffin."

"I'm enjoying sitting here with you right now."

"You're sweet."

After we finished, well, after I finished—Drew broke down and had a cup of tea —we exited the dining hall. Brian informed us we had to head to the airport in a few.

Other guests piled into the van, picking and choosing their seats. I knew Brian would reserve two in the front row for me and Drew so felt no urge to go claim some.

We hustled back to my cabin to retrieve our bags. We loaded them in the back of the van with all the other guests' luggage. My guitar case remained firmly in my grasp, the same as when I'd arrived.

The ride to the airport felt shorter than the ride to the ranch because I had Drew tucked underneath my arm. Layla, Brian, and I chatted during most of the trip. Drew slept, her head resting on my shoulder.

My adrenaline rose the closer we got to the city. As recharged as I felt spiritually, I wasn't quite ready to get back into the craziness of my life.

Once at the airport, we said our good-byes to Layla and Brian as well as the other guests. Two of the teenage girls from the ranch asked for a good-bye hug. Drew beamed on the sidelines when I gave each of them one.

We checked in with an attendant. Drew's baggage required tagging. I planned on carrying my bag on board. I knew how to travel light, clearly Drew didn't.

We had about an hour and a half to kill, so we sat our asses down at the semi-crowded terminal. I brought my phone to life and switched it off airplane mode, so not happy to face the music.

My cell took me aback, lighting up like the Fourth of July, an explosion of text messages and missed calls rapid firing on the screen, most of them, if not all, from the guys and Camilla. Something was definitely up. I didn't know who to reach out to first. I figured I'd go with Joey via text in case the shit had hit the fan, which in all probability it had. I also didn't want others around me hearing my conversation with him.

Joey: *Seems someone had a good time.*

Sarcasm filled the words he'd typed.

Logan: *I did, always do. What you mean by seems?*

Joey: *Have you not seen the pictures posted all over the net yet?*

No, I hadn't seen any pictures because I had been isolated from the Internet world over the past week and wanted to disconnect from all forms of social media, period.

. . .

Logan: *What pictures are you referring to? I've been in the middle of nowhere for a week.*

Joey: *Is the girl in the pictures who I think it is?*

What the fuck? How did he know about me and Drew, if she was in fact the girl he referred to?

Logan: *What girl?*

Figured I'd play stupid and ask.

Joey: *The girl at the ranch you've been touchy feely with, the one from your past who you used to be in love with, if I'm not mistaken.*

Double what the fuck? My adrenaline surged. Joey knew Drew all too well, which meant whatever pictures he spoke about displayed her face clearly enough for him to recognize her.

Logan: *Where are these pictures posted?*

Joey: *Where most of our fans post pics.*

I searched Steam on Instagram to see what action I had missed out on.
    The wind almost got knocked out of me when I saw not one, but

picture after picture of me and Drew. Some had the two of us locking lips. Others had us strolling hand in hand around the ranch.

Who took the pictures? I scratched my head, contemplating the thought. The Addison family made it a top priority to respect my privacy. They would never set me up for anything like this.

That was when it hit me. It had to be one of those teenage girls at the ranch. How they uploaded pictures when the Internet service at the ranch sucked ass was beyond me. What pissed me off more was that Susanna had specifically asked the guests not to take any pictures of other guests without prior approval. In all my years visiting the place, I'd never once had an issue of my privacy being violated. I guess things were changing with the recent popularity of the band. My one place of escape and solitude had now been tarnished.

How was I going to tell

Drew about this situation, and when? I didn't want paparazzi eating her alive, and they took pleasure in doing just that when they saw me with women in pictures, usually multiple women over short time spans. Entertainment reporters had a field day with me.

Logan: *I see the pictures now. I'm screwed, man.*

Joey: *Did you and Drew have this secret get-together planned all along?*

Logan: *No. Sheer coincidence, if you can believe it. A great one, I must say. I'm not going to get into it now because I want to tell Drew about the pictures. I don't want anyone to say anything to her about them without me telling her first. Don't know how she's going to handle this. Camilla left me multiple voice mails. Is this what they're about?*

. . .

Joey: *Yup. She called me repeatedly, telling me you were purposely avoiding her calls because you didn't want to deal with the media while on vacation. I assured her that you had relatively no Internet service at the ranch and the little you did have, you didn't take advantage of. You went there to ride solo. Guess you didn't. LOL. I have to say, I can't wait to hear the details. This is the last sort of drama I expected to transpire. Usually your visits to the ranch remain under the radar. Drew. I can't believe it. She looks good, but then again, she always did. A word of advice. I'd call Camilla prior to takeoff. She probably wants to do damage control.*

Logan: *I hear you. I'll speak to you when I'm back in town. How's your trip with Teva going?*

Joey: *Amazing. We'll be back in a few days. Camilla wants all of us to meet up before we head to NYC for the video shoot.*

Logan: *Very well. Enjoy the rest of your vacation. Sadly, I might be in need of another one in the near future.*

Joey: *LOL*

At least someone found humor in my situation. I, for one, didn't.

Drew strolled toward me, coffee cup in hand. She had gone to get some while I texted Joey. Lord help me. I hoped she wouldn't toss the hot liquid on me when she heard the terrible news.

She frowned upon seeing me. "What's wrong? You look like you've seen a ghost." She sat next to me, her body in my direct line of sight.

"I have to tell you something." I glanced at the evil device sitting in my hand, figuring it would be better to show her rather than tell her.

Her eyes narrowed and she bit her bottom lip. Time to get the big reveal over and done with.

I held the phone between us so she had a good view of the screen. I scrolled through the four or five pictures taken of us at the ranch.

She shrugged.

Shit, she didn't understand the meaning or magnitude behind my sudden show-and-tell.

"Where did you get those pictures?"

"My gut is one of my fans took them at the ranch and posted them online. They're all over the net. The guys and my manager have blasted my phone with messages and texts about them."

The cup trembled in her hand. I reached over to steady it. I didn't want the hot liquid to spill on her.

When I saw my gesture didn't resolve the problem, I retrieved the cup from her.

"You mean to tell me these pictures are out there for the world to see?"

I hated to agree but didn't want to lie. I nodded. She covered her mouth with her hand, her disbelief clear as day.

"Tell me what you're thinking?" This type of shit typically didn't bother me. I had accepted it as part of my life, pretty much ignoring the bad and taking pride in the good. But now someone I cared about had become involved. That didn't sit well with me.

"Too many things. I guess the main one is that I don't want any slanderous comments made about my character. I can't imagine how horrible it would be to experience something so life changing." She sighed heavily and rubbed her palms on her pants. "Did you just find out about this?"

"Yeah. When I turned my phone on and saw the shitload of messages from the guys and my manager, I knew something had happened. I texted Joey, and he informed me about the pictures."

"Maybe I should check my phone too." She dug inside her purse but paused. She placed it on her lap instead, where she resumed rubbing her palm back and forth on her pants. "On second thought, maybe I shouldn't."

"The good news is nobody knows you by name."

"But people who know me will recognize me. And how long will it take before my name is next to the pictures?"

She had a point.

"Let me call my manager. She's good at sorting this type of shit out."

If Drew continued to rub her hands against her pants, she would burn a hole in them by the time our flight took off. I offered her some coffee. She shook her head, rejecting it. I set the cup on the ground next to my chair and covered her hands with mine to stop them from fidgeting. I dialed Camilla's number with my free hand.

"Hello."

Fuck, Camilla sounded pissed.

24

DREW

Nervously, I watched and listened to Logan engage in a conversation with his manager, tapping my foot nonstop. But I couldn't sit tight any longer. I had to move. I paced back and forth in front of our chairs. It did nothing to calm me.

Pictures of me were posted online. It made me realize how different Logan's life had become. I bet he dealt with this type of thing daily. Well, I wanted no part of it. I didn't relish the spotlight.

I guess the two of us being at that ranch together gave me a false sense of security that things could remain the same between us, the two of us in our own private world. But reality set in fast and furiously. We wouldn't experience that kind of privacy again unless isolated on a deserted island.

Where was the bathroom? I needed to splash some cold water on my face. My hands were clammy, my head dizzy. It didn't help that I hadn't eaten anything prior to leaving the ranch. I figured I'd eat on the plane, but now I had no appetite, even though my stomach gurgled for food. I whispered to Logan, informing him I had to use the restroom. He nodded and continued talking on the phone with his manager.

The cold water on my cheeks did me good; the dizziness somewhat fading.

I dried my face and took some deep breaths to relax. I had no clue what news Logan would give me next.

A bubbly teenage girl approached me at the vanity in the bathroom. "Hey, you're the girl dating Logan Trimble of Steam, aren't you?"

She had to be kidding. I already got recognized? Better yet, at an airport in the middle of the boonies? What the hell? I tried to stifle my angst.

"Sorry. You must have me confused with someone else." I played it off as best I could, on the outside. On the inside, my heart was racing, I had a pounding sensation in my forehead, and my legs felt weak. So much for trying to relax. I was in a worse state now than when I'd entered the bathroom.

"Oh, I'm sorry. I thought you were someone else."

My lips twitched with my fake smile. I dashed out of the bathroom, almost crashing into Logan outside the exit. He steadied me, assessing me, his lashes fluttering with worry.

"I wanted to make sure you were okay. You rushed off."

"I'm fine." I shuffled from foot to foot, too full of anxiety to keep still.

"Oh my God, you're Logan Trimble!"

The same teenage girl I'd met in the restroom appeared, bouncing up and down with glee. Her enthusiasm took a hike south along with her brows when she caught sight of me, pointing at me accusingly.

"Then that means you *are* the girl in the picture who's dating him."

Logan looked at me with question marks. I couldn't deal with this shit, so I raced back to the terminal where I planted my butt on an uncomfortable chair. Logan joined me not a second later, taking my hand in his, tugging it to get my attention.

"What did your manager say?" I blurted out, dying to know the next scene in the soap opera presently called my life.

He rubbed the back of his neck, his outward level of anxiety matching mine.

Shit.

I closed my eyes, leaning back in my chair. I took slow, deep breaths.

"She's on it."

My eyes flicked open. I put my hand out, palm up. "What the hell does that mean, *she's on it*?"

"Camilla's a guru at spinning stories in the band's favor."

Sitting up, I crossed my arms over my chest. "The band's favor? What about me?"

"I told her you're important to me, that you're not the same as the other women she's seen me in pictures with online or after shows."

He rubbed his neck more vigorously. I found his comment endearing but still, I didn't want my reputation tarnished. For him, it didn't matter what people said, he'd still sell records and as a result, become more popular from all the free publicity. Not me. I had a lot more to lose, most importantly my integrity.

The flight attendant called for first-class passengers to board. Logan had tried to upgrade my ticket when I checked my baggage, but the flight had been completely sold out, being there were only a limited number of flights arriving and departing each day from this small city.

He sat tight, not budging, his feet remaining glued to the floor. He kept my hand in his, swiping his thumb over my knuckles.

"Go on." I shooed him off with the back of my hand.

"I don't understand why you're mad at me. I didn't post the damn pictures. I did nothing wrong, Drew."

"I know." I closed my eyes for a second in an effort to collect my thoughts. "It's not your fault. I'm sorry if I'm making you feel that way. But it's a lot to take in. This is only the beginning of the media circus I'm sure will ensue. What happens when we get home?" I studied him, waiting for and wanting an honest reply.

. . .

"What do you mean? We're going to spend quality time together until I leave for New York and then again when I get back. I don't hit the road for a while yet."

He sounded so optimistic about the possibility.

"I don't want to be followed around by reporters everywhere we go. Is that what your life has become?"

"No. When the guys and I do band performances, yes, a lot of pictures are taken by fans and photographers. But when we're living our lives, doing our thing, we're pretty much left alone unless a fan happens to spot us like the girl did back at the ranch or outside the bathroom a few minutes ago."

"Maybe I'm overreacting." I prayed desperately for that to be the case.

"Please, don't let this ruin the great week we've spent together." He tilted my chin up to meet my gaze. "Please?"

How could I resist the sadness in his eyes?

"Fine," I agreed, not sure how convincing my affirmation sounded.

He leaned forward, brushing his lips against mine, then whispered in my ear. "I'm assuming you're not a member of the Mile High Club yet, since this trip was your first plane ride. Am I correct?"

My jaw fell slightly open in surprise by his question, which had come out of nowhere. Leave it to Logan to think about sex in any situation.

"No, I'm not. You are in fact correct."

"How about you let me initiate you into the club, baby?"

The warmth in my cheeks spread to the rest of my limbs. Sure, I had heard about the Mile High Club but never imagined myself being a member, until now. Damn Logan and his bad influence over me.

"I'm assuming you're already a member." A tinge of jealousy flowed through me because I knew what his answer would be. His expression said it all.

"It'll be different this time, though."

Yeah, right.

"Are you playing me right now?"

"The only thing I want to play with right now is you in the bathroom of that 737." He nodded toward the floor-to-ceiling window, the jet parked outside.

"I don't know. I haven't seen the bathrooms yet but I'm sure they're tiny. Would both of us fit inside one?"

"Trust me. I'll fit in you perfectly."

My cheeks burned, for sure red to match the heat in them. I covered my mouth in embarrassment.

"I'll take that as a yes." His lips curled up devilishly.

"But I'm not in first class. How would it possibly work?"

"Not to worry. I'll take you in back."

Logan worded things so sexually. My entire body seared with shyness, naivety, and more importantly, desire.

"I can't believe you just said that." I stifled a laugh.

"If your body has anything to say about it, you're basking in the glory of it. Don't think I can't read the *please fuck me* vibe your body is giving me."

"Oh my God. Please go board the plane before I die of humiliation."

He planted a soft kiss on my lips. "I have to give you a quick rundown first on how this little scheme of ours will play out."

"Are you telling me there's actually a right and wrong way to do this?" I couldn't believe I considered going through with his request. Screwing in an airplane bathroom? *Holy shit.* Heat pooled between my thighs.

"It's all about timing, babe. I have to be honest and say I've never done it in coach nor have I done it during daylight hours. It's best at night, when people are asleep, but it's not to say we can't pull it off. Here's what I want you to do…"

He contemplated for a minute.

"Wait until the attendants finish serving drinks, because their carts will block the aisles. When the coast is clear, come up to first class. A flight attendant will most likely say something to you about being up there, but it's crucial that I see you to make this work. Make sure I do, then turn around and head toward the bathrooms located in the back of the plane. Use the one on the left. Once inside, lock the door behind you. I'll be on your tail. I'll give you a heads-up with a one, two, three, knock when I get there. Unlock the door, leave it slightly open. Whatever you do, don't undress until both of us are locked inside in case someone else enters the bathroom. Trust me, I don't want anyone else seeing your smoking-hot body. I'll come in and lock the door behind me. We have to be quick. When we're done, we'll make a prompt exit and return to our seats. Usually after beverage service, passengers use the restroom which means we can't occupy it for too long. That's all there is to it."

That's all there is to it?

He made it sound *much* easier said than done. My palms became damp because of the precise order of steps he'd instructed me to follow. I didn't want to screw anything up.

"I don't know. It sounds kind of dangerous."

"Danger can be fun, Drew. Think of the story we'll have to tell."

"To who? I'll be too embarrassed to tell anyone."

"But you and I will have a really good secret. Won't we?"

"I can't believe I'm agreeing to do this. I don't want to get into trouble."

"You're with me now, babe. I'm *all* about getting in trouble."

"I know. That's what I'm afraid of."

"See you in the bathroom." He winked, satisfaction written all over him. He headed toward the line for boarding, leaving me in his dust with an abundance of nervous energy.

What in the heck was I thinking by giving in to such an asinine request? What if I lost my nerve? Things like this put me on edge. I could already see it, a picture of me and Logan posted on the net, the two of us coming out of the same bathroom, our hair disheveled, our clothes not properly tucked in. *Holy moly.*

Most of the others sitting around me were engaged with their electronic devices. No one paid me any mind. My hope was they'd be as intently engaged with their tablets and phones when Logan and I pulled off our stunt in the bathroom.

Seeing people mesmerized by their phones made me think of mine. I retrieved it from out of my purse to check for any urgent or important messages I might have missed over the course of the week.

Surprisingly, the only texts I got were from Eric, my best friend. I scanned through them, most of them *I miss you* and *I can't wait for you to come home* messages. I loved that man. He made me so happy. When I told him who I'd spent my week with, he would shit. I'd have to tread those waters carefully. Eric still held a grudge against Logan for the way he'd hurt me all those years ago.

My lower lip got ample attention from my teeth as I chewed on it, my mind pondering how I'd break the news to him and convince him Logan had changed. Maybe I would ask him about his relationship status first. He loved to feed me details about his dates. I often tried to reiterate how he could share his enthusiasm without a play–by–play but God bless Eric, he continued to feed me specifics in all of their juicy explicitness.

When my section was called I boarded the plane, in somewhat of a daze. The cool air hit me, but not enough to bring down my body temperature, which had elevated for multiple reasons.

Luckily, I had an aisle seat. A couple sat in the two seats next to me, too busy with their tablets to even acknowledge my presence. Sweet relief. It meant they wouldn't notice my absence either.

I twiddled my thumbs nervously until the beverage carts came and went.

I surveyed my surroundings to discover passengers napping, reading, or watching the small television screens in front of them.

Okay, it was time to set our plan into action. Lord help me. Talk about walking to the guillotine. With each step I took toward first class, both feet felt heavier, making the task of walking a conscious effort on my mind's part. I took deliberate and steady breaths, but it did nothing to slow my pounding heart. I should've brought my club soda along with me on this excursion. I could barely swallow due to the dryness in my mouth.

When I got to the curtain which led to the first-class area, I stopped, second thoughts having a field day inside me, begging me not to go through with this absurdity. I glanced at the passengers sitting in the aisle seats to my left and right. Neither of them paid me any mind, the one to my left fast asleep and the one to my right engrossed in a movie.

I can do this. It'll be fun. I gave myself a quick pep talk, the thrill of getting away with something like this insanely enticing.

I reached for the soft gray curtain in front of me and slid it partially open, leaving enough room for me to get on the other side of it.

Adrenaline rushed through me, my eyes not knowing what to focus on first.

Logan's messy hair couldn't be missed. He sat in an aisle seat with earbuds plugged in. He watched a movie on a larger screen than those we had in coach.

Now my feet felt light. I speed walked to the bathroom when an attendant stopped me in my tracks, informing me to use the restrooms in the back of the plane. With a snooty attitude, I might add. Talk about feeling demeaned.

While strolling back down the aisle, I purposely bumped into Logan's arm, not that he didn't see me. He sported a big stupid grin.

What am I doing? This is ridiculous.

Positive self-talk drowned out the negative as I went to the back of the plane. One passenger stood in front of me, waiting to use the restroom.

My fingernail would need fresh polish. I chewed on it, my thoughts too scattered to remember which bathroom he'd told me to use.

Shit!

Is it the right one?

No, it's the one on the left.

Which bathroom was I supposed to go into? I had been so nervous when he gave me the instructions, my thoughts had gone into overdrive. I'd obviously missed some of the finer details.

The lady ahead of me took the vacant restroom on the right. I tried to replay Logan's exact words in my mind.

Yes, I had it now. Enter the bathroom on the left.

Once the passenger who occupied it exited, I stepped inside the small space but not before glancing down the aisle to see if Logan was coming. I rolled my eyes at the sight of him strutting in my direction, as if his overenthusiastic waltz wouldn't give us away. Be real.

Hesitantly, I locked the door behind me, doubting whether I could go through with this. I stared at the door and rocked back and forth, waiting impatiently for his knock.

He did his one, two, three, thing. I opened the door slightly. He stepped inside, locking it behind him.

"Hi, stranger. Fancy meeting you here." He had hunger in his eyes.

If he wanted or expected my eyes to reveal the same amount of desire as his, he better start touching me with those magic hands of his. I just about shitted bricks over the fear someone would catch us. Good thing we stood in the bathroom.

"Calm down, babe. You're going to love this."

My stiff posture and shell-shocked pose must've given him insight into my nervous state. His attempt at trying to relax me didn't work. It also didn't help that I felt cramped and boxed in a urinal, one which smelled equally offensive to put it mildly.

He and I faced each other. I stood still. I wanted him to take the lead, since much to my dismay, he had experience with this sort of thing.

Fortunately, I didn't have to wait long. He wrapped me in his arms, his lips getting friendly with mine, his tongue slipping inside with a sense of urgency.

My mind kept drifting toward the other passengers who might be waiting outside to use the bathroom.

As crazy as it sounded, these thoughts were erotically enticing, a fantasy about me and Logan pulling off our very own *Mission: Impossible* caper, this one sexual in nature, in an airplane bathroom nonetheless. Combine that with the sneakiness we had going on with Logan's hands exploring my thighs, my ass, my waist, my breasts.

Our kiss had primal need in it. I took off on my own flight. Destination: the vivid imagery playing in my mind.

One of my hands went into his hair, the other down to his firm, gorgeous ass. He brought his hand forward to the waistband of my joggers. I had intentionally dressed comfortably for a long day of travel. Glad I had thought ahead for reasons other than this one: easy removal.

He grazed the skin slightly under my belly button, down to the waistband of my undies, then lower.

I melted into his touch, his manner of rubbing causing me to writhe against him. Nirvana.

"Ah." A moan slipped out.

Wanting to make sure we both had the same heat index going on, I cupped his erection over his jeans, finding him to be equally reactive and ready for action. *Yay!*

He yanked my joggers down. I, in turn,

scanned the space, confirming in my mind that my ass and the toilet seat positioned a foot in front of me would never meet in this lifetime. I had to set limits and boundaries somewhere.

He unfastened his jeans, jerking them down and letting them drop to his ankles. I was still trying to figure out how we were going to get this feat accomplished. There were only so many options I could come up with to get this task underway, but I had run out of creative ideas. He had other things on his mind such as wrestling my pants down to my ankles.

"Put your hands on the wall, Drew."

He flipped me around so I faced it. I cringed at the thought of touching anything but took him up on his request, telling myself I could wash my hands afterward.

"Now bend over slightly."

Ah, now I knew his plan.

He stood behind me, using his palm to start the party, rubbing it against my now hypersensitive flesh. *Mmm.* He had so many tricks up his sleeve, this one by far an effort to make sure I still planned to attend the fiesta he so diligently organized. Oh, he needn't worry, I had no intention of skipping out. In fact, I'd be the life of the party, that was how full of lust he had me.

"So wet. I fucking love it."

When he ran a finger down my spine, I shivered, closed my eyes and arched my back. For a minute I wondered whether he'd get me off with his hand alone because it did a splendid job of winding me up, to the point my body felt ready to unravel.

His other hand spread my ass cheeks wider so he could better align himself up front. My anticipation blossomed like wildflowers. I couldn't wait.

My body trembled, but it didn't stop it from sucking his cock in whole, my palms unsteady on the wall supporting them, my knees already weak.

"Fuck yes, Drew," he huffed against my ear, moving in and out of me at a steady pace, his body slapping against mine more vigorously with his increase in tempo.

"Logan." I tried everything within my power to hold back the screams dying to come out. The fantasy playing out in my mind along with the reality of our situation had me on the edge of a tall cliff, ready to take the plunge with my bungee cord intact.

He again picked up the speed, my legs barely able to keep me upright. No way was I about to allow myself to fall in dried-up puddles of urine. *Gross.* I willed and demanded my limbs to hold me up.

It was ironic that I saw stars, Logan being one and me flying in the clouds closer to them.

My eyes rolled back, the juncture where our bodies connected sending fireworks of pleasure throughout.

I arched my back more, thinking it would enable him to fill me deeper even though he filled me to the rim.

Sweet heaven above.

. . .

I floated inside the small confines of the bathroom, miles above the ground, now an official member of a club I'd only read about in magazines or heard others speak about.

My body exploded around him, shattering into a million pieces. His went still. He tensed inside me, only for him to put me back together again when he pulled out, the two of us breathing heavily.

Holy shit.

I closed my eyes. The thrill of the ride far surpassed anything I had conjured up in my mind.

He helped dress me, hiking my pants up, my limbs too weak and heavy to assist.

We didn't speak. Instead we got ourselves presentable and washed up in the small sink to prepare for our grand exit.

My nerves kicked in again. Who knew if a line had formed down the aisle, people arguing, cursing us because they only had one vacant bathroom to use, that being the one on the right?

"I'm going to exit first. If things seem suspicious, I'll come back inside, complaining of stomach pain. I'll hold my stomach too. That'll prevent people from questioning me. If all is good, I'll head up front to my seat. In about a minute or two, you do the same."

People were going to wonder why the door remained locked after he exited. The man had basically thrown me under the bus in this operation because passengers would look at me as the guilty party when I made my getaway.

"Nobody gives a shit. If anything, you'll get high fives."

What? I stared at him in awe. He was serious too, *and* he had read my mind.

"You're not funny."

"And you're hot. Welcome to the club, babe. I'll see you shortly." He kissed my lips and unlocked the door.

Oh my God. I fidgeted in place, praying desperately this part of the plan worked.

When he
opened the door. Panic set in.

He faced me prior to leaving, his demeanor calm, as opposed to mine. "Embrace the danger. It makes life more fun." He blew me a kiss, winked, and left.

Embrace the danger? I wasn't sure about that.

One thing I was sure of—the uneasy sensation in my gut telling me a lot of it would be coming in the near future.

25

LOGAN

Prancing back to first class, I got a few stares. Not that I gave a shit what anyone thought about me or my actions. My worry lay in thinking about whether Drew could handle it.

The rest of the flight went by in a flash. It felt great to be on home turf again. I waited for Drew to exit the plane and escorted her to baggage claim to retrieve her suitcase. Kate and her runaway groom greeted her with hugs. If I could have my way, Drew would spend the night at my place. But I understood her eagerness to go home and sort things out with her sister and parents over the entire wedding and honeymoon shenanigans that had taken place.

Before we parted, I made sure she had all my contact info, a somewhat awkward experience. As much as I wanted to cuddle her in my arms and kiss her good-bye for the world to see, I couldn't. I had to keep things on the down low, at least for now, a challenging concept for me to face and accept.

Once I got home, familiarity settled in. I rarely had the opportunity to spend long periods of time in my small house, a place I loved to chill out and relax in. I had bought it a year or so ago. Not the most extravagant of places but definitely a step up from homes I had resided in prior to fame settling in, if one could call some of the shit-holes I had slept in that. I didn't feel or see the point in playing show-and-tell with my residence when I rarely stayed in it, for good reason too. It meant the band did well, and we were in high demand.

After taking a hot shower, I sorted through my mail, discarding the junk from the bills. My neighbor had been kind enough to get it for me, something he did on a regular basis. Most of my bills were set up on autopay, so I didn't have too much to deal with. He also had a key to turn on lights, flush toilets, and such when I traveled for extended periods.

It was nice to have someone I trusted with my personal shit, since I had no family close by to help. It also didn't hurt that the guy was a judge, his partner a happy homemaker. Every now and then I'd come home to discover new flowers planted in front of my house. His partner loved to garden.

It also didn't hurt that I paid them a nice chunk of change to take care of my shit for me. I considered it to be one of my better investments, because in my business, finding trustworthy people who didn't want to suck you dry or steal from you didn't come easy.

Two envelopes stuffed in the pile caught my eye. They were thick, larger-than-average envelopes, similar to those that held birthday cards. My lip did its best Elvis impersonation, slightly lifting at the corner. My birthday had passed months ago. Who in the hell had sent me cards?

I opened the first one.

Dear Logan,

I miss you. I used to love hearing you guys practice back in the day and play local gigs, but now you travel so much, it's hard to keep up with you. Social media has been my saving grace, but it's not enough anymore. I like knowing what you're up to. It's probably no good, you bad boy. I wouldn't mind being bad along with you. And now that you're on break for a few weeks, it might be the perfect opportunity for me to do so. I'll be in touch.

. . .

What the fuck?

I tossed the note aside and opened the second envelope.

Dear Logan,

I didn't know you were traveling with a companion. Usually shots of you posted online with women are singles, meaning there's one pic of you and your bimbo for the night, but there are multiples of you and your new friend together. It bothers me you'd betray me this way. Here I was looking forward to your return home and come to find you have a girlfriend. I'm not sure what to do with my feelings. I'm both baffled and hurt. I'm beyond surprised you'd slap this in my face without even considering how your behavior would affect me.

I squeezed the card tighter, grabbing hold of the envelope to check for an address and postage. Nothing on either one. How did she know where I lived? And how would she have been able to reference me and Drew when the news of our relationship only broke recently?

With deep focus I reread the first letter, noting how the person stated knowing me back in the day. It'd be impossible for me to figure out who the hell the note had come from. I might as well pick a name out of a hat because that was how many women there had been over the years. I had no fucking clue whatsoever. For all I knew, if could've been a dude. But I seriously doubted it.

Camilla needed an update on this situation. I snagged my phone from the counter and called her. I wondered whether this was the same fan she'd been receiving e-mails from, the one she'd warned me about after our last show. The e-mail I had blown off as nothing to worry about.

She asked me to send her pictures, so she could see the letters for herself. I used the camera function on my phone and snapped a few shots, sending them to her via text.

"I can't say for sure if it's the same girl, but the wording is awfully similar to the other e-mails we received. My gut tells me we're dealing with a love-obsessed stalker."

Pacing back and forth in my living room, I rubbed my fingers over my brow, my worry growing frantically by the minute. Camilla spoke in a foreign language. I had no idea what she talked about.

"Please explain that in plain English."

"It's a psychological disorder where one person becomes fixated on another person and believes their feelings are reciprocal. The people might be complete strangers and know nothing about each other personally. In other words, in this person's mind, she thinks you're in love with her, and, by the tone in those letters you received, feels you're cheating on her with the woman in your pictures. Something else we need to discuss in more detail."

Fuck! I didn't want Drew dragged into this mess.

"Please tell me how the hell we stop this nutcase."

"Well, since she hasn't made any type of direct threat, there's not much we can do right now."

"She hand-delivered letters to my house, which means she knows where I live. Neither envelope had postage. I don't like this, Camilla."

Anger at the situation consumed me as did a bit of fear. The guys and I had received many fan letters over the months, women telling us how much they loved us, some claiming to want to bear our children, and such, but we regarded them as nothing, feeling untouchable. This shit came too close to home for my comfort level.

"I understand your concern. But there's nothing we can do. This woman hasn't posed any type of a threat to you. Usually, there has to be some type of criminal intent on the part of the stalker to create fear. She's done nothing so far to indicate any of that."

"Key words being *so far*."

"I thought you had an alarm and security cameras around your place."

Fuck, yes! Why hadn't I thought about that?

"I do. I totally forgot about the cameras."

"Why don't you review some of the footage recorded over the last week and see if you spot anything unusual? And don't your next-door neighbors take care of your property for you? Maybe you can ask them if they noticed any odd or suspicious activity around your place."

"I'm going to take you up on both of those suggestions. My neighbors know how to get in touch with me at all times, even at the ranch, in case of
emergency. So I'm sure if they saw anything out of the ordinary, they would've contacted me. But still, I'm going to speak with them."

"Now, about the girl in the pictures, care to elaborate? You only gave me a brief rundown when I spoke with you earlier. I want to know what kind of damage control I'm dealing with."

Camilla had a knack for making me feel like the runt of the litter, the odd guy out who always caused trouble when it came to the band.

"I already told you. She's an old friend."

"Don't forget who you're talking to. I'm on your side, remember?"

It was instinctive by this point to get defensive with her since she blamed me for everything under the sun. But for once, I hadn't done anything wrong.

"She's my ex. She happened to be at the ranch."

"Coincidence?"

"Yes, sheer coincidence. Both of us were beyond surprised, to say the least."

"So what's the status of this relationship with your ex now?"

"I honestly don't know how to answer your question. Things were great between us at the ranch, but now that we're back home, in the real world, my crazy-as-fuck world, who knows?"

"Very well. Do me a favor and try to keep a low profile. We're not sure whether the woman sending you the notes is stalking you, watching you from afar, you know? I would consider taking on extra security. I'll see if Tomas knows of anyone who might be interested in a side job."

This sucked. Being followed around by a bodyguard was the last thing I wanted to deal with. I wasn't ready to take that drastic of a measure yet.

"For now I want to check out the footage and speak with my neighbors before I agree to put a guard on my tail 24/7."

"Don't take this lightly. This type of a situation could turn ugly fast."

"I'm not taking it lightly. That's why I called you. I'm freaking the fuck out."

"And with all good reason. Let me know if you find anything interesting on the video footage or if your neighbors have any information that might help us figure out who this woman is. It's important for us keep abreast of this situation and journal the happenings, so if and when the police have to get involved, we can present them with evidence to support our case."

"Will do."

I disconnected the call and set my phone down. I went into my office and brought my computer to life, wanting to check out the surveillance footage. Joey had requested that both me and Trevor step up security measures at our respective places several months back to prevent situations like the one I currently found myself in from occurring. It seemed the more popular we became, the more hard-core our fans became as a result.

Since the second letter had to be delivered within the last twenty-four hours, I began watching recordings within that timeframe.

On a positive note, I didn't see anything out of the ordinary around the immediate borders of my property.

My next step was to search my name online to see what new and disturbing press and pictures had popped up while I'd escaped to the mountains. The band had a social-media team who managed our posts, since it had become a round-the-clock job that required constant monitoring. Fans loved to post all kinds of crazy-ass shit, some of which our team tried to remove whenever possible.

Other than the few pictures I had already seen posted of me and Drew on my phone at the airport, I didn't see anything new.

While at my desk, I also took care of other business and dropped

Drew a text. How bizarre that I missed her so badly when we'd only been apart for several hours.

Logan: *How does it feel to be home?*

Drew: *It felt better at the ranch. My parents are still pissed at me for taking off with Kate.*

Logan: *I'm sure they'll get over it. Besides, Kate ended up getting married anyway, so everything worked out for the best, especially the part about us finding each other again.*

Drew: *Aww, how sweet.*

Logan: *But so true.*

Drew: *Yes, I'll agree with you on that one. As far as my parents go, you and I see the logic, but they aren't the most rationale people, so they only see the negative in the situation. Whatever. I'm too old to have to deal with this shit. I'm an adult and they still treat me like a child.*

Logan: *A mighty sexy one too if I do say so myself.*

Drew: *Sexy adult or child?*

Her witty sarcasm made me smile. I typed my reply.

. . .

Logan: *Oh, there's not a hint of adolescence on that flawless body of yours, baby. You're all woman.*

Drew: *Now you've gone and made me blush. FYI, my body is not flawless. I think you're referring to yours.*

Now I think I blushed, a difficult feat for her to triumph. Warmth spread across my cheeks.

Logan: *How about flawless when we're together?*

Drew: *Such a charmer, Mr. Trimble.*

Logan: *I only speak the truth, especially to you. Do you feel like getting out?*

I did. I had just gotten home from vacation and felt I could already use another one.

Drew: *I'd love to. What do you have in mind?*

Logan: *Thoughts not appropriate for a text.*

Drew: *You're quite funny too. Seriously, though, what do you have in mind?*

. . .

Logan: *I was being serious.*

Drew: *Do you think of nothing else?*

Logan: *Not where you're concerned. Fine, how about dinner? Are you hungry?*

Drew: *I could eat.*

So could I, my cock and mouth in agreement with her statement, neither with thoughts about food.

Logan: *Shall I pick you up in an hour?*

Drew: *How about I meet you?*
    Logan: *Don't tell me, you happened to leave out the part about meeting up with me at the ranch when you told your folks about your stay there.*
    Drew: *Trust me, I got an earful from them without doing so. I didn't want to hear any more negativity. I can't believe Kate never mentioned our meetup to them either. Hmm, there must be some goodness in her . I'm sorry. I hope you're not angry.*
    Logan: *First of all, there's no need for apologies. Second, I'm not angry with you. It's quite the opposite. But I'll go on a hunch and say I'm still on their shit list.*
    Drew: *You could say that.*
    Logan: *I guess I'll have to change their minds.*
    Drew: *Good luck with that. Where do you want to meet?*
    Logan: *Come to my place. We'll head out from here.*
    Drew: *Am I to believe you?*
    Logan: *Believe what you will.*

Drew: *I'm shaking my head at you right now. Send me the address.*
Logan: *Already did.*

I couldn't wait to see her, the few hours we'd been apart too long for my satisfaction.

Fuck, this woman already had me by the balls. Again.

26

DREW

Now I would have to deal with the *Twenty Questions* game of my plans, who with, etc. It's ridiculous that in my twenties I still had to tell my parents about my whereabouts. I so had to move out of their place.

They didn't give me a welcome reception when I got home from the airport, not that I expected them too. Surprisingly, Kate had taken the blame and told them she'd been the one who came up with idea of me going with her to the ranch. Usually they faulted her for everything. I think my parents still felt bad Joe had left her stranded at the altar in front of all their family and friends, so they took their anger out on me instead.

After putting my last load of laundry in the dryer, I got dressed. My mom happened to walk by my room as I spritzed on perfume.

"Where are you headed off to?"

"Dinner with a friend."

"Eric?"

Such a moral dilemma faced me. I hated to lie. I cringed inside because I so didn't want to, but I couldn't tell her the truth about Logan because I myself didn't know the status of our relationship.

"Just catching up."

That didn't answer the question one way or another and she looked pacified. A win-win for all.

"Did you at least have fun on the trip?"

Surprise, surprise, she actually cared enough to ask. All our conversations prior to this one had been me on the receiving end of her rants.

"Yeah, I had a blast. But I have to go or else I'll be late for dinner. I'll see you later."

I brushed past her and left the house. My heart pounded in my car. I didn't take comfort in keeping secrets, especially when there were pictures floating online of me and Logan. Not that my mom was an Internet junkie, but still, news traveled fast in this town and would get back to her. I could almost bet someone would bring it up at the pet clinic the following morning too.

Logan's directions were superb. I located his neighborhood with ease. He had definitely moved up in the world, the neighborhood he lived in luxurious and well-maintained. I wouldn't say the houses were mansions, but they weren't small cookie-cutter homes either. They were stately with freshly manicured lawns.

The closer I got to his house number, the slower I drove. I didn't want to pass it. I parked in the empty driveway in front of his three-car garage.

My heart pounded harder and now my palms sweated. I didn't understand my nerves. I had spent an entire week with the man at the ranch. I guess it was because we were now back on familiar territory.

Old memories flooded me, most of them good. Rewind, *all* of them good except for the one when I caught him cheating on me. I forced myself to push that thought aside, praying I wouldn't have to live through a repeat of that disaster. Once had been enough.

Beautiful flowers trailed the path to the front door.

My finger slightly trembled when I rang the doorbell.

"I'll be right there!"

My breath picked up speed, waiting for him to greet me.

The lock clicked, and he opened the door. He beamed upon seeing me. I was sure I beamed as well.

"Come in."

He stepped aside so I could enter.

The smell of something mouth-watering filled the air, and I wasn't referring to Logan, who had been born with the privilege of smelling divine.

The living- and dining-room areas were scarce of furniture.

"Did you just move in?" I followed him into the kitchen and den area. At least those rooms were furnished. He had a huge television mounted on the wall with soft plush leather couches in front of it. The kitchen consisted of dark wood cabinets with light granite countertops.

Wait a minute, he had the table set for dinner with the napkins folded just so. He'd told me we were going out to eat, not dining in. The fact he had cooked dinner for the two of us touched me.

"No. I've been here about a year, but I'm not home to entertain much, so decorating hasn't been a priority."

My anxiety increased. In a sense, as odd as it sounded when I'd known the man for years in every way possible, I felt as if we were about to have another first date.

"It's a beautiful home."

"Thanks. Can I offer you a drink?"

I shook my head. Even though my mouth felt dry like the desert, I didn't want anything. Instead I pulled a mint out of my purse and popped it in my mouth.

"I thought we would eat in. It's been a long day, and I'd rather hang tight and chill out, if you don't mind?"

"No, not at all. It smells delicious, whatever it is."

"I had nothing in the house to eat, so I went food shopping. I make a mean Chicken Parm. It's about the only thing I know how to cook other than eggs and toast."

"You seriously cooked us dinner?" I still couldn't believe his considerate gesture.

"Yeah. Why?"

"I didn't mean to put you through so much trouble. We could've ordered in."

He came closer and embraced me. "It was no trouble whatsoever. I wanted to act selfishly and not share you tonight. I knew if we went out, I'd have to."

"You always were a charmer, Logan."

"Are my charms working on you."

"You know they are."

He flashed me a crooked smile before his lips crashed down on mine. His tongue slipped inside my mouth, engaging mine in a merry-go-round of sorts, our tongues rolling over each other in a gentle manner.

The warmth in my cheeks spread throughout the rest of my body. I clenched my pelvic muscles, Gosh, could Logan kiss. And he did it with such passion, almost as though he wore his heart on his sleeve when his lips touched mine.

It made me wonder whether he exposed the same vulnerability to other women he'd kissed. A yucky thought if I ever had one.

He picked me up and set me on the kitchen island.

He stepped between my legs and ran his hands through my hair. I did the same to his. He lifted my shirt, breaking our kiss for long enough to get it over my head.

Heat flickered in his eyes as he gazed at my lacy push-up. I had put some forethought into the one I had chosen to wear.

"I like."

He leaned forward and kissed each breast on the outside of the bra.

I wouldn't feed his ego and tell him I'd worn it especially for him.

He trailed kisses up my neck, ending on my lips.

"What do you say we have appetizers upstairs in my bedroom?"

Too hot and bothered to reply, I simply nodded.

He hoisted me off the counter and carried me to the stairs, where he set me down on the first one. He stepped around me, took hold of my hand, and led me upstairs.

There were four doors on the second floor. I assumed three were bedrooms, the fourth a bathroom. I'd find out sooner or later.

We went to the room in the corner, the master, a big-ass one to say the least. He had a king-size bed and a second huge TV mounted on the wall in front of it. His furniture was crafted from simple wood, nothing elaborate. Logan, Mr. Casual, didn't give a shit what people thought about him. He had always been confident in being true to himself.

He couldn't get his hands on me fast enough. One would think we hadn't seen each other in forever. He unbuttoned my jeans. I jacked his T-shirt up and over his head. We couldn't undress the other fast enough, as if a timer would go off, telling us to stop.

Once we were both naked, he picked me up again. I straddled my legs around his waist. He kissed me, our tongues swirling in a mad race to the finish line. The softness from earlier in the kitchen became replaced with lust.

He dropped me on the bed, his body lowering with mine, the two of us falling onto the mattress. He kicked my feet apart and rubbed his hardness against me.

The sensation made me delirious. I felt sex deprived, despite Logan having satisfied me to the hilt this past week, including earlier on the plane.

"I want you so badly right now."

His kisses alone had all but done the foreplay trick.

"What are you waiting for? Take me."

Those magic words.

He reached for my leg and wrapped it around his waist. He did the same with the other leg. His fingers got busy between my folds.

"So wet, baby."

"Only for you."

Guess I fed his ego after all because the hunger in his eyes quadrupled after hearing my comment.

He aligned himself with my opening, inching himself in slowly. My eyes closed, the fullness engulfing my entire being.

"Aah." My hips met his in an up-and-down rhythm.

"You feel so fucking good inside."

His whisper lit me up even more.

I wanted to kiss him, yearning for that connection with him as well, so I did.

Our mouths and bodies became entwined, our breaths became panted. He penetrated my core, deep. He throbbed inside me, thickened. His body tensed over mine, and he stilled.

I balled my hands into fists on his back, crying out, my orgasm ripping through me, the two of us coming together. He remained locked in place, the pulsing of his cock taking me higher.

Fuck.

That was basically what we had just done, fast and furiously. But now he acted tender and sweet, planting delicate kisses on my neck.

"You're incredible." He swiped hair off my sweaty face.

Years of pent-up feelings and emotions came to the surface at once. I didn't want them to come out yet. I swallowed hard in a last-ditch effort to bury them. My heart demanded protection, because as desperately as I wanted this to happen between me and Logan, I still had an array of doubts and fears to go along with it.

27

LOGAN

Of all times for the oven timer to go off. I didn't want to get up because I still had Drew in my arms. But I didn't want the chicken to burn.

I gave her a peck on the lips and took the stairs in pairs to the first floor. She followed suit a few minutes later wearing too much clothing. She'd put her jeans and shirt back on.

"If you want, I can take care of this while you clean up."

"Why clean up when I plan on getting dirty again?" I raised my brows flirtatiously. Still, I agreed and gave her the silicone oven mitts. "The salad is good to go. It's in a white bowl in the fridge, and the pasta's in the strainer in the sink. Her eyes opened wide. "What?"

"I can't believe you went to all this trouble." She rubbed her hands on her jeans.

"I told you, it's no trouble at all unless it tastes like shit. If it does, we'll have to order in."

She laughed, seizing the mitts from me. I went upstairs to the bathroom to wash up and get dressed.

When I returned she had everything on the table, ready to eat.

"This looks fantastic. Thank you again."

Nodding in acknowledgment, I assisted her into her seat. I took my own next to her. I couldn't remember the last time I had cooked for a woman other than Dani, who didn't count because I considered her a sister. Now and then the guys and I would prep meals before rehearsals. The thought brought a suggestion to mind.

"After dinner, how about I show you my ministudio and we lay your song down on a track?"

"Two things." She held up two fingers. "First, you have a recording studio here? And second, I told you I prefer to play for and by myself, not in front of others."

"I don't consider myself to be in the others category because you've already played the song for me. I want you to hear how good it sounds professionally recorded. I think it's a really great song. And yes, I have a recording studio here, albeit a small one."

"I appreciate your enthusiasm and compliment, but I'm not sure about taking you up on your offer."

"Come on, it'll be fun. I have a few guitars. You can pick whichever one you want. I'll even play along with you."

"And steal my thunder from my awesome guitar-playing abilities?"

"On second thought, maybe I'll let you play. I'm used to the spotlight being on me. I would hate for you to upstage me."

She smiled and sampled her chicken. "Oh my God, this chicken is to die for."

"I'm glad you approve. For the most part, me preparing food is hit or miss."

I ate some as well. I had to agree with her. I did have the Chicken Parm thing down to a science.

"I love it. You'll have to give me the recipe."

"I could, but then I'd have to kill you."

She laughed then ate some more. I could tell she enjoyed her dinner because when she brought her dish to the sink, it was empty.

We cleaned the kitchen together, working proficiently as a team.

I gave her the grand tour of the house, ending with the garage, which I had converted into a soundproof studio.

"Wow, this is so cool." She surveyed the room, her eyes lighting up. "Do you guys practice here?"

"We do." Which explained my reason for having a drum kit and keyboard in the studio as well.

"I'm so happy for you guys. Who would've thought playing in Trevor's garage would have turned into something so huge." She gestured to the room.

"I'm thankful each and every day. So, are you ready to make some music?"

She shrugged, twisting her fingers.

"Don't be nervous. You're going to love this. It's going to be awesome."

My adrenaline kicked into full gear. I brought the room to life: flicking on the computer, the mixer, and lowering the mic stand adjusted for Joey's height. I loved my ministudio. Trevor, Joey, and I recorded our songs in professional studios, but I had to say, I'd invested a shitload of cash into mine and could get equally impressive results for simple jobs like laying down a few tracks for Drew's song, which wouldn't require a ton of postproduction.

I tested the sound, making sure it came through the speakers clearly. I grabbed two guitars, one for each of us, and placed one in her hands. She strummed a few chords. I handed her the other one, so she could decide which one she preferred. She chose guitar number one.

"I can't believe we're about to do this. I'm so excited to hear what the end result will be."

Me too.

"It's going to sound great because the song is great."

She took a deep breath and stepped in front of the microphone.

"We're going to lay the music track down first. If you want, you can run through it a couple of times to get comfortable. After we record, and you're satisfied with the sound, we'll lay down the vocals."

She breathed deeply again and shook her hand out, stretching her fingers. "I feel so nervous."

"I get it. Remember, this is for you. It's not going to be distributed worldwide, *yet*." I winked.

"You're quite the comedian this evening."

"Hey, you never know."

"I do know, because no one will ever hear it."

Not if I have anything to say about it.

I dared not vocalize my thought.

She rehearsed the song, each run through sounding stronger, with more passion and feeling to it. These practice rounds were a great way to release pre-performance jitters.

Once I had everything set and ready to go on my end, I gave her a heads-up. She confirmed we could begin. We ran through the song three or four times, until the two of us were satisfied. She did well. I would enhance the sound later, but I had to get her vocals down first.

She stood still while I placed headphones over her ears. I planted a kiss on her lips.

"You'll be fine. There's no rush or limit, no studio charges. We can record until you're pleased with the outcome. So kick back, relax, and most of all, have fun."

She nodded but didn't seem pacified. I found it adorable how anxious she became about doing this. For me, performing was second nature. I never felt stage fright but that didn't mean I wouldn't support Drew and try to put her mind at ease.

After adjusting the sound in her headphones, I told her to go with it and sing her heart out.

The first go-round she missed her cue.

"I'm sorry." She withdrew.

No big deal. I made that point clear to her.

The second go-round she made it through the first three lines then panicked. I let her know I had all night to kill if that's how long it took her to chill out and sing the song.

The third go-round she made it through half the song. We were making steady progress. I recorded everything she did because we could pick and choose the best parts and mix them together.

To help ease her tension, I suggested she close her eyes and *feel* the music. I also dimmed the lights.

It worked. About the fifth or sixth take, she loosened up and became more relaxed with the process. Still, I had her sing the song again, so we had several variations to choose from.

The final run-through was by far her best vocals. She had lost her inhibitions. With her hand on her heart and tears sliding down her cheeks, she sang. The words flowed with perfect pitch and cadence.

> *An internal walk*
> *That led nowhere good*
> *Eyes wide open*
> *From where I stood*

> *Is it something I did*
> *Is it something I said*
> *A heart full of love*
> *Now forever broken instead*

This part hit hard because I'd never intended to hurt her and didn't want her blaming herself for my stupidity. It destroyed me that she'd felt her heart had been forever broken because of me too. I had no choice but to mend it and put the pieces back together. I just had to convince her to give me the opportunity to do so.

> *Shadows of you*
> *Are all that remain*
> *If only the real you*

Could take away all my pain

The real me currently sat at my mixing station, kicking myself in the ass for betraying Drew. She deserved the world.

Did you mean what you said
Did you say what you meant
Why bother to ask
I came, I saw, I went

Even though I'd already heard the song multiple times, it didn't get easier hearing the lyrics. The memory of Drew walking in and finding me with that slut still caused excruciating pain in my heart. I had learned over the years not to give a shit when it came to women. Fuck 'em, move on. But not Drew. She had been the only exception to my rule.

Find your truth
I now know mine
We were too young for a love like ours
To stand the test of time

I shook my head in disagreement, but I couldn't look at her because I didn't want her to see the emotions seizing control of me or how my eyes had started to water.

Moving on

Risk Worth Taking

The hardest thing so far to do
Moving forward
My hope is that you did too

My hope encompassed the idea that we could move forward together like we should have done all those years ago.

Shadows of you
Are all that remain
If only the real you
Could erase all my pain

Shadows of you
Are all around me
I'm still trapped in your heart
Please set me free

Buried, I can't seem to find my way out
Buried, from a cheatin' heart no doubt
I'm still buried, buried, still buried

Another knife stabbed in my heart.

Shadows of you
Are all that remain
If only the real you

Could erase all my pain

Talk about feeling stripped to the core. I'd fucking erase all her pain if it was the last thing I did.

The song ended. I spun my chair around to find her wiping her eyes. I gestured for her to come to me. She removed the headphones and set them on the mic stand. She walked toward me, her hands clasped together. I patted my lap for her to sit on.

"That was fantastic." I complimented her, not getting into anything heavy.

"Do you really think so?"

"I'll let you hear for yourself. Now comes the fun part. Ready to mix it?" She nodded excitedly. "Excellent. Let's do it."

We worked on the recording for several hours. She couldn't stop yawning.

She checked her phone. "Oh shit. It's so late. I have to be at work in a few hours."

"Why don't we go upstairs and crash?"

"I can't." She frowned. "I don't have any clothes with me. I have to go home. Besides, my parents will freak if I'm not in my bed when they wake up in the morning."

This parental overinvolvement in Drew's private life required an intervention ASAP.

"I love how the song came out. I can't thank you enough for letting me record it. I had a ball. You made it sound amazing."

"No. You made it sound amazing. I just tweaked it."

"For hours. But still, thank you."

"Anytime."

28

DREW

*B*est night ever. I couldn't stop thinking about how much fun we'd had in his studio during my drive home. He had the patience of a saint too. I'd kept screwing up, and he never once got frustrated or annoyed with my inexperience with recording. And the best part—he made it all about me. Such a selfless man.

Entering my house, I remained mindful not to wake anyone. Tomorrow I would be functioning on about three hours sleep, but I didn't care. Logan had totally made it worth my while.

When my alarm sounded, I kept hitting the sleep button until my mother came in and ordered me out of bed, telling me I'd be late if I didn't hurry my butt on up.

"What time did you get home last night?"

"I'm not sure." I didn't give specifics.

"I thought you were just going to dinner?"

"I was. What's the problem?" I hadn't intended to come off in such as crass manner.

"What's going on, Drew?"

"Nothing. I have to get ready for work, so if you'll please excuse me, I'm going to go take a shower." I brushed past her and locked myself in the bathroom. I hated to sound so bitchy, but I didn't want to be questioned. I guess a part of me felt protective over Logan, like I had to defend him because I knew she wouldn't take the news about the two of us seeing each other again well.

My parents weren't exactly part of the Logan Trimble fan club, especially after he broke my heart. My mother used to preach how I could do better than a musician. Huh, what a hypocrite. The woman majored in musical theater but gave up her passion when my father got into vet school. One would think she would have respected Logan's aspirations to turn his passion into a career, a successful one too. But nope. She only saw the negative in him. Her problem now, not mine.

As soon as I got dressed I left for work. My mother typically showed up midmorning, so I had a few hours reprieve from having to deal with her again.

Eric sent me a text, saying he had seen the pictures online and wanted to meet up later, so I could fill him in on the situation. I agreed to meet him for dinner, unsure of what his response would be when I gave him details. He didn't think highly of Logan, which I understood. But Logan had changed. I hoped I could convince Eric to keep an open mind about the possibility.

Mia, our vet tech, escorted a new patient to the front desk. The woman cuddled her Teacup Yorkie in her arms. Mia handed me the woman's billing sheet. She reiterated the suggestions my father had given the patient regarding her dog, then left. I scanned the sheet, remembering the woman had brought her Yorkie in for an emergency visit, something about odd-eating behavior on her pet's part.

"Was Dr. Sanders able to help you with Logi's eating issue?" I asked.

"Yes. He thinks my little man here is picking up on my nervous energy at home." She nuzzled and kissed him.

This woman had some issues going on. I too felt her nervous energy, so I understood Logi's problem.

"I hope Dr. Sanders' recommendations work with Logi."

"Yeah. Hey, you look familiar to me. Have we met before?"

She brushed off my comment about her dog, now more interested in me for some strange reason. I had never seen this woman in my life.

"I don't think so."

"Hmm... I know you from somewhere, but I'm having trouble placing where."

"It is a small town."

"No, not from here. Wait a second, I know where I've seen you. You're the girl in the pictures getting hot and heavy with Logan Trimble from Steam, aren't you?"

Oh no.

"I'm a big fan of the band. This is so cool." She bounced from foot to foot, her grin wide, teeth and all.

Of course my mother had to pick that moment to approach the front desk. She stopped dead in her tracks, her body language speaking a thousand words, none of them nice. Mia's ears perked up in the hallway. She rushed back to the counter to hear my answer. So much for keeping it quiet for as long as I could.

"Please tell me about him." Logi shook in his owner's arms, her animated movements jerking the little guy around.

"I'm not comfortable discussing my private life. But I'll make sure to let him know I met a fan."

"The *biggest* and *best* fan ever. I see him in concert whenever he's in town or nearby."

My mother placed her hands on her hips, scowling at me.

Yeah, yeah, bring it on.

I had all but hit my boiling point with her.

Mia couldn't contain her excitement but remained silent until I finished with the patient.

"Dr. Sanders wants you to schedule a follow-up appointment to make sure Logi doesn't lose any weight. I can go ahead and make that appointment for you now." I got back to business.

She reviewed the calendar on her phone and scheduled one.

"You're pretty. I can see why he chose you."

She stared at me. Something about her didn't seem right. She gave me the creeps, sending shivers through me. But still, she was a patient, so I had to treat her with respect. I gave her a polite thank-you.

As soon as she exited the clinic my mother all but attacked me. How mortifying to be reprimanded at my place of work, about my private life nonetheless.

"Is that where you were last night?"

"Can we please discuss this later, Mom?" I prayed to God she'd give me an affirmative reply.

Mia stood nearby, trying to hide her enthusiasm about me and Logan.

"Oh, we'll definitely discuss this later. There's no question about that."

How dare she treat me like a child? Did she not think I could make healthy decisions for myself? I didn't need her permission on who I chose to date. Sure, I would love for my parents to be supportive, but did I *need* them to be? Hell, no.

My mother bolted for her office, a gust of disappointment lingering behind her in the form of me. I didn't give a shit.

"Tell me, tell me." Mia flashed me her phone to reveal one of the pictures of me and Logan making out at the ranch.

Oh my God. I so didn't want to do this. What happened to private moments being private? I guess in Logan's world they didn't exist.

"I'm not sure if you know this, but Logan and I were in a steady relationship back in high school."

Her jaw fell open. "Are you for real? You never told me that. I'm so jealous."

My past relationship with Logan, how it ended or why, wasn't something I advertised.

"So are you guys like, back together?"

"I'm not sure what we are, Mia, so I'd rather not discuss it."

She sighed dreamily. "I love Steam. Joey Fine? OMG. I love the man."

"I'll be sure to let him know he has another fan." I shifted my focus to the patient billing sheets in front of me, not wanting a back and forth with her about the band.

"Say what? You've met Joey Fine?"

Ugh! Why wouldn't she let me get back to work?

"Yes. Logan and I dated for several years. He and the guys have played together since they were teenagers."

"Do you think you can get me a meet and greet? I don't think you realize how much I love them." She placed her hand over her heart.

"I'll see what I can do. But no promises, okay?"

She bounced up and down like a teenage fan, then skipped down the hall to assist my father with his next patient.

Jeez.

The rest of the day flew by. The hectic schedule helped because it meant I didn't have to speak with my mother. I had an excuse whenever she tried to approach me. *"Sorry, I'm busy."*

I'd just finished checking out a patient when my phone signaled an incoming text.

Logan: *Hey gorgeous. What time do you finish work?*

. . .

Drew: *Five.*

Logan: *Can I take you to dinner?*

Drew: *I would love for you too but I'm meeting up with my friend Eric. You probably remember him, Eric Fields, from high school? He used to hang out with us sometimes. We became the best of friends after you and I broke up. He's a great guy.*

Logan: *Rub it in why don't you. Should I be jealous? Has he changed his ways?*

Drew: *I think you should. He woke up one morning and decided not to be gay anymore. And he thinks I'm super hot. You have some stiff competition, buddy.*

My joke made me smile.

Logan: *I'm stiff alright.*

That wasn't the joke I found comical but Logan took the opening to toss in a sexual innuendo. Hence, my grin widened.

Drew: *Funny too.*

. . .

Logan: *But I speak the truth. You have that effect on me.*

He said the kindest things.

Drew: *Do you want to join us?*

Logan: *I'm sure I'm the last person on earth Eric would want to have dinner with.*

Yup, his words rang true.
    Drew: *I bet you could win him over.*

Logan: *In which way are you referring?*

Invariably a tease. I loved that about him.

Drew: *Are you trying to make me jealous?*

I could tease as well as the next gal.

Logan: *Is it working?*

Warmth spread across my cheeks. I felt so off-balance whenever I thought
    about or spoke to Logan.

. . .

Drew: *Sorry to say, in this case it's not.*

Logan: *Bummer. Why don't you give me a call after dinner?*

Drew: *Don't tell me you're afraid of Eric? Although he has bulked up a bit since you last saw him.*

Logan: *I'm not afraid of anything, baby.*

Drew: *My hero.*

Logan: *Damn right.*

Drew: *Fine. I'll give you a call later.*

Logan: *Very well. Hey, I listened to your song again. It's really good.*

Drew: *Thanks. I mean it. You've been so encouraging and supportive about it.*

Logan: *You have talent. Don't let it go to waste. You should let me give it to someone. I think it has potential.*

My heart fell into the pit of my stomach. He thought it had potential, good enough for someone in the music business to hear? Wow. I broke out in a sweat and tapped my foot nervously on the floor. I'd never expected to hear him say that, the ultimate compliment.

Drew: *I'm not sure about that. You know how I feel about performing in front of people.*

Logan: *You wouldn't have to perform it in front of anyone. The song speaks for itself. Someone else could record the vocals. Even though your voice kicks ass.*

Drew: *I appreciate the accolades. To be honest, I've never given this any thought. As I've told you, I've solely played and written for myself.*

Logan: *Well, maybe it's time to think outside the box. You have a gift. Share it with others.*

Drew: *I'll think about it.*

Logan: *Do that. I'll speak to you later.*

Writing had always been my escape, my outlet, a mechanism to purge my feelings by putting into words what I found difficult to say out loud. *I* discovered writing about them could be both cathartic and healing. And if anyone had the connections to get my songs into the right hands, Logan did. But sharing my innermost thoughts with others? I wasn't sure how I felt about putting my life out there for others to scrutinize.

I'd have to give his suggestion serious consideration. But later. Another patient had entered the clinic and needed my attention.

29

LOGAN

*T*revor, Dani and I indulged in a late lunch together. Joey would be returning from his trip with Teva the following day. Things would pick up speed after he came back, and my free time would lessen.

Camilla requested a meeting with the band to discuss our schedule for the upcoming weekend in NYC as well as pertinent information about resuming our tour. She also wanted to discuss the video shoot, and our planned visit to the hospital, something that ripped me to shreds; nothing worse than seeing kids fighting for their lives. It truly brought things into perspective and made me grateful each and every day I had my health.

"So, are you and Drew back together?" Dani took a bite of her hamburger.

"We haven't really talked about what we are. All I know is I can't get enough of her. I want to see where things go."

Trevor flashed me a half-smile. "What are the odds of Drew showing up at the same ranch as you, the same week?"

"Maybe it was fate." Dani sighed, clasping her hands together, forever a romantic.

"I don't know, but I can definitely say it feels like we've picked up where we left off."

Dani frowned. "If I recall correctly, you didn't leave off on such good terms."

"Minus that part. Trust me, I'm surprised she even gave me the time of day."

"Me too. You guys were inseparable. I have to say it took me a while to forgive you for the shit that went down and how you disrespected her."

Guilt consumed me, especially after hearing Trevor's words.

"I know. I fucked up. I'm trying to make things right."

"Good luck. Drew always was a nice girl. I'd love to see you settle down and stop with all the bimbos."

What nerve Trevor had for chuckling at Dani's comment. Prior to being in a relationship with her, he had engaged in more than his fair share. Sure, for the most part he'd kept his trysts hidden, but the guy was far from celibate. My how things had changed for him. For the better.

"Go ahead and laugh, asshole. Your past doesn't portray a pretty portrait either." I put him in his place to silence him.

He put his hand up in surrender, clearly not wanting to go down that path with Dani sitting next to him. She wrapped her arms around his neck and planted a kiss on his cheek.

"Only the part that includes me." She smiled warmly at him.

"Damn right. That's the only part that counts when it comes to women and my past."

She smiled wider at his response and rested her head on his shoulder. What a fucking pussy he had become.

"No comment." I looked him square in the eye. I would never throw him under the bus, especially when he tried to impress his girlfriend. "So you guys ready for New York?"

"I'm excited. Trevor and I are going to catch a Broadway show." Dani dug into her food again.

Things had certainly changed. Trevor, Joey, and I used to party hard whenever we had a break, but now two thirds of our group was tied down.

Thoughts about the video flashed through my mind. The director expected me to kiss and grope the hired model, since Trevor and Joey refused. When I originally agreed to do it, I had no issues with it. Engaging with models during video shoots usually ended up with me bringing them back to my hotel room. Therefore, I never had any complaints about doing so.

This time would be different. Remorse filled me, and I hadn't even filmed it yet. Because I knew once the video went viral and Drew saw it, she would see me as a cheating son of a bitch again, despite the fact I'd be innocent. I couldn't make a request now to change things up. The director had already been hired, scenes had been discussed and agreed upon, and preparations had been made.

After lunch I went home and visited my neighbors. They said they hadn't seen anything out of the ordinary at my place and checked in daily. So whoever this psycho stalker was, at least she didn't seem to be hanging around. I hadn't received any more letters. Sure, it had only been a day, but I took that as a good sign.

Drew texted me a few hours later to say she was free to meet up. She offered to come to my place again. It pissed me off that I couldn't pick her up and take her on a proper date.

The minute she entered my house I pulled her into my arms. She sported hip-hugging jeans with an off-the-shoulder top. My cock noticed immediately.

"You look beautiful as always."

I kissed her sweet lips.

"As do you."

"Is there any place in particular you want to go?" As pussy as it sounded, I didn't want her thinking sex was all I wanted from her. But I couldn't deny when I engaged in it with her, whew, an added bonus times ten.

"I actually do have something in mind."

"And what would that be?" Nothing like seeing a woman make a decision and assert herself.

"Do you remember when we used to park at the airport and watch the planes land and take off?"

I recalled all too well. I also remembered that we didn't do too much watching during those little trips.

"How could I forget?" I raised my brows in anticipation. My dick rose too. I loved how pink her cheeks became when she got embarrassed. "Let me grab my keys."

She nodded and followed me into the kitchen, where I shoved my phone into my pocket and retrieved my keys off the counter.

When I'd converted the garage into a studio, I hadn't converted the entire thing. I kept my car parked in the single portion.

"You're a big famous rock star, and you drive a Mustang?"

"What? I love my car." I assisted her into the passenger seat, then went around to my side.

"It's good to see fame hasn't changed you."

"I'm still me, Drew." I gazed into her eyes.

"I know."

The air suddenly thickened in the small space.

Time to get moving to thin it out. I backed out of the garage and drove to the airport. I kept her hand in mine during the entire drive. We didn't speak much. Rather, we listened to the radio.

Off the main road, I parked in front of the same old fence, the very one we'd parked in front of several years back. The scenery hadn't changed much at all.

"Gosh, it brings back so many memories, huh?" She reclined her seat, leaning back against it and staring out the front window, watching as a plane departed.

Squeezing her hand, we sized each other up. She tore me apart inside. My heart pounded, her eyes taking me in. I could swear she saw through me. She probably could.

"It does. We had some good times in this very parking spot, didn't we?"

She smiled. "It's still relaxing to sit here and watch the planes."

When I stopped to think about it, it was relaxing. My life seemed to be a constant whirlwind of events, which was why I valued my visits to the ranch so much. But sitting here right now with Drew made me realize I could have some of that detachment at home too. I didn't have to travel far from home in order to get it.

"I'm glad you suggested this."

She grinned. "Me too."

"So does Eric forgive me?"

"Eric just wants me to be happy."

"And are you?"

"Very. You? "

"Extremely."

I leaned over and kissed her, our tongues gliding around each other with ease. The console presented a barrier between us. She cupped my cheek. I snaked my hand behind her head.

Man, making out with a woman without going further didn't exist in my world anymore. Until now. Sure, my hand copped a feel underneath Drew's shirt. But in my defense, the thing hung off her shoulder and provided easy access, so how could I not? I flicked her hard nipple and rolled it between two fingers. She purred.

We worked each other up into quite a frenzy. She unbuttoned her jeans. So much for just making out. No complaints on my behalf whatsoever. I jumped on board and did the same to mine. I didn't know what she had in mind, but I didn't care, game for whatever she suggested.

She shimmied her denims down. Her underwear came along with them. Fuck. I could already smell her desire.

Enough sitting and watching. I lifted my ass off the leather seat and got rid of my shoes, jeans, and boxer briefs, chucking all of them in the backseat.

My chair could only recline so much. I'm talking tight quarters, but damn if she wasn't crawling over the console and sitting on my lap, facing me.

"Hi, there." She faced me, eyes wide, hunger in them.

"Hi, yourself. Getting mighty bold in your old age, aren't you?"

"It seems that way, doesn't it?"

She leaned up on her knees and fisted my cock.

Shit.

She pumped me good and plenty, seeing for herself I hadn't been lying earlier when I said she made me stiff.

To my surprise, she aligned her pussy over me and came down, my cock easing inside her with no friction whatsoever.

I reached for her hips, controlling the speed and tempo.

She kissed me fervently, our tongues again getting acquainted but now in a more aggressive manner.

She became more forceful in her movements as well, the feeling fucking nirvana, Drew as magnificent as the Sistine Chapel. She too had an entrance hall, which my cock currently buried itself in, her side walls just as splendid. And her ceiling? Fuck, my dick couldn't get there fast enough. And trust me, similar to Michelangelo's scene depicting *The Separation of Light From Darkness*, Drew had brought light back into my life that I forgot existed. I experienced my own kind of last judgment. I hoped she would consider me one of the blessed rather than one of the damned to be sent to hell to be tortured by demons. I longed for her forgiveness.

"Logan." She breathed warmly against my cheek.

I grazed the soft skin on her back, up to her neck. I brought her face to mine, yearning to kiss her again, to taste her.

She slowed the tempo.

We got a steady groove going, her flesh no longer slapping against my thighs as she rocked up and down on top of me.

I circled my hips. She followed my lead.

I didn't want to come before she did. The girl had an edge on riling me up prematurely.

She rested her hands on my shoulders for leverage, my dick content with its present location. Guess she wanted the mood a little less fucking and a lot more making love, but shit if her pussy clenching my cock didn't encourage me to pump into her harder. I had obviously hit her gold mine.

"Aah!" Her body gave itself over to her orgasm, shuddering over mine.

My dick required more action. I first allowed her to ride her wave out to its finish. But then I became selfish. I steadied my hands on her hips and picked up the pace again, bringing her down on me with more energy, my buildup coming on strong.

I released myself into her, locking her in place over me, the connection between us all about making love. Me too craving that type of connection to her right now.

Fuck, fuck, fuck. How will I make this work when I leave town?

I had no clue other than I had to. I just had to.

"That was unbelievable." Her eyes were still heavy with intoxication.

More than unbelievable.

She raised her hips and my dick popped out of her. I reached for some napkins stuffed in the door pocket and wiped us both clean.

While she dressed herself, I retrieved my shit from the backseat and put it back on.

We reclined in our seats, our hands joined on the console between us. I caressed her knuckles with my thumb.

"Are you excited to go to New York?"

"No. It's not a pleasure trip." Again I thought about the model I'd have to kiss.

"Still, it's a video shoot. That must be cool, huh?"

"I want to tell you about it." I had to get the truth off my chest.

She nodded excitedly. Too bad her mood would change as soon as I gave her details about the video.

"The song's a new one. It's a ballad." I tried to put it lightly.

"Joey always did have a thing for ballads." She caressed my fingers.

"Yeah. So… uh… the video is about finding lost love."

Her eyes went to mine. I hadn't given real thought into how much meaning the lyrics had to them in relation to me and Drew.

"The band agreed I would do the scenes with the actress, since Trevor and Joey are in committed relationships. They didn't feel right about touching another woman, even if it was only acting."

Her hand tensed in mine.

"I understand. It's part of the job, right?"

Understand, my ass. She lied through her teeth.

"I agreed to it before you came back into my life."

"You don't have to explain yourself. We've spent a week together. That hardly constitutes a relationship."

The hurt in her eyes pained me beyond belief. She bobbed her foot up and down on the mat and stared out the front window.

"Hey, look at me." I shook her hand in mine and she did. "You know that's not the truth. We go way back, more than just a week together."

"I don't know how to feel. Last week felt like a fantasy, but now we're back home. There are pictures of us posted on the Internet, and one of the patients at the clinic today recognized me. She told me how she's a big fan, and blah, blah, blah. Unfortunately my mother walked by while the lady spoke. I've managed to brush off speaking to her about the two of us, but I can't do it much longer. She wants to know what the deal is. I can't tell her because I myself don't know what the deal is. What I do know is that you're leaving town for the weekend and go on tour shortly afterward. I don't see how I fit into that picture." Her voice escalated as she put all her fears and insecurities out on the table.

Sighing heavily, I rubbed my chin. I didn't know how we would make it work either, but I damn well wanted to try.

"Listen, I've never been in this type of a situation either. It's all new for me as well. Why don't we try to figure it out together?"

"You're going to be on the road for months on end with various women throwing themselves at you. As much as I trust you right now, I don't know how I'll feel once you leave."

How could one mistake carry over and ruin everything years later?

"Drew, I fucked up. I've already apologized. Please give me a chance to prove to you I won't fuck up again."

"I want to be with you, more than anything, but I don't think I can go through that pain again, especially with how the social media portrays the band, you especially. I've done research. You were right when you said they love to portray you as the bad boy who screws anything with breasts and a vagina."

Anger boiled inside me. "Do you really think I have that little self-control?"

"I don't know what to think."

"You have to decide whether you're willing to take a chance on us or not. But my heart's vested in this union as well. I don't give of it freely. In fact, you're the only woman I've ever given it to." Tears spilled from her eyes. "Tell me what you're thinking."

She shook her head and brushed me off with the back of her hand.

"You have to be able to talk to me, babe, if this is going to work."

"Logan…" Her lids were heavy.

"Please talk to me."

"I'm scared."

"I am too. I lost you once. I don't want to lose you again."

She swallowed and wiped her tears. "That's exactly how I feel."

"At least we're on the same page."

She forced a smile. God, did I want to tell her how much I loved her. How I had never stopped loving her. I knew the road ahead of us would be rocky as hell, but I wanted more than anything to take the journey with her, hiking boots and all.

30

DREW

*L*ogan and I spent as much time together as possible prior to his weekend trip to New York. I hated to see him go, emptiness filling me with each passing minute, a feeling that would become my new best friend, since he would be resuming his tour in the next few weeks.

My mother finally got me alone at the clinic during lunch hour when the others weren't around.

"You've been avoiding me like the plague." She took a bite of her turkey sandwich.

"I don't want to get into it with you right now."

"How about I listen while you speak, no rebuttal?"

She had to be kidding. "No rebuttal?"

"You're a grown woman. You're going to do what you want anyway, so it's not worth arguing about. If you and Logan are back together, as your mother, I deserve to know."

"Yes, he and I are back together." I dared to peek up at her. She forced her lips together in a hard line but didn't say a word. "He happened to be at the ranch the week Kate and I visited. I had no clue he would be there. Serendipitous, huh? Well, the two of hung out, and things kind of picked up where they left off."

"If I may interject, even though I said I wouldn't, my recollection is you finding him with another woman. Isn't that how things left off between the two of you?"

My hand balled into a fist. I knew she would bring this up. I wouldn't let her manipulate me, though. Logan had matured. Both of us had.

"We've spoken about it, and he apologized. He can't apologize enough, and I've accepted it. He made a mistake. People do that, you know."

"And you believe he's being sincere?"

She obviously didn't.

"I do. People make mistakes. Take Joe, for example. Why aren't you giving him a hard time for abandoning Kate at the altar? And then he married her in Vegas at one of those Elvis chapels after you spent thousands of dollars on a wedding." My anger came out in my tone.

"First of all, they didn't get married by an Elvis impersonator, so you can drop the sarcasm. Second of all, I'm of the belief that once a cheater, always a cheater. Joe didn't cheat on your sister."

Christ. I couldn't believe she stood up for Joe. The man ditched my sister *at the altar* and broke her heart.

"Go ahead and defend him. And here I thought you said this wasn't worth arguing about, that I'm an adult who can do whatever I want. Well, I want to be with Logan, so that's exactly what I'm going to do, whether you approve or not."

"Please don't make threats. I may not agree or like your decision, but I can't stop you from seeing him. All I ask is that you acknowledge he's in a band. He lives the fast track, touring the country, boozing it up with women. How do you expect this to work? Your life is here. His is anything but."

My eyes widened. "He's not *boozing* it up, Mom. He's never been into drinking or drugs. You know that as well as I do, especially with Joey and Dani's history with their alcoholic father. So please don't make accusations you can't back up. As far as touring the country, I understand your concern in that respect. I'm concerned as well. But

I'm in love with him. I always have been. I never stopped. And whether you accept it or not, I'm going to give things another shot between us."

Her disappointment was clear as day, but I didn't care.

"I hope you know what you're getting yourself into. Maybe you don't remember how devastated you were when he cheated on you. But I do. I lived with you and held you when you cried nonstop for months on end. Don't expect me to forgive so easily."

"It's your choice. I believe in second chances. It's safe for me to say Kate does too."

"This has nothing to do with your sister, so leave her out of it."

"Really? Kate has been a screwup most of her life. Yet you never came down hard on her. I never gave you a moment of grief, and here you are, giving me an earful."

"I'm not giving you an earful. You're a competent adult who can make your own decisions. Do I think getting involved with a rock star is a good idea? Absolutely not. The only thing Logan can offer you is financial security."

My jaw fell open. She had dared to stoop that low.

I rose, grabbed my cell off the desk, and retrieved my purse from the floor. I hustled around the counter toward the exit.

"Where are you going? The schedule is full after lunch. We need you here."

"I'm taking a sick day. I'm sure you can handle things up front."

I stormed out the door without waiting for a reply.

In my car, I started the engine, my hands trembling against the steering wheel. My heart pounded so hard I almost couldn't breathe. She made me so gosh darn angry. Did she not think I hadn't thought about every point she'd mentioned? And for her to insinuate Logan had nothing to offer me except his money. That was the final straw. Logan had a heart of gold. So he screwed up. We all do. It wasn't the first time, and I could guarantee it wouldn't be the last. But I knew what I felt for him and from him was real, not a wham-bam-thank-you-ma'am hookup. We cared deeply for each other. Sadly, she wouldn't get to see how much.

My cell rang while I drove about, unsure of where I was headed. I checked the caller ID. My mother. I let it go to voice mail. Usually I would call Eric in a situation such as this, but I called Logan instead.

"Hey babe." His chipper voice did wonders to help calm me.

"Hey. How's the shoot going?" I didn't want to dump my troubles on him so fast.

"What's wrong?" Guess he could hear the anger in my voice.

"I had a fight with my mom and left the clinic."

"About?"

"About you and me being together again."

"I'm assuming I don't have her blessing?"

His displeasure made me feel worse. I pulled into a small shopping center and parked the car, too riled up to continue driving.

"I don't really care. I'm so tired of trying to please my parents. Nothing I do is good enough for them."

"Where are you now?"

I glimpsed at the stores in front of me. "Parked in front of Bed, Bath & Beyond."

"Why don't you go to my place?"

"It's okay. I'll call Eric and go to his."

"Go to mine. My neighbor has a key. I'll give him a heads-up you're coming to get it."

"It's not the same without you there."

"Fuck, babe. That's sweet."

"It's the truth."

"Seriously, go to my place. I don't care if you stay there until I get back. Hell, I'd love it if you did. That would mean you'd be there when I get home."

"I can't hide out in your place. I have to face my parents."

"Whatever you want, but the invitation is out there. Let me know if you change your mind so I can have my neighbor give you the spare key."

"Thanks. I appreciate the offer. How's Hollywood?"

"It's New York, babe. We're on a lunch break."

"How's the actress?" I hated to sound so infantile and jealous.

"You're much prettier."

Finally I could smile. "Thanks, smooth talker."

"What? You are. Listen, the director's calling for me. I'll give you a call after we wrap up for the day."

Why did that seem too long to wait?

Knowing Eric would be at work, I called anyway. He told me to go to his apartment and wait for him. I had a key to let myself in. First I stopped by my house to get some clothes. I told Eric I wanted to spend the night. He informed me he had a date later but didn't mind if I crashed there. I figured I'd rather hang at his place alone than at mine with my parents.

My mother tried calling me again, but I didn't answer. When my father called, I did.

"You can't just pick up and leave work because you're upset. Behave responsibly. We have a lot of patients to see, and now your mother is stuck up front instead of taking care of her own work in the back office."

I should've figured he'd call to reprimand me rather than ask about my emotional well-being. I had never once called in sick, at his beck and call any and every time he or my mother asked for help. So he could take his explanation about me behaving responsibly and shove it up his ass.

"If Mom didn't upset me, I wouldn't have left. If she wants to keep our business and personal lives separate, she shouldn't bring up personal shit at the office."

"Language. Please show some respect."

I rolled my eyes. "I'll be in on Monday."

"Mom tells me Logan's back in the picture."

Of course she did.

"Yes, he is." My inner child had her boxing gloves on, ready to fight and defend.

"I see."

The front door opened, and Eric strolled in. I held up a finger, so he'd know to give me a minute. He set his stuff on the kitchen counter and plopped on the couch next to me.

"Dad, I'm hanging out with Eric. Is there anything else you need?"

"Yes, for you to get your head out of your ass and grow up. You're behaving like a child."

Such harsh words. How dare he!

"What an awful thing to say to me. I've always been reliable and dependable so let's stop with the insults."

"I don't appreciate your attitude."

"I'm sorry to have to say this, but I'm not a little girl anymore. Why can't you accept that?"

Eric's eyes went wide. I shook my head, letting him know I had run out of patience with this nonsense.

The problem I faced was that my father allowed me to work around my school schedule. Every semester it changed. Some of my classes were only offered at certain times of the day. He never complained, telling me my education should come first. I kept reminding myself I wouldn't be his employee forever. I simply had to bide my time, but it became more difficult as the seconds ticked by. I didn't know how much longer I could remain sane living under his and my mother's roof.

"I know you're not a child. Please don't speak to me in such a condescending tone. Case in point, when you behave like one, I treat you as such. And right now, you're acting spoiled. You had a tizzy because you didn't agree with what your mother said to you, so you threw a fit and left work. That's both irresponsible and childish."

"I'm sorry I left you in a bind." I said what he wanted to hear in an attempt to get him off my case. Plus, I knew part of his accusation was true.

"Thank you for taking personal responsibility for your actions. I understand you're an adult. I'm not trying to baby you. But while you're living under our roof, your mother and I would appreciate if you gave us a heads-up about your comings and goings. We don't want to worry at night if you don't come home. All I'm asking is that you show us some respect. Fair enough?"

"Fair enough."

We finished the call, and I sighed. I properly greeted Eric with a giant bear hug.

"What was that all about?"

He listened to the day's events.

"Sorry. That sucks. You know you can stay here whenever you want, unless I have a night guest." He winked.

My mouth opened in faux surprise. "You'd kick out your best friend for sex?"

"You know it."

Knowing he teased, I laughed.

"Tell me about your hot date for tonight."

"I met him through a colleague."

Using my hand, I made a rolling motion, prompting him to elaborate. "And…"

Eric worked as a paralegal in a law firm and attended law school on the weekends. He lived an obscene schedule. I didn't know how he did it, but he knew in the end his sacrifice would pay off. I only hoped mine would too.

"He's a bankruptcy attorney, thirtyish, single, and handsome."

"So you've seen him already?"

"Not in person. He's so good-looking. Want to see?" He brought his phone to life and showed me a picture.

"Wow. He is nice-looking. Too bad he's gay."

"Stop being selfish. You're spoken for, woman."

Hmm, that sounded nice, being spoken for. Logan and I hadn't discussed not seeing others, but I knew that's where we stood.

"What time are you picking him up?" I had to know when to make my exit.

"In about an hour. I have to shower and change first. You know you can stay here for as long as you want."

"Thanks, but I'll leave when you take off. I want to see how cute you look for your date before I go."

He beamed and headed to his bedroom. I clicked on the television with the remote and watched garbage reality shows until he came back out, all debonair in slacks and a polo. He smelled even better. Eric was a prize: smart, gorgeous, and a heart of gold. Any guy would be lucky to have him.

He escorted me to my car, and we parted ways. When I got home, I saw Kate's car parked in the driveway. *Great.* Now I'd have to deal with her too.

"Hey Drew." She sat at the kitchen table, drinking tea with my mother whose eyes pierced into mine.

"Hey. How's Joe?" I knew they'd been talking about me by the silence that took place when I entered the room. I cringed at the thought. My mom used to sit in that same seat and complain to me about Kate.

"He's working late, so I figured I'd stop by."

Sure she did. I bet she had called, and my mother filled her in on all the juicy drama taking place at home, so she came by to become an active participant in it.

"I'm going to take a shower." I went to leave.

"Why don't you join us?"

Damn Kate!

I knew if I stayed, they'd push me over the edge, and my feet stood too close to it. If I left, they'd continue to talk about me. Since it was a no-win situation, I chose to excuse myself and take a shower.

31

LOGAN

After the video shoot, I called Drew, then went to dinner with the guys and Dani. Camilla tagged along with us.

"We received another e-mail from your fan." Camilla focused her attention solely on me while speaking. All the other eyes at the table went to me too.

"What did it say?" My knee shook underneath the table. I hated this situation.

Camilla opened the e-mail app on her phone and showed us the letter.

Dear Logan,

I know you're out of town for the weekend. Your social-media pages say you're in New York City with the guys taping a music video. I can't wait to see it. I met your new girlfriend. She's cute. Not the type I thought you'd be interested in. I thought you preferred more voluptuous women, like me. You're surprising me in so many ways. I know you have a few weeks off before your tour resumes. I want us to meet up again. It's been too long. I'll be in touch next week.

I pounded my fist against the table. It hurt too.

"She met Drew? Where? Drew never mentioned anything about it. This has to stop, Camilla."

"Like I said previously, since no physical threat has been made, there's nothing we can do. I made a file and am saving all correspondence from this fan in it."

"I have to warn Drew. The sad part is I don't know who the fuck this woman is, so how can I effectively warn her? According to this psycho, she and I have met. That doesn't help for shit."

"This is worse than I thought." Joey sighed.

"No shit. It was bad enough when the lunatic sent me letters, but now she's bringing Drew into the picture."

"I think you should call the police and let them know what's going on," Trevor advised.

"And I think you should take me up on the suggestion to heighten security until we figure out who this woman is," Camilla added.

Maybe she was right. I wanted to get this video shoot over and done with, so I could get home. I hated being on the other side of the country while this crazed fan remained in the same town as Drew. I also didn't want to add to Drew's stress. She sounded pissed about her mother on the phone earlier.

The following morning the guys and I picked up on set where we'd left off. The model understood she could only touch me during scenes. She had inquired about taking our onscreen kiss backstage. Crazy enough, I didn't think I had ever rejected a come-on from a hot chick, this being a first for me. That's how pathetically I had behaved over the years, something I wasn't particularly proud of.

The director kept badgering me to kick up the sex appeal when I had the girl in my arms. I never had a problem doing so in the past. I did now. The dick wanted tongues, touching, as much as television would allow, which in this day and age, I considered too fucking much.

It felt so wrong to have my tongue down another woman's throat. I could only imagine how Drew would feel when she saw the finished video. The guilt penetrated deep, as if I blatantly cheated on her all over again, even though this time it wasn't intentional and merely an act, with a limp dick to prove it.

After the hot-and-heavy scenes finished, I took a well-deserved break.

"Excuse me, Mr. Trimble. I'm Lorraine from Entertainment News Daily. We're here getting some footage of the video shoot and to help promote Steam's new song. I wondered if I could ask you a few questions."

My jaw clenched with tension. Nobody had mentioned anything to me about an entertainment reporter with her camera crew in tow coming on set to take footage. I put my finger up and excused myself, finding Camilla ASAP.

"What the fuck, Camilla. Why didn't you tell me reporters were going to be here?"

"I didn't think it was a big deal. We want to promote the new song, don't we?"

"Drew's going to shit when she sees the footage." I balled my hand into a fist.

"Wow, I've never seen you act so smitten over a woman. I have to say, I find it kind of cute."

Really? I smirked as her sarcasm. "Cute?"

"Yeah. You're my bad boy, and here you are, turning all soft on me."

Female bullshit. "Whatever. So yeah, about the reporter. She wants to interview me."

"So go get interviewed. You've never been one to act shy around a beautiful woman. You surely aren't with Hauser. As cute as it is that you're gushing all over this girl, Drew, we still have an album to promote and records to sell. We're here to do a job. Now please go and do yours."

God bless Camilla, all business.

The reporter sat on a chair, waiting for me. She hiked her leg up, giving me a nice view of her gams. Sadly for her, I showed no interest. It didn't stop her from continuing to flirt. I ignored all her subtle gestures.

She asked basic questions about the new album, easy stuff. She wrapped up our session by asking questions about the mysterious girl with me in the pictures on the Internet. I told her I didn't want to discuss it. I kept my private life just that, private. She tried to rebut. I reiterated my stance on the subject.

After the interview, I headed back to the set. The shoot took hours. We didn't end until almost midnight. I didn't want to call Drew so late.

The following morning the guys and I got up at the crack of dawn to visit the hospital. As sad as the visits were, I took pleasure in participating in these types of events. I felt humbled that I could bring joy to sick children. It made me appreciate my job immensely.

We took pictures and sang a few songs, then hit the road for lunch. We didn't get back to the hotel until early evening. Trevor and Dani had taken off earlier for a Broadway show. Joey and I did a bit of shopping. I picked up a toy airplane at a kid's store as a gift for Drew. I wanted it to remind her of our night at the airport, where we'd parked and *kind of* watched planes take off and land as well as remind her of her initiation into the Mile High Club.

I left her a voice mail. Joey came with me to Camilla's room so I could play Drew's song for them. I knew Drew had told me she wanted to think about me sharing it with others, but the timing was perfect, especially since we were in Manhattan, and Camilla planned to stay in town for the week to meet with record execs. I couldn't with good conscience let Drew miss out on an opportunity of a lifetime.

Camilla and Joey sat tight and listened to the rhythm and lyrics. When the song ended, Joey glared at me. "Fuck, you did a number on that poor girl."

"Thanks for sharing, asshole."

He chuckled. "Just sayin'. I guess I could also say you did her a favor because that song rocked!"

"I agree." Camilla leaned forward in her chair. In Camilla's world, that meant it piqued her interest. "Does she have others?"

"I think so. She loves to write. She hasn't played me any others, though."

"Would it be possible for me to speak with her?"

"Can you get me some feedback first? I would hate to get her hopes up for nothing. She's kind of shy about performing in front of others. Besides, she doesn't know I played the song for you."

Joey pressed his lips together as if he wanted to whistle but didn't. He spoke instead. "You're digging yourself into a deeper grave, my friend."

"No, I'm trying to pull her out of the shithole she's currently in. If her song sells, it's worth it no matter what the outcome."

"I hope you know what you're doing."

No need for Joey to warn me. I did. I knew in my heart I did right by her. My gut told me so.

"If that's how you want it, I'll bring it with me to my meetings this week and try to shop it around. You know if there's an interest, she's going to have to get involved, possibly perform."

"Of course, but I'd rather give her good news than bad."

"Listen to you, Trimble. If I didn't hear it with my own ears, I wouldn't believe it." Camilla grinned.

"What?" I was clueless as to what she referred to.

"She's referring to you being pussy-whipped." Joey chuckled.

"Call me what you want. That's how it is."

Camilla frowned. "You're being too nice. I miss all your drama."

No comment.

"I'm all for the union. Drew is far from the trash you bring into your room on a nightly basis. And she won't intentionally screw you over."

I nodded in agreement with Joey's sentiment.

"Okay. You guys sound like a bunch of women. Go back to your rooms and resume whatever it was you were doing prior to your spontaneous visit." Camilla chased us out.

"Want to shoot pool?" Joey asked as we strolled down the hall to the elevators.

"You bet."

A short walk outside led us to a pool bar. We tossed back a few drinks and played a few rounds. It felt great hanging out with him without Teva in tow. She'd remained at home.

"How was your vacation?"

"Incredible." Joey hit a striped ball into the corner pocket.

"Things are serious between you and Teva, huh?" I stood with my cue stick, waiting for him to miss a shot.

He looked up at me from a bent-over position before hitting his next ball. "She's the one." He took the shot, getting it in the side pocket.

"I'm happy for you."

"Yeah. I'm happy for me too. I'm also happy for Dani. As much as I argued against her and Trevor being together at the beginning, he's the best thing that's ever happened to my sister. And the fact I know him so well means I know he'll do right by her. He's a good guy. Solid, you know? What about you and Drew? What're you going to do when we go on tour?"

"I don't know, man. It's going to be hard. I can't stop thinking about it."

Yes! He missed the right corner pocket. Finally, I could do some damage.

32

DREW

Trying to kill time, I flipped through various channels on the television, bored out of my wits. Classes started up again on Monday. A part of me couldn't wait to go back. If anything, school would occupy my mind.

For the most part, my parents left me alone all weekend. Eric had a blast on his date so asked the guy out again, therefore, I spent my Saturday night watching the tube. Logan had texted earlier that the video shoot ran late, and he didn't know when he'd be finished.

Nothing caught my attention on TV. I settled on an entertainment show, figuring I'd catch up on the celebrity lifestyles. Not that I cared, but it gave me something to do.

With my pillow fluffed behind my head, I played with the remote. It fell out of my hand when the reporter said there would be some footage from the new Steam video shoot after the commercial break.

My heart raced and I clapped my hands, cheering for Logan, so utterly excited for him. He had gained enough fame to land on an entertainment show. Wow. He had come so far. I couldn't be prouder of him for never giving up on his dream.

The commercials went on and on. It made me bonkers.

Impatiently, I waited for the show to resume. I raised the volume when the reporter came back on the screen.

"Our very own Lorraine Whitaker is on location with the band Steam. They're shooting their new video for their latest release, "Still Dreaming of You." Lorraine is taking you live and behind the scenes."

The scene changed to one that resembled a movie set. Trevor sat behind his drum kit, Joey held his mic, standing in front of his keyboard, and my beautiful Logan held his guitar. I couldn't wipe the goofy smile off my face at his devilishly handsome appearance.

"I am here on the set of Steam's *steamy* new video to give you a sneak peek."

The reporter played some footage of the guys jamming and shots of Logan with the actress he had mentioned to me. He had conveniently left out the part about her being a supermodel. I reeled in my jealousy until a scene flashed of him with his arms around her, the two of them making out. Logan held her leg against his thigh and gyrated against her.

My mouth fell open. It felt like déjà vu. I knew the video portrayed a make-believe scenario but this, the acting too real for words.

Tears flooded my eyes. I wanted to change the channel but couldn't, aching to see the ending.

I didn't think it could get worse.

But it did.

"Logan Trimble, Steam's guitarist, met up with me during the shoot."

The reporter sat opposite Logan, the two of them sitting face to face. She asked him questions about the new song and other trivial stuff.

"There have been a few pictures floating around the Internet of you and a mystery woman. Care to share?"

Bitch!

"I keep my private life private."

Thank you, Logan.

"This new video is quite provocative. How did it feel working with model Jessica Hauser?"

Why doesn't she just jump on his lap and fuck him with her clothes on?

I couldn't be the only person on the planet who saw the reporter's obvious flirtation and liking of Logan.

He put his hand out. "It's a tough job, but somebody's got to do it." He chuckled.

Is he serious?

The reporter giggled; a stupid fake one too.

"I guess you got to be the *lucky* one." She teased him.

"You don't hear me complaining one bit."

Excuse me? I picked up the remote that had fallen on my comforter and shut off the television. That was not my Logan. My Logan would never behave so pompously.

So which was the real Logan? The one he showed me in private, or the jerk he portrayed on television?

Resting on my side, I pulled a few tissues from the box on my nightstand, and cried into them. I couldn't do this again. Seeing that news story only confirmed it. Logan would be on the road for weeks, months at a time, and I would see similar reports nonstop. After all, he had been depicted by the media as Steam's bad boy. I wanted to kick myself for falling so hard and fast.

The following night when he called, I let the call go to voice mail. I couldn't speak about my feelings regarding the entertainment story over the phone. I had thought long and hard since seeing the interview. As much as I hated to admit it, my mother had been right. Logan lived his life on the road, in the fast lane, whereas mine belonged here in Boringville. How could I have been such a fool to believe it could ever work between him and me?

The sad realization had me moping around, bringing my horrific mood with me to the clinic on Monday. My parents kept asking me about my depressed state. I wouldn't tell them they were right, so I blamed it on my hormones, PMSing, the only excuse I could come up with to get them off my back.

Logan would be returning later in the day. I knew he'd reach out to me when he got home. Luckily for me, I had an afternoon class. I prayed those three hours in school would help divert my attention from Logan Trimble because working at the clinic did anything but.

Mia brought me the form for the patient my dad had just finished with. "I'm giving you a heads-up, the lady about to come up here is a cuckoo." She gestured, her finger going in circles to indicate the lady had some mental issues.

I giggled.

"Laugh all you want. She's a head case."

Mia took off for the next exam room.

While entering the patient's information, I realized it was the woman with the Teacup Yorkie
. Christ. I must've been in the bathroom when she checked in and didn't recognize her name on the schedule.

"How's Logi?"

She shook her head as in so-so.

"Dr. Sanders indicated he wants to see him again next week because he lost a pound. Logi's a small dog, so every pound counts. He also indicated that for now, he wants him on a special high-calorie diet. You can purchase the food here as a convenience or at a local pet store. It's your choice."

"I'll get it here. Add it to my bill. Hey, did you happen to see the entertainment news this weekend? Seems your boyfriend is hooking up with Jessica Hauser. She fucks anything with a dick."

Disgust overtook her. I understood, I felt the same. Still, I hadn't expected all of that to come out of this woman's mouth. Mia was right when she called her a head case.

"I must've missed the story." I had no intention of commenting on the subject. I had done a superb job of keeping my emotions in check in front of patients and didn't want to ruin a perfectly good track record.

"Oh yeah, his tongue was down her throat and he groped her perfect model frame." Her eyes widened as she spoke. This woman didn't hide how she got a kick out of digging the news into me.

"If you'll please excuse me, I'm going to go get Logi's food."

Mia happened to be standing in the lab as I gathered a few cans from off the shelf.

Sweet relief.

"Can you please do me a favor and check out the nutcase up front? I'm going to explode if I don't go to the bathroom." My hands trembled when I handed her the dog food.

"Are you okay?" Her brow furrowed with concern.

"I'm fine. But I have to pee." I tightened my legs together to add to the believability of my made-up story.

She took the cans from me. I knew she didn't believe my lie about being okay, but I didn't care. The bathroom would provide me with a breather.

Once in the confines of the small space, I splashed cold water on my face.

What the hell was that all about with that crazy lady? She obviously took pleasure in seeing me squirm.

Not wanting to run into her again, I hid out in the john for a few minutes, hoping she'd be gone when I returned to my desk.

Damn. There she stood up front, chatting with Mia, who gave me a sideways glance, begging for me to rescue her. What about someone rescuing me?

"Dr. Sanders needs your assistance, Mia."

"Okay. Thanks." She bolted like a bat out of hell, leaving me stuck with the looney toon and her Yorkie.

"Did Mia check you out and schedule Logi's follow-up appointment?" I got right down to business, anxious to move her along.

"Yeah. She and I were chatting about Logan Trimble too. She's also a big fan. We're so jealous of you. Although, I do know how great he is in bed." She whispered the last part, shielding her words from others with her hand.

"Excuse me?" I did a double take, unsure if I had heard her correctly.

"He fucked me after a show one night. What a head rush, right? That man packs a punch." She thrusted her hips forward and smiled at whatever crazy memory she currently relived in her demented mind.

"If you don't mind, I have a ton of work to attend to and patients to check in." I clasped my hands together in front of me.

"Oh, of course. Listen to me, blabbing on about bedtime stories with Logan's new fuck buddy. I apologize."

I'd had it with this woman. "Please don't refer to me as that, and please don't speak about Logan to me anymore. This isn't the place for it."

"We could meet for dinner or something?"

She had to be kidding me.

"I'm sorry, but I'm going to have to ask you to leave the clinic."

My father would have my head if he knew I kicked a patient out of his office, but this lady had totally crossed the line.

"It sucks hearing the truth, doesn't it? You'll see. He'll toss you aside. He throws all of his beauties in the trash, me included."

Oh my God. This girl spoke in deranged stalker-fan mode. Logan had to be warned about her when I spoke with him. I'd had a gut feeling about this woman from the beginning. I had to tell my father to discharge Logi as a patient. I didn't want his owner ever stepping foot inside the clinic again. And I'd make sure he knew that if he refused my request, I wouldn't be present when she came in for her visits.

I rose and ushered her to the waiting room, where I called in the next patient.

The whack-job stormed out of the clinic in anger. The incoming patient raised her brows. I breathed in acknowledgment that both of our thoughts were on the same page.

My nerves were fried by the time I left for class. I'd have to wait until I got home later to discuss the unhinged patient with my father.

Arriving early to the university gave me some time to chill. I sat on a bench outside my building and listened to music from my earbuds. The minutes ticked by. Whoever thought I'd be this excited for statistics, a boring prerequisite?

The three hours sitting in class passed second by agonizing second. I could barely keep my eyes open while trekking to the parking lot. I checked my phone for any missed calls or messages, finding one text from Eric and three missed calls from Logan along with voice mails. I had silenced my phone during class.

Logan: *I'm home. Please give me a call.*

Logan: *Hope everything's okay. Tried calling you last night, but never heard back from you.*

Logan: *Where are you?*

I shoved my phone inside my purse and continued toward my car. That was when I sensed an off-kilter presence behind me.

I clutched my bag against my chest and picked up my pace. My mother begged me to carry mace, since she knew I walked alone on campus at night, but I kept shrugging her off. Wouldn't you know it, she was right again.

The footsteps behind me got louder as the person got closer. Panic set in. My hands shook and my heart beat a million miles per second.

Get to my car. Get to my car.

Left and right, I surveyed the area, trying to find someone I could approach for help. There was nothing but darkness and emptiness along with the tapping of feet behind me.

Fuck!

Naturally, on this night the lot was quiet. It had been so full when I arrived, I'd no choice but to park in the boonies, far from the building where my class was held. Big mistake.

I adjusted my keys in my grip to use as a weapon if necessary.

The footsteps got closer.

My heart pounded faster.

I sped up.

The footsteps got louder.

I ran.

Faster.

Faster.

Until I reached my car.

What the hell?

My windows had all been smashed.

I spun around to see if the person I sensed lurked behind a car or something.

Nope. Whoever had been following me had all but vanished, gone like the wind.

Oh my God!

The words *Stay away from Logan Trimble* were scribbled on the windshield in red lipstick.

Hugging my purse, I took off running as fast as my legs would take me, back to the main campus. Many students were scattered about. My hands trembled too much to hold my phone steady. Two girls passing by stopped when they noticed my shaken state.

"Please call the police." My voice quivered, my entire body shaking from nerves.

One of the girls agreed to stay with me until the police arrived. She put her arm around me, comforting me as best she could.

"Do you want me to call anyone else?"

Unable to think clearly, I closed my eyes. "Um... My boyfriend." *Is he?* Whatever.

How I managed to find his name under my contact list, a miracle in itself with the unsteadiness of my hands. The thought came to me that if he showed up, his presence would create a mob scene due to his celebrity status. Again, whatever. I'd deal with the consequences later. I asked her to call him. I couldn't talk, my mind and body in too much shock.

I didn't tell the girl the specifics about the message written on my car or about Logan's true identity, that information irrelevant.

She handed me the phone. "He wants to speak to you."

"Lo…gan…you're…not…going…to…believe…what…happened." My words were broken up between tears, and choppy breaths.

"Where the hell are you? What's going on?" I heard his distress.

"I'm at school."

"I'm coming."

"No," I snapped.

"What do you mean, no?"

"The police are heading here now. We'll talk after I leave campus, but it's important for you to know what's going on."

"You can't call me in a panic and tell me we'll talk later, especially if the police are involved. You're freaking me out. I'm coming whether you want me to or not."

"You can't. It involves the band. The publicity would be bad."

The girl standing next to me cocked her head to the side, eavesdropping on my conversation, getting more interested by the minute.

"About the band?"

"Yes. I don't want to get into specifics now."

"I don't give a shit about the fucking publicity it brings. You obviously need me right now, and I'm coming for you. Please tell me where you are on campus."

After informing him of my location, I disconnected the call and buried my face in my hands, sobbing because of this unexpected turn of events.

33

LOGAN

My keys couldn't get in my hand fast enough.

I jumped in my car and took off for the university. I had no clue what was taking place or what the situation was. Drew hadn't given me any indication as to why she'd been crying on the phone.

My nerves heightened the closer I got to my destination. I vigorously tapped the steering wheel.

A thought flashed through my mind about the stalker girl who had sent me the notes. The last letter Camilla received stated she'd met Drew.

Fuck!

I slammed my hand against the wheel, praying for my higher power to keep Drew out of harm's way.

Talk about a massive campus. Luckily, I saw several police cars in front of one of the buildings, their lights flashing. I illegally parked next to them, hopped out of my car, and ran to Drew. She had no color to her, standing with another student.

"Baby." I reached for her.

When she caught sight of me she buried her face in my chest, crying. I held her in my arms, resting my head on top of hers.

"It's okay. I'm here now."

"It was awful." She cried harder.

One of the cops addressed me. "You are?"

"Logan Trimble."

His eyes went wide as did the girl next to us. A big smile took shape on her face.

"Your name is the one scribbled on Ms. Sanders' vehicle."

"Excuse me?" *Fuck! Fuck! Fuck!* I should have told Drew about the psychopath on my tail.

She dislodged herself from me enough to get in on the conversation.

"I think I might have a clue about who did this." I spoke in a quiet tone. Drew as well as the cops standing around us gave me their full attention. "I also want to file a police report."

Drew tilted her head to the side. "For what?"

"I've received a few suspicious letters from a fan. My manager informed me that since no threats had been made, I didn't have a case. I'd like to show you the letters."

"I'm sure you have a lot of fans, Mr. Trimble, whom you receive letters from on a regular basis. What makes you think the fan involved in this incident is the same one you're receiving suspicious letters from?"

"Because this fan specifically mentioned she had met my girlfriend."

Drew covered her mouth. "You never told me that."

"The latest letter came over the weekend while I was in New York.

I planned on telling you when I spoke with you but haven't had the chance until now."

She pushed me. "Oh my gosh, Logan. You should've told me this as soon as you heard about it. That lunatic followed me in the parking lot and destroyed my car. What if she had tried to hurt me?"

My head fell in shame because I couldn't dispute her point. I should have continued to reach out to her until I'd gotten hold of her.

When I lifted my head, I realized we had a small crowd gathered around, some with phones. I couldn't do this here, highly unfair to Drew. I didn't give a fuck if the people recorded me, but Drew didn't deserve to be put in that position, especially in her frantic mood.

"Can we go back to my place and discuss this somewhere private? This is only going to get worse." I gestured to the group of students assembling around us, their numbers increasing by the minute.

"Why don't we go to the station?" the cop suggested.

"I'd rather go to my house, so I can show you the letters I received."

"Very well. A few of our officers will remain here to check for fingerprints and any other information they can gather from Ms. Sanders' vehicle. My partner and I will follow you to your home. A tow truck is en route to remove Ms. Sanders' car from the lot."

Drew got into my car. She leaned back in her seat and closed her eyes. I shot Camilla a quick text, informing her of the situation and asked her to forward me the e-mails she had received from the fan, so I could show them to the officers as well. I set the phone on the console.

"I'm so sorry, babe. I wanted to tell you. None of the letters said anything about physical threats or danger." I rubbed Drew's leg.

"If this person mentioned me, I had a right to know about it."

. . .

"You're absolutely right. I apologize. Do you want me to call your folks and fill them in on what's going on?"

She shook her head. "No, not yet. I can't deal with them right now." She paused. "Actually, maybe I should contact them, so they can wait with the car until the tow truck arrives."

"Sounds like a good idea."

"This is crazy. I can't believe someone broke the windows of my car."

"I can't say how sorry I am that whoever this person is got you involved. I'll pay for the damage." I squeezed her hand.

"Don't worry about it. I'm sure insurance will cover it."

"Still, I don't want a dime coming out of your pocket for something that happened because of me."

"Thanks. I appreciate that. Can you tell me about the letters?"

"I'll one up that. I'll show them to you."

"I wonder if it's the same weirdo who's come into the clinic twice with her dog. Today she told me the two of you had sex."

Say what?

I clenched my jaw and steadied the car after almost swerving off the road. Luckily, there were no cars to my left, or we would've crashed. A feeling of gratitude swept through me that the cops behind us didn't give me a ticket for reckless driving.

"Come again?"

"She said you had sex with her after a show one night. She referred to me as your *fuck buddy*. She also ranted on about the entertainment story, which aired this weekend with footage from your video shoot. You know the one where you made out with Jessica Hauser and practically felt her up? And when asked about it, you said it's all part of your job, somebody has to do it. Yeah, I happened to watch the show too." She shifted her body toward the passenger window. She also slipped her hand out of mine.

Point taken.

"You knew I had a video shoot with an actress. I already told you it didn't mean anything."

She shrugged, not looking in my direction.

"Drew, do you honestly think I did something with that woman?"

"I don't know what to think right now, Logan. All I know is your world has a lot of crazy in it, and I'm not sure I can or want to be involved in it."

"Fuck. When are you going to trust me? I'm trying to move forward, but the past keeps getting in the way."

She finally gave me a visual of her teary-eyed face. "You want me to trust you, when you received correspondence from a fan who stated she'd met me without even telling me about it. Regarding the video, you mentioned shooting one with an *actress*, not a supermodel, and more importantly, you left out the part about you kissing and touching her. Why didn't you at least give me a heads–up, so I could prepare myself instead of having to see it firsthand on TV along with the rest of the world? There are already too many secrets for my comfort level."

"I wanted to tell you but didn't know how. I didn't realize the story would air so quickly. And just so you know, Jessica did come on to me. She asked if we could take the party back to my room, but I told her no. I've never told a woman no. It doesn't make me feel proud to admit it, but it's the truth. I don't want to be with anybody else, and the last thing I'd ever do is repeat a mistake I still can't forgive myself for making. For the record, I left you a few messages. You didn't return any of my calls."

She sniffled. I handed her a tissue. I kept them stashed in the middle console.

"You're right. You did call, but I was too upset about the entertainment story to speak to you. I wanted to talk about my feelings with you in person. I'm sorry for jumping at you about that, and I appreciate you sharing all this with me. It means a lot. I guess seeing the video and then having that whack-job intentionally rub it in my face hurt me. The sad part is I know this isn't a one-time occurrence. This insanity probably happens to you nonstop. I don't know if I can handle it."

"If you don't trust me, this thing between us will never work."

She sat upright and exhaled. "I know. It's not something that will happen overnight, though."

"I get it, and I'm trying to prove things are different. I wish you would've spoken to me after you saw the report on TV."

"I felt too angry. The reporter spun the story to portray—how can I say this politely? It doesn't matter. She portrayed you as an asshole. I think she wanted the viewers to think something went on between you and Jessica Hauser."

"Nothing went on between us that you didn't see. I can assure you of that. As soon as we wrapped up shooting, I went to sleep. The following morning the guys and I visited the children's hospital. Later that day Joey and I had dinner and shot pool. I couldn't wait to get home to see you."

She gave me a faint smile. "I think I better call my parents. We're almost at your place."

Her fingers drummed nervously on her lap during her conversation with her father. I lowered the volume on the radio. I couldn't hear what he said but could tell he blamed me for what went down based on her replies to him.

She began using hand gestures, arguing that I had nothing to do with it. I remained silent until she finished the call. When she did, she tossed her phone in her purse. "What a crock of shit."

"What did he say?

"He's not happy I left the car. He said I should've waited until the tow truck arrived. I'm sure you heard me tell him we're meeting with the police at your place because a crowd gathered around, wanting to see you. He and my mom are heading to the university now. I'm so tired of them." She grunted her frustration.

"You're more than welcome to stay at my house whenever you want. Just say the word."

"That's nice of you to offer, but it wouldn't be much fun staying at your place without you there, since you're leaving soon to go back on tour."

Not having a response to give her, I sighed. I didn't want to leave her behind. I prayed Camilla would work her magic with some of the music execs and get Drew's song heard. If others heard the potential I did, Drew wouldn't have to worry about her financial status anymore. Songwriters made a shitload of cash when their songs hit the charts. I felt confident hers had the potential to do that. Not that I wouldn't help her out financially if things didn't turn out as I hoped.

We pulled into my driveway with the cop car in tow. We went inside the house, and I showed everyone to a seat in the living room. I went into my office to collect the cards I'd received in the mail from the fan as well as printed out the e-mails Camilla forwarded to me. I clipped all the papers together and brought them to the living room, handing them to the officer with the mustache. I believe Fields was his name. I couldn't read his nametag.

He scanned through them. "We have no proof that the person who sent these letters is the same person who damaged Ms. Sanders' vehicle this evening."

"I do. The one e-mail she sent me states she met Drew. And Drew informed me that a woman came into the vet clinic where she works and told her she's a fan. I think it's the same girl."

"We have no proof of that, Mr. Trimble. We'll see if the university has surveillance cameras on campus. In addition, Ms. Sanders, can you please provide me with the name of the patient whom you had the interactions with at work? We can do a background check and see what we find," the other officer requested.

"I can get you the information right now. All I need is a computer with Internet access, and I can log into the office network."

"That would be great," the second cop replied.

I led Drew to my office, so she could use my computer. Her hands trembled as she typed on the keyboard. I rubbed her shoulders.

She logged into her office system and printed out the patient's demographics. I took a gander at the woman's name but had no recollection of it. We brought the info to the living room, where the officers sat waiting for us. Drew handed one of them the paper.

"My parents are headed to the university now. The car's registered under my father's name. Can you please let the remaining officers at the scene know he and my mother will be arriving shortly?"

"Will do," Fields replied. I saw his name tag clearly now. He promptly made the call.

"How do I know this woman isn't going to try to hurt me?" Drew sat huddled on the couch.

I sat next to her and put my arm around her. She leaned into me, a bundle of nerves. I couldn't blame her. I felt her anguish.

"Right now, there have been no physical threats. There has been a written warning, which we will investigate and see what we come up with. The woman sounds like a love-obsessed stalker."

That was the same terminology Camilla had used to describe the fan over the phone.

"This type of stalker becomes obsessed with another person, usually someone he or she has had no relationship with. In this case —according to the stalker's letter, Mr. Logan—it appears you have somewhat of a past with the woman involved, however minimal." The second police officer directed his attention toward me.

Drew sighed heavily and closed her eyes.

"These types of stalkers usually expect the victim, in this instance you, Mr. Trimble, to have reciprocal feelings, even though it's all a fantasy inside his or her mind. Your fan is reaching out via e-mail and letters to make her awareness known to you. But you should understand that this situation could easily escalate to physical and verbal threats, which Ms. Sanders received earlier with the vandalization of her car. That is, *if* we are speaking about the same woman. We have no proof or conclusive evidence to support that at this point in time."

Drew twisted her fingers on her lap. I took her hand in mine and caressed her knuckles, trying to calm her. Sadly, nothing I did to try and soothe her pacified or helped her relax. She bobbed her foot nervously on the floor.

"Unfortunately, we aren't able to provide you with round-the-clock protection. I have no idea what plan of action this fan has in mind. All I can guarantee is that we will do our best to see what information we can gather with the evidence we have so far."

"And what if this lady knows where I live? She already knows where I work and go to school. I'm scared." Drew sniffled between her tears.

"For now, my suggestion is to keep a running log of the stalker's attempts at contacting either one of you, whether through e-mail, telephone, letters, anything. You might consider hiring personal security protection unless you already have security personnel, Mr. Trimble. Please be alert of any unusual packages or envelopes you receive. You might also consider changing your telephone number and keeping it unlisted as well as informing neighbors, friends, and coworkers about the situation, so they too can keep an eye out for any suspicious activity. Ms. Sanders, I strongly urge you to have someone escort you to the university, since this person clearly knows when you attend class. You should also park in well-lit areas, and check your vehicle whenever you enter or leave it unattended. Make sure to lock all the doors, and keep your car in a garage, if possible. If you notice somebody following you, drive to the nearest law-enforcement agency. Do not take the person on a wild-goose chase."

Drew cried harder. She rose from the couch and paced in front of it.

"I'm sorry there's nothing more we can offer you at this time. Here's my card."

Officer Fields handed me and Drew cards.

"If you think of anything else that might help assist us with this case, please contact me or Officer Edwards. We'll be in touch as soon as we have more information to provide you with."

Officer Edwards now **handed us his cards.**

"Thank you." I led both men to the door and escorted them out.

34

DREW

Why won't my hands stop shaking?
Did I really have to ask myself that question? PS, the rest of me trembled as well, from head to toe.

My throat felt so dry, I could barely swallow. I went to the kitchen to get a glass of water.

Logan spotted me sitting on a stool next to the kitchen island. He spoke on the phone, talking to someone about private security.

What the hell had happened? My life had turned completely upside down in the course of a few short weeks.

"That was my manager on the phone. The band hasn't required extra security, but that's about to change. Our guy, Tomas, will be contacting me in the next hour with the name of someone who does personal security. I don't want you going anywhere alone until we catch this woman."

"I can't walk around with a bodyguard 24/7, yet I feel afraid not to. I'm scared to walk outside your front door. What if she's out there right now? I fear for my parents' safety at the clinic. This person knows who we are. What if she follows my family? What if she tries to hurt them?" I rambled off questions as quickly as they came to mind.

"It's a lot of what-ifs, babe. We don't have any idea how far this lunatic is willing to go, but we're not going to take any chances to find out. We'll have to stay one step ahead of her."

My cell rang. I checked the caller ID and answered.

"Hi, Dad."

"We're getting ready to leave the university. Your car's about to get towed. Is there anything you want me to grab from it before we leave?"

"Please check my trunk. I should have everything, but just look around in case I left a jacket or books for school in there. I'm having trouble thinking straight right now. Did the police give you any information?"

"No. They took pictures and inspected the interior of your car to make sure nothing was tampered with. They also checked under the hood. Your mother and I aren't happy with this situation, as I'm sure you can imagine. Please ask Logan to bring you home. You mother and I want to have a serious talk with you. We don't need Logan's celebrity lifestyle affecting the safety of our family. The man has been nothing but trouble to us, both in the past and now."

"Dad, this isn't Logan's fault, so don't even go there. Trust me, he's doing everything he can to keep me safe. As a matter of fact, he's waiting for a call now from someone on his security team."

"That's great. But we don't have his kind of money to pay for bodyguards."

It pissed me off how my father kept bringing up Logan's money.

"The security's for *both* of us," I enunciated with anger.

He sighed heavily into the phone. "I'm not pleased with the changes taking place in you. But we'll speak about it later. Please meet me and your mother at home."

After disconnecting the call, I cried again. I couldn't seem to stop blubbering.

Logan wrapped his arms around me. I swiveled my stool around, so I could bury my face in his chest.

"My parents want me to go home. They want to talk to me. I think they're going to ask me not to see you anymore."

He released me but held on to my arms.

"Fuck that. I hope you're not considering it?"

"I can't think right now. Maybe you should take me home. I've caused my parents enough grief for one night."

"Do you hear yourself? You're blaming yourself for something that has *nothing* to do with you. Letting your parents guilt you into thinking so is absurd. This is a serious situation. I don't think they realize just how much. Please wait until we hear from Tomas before leaving the house."

"This girl could be anyone. How in the world are the cops supposed to find her? And the woman who came to my father's clinic might not be the guilty party, though she did give me the creeps. She could simply be another whacko on the prowl."

He sighed, and began pacing back and forth in front of me. "You don't think I'm upset about this? It's tearing me up inside."

He went to the fridge for a bottle of water. He'd seen mine, so he didn't offer me one.

I nervously picked at my nails. I had been so consumed with my own worry I hadn't given a thought about Logan's feelings.

His cell rang and he promptly answered it. I continued to pick at my cuticles while he spoke to who I assumed to be his security manager. I excused myself to go to the bathroom, so I could clean up and take a mental timeout, not that the change of scenery gave me one. My thoughts followed me wherever I went.

When I exited, I retrieved my phone from my purse. I checked my Facebook page to make sure my settings were private. Nothing struck me as out of the ordinary. I checked my e-mail in-box, nothing. I shot

Eric a quick text to let him know the story. I then checked for any missed texts. Nothing.

Suddenly, a reminder alert signaled. How odd. I didn't recall setting any reminders to go off.

"What?" I gasped when I saw the unexpected message.

My phone fell out of my hands and onto the floor in front of me.

"Logan! Logan, please come here!"

He came running in from the kitchen, telling whoever was on the phone he'd call them back.

"What is it? You scared the life out of me." He held his chest, panting heavily. "Why is your phone on the floor?"

"Read the reminder alert on it."

He cocked his head to the side. "What?"

"The message on my phone, dammit, read it!" I hated to yell, but I couldn't hold back my anger any longer. My emotions were bursting at the seams. I couldn't breathe.

"Drew, you need to calm the fuck down. Do you hear me? Now please, I want you to take slow, deep breaths. I'm not going to read the message until you calm down."

He was one to talk.

I rocked back and forth like a psych patient, crying into my shaking hands. He snuggled me in his arms and stroked my arm.

"Ssh. It's going to be okay. I won't let anyone hurt you."

"What about you? I don't want anything to happen to you either. I lost you once. That's enough for me."

He mumbled the word fuck under his breath.

True to his word, he didn't look at my phone until my breathing pattern steadied. I rested my head against his strong chest.

Hey bitch. I bet you're wondering how I got hold of your phone. You're in the back now, getting Logi's food. You were dumb enough to leave it on your desk. As an FYI, I'll be following you after you leave this shithole. Not sure where you're going so can't give you a heads-up as far as what I plan to do to you. Either way, whatever it is, just know this is only the beginning unless you wise up and stay away from Logan Trimble. Oh, I see you sent your peon to come and do your dirty work for you. Pussy. You'll get this reminder later. Take me seriously. Ta-ta for now.

"Fuck!"

Logan tensed under me. He took a picture of the message and called one of the cops who'd just been here.

"Office Fields, this is Logan Trimble. You left my house a little earlier regarding one of my fans damaging Drew Sanders' car."

While Logan spoke with the cop, I continued to focus on my breath.

"The woman who came into Drew's workplace just answered the question as to whether she's the psycho after me. I'm going to forward you a copy of the reminder she set on Drew's phone where she specifically threatens her. The lunatic helped herself to Drew's phone when she left it on her desk to go get food for the woman's pet. I'm hopeful it'll help our case. You have the woman's contact info on the paper we gave you from Drew's office."

Officer Fields must have been talking because Logan kept saying, "Uh-huh... Uh-huh."

He wrapped his arm around me and led me into the living room. He hung up from the officer and made another call.

"Drew got a reminder message from the person of interest, Tomas. I'm forwarding it to you now." He removed the phone from his ear so he could send the picture he'd taken of the reminder note. "I need your security guy, pronto."

I zoned in and out of his conversation, getting comfortable lying down on the couch with my head resting on Logan's lap. I closed my eyes. He played gently with my hair.

The next thing I knew, I awoke to find Logan sprawled out on the couch, passed out, with my head still resting on his lap. I reached for my phone to check the time.

"Shit." There were a ton of missed calls and text messages from my parents. They were going to kill me.

Logan stirred beneath me, stretching his arms up and over his head. "Hey. What time is it?"

"Nine thirty. My parents are going to murder me. I never went home last night, I never called them, and I should've been at work half an hour ago."

He lightly knocked on my head. "Hello? Do you not realize the severity of this situation? You can't go back to the clinic until you have someone there to protect you. We can't take a chance. I'm sure your parents will understand."

"I could say you don't know my parents very well, but in this case, you do. You also know how hardheaded they are."

"Give me the phone." He put his hand out. "Let me call them."

"No. I may as well face the music and get it over with." I hesitated, then dialed my dad's cell. Believe it or not, he was the more rational person to deal with in crisis situations. Besides, my mother was still angry at me, so I didn't want to speak with her.

Fortunately, he wasn't with a patient and answered on the second ring.

"Thanks for coming home last night, returning our calls, and showing up to work this morning. Your mother and I have been awake all night, worried sick. We have no clue where Logan lives so didn't know where to find you. He's unlisted. We want you home, *today*. You are not to see him again. Do I make myself clear?"

"Dad, please, this isn't a joke. The girl who smashed my windows got hold of my phone at the office yesterday. We think the girl responsible for this is the patient who brought that Teacup Yorkie, Logi, into the office. You know, the dog with eating issues? When I went in the back yesterday to get the food you prescribed, she snatched my phone off my desk and sent me a reminder message. She said she was going to follow me after work and threatened to do something to me.

The maniac set the message to go off after everything had already transpired. We've notified the police about it."

"What?" Concern now filled his tone.

"I logged into the office computer last night so I could give the police her contact information. They're going to do a background check and see if they find anything. Please don't let her inside the clinic. I don't care if you have to lock the door and let patients in one by one. This girl is dangerous, and I don't want her hurting you or Mom. As of now, I don't think she knows I'm your daughter. But it's better to be safe than sorry."

"For heaven's sake. What the hell kind of mess have you gotten yourself into? I can't hold down the office without you. And what about your classes? Don't you have one later this afternoon?"

I nervously picked on my nails again. Logan held my hand to stop me. I flashed him a menacing scowl. The stupid ass grinned at me.

"Do you think I asked for any of this to happen?"

"To be honest, I don't think you're using your brain at all lately. You took off with Kate on her honeymoon against our wishes. You came home to inform us you're back together with Logan Trimble, who isn't the most ethical of men."

"Stop it! Stop insulting him. People change. Why can't you accept that he makes me happy?"

Logan squeezed my hand and smiled sweetly.

"I don't know. You seemed pretty happy prior to taking off with Kate. You do an outstanding job at the clinic, and you get excellent grades at school."

"Did you ever think I want more?"

"More what? What is it you feel you lack?" His sarcasm had my hand balling up into a fist.

"Please forget I said anything."

"No, I won't forget it... Mia just informed me I have a patient waiting, so I have to cut this short. I would appreciate it if you would please answer our calls and texts and let us know when you'll be coming home. I also don't want you missing class. Your mother called the insurance company this morning. We can get you a loaner until your car is repaired. In the interim, either call a service or ask Logan to take you wherever you need to go."

He disconnected the call.

"I can't stand them! And it's obvious my father can't stand the fact he can't control me like the puppet he thinks I am. I can't do it anymore."

"As I said, you're more than welcome to stay here whenever and for however long you want."

Didn't he get it? I didn't want to be in his big house without him. I wanted to be *with* him. Sadly, that wasn't an option or a possibility.

35

LOGAN

We took an uneventful shower, both of us lost in thought, and went downstairs for some necessary caffeine. Tomas sent me a text, informing me that two private security guards would be showing up to my place in about an hour's time, one for me, one for Drew.

I called Camilla to give her an update on the situation.

"I'm not happy about this situation."

No shit. Me neither. The last thing I needed was her fucking attitude. I had enough stress to deal with.

"I hear you. I'm not jumping up and down for joy about it either. We have to catch this woman, Camilla. We can't be dealing with this insanity when we're back on tour. Break is over in a week."

"Trust me, I know that all too well.

By the way, I played Drew's song for one of the record execs at your label."

"And?"

My heart pounded. Camilla's reply would carry a shitload of weight.

"He loved it! So much so, the label wants to buy and record it. They also want to know if she has anything else."

"You're kidding me?"

Drew's eyes brightened at my transformation. I had the hugest fucking grin in the universe on my face. She put her hand out in question.

I held up a finger so she'd give me a minute while Camilla continued to fill me in on the details.

"I'd like to speak with Drew directly to give her more specifics."

"You got it. I'll have her get in touch with you after we meet with the security team."

"You have a good ear, Logan."

"No?"

"Okay, smartass. You did good. I'm excited to see what happens with her song and any others she might have."

"So am I. More than you can imagine."

I disconnected the call, climbing out of my skin with elation.

"What is it?" Drew wore a big smile even though she had no clue my conversation with Camilla had anything to do with her. Still, seeing her look anything but sad lit me up inside.

"Come with me into the living room."

"What's going on?"

"Come with me." I took her hand and led her over to the sofa where we both sat. "Remember when I told you Joey and I had dinner and played pool on Sunday night?" She nodded. "Well, I left out the part about us hanging out with our manager, Camilla. I know I went behind your back, but I also knew it was your chance of a lifetime. I didn't want you to miss out on it."

She furrowed her brows. "What're you talking about? Miss out on what?"

"I played Camilla your song."

She covered her mouth, staring at me with wide eyes. "You what?"

"You hadn't given me an answer, and Camilla has meetings with music execs all week. I didn't want you to lose out on your song getting into the right hands. I asked her to shop your song around, and guess what? Our band's label wants to buy the song from you. They're also interested in hearing what else you've got." She stared at me, frozen. She blinked. "Drew, did you hear me?"

She snapped out of whatever shock she'd gone into. "Are you kidding me?"

Those were the exact words I had said to Camilla.

"No, baby. I would never kid you about something so wonderful. Camilla wants you to call her, so you can get the ball rolling. Do you realize what this means?" She shook her head, still visibly stunned. "If the label accepted and approved of your first song, it means they'll probably want others from you as well. Do you know how much money can be made in songwriting?"

She remained silent.

"If your song takes off, you won't have to worry about living under your parents' roof anymore. Joey and Dani make a fortune writing our songs."

"Oh my gosh!" She leaped into my lap and hugged me. So much for her silence. "I don't know how I'll ever be able to thank you. I have no clue how any of this works. Oh my God! I'm so excited. I can't breathe." She climbed off me, spread her legs wide, and bent forward, resting her head between them, taking slow, deep breaths.

It felt good to give her good news amidst all this chaos.

"I don't think I can speak to Camilla in my current mental state," she said between hyperventilated breaths. She spoke with her head tilted downward toward the floor, her voice somewhat muffled. "I mean, who will sing my song? I hope I don't have to. You know I can't sing in front of people. And they won't make me play for anyone live, will they? No. No. No." She shook her head. "You know how I feel about doing that."

She rambled on and on. I couldn't help but laugh.

"No, you won't have to audition the song for music execs. They've already heard it and accepted it. I do want you to speak with Joey and Dani, though, before signing a contract to make sure you don't get screwed. Although Camilla is a tough cookie when it comes to the biz, and we also have an excellent entertainment lawyer who doesn't take any shit. Between all of them, I'm sure you'll get what you deserve for the song. If you choose not to sell it, you'll earn royalties on sales, no matter which artist records it. You'll have to speak to Camilla about specifics. I'm not exactly sure what they're offering. She'll be able to fill you in on all that."

"Oh my God! I can't believe this!" She sat upright with a shit-eating grin. She jumped on my lap again. "You, Logan Trimble, are something." She kissed me.

"As are you, babe." I considered her to be more than something. Try the love of my life. She always had been and always would be.

I traced her lips with my tongue, eagerly sinking it inside her mouth to be greeted by hers.

Drew hauled up my T-shirt. I raised my arms so she could get it over my head. She tossed it on the couch. I did the same with the T-shirt she sported, one of mine, since she didn't have any fresh clothing to wear.

I flicked my tongue against her hard nipple. She moaned. I cupped her soft flesh, enveloping her areola, sucking on it, delighting in it. She had the primo amount of pink, the perfect sized nipples, and I had seen many in my day.

She danced against my raging hard-on. The confines of my denims didn't provide much breathing room for my poor cock. The suckers needed to take a hike. I shifted her off me, into a reclining position on the sofa.

I unsnapped and unzipped my denims, kicking them off. She did the same with the sweatpants I'd lent her. They were the only thing that fit her small frame, since they had a drawstring.

Her eyes glistened; lust, possibly love, filling them. I preferred to go with the latter. I for one felt that strong feeling toward her.

I kissed my way up her legs, stopping above the knee. I spread her legs wider, kissing her inner thighs, the crease on the side of her pussy. I lifted her hood and licked her clit. We didn't require foreplay, the sucker already erect, the area swollen. I flattened my tongue, bringing it up and down in a variety of patterns, only to finish with her clit, teasing but retreating whenever I sensed her body climbing.

In and out, my thumb pumped her. She dug her hands into my hair, gripping it, her thighs shaking.

"Right there... Please... Don't stop."

No worries. I had no intention of stopping. My cock was in some serious need of release as well. I would have to get it involved pretty fucking soon.

My thumb got replaced with a finger. I circled her clit, allowing my tongue to go to town again.

She convulsed underneath me. I continued to feast on her, never able to get enough, never feeling sated.

I kissed her belly button, and moved upward, ending where I started, with her breast, teasing her by tugging her nipple between my teeth.

She reached down and lugged me on top of her. "Make love to me."

"With pleasure."

She spread her legs. I probed her entrance before heading in.

I rested on my elbows, taking in the beauty of Drew, her eyes heavy, trying to focus on mine without much success. I swiped her damp hair off her face.

The intensity of our stare became stronger the faster I moved.

The back of her hand glided over my cheek. She smiled. I brushed my lips against hers. My heart pounded. I perspired like I'd run a marathon. I had so much pent-up energy, both good and bad, over everything that had gone down the last few days. It finally had a chance to release itself. But I allowed it to do so in a gradual manner, not in the mood for a quick fuck. My head and cock were on two different pages reaching for the same finish line. Not only was my cock getting satisfaction but my head and heart were as well. Every part of me happy.

Drew wrapped her legs around my waist. I kissed her neck,

nipped her silky skin, up to her ear. I took her earlobe between my teeth.

She curled her arm around my neck, snaking her fingers into my hair and fisting it.

Our bodies became slick with sweat. Her pelvis met mine thrust for thrust, the two of us perfectly synchronized in our movements.

Things became more forceful, but still, I didn't consider it fucking. I claimed her mouth, my tongue finding hers, dancing with it to the rhythm our bodies played.

She reached for my ass. I reached for hers, underneath it. I tilted her pelvis, giving my cock the perfect angle to hit her where it mattered the most.

"Logan..."

Pressure rose in my dick, the feel of her skin surrounding mine with no barriers the icing on the cake.

My mind shut down. No thoughts, only sensations overtaking me, a sense of sheer love and admiration for the woman beneath me. My body stiffened over hers, going numb for a few seconds, as I released myself into her.

She dug her fingers into my ass, holding it in place. I buried myself inside her as she too found her sweet release, shattering underneath me, her pussy clamping down on my cock.

"Logan!"

My pace slowed. I collapsed on top of her, breathing heavily. Her warm breath blew against my cheek.

We remained still for quite some time until I raised my head and looked into her eyes. "I love you, Drew." The words slipped out.

Her eyes widened. A stream of tears leaked out. I tensed, unsure if I had said the wrong thing. She placed her hand on my cheek.

"I love you too, Logan. I never stopped."

Well, fuck.

I kissed her, a passionate kiss to express my feelings toward her.

The ringing of the doorbell startled both of us.

"Shit. It's the security guys. For a minute I forgot they were coming." I jumped off her and stumbled to my feet.

She hurriedly sat up. "I'm going to clean up in the bathroom while you greet them."

"I think I should clean up to, babe. My mouth could use a little mouthwash action." I winked.

Her mouth fell open. "That's disgusting."

"No, you're fucking delectable, but I still don't believe in sharing." She blushed.

On our way to the bathroom,

I shouted toward the door that I'd be right there.

36

DREW

*L*ogan left the bathroom to answer the door. I hung tight for a breather. So many feelings and thoughts consumed me. I couldn't believe he had given my song to his manager, more than grateful he'd taken it upon himself to solicit the song on my behalf. I couldn't wait to call Camilla to find out the next steps. I prayed I'd be able to move out of my parents' house. I didn't want to jump the gun and get ahead of myself by thinking about the million possibilities and paths my life could take as a result of the gift he had given me.

Logan, the love of my love. He'd professed his love to me. Man, his confession had put me over the edge. I was so happy, giddy. Nothing could bring me down, absolutely nothing.

With my elated state intact,

I entered the living room to see two bodybuilder-type guys sitting in the loveseat across from Logan. They made him appear small, and he was anything but.

"Here she is." Logan gestured toward me. "Drew, this is Tyler and Steve. They work with Tomas, the security guard who helps with the band. Steve here has agreed to keep an eye on you while Tyler's going to hang with me."

Taking them in, I gave a slight wave. I didn't know their backstories. Tyler wore a dress shirt and slacks. He probably had the shirt custom-made to fit the Hulk-sized arms he had going. Damn, they were scary big. I certainly wouldn't mess with the guy.

Steve's arms were equally impressive. Both men were clean-cut, hair gelled, slicked back. I didn't know what I had expected. Maybe guys sporting wife-beater tanks and basketball shorts. These guys were totally professional.

Logan continued to make arrangements with them. I sat next to him on the couch and listened. The band's label agreed to cover Tyler. Logan agreed to compensate Steve, which upset me. I didn't want Logan shelling out money on my behalf, but I also didn't have enough dough to afford a bodyguard myself.

We discussed the plan. Basically, any time I had plans to go anywhere, I'd have to let Steve know in advance, so he could come with me. The only place I could roam freely would be in my house. I had to fight on that one. I knew my parents would never allow a strange man to hang out in our home for hours on end.

Both men would be staying at Logan's place, since he had several guest bedrooms. Turns out Tyler and Steve were retired marines. They both carried concealed weapons.

The reality of the situation hit me hard. This reeked of the kind of stuff I read about in gossip magazines or heard about on the evening news. In my wildest dreams, I would've never figured me, of all people, would require personal security to protect me from a stalker.

After our meeting, I called Camilla. I put the phone on speaker mode, so Logan could hear the conversation. I knew nothing about the music business.

"Drew, I wish we could have this discussion in person, but under the present circumstances, this will have to do. Legendary Records, the company that represents Steam, loves your song. You have several options. You can sell it to them, which means you'll be relinquishing all rights once the contract is signed. Or you can have creative say in the process. I don't know how much they'll be willing to give an unknown but at least you'll still have rights to the song and any profits it brings in in the future."

Camilla sounded like a tiger but one I definitely wanted to protect me.

I had no clue whatsoever about right from wrong regarding the process.

"If you ask me..."

Which I didn't but was glad she continued to speak because I had so many questions swirling around in my mind I couldn't concentrate.

"I've always advised Joey and Dani, the main songwriters for Steam, to keep the rights to their songs. If you sign off from them, the record label can do with them what they will. You may not approve of the outcome, and your word will mean nothing."

Logan nodded in agreement with her words.

"Okay. Then I'll do that."

Logan would never steer me wrong and keep my best interest at heart. Deciding to keep my song gave me a sense of comfort, to know it would forever be tied to me. My songs were my babies. I wasn't ready to let go of them so quickly.

"Excellent decision. Do you have any other songs you could forward me?"

Logan had only recorded the one. The others were still raw.

He looked at me for an answer. I nodded.

"She does. But you'll have to give me time to work some magic in my studio."

"Then do it and send it to me. I've spoken to Mr. Epstein, the band's attorney, and he has agreed to read through whatever contract Legendary Records offers you. Being you are a close friend of Logan's..." He and I exchanged glances. I guess she didn't know the status of our relationship. I now did. He loved me. I loved him. "He has agreed to take you on as a client, out of professional courtesy."

"Thanks, Camilla." Logan spoke with sincerity.

. . .

The enormity of this event became difficult to process. The entire situation had come out of nowhere, so much happening and so fast.

The conversation with Camilla lasted for quite a while.

When we hung up, I gave Logan a big smile.

"Come on. We have a lot of work to do. Let's go lay down some kick ass tracks."

Yay! I couldn't wait to record more songs.

"I need to go home after we're done, though, so I can speak with my parents."

"No problem. Give me your phone. I'll put Steve's contact information in it."

The private security escort would start later today. If I left my parents' house, Steve would come with me.

The two men agreed to meet back at Logan's at six in the evening to discuss the touring schedule. Tyler would be staying with Logan until law enforcement caught his stalker. Logan didn't want to take any chances. Neither did I.

This time I felt more comfortable in the studio.

The name of the song I chose to record was "*End It*," a song I had penned for him and one of my favorites. He hadn't heard it yet.

He got me situated with the guitar I'd used during our previous session. I strummed a few chords to warm up and he busied himself with the equipment on his desk and around the room. Content everything was to his liking, he put on and adjusted my headphones.

"You ready, or do you want to practice some more?"

He had such excitement in his expression. It made me happy to see his enthusiasm over something that had nothing to do with him and benefited me. Well, other than the lyrics, which he hadn't heard yet.

"No. I think I'm good."

"All right. "*End It*." Take one." He gestured for me to begin.

First I laid down the music. Once we agreed with the sound, I recorded the vocals.

End it, end it,
Walk away
I'm not going to join you
In the game you want to play.

Send him, send him
On his merry way
I deserve so much more
It doesn't matter anyway.

Tears slipped down my cheeks because my feelings related to these lyrics had changed tremendously. I didn't want to end things with Logan all those years ago and never wanted to again. I also had no intention of leaving him. Tears pooled in his eyes as well.

Down the path of least resistance
Walk down the one that feels right inside
Keep my truth and do what's right
I will walk tall, hold my head up with pride.

Be who I am
Be who I want
It's all in the palm of my hand
Ain't nobody going to hold me back

FAITH STARR

I've now got the power to stand

This part I agreed with. I wanted to be my own person without my parents or anybody else, for that matter, holding me back, something my mom and dad tried to do for whatever insane reasons.

My tears ceased, and I stood taller, feeling empowered by my lyrics.

The past is behind me
The future's ahead
Today I know who I am
I'll now forge my own path
Without you instead.

Down the path of least resistance
Walking down the one that feels right inside
Keeping my truth and doing what's right
I'm walking tall and with pride

Sometimes sorry isn't good enough
To take away someone's pain
I look to you and thank you,
For all that I have gained.

Logan had more than made up for his mistake. I believed in forgiveness and in giving second chances, in contrast to my parents. Logan deserved that, and I was grateful I had given him the opportunity to prove through his actions that he had, in fact, changed. And for the better. Still the man I forever loved but a lot wiser.

Down the path of least resistance
Walking down the one that feels right inside
Keeping my truth and doing what's right
I'm walking tall and with pride

Down the path of least resistance
With my confidence fully intact
Keeping my truth and doing what's right
I'm never going back

Finished, I set the guitar down, removed the headphones, and went to Logan, sitting next to him by the computer desk.

"Who would've thought me breaking your heart would make you millions?" His eyes were still wet.

"From your mouth to God's ears, but that's not what I'm in this for."

"I know, babe. I know how it feels to do something you love. Getting paid to do it is just icing on the cake." He smiled, but I sensed sadness as he shifted his attention toward the computer screen.

I turned his head toward mine. "Logan, it's in the past. I want to move forward with you."

A tear slipped out of his eye. I dried it.

"I want that more than you can imagine."

"I know." I nodded. "I know."

37

LOGAN

When we arrived at Drew parents' house, I got a feeling of déjà vu. I used to visit it so frequently years ago. I wanted to inspect it, make sure all was copacetic, before leaving her alone.

"I'm going to finish working on your song and meet with the security guys. Let me know what happens with your parents. If you want to escape, all you need to do is call me and I'll come get you at a second's notice."

She squeezed my hand. "I might have to take you up on that offer."

"It's on the table. Come. Let's go check out the house."

Everything looked clean, but it didn't make me feel any better leaving her by herself.

"I don't know, babe. I have a bad feeling. Maybe I should hang out with you for a while."

"I'll be fine. Besides, my parents will be home within the hour. You've checked every nook and cranny in this house. I feel perfectly safe."

"You sure?"

She hugged me. "Yes. Thank you for watching out for me."

"I always will."

She touched my cheek. "And I will for you as well."

"Remember, I'm a phone call or text away."

She nodded and walked me to the door.

"Promise me you'll stay tight until your folks return. Don't go outside for any reason."

"I promise." She crossed her heart.

She waved me off, blowing me a kiss, then closing the door. My gut clenched.

At least later I knew she'd have security watching over her. That gave me some solace.

Back home I worked on Drew's song for hours. It came together brilliantly, the melody phenomenal. She had another hit, a masterful songwriter to say the least. I hoped no one would ever find out who the two songs had been written about, or I might start getting hate mail instead of fan mail.

After eating dinner with Steve and Tyler and discussing the details of their security and my upcoming tour, I isolated myself in my studio to continue mixing the song.

Joey, Trevor, and Dani were ecstatic when I informed them about Drew's song via telephone hours later.

I invited them over the following day for a jam session.

Maybe things were changing for the better. We had security measures in place, I had no doubt Drew's songs would take off, and she'd told me she loved me. That topped everything. I only prayed her irrational parents wouldn't take the thrill of this news away from her.

Just when

I began typing her a text, my cell rang.

"Hello?"

"Mr. Trimble, this is Officer Fields. We met last night when you filed a claim against a fan stalking you."

"And?" My heart pounded. Maybe they'd caught the psychopath.

"I'm calling to inform you that a woman broke into Ms. Sanders' home this evening and assaulted her."

What? My heart fell into the pit of my stomach. I grabbed onto the wall for support, my legs like jelly.

"Is Drew okay?" That's all I cared about, my number-one priority right now.

"She was alert but confused when the paramedics took her to the hospital."

Paramedics? Hospital?

What the fuck?

"She rode to the hospital in an ambulance? What happened to her?"

"We're not sure yet. We're still trying to gather pertinent information. It would be helpful if you could come down to the station to see if you can identify the intruder we found at the scene."

"I need to see Drew first. Did anyone else get hurt?"

"No, it doesn't appear as such, other than the suspect. She's been cleared by the paramedics and will be taken to the station to begin booking procedures."

Fuck!

"Is Dr. Sanders available to speak on the phone?" Maybe he could provide more information than this guy offered.

"He's currently speaking with an officer."

Triple fuck! I swiped my hand through my hair. I couldn't breathe. A wave of lightheadedness had me sitting my ass on the couch again where I hyperventilated. Yup, I was tough as nails at the moment. Not.

"I'll meet you at the station." I disconnected the call without mentioning it would be after I saw Drew at the hospital. I had to see for myself the extent of her injuries.

"What's going on?" Tyler asked.

Shit. I had forgotten he was in the room. No doubt he'd witnessed me disintegrating in front of his very eyes.

I leaned forward, rested my elbows on my knees and buried my face in my hands, similar to what Drew had done just a few short hours ago. I inhaled slowly, exhaling in the same precise manner.

Once I got my bearings, I filled both men in on the situation.

Dammit!

I had forgotten to ask which hospital they took Drew to. There were only two local hospitals, one better and bigger, the other not a top pick. I would assume the paramedics brought her to the larger of the two. *Whatever.* Even if I had to drive to both, that's what I'd do. And I wouldn't stop searching until I found her.

"Let me drive you to the hospital." Tyler already had his keys in his hand.

"<u>Us,</u>" <u>Steve chimed in.</u> "I'm coming with."

Their protective services weren't required anymore, but I didn't rebut their request, knowing it wasn't safe for me to be behind the wheel in my current state of worry.

"Thanks, guys."

We drove to the major hospital first. The receptionist in the emergency room wouldn't give me any information regarding Drew, stating it violated patient privacy or some shit.

I argued with her, informing her I was Drew's boyfriend. She shook her head, not budging whatsoever with her decision.

There had to be a solution, and I'd find it.

"I demand to see Drew Sanders!"

That one wasn't it. The bitch threatened to call security if I didn't keep my voice down and stop arguing with her. Fuck her. She hadn't heard anything yet.

Another nurse with a softer demeanor approached.

The nice nurse's eyes went wide with recognition when she saw me. She covered her mouth.

"Oh my God, you're Logan Trimble of Steam, aren't you?"

"In the flesh. Listen, I could seriously use your help." Sometimes I loved playing the celebrity card, this being one of them.

"Anything. I'm a *huge* fan." She bounced up and down, giddy with joy.

"How about this, you help me find my girlfriend, and I'll get you a personal meet and greet with the entire band plus backstage passes and front-row seats."

Her jaw fell open.

"Carol," the other nurse snapped. "You know you're not allowed to give out patient information."

"Give it a rest, Ursula. I'm not giving the man her Social Security number."

You tell her, Carol!

The evil nurse shook her head in disappointment. I stood there, tall and proud. Ursula typed on her keyboard in a huff, focusing on her monitor instead of us.

My new buddy, Carol, identified Drew's name in the system and sent me on my merry way.

Mrs. Sanders eyes widened in disbelief when I entered Drew's room, the bed empty. *Oh no, where is she? What happened to her?*

My heart raced double time. I had forgotten her mother was in the room until she spoke. I had been too deep in thoughts about Drew.

"Logan, what're you doing here? How did you know where we were?" Her tone was harsh, her eyes swollen and red from crying.

"Why do you think I'm here? How's Drew? Where is she?"

"She was a lot better until you came back into the picture."

Screw her.

She shifted her attention away from me. The woman despised me. I felt it as much now, if not more, than I had years ago. Back then she doubted my music career, called it a dead-end road, and felt Drew could do better. Guess she'd been wrong. Bitch.

"I'm not here to argue. I just want to know how Drew's doing."

"I don't have to tell you a thing. In fact, I think I'll call security and have you ushered out."

"Drew's not a minor. She can make the call if she wants to see me or not. I'm going to place bets on the fact she will. So please stop with the threats."

"She's still my daughter and as her mother, my job is to protect her, no matter what age she is. So *you* can stop with the threats. Drew's life has turned to shambles ever since you've come back into the picture, with this being the final straw. My poor daughter got clocked over the head, broke her arm, and got dragged through our house by some crazed fan of yours. This is all *your* doing." She pointed at me, giving me the evil eye.

Holy shit. All that had happened to Drew? I swallowed hard, guilt consuming me. Yet I wasn't the person who'd committed those horrific acts.

"This is not my doing, and you know it."

"What I do know is you broke my daughter's heart years ago because you couldn't keep your zipper closed, and now here you are again, same scenario, different day."

"What're you talking about?"

"The woman who broke into my house claimed you two are involved and said you slept with her. You should've heard the things she said to the police. Ugh, I'm disgusted. Please leave." She shooed me away with the back of her hand.

"That woman has been stalking me. She's crazy. You can't believe a word that comes out of her mouth. Wait a second, why am I trying to explain myself to you? I don't owe you a God-damn thing. I'm here for Drew."

"I don't care who you're here for, but you're not seeing my daughter. Stay away from her. She's been through enough. Every time you show up, you bring harm with you and hurt her."

"I think you're the crazy one, Mrs. Sanders. Here's the deal. I love Drew and there's not a thing you can do about it. If I were you, I'd start getting used to the idea of me being around more. The sooner you accept it, the better things will be between you and Drew."

She gritted her teeth, her pupils flared, as did her nostrils. "You don't intimidate me. Maybe your fans and groupies bow down to you, but I won't and never will. My daughter is getting an X-ray right now because one of your ex-lovers chased her down. She doesn't need or deserve a man loving her who can't keep his dick in his pants."

It took everything I had to reel in my anger. What a fucking nerve she had to judge me. She knew nothing about me.

"I told you, I'm not going to argue with you. I merely wanted to check on Drew before heading to the police station to see if I can identify the woman who attacked her."

"She'll probably be in testing for a while, so you may as well leave. There's clearly not enough room in here for the two of us, and I don't plan on going anywhere."

Fucking bitch. I knew she wouldn't call me with information regarding Drew either.

"I'll be back."

I returned to the waiting room. I was powerless over the situation, couldn't do shit about it until Drew had her tests done, so figured I would visit after I took care of police business.

"Let's go," I advised Tyler and Steve.

A short time later, Tyler dropped me off in front of the station and parked the car. A woman at the front desk escorted me to Officer Fields' office.

"Have you heard any news on Ms. Sanders' condition?"

"Sadly, no. She's still having tests done." I sighed in defeat.

. . .

"Very well. I'm going to show you some pictures on my computer screen. Please tell me if any of the women look familiar to you."

He tapped a few buttons on his keyboard, and six pictures sprang to life. All of the women were similar in appearance: long dark hair and brown eyes.

I studied each one for several minutes, the fifth sparking recognition. I didn't know where I knew her from, but I recognized her from somewhere.

Holy shit!

It came to me.

"Do you spot someone you know?" Fields asked.

"Yes, this one right here." I pointed to the fifth picture. The woman scowled and had a bruise on her face. "She used to come watch the band perform back in our earlier days. Wow, I never thought anything of it. One night after playing, she came on to me. She ended up in my bed. I never saw her again. It's been years."

He nodded in acknowledgment, making some notes.

"Is she the woman who attacked Drew?" I didn't get this woman's motive. It had literally been years since I'd fucked her.

"She is. Her name is Liz Piper."

"Liz Piper." I thought long and hard, recalling the name. "Yes, believe it or not I remember that being her name."

He twisted his lips. I didn't give a fuck. He could judge me all he wanted. I couldn't deny I'd slept with my fair share of women.

"Did she admit to committing the crime?"

"At first, no. She claimed to be your girlfriend, and said that the two of you have had an ongoing sexual relationship. Upon further probing, she opened up and confirmed she had broken into Ms. Sanders' home with intent to cause bodily harm. She also confessed to meeting Ms. Sanders in her workplace and vandalizing her car. She stated she didn't want another woman having what's hers."

"Fuck!"

He eyed me. I put my hand up in apology.

"I want to press whatever charges I can against her."

"She will be charged with aggravated stalking, since you previously filed a claim, and she assaulted Ms. Sanders. The latter adds more severe charges. Don't you worry, Mr. Trimble, Ms. Piper will definitely serve time for her crimes."

Excellent. I sighed, relieved the police had caught the bad guy, or in this case, the bad girl. Drew and I could finally move forward. Our next cross to bear—her parents, another story altogether.

We finished up, and Tyler drove me back to the hospital, with Steve sitting in the back seat. During the ride, I

phoned Camilla to update her on the situation and texted Joey and Trevor. I wanted to keep them in the loop as well.

Drew had already been placed in a private room. Of course her parents and Kate were sitting in it when I entered. Drew slept soundly.

Christ. I gasped upon seeing her, guilt filling every fiber of my being. Her arm rested next to her side in a sling, her head was wrapped in gauze with an ice pack sitting on top, and her cheek had bruises.

Dr. Sanders got out of his chair and approached me. "Don't you think you've done enough?"

He didn't intimidate me. I had inches in height and width on the twig of a man. Not that I would ever hurt him, but still.

"How is she?" I ignored him, focusing on Kate instead because I knew she'd answer me.

Mrs. Sanders took the floor, anger seething from her pores. "How would you feel if you got hit on the head with a baseball bat, only to black out and break your arm, and let me not leave out the part where you fall unconscious to the floor? I'm sure not too good. And that's not all of it. That lunatic woman dragged Drew down the hall, unconscious with a broken arm, by her feet nonetheless, with the intention of drowning her in the bathtub. If my husband and I hadn't shown up when we did, Drew might not have been so lucky."

Kate cringed and closed her eyes, wiping tears from her cheeks. Mrs. Sanders glared at me. Dr. Sanders now stood next to her.

"What's the prognosis?" I wanted answers.

Kate interjected, cutting off Dr. Sanders. "She has a minor

concussion and a cut on the back of her head where she fell and hit the floor. It's stapled together. She'll have to go to an orthopedist to get her arm casted once she's released."

Relief crashed through me. I held on to the edge of the bed to steady myself because the enormity of the situation hit me like a ton of bricks.

"They're keeping her overnight for observation. If all goes well, she can leave in the morning. I'm sure she'll get in touch with you. That is, if she wants to." Mrs. Sanders spoke snidely.

"No, I think her phone broke during the accident," Kate informed me.

"I'll come by and see her at your place, then."

"No, you won't. You're done with our daughter. You're not welcome in our home," Dr. Sanders replied.

"You can't keep me away from Drew. I love her, and she loves me."

"Like hell I can't keep you away from her. I'll get a restraining order if I have to." Dr. Sanders stood in front of me again.

"For what, loving someone?"

"Just get out and leave my family alone, Logan." Mrs. Sanders stepped closer to me, tears falling down her cheeks.

Fuck, my head ached. One would think I had gotten clocked over the head with a bat.

"Lo...gan..." Drew whispered.

"Baby, I'm here." I moved around Dr. and Mrs. Sanders and ran to the side of the bed, taking Drew's hand in mine, holding our joined hands against my heart.

"Now you've woken her." Mrs. Sanders sneered at me in disgust. "Drew has to rest. She shouldn't be upset right now, which is exactly what you're doing to her. She's been through a very traumatic experience, all thanks to you. I think it's best if you let her family take care of her tonight." She rushed to the other side of the bed.

Her parents didn't fucking get it.

"I'm not going anywhere unless Drew says otherwise."

Everyone turned their attention to Drew. She winced in pain as she shifted on the bed. I wanted to stroke her hair but didn't want to hurt her. Her bruises were on full display. Her suffering pained me even more.

"Don't go." She weakly squeezed my hand.

"I'm right here with you, baby," I assured.

"Drew, you need your rest." Her mother spoke through gritted teeth. "There are too many people in this cramped room. I think it would be best for Drew if everyone left. I'll stay here with her." She now focused on Drew. "You can speak with Logan when you're home and feeling better."

Drew swallowed, briefly closing her eyes. Her hand had no strength to it. Her eyes went to mine. "Stay."

"Drew!" Mrs. Sanders admonished.

"It's not good for her to get upset, Mrs. Sanders." I couldn't help but spit her words back in her face.

"I've had it with you, you bastard!" Dr. Sanders sprung toward me with his fist in the air. I moved swiftly enough to prevent it from making contact with my face. The women in the room gasped. Drew started crying, as did Kate, who ran out of the room. She returned with a nurse.

"What in heaven's name is going on in here? Ms. Sanders should be resting."

How many more fucking times did I have to hear that recommendation? I knew it already!

Dr. Sanders stood in front of me, his chest rising and falling rapidly.

"You might want to rethink that restraining order because I could swear you just attempted to punch me." My own chest heaved with a surge of adrenaline.

"Screw you, Logan."

He stormed away from me.

"I'm sorry, but I'm going to have to ask all of you to leave this instant," the nurse ordered.

Standing next to the door, she gestured for all of us to exit. My feet remained glued in place. I didn't intend to go anywhere.

"Excuse me, sir, but that means you too." She motioned to me.

"I'm not going anywhere," I advised.

"I want him to stay," Drew whispered.

"Very well. I want everyone else to please leave and let this patient rest. If I find any of you in here again tonight, I'll have security escort you out," the nurse warned.

Dr. Sanders turned toward Drew. "You better start thinking about consequences of your actions, young lady. This conversation is far from over." He careened out the door with Ms. Sanders following closely behind.

Kate looked at both of us and mouthed, "I'm sorry."

The nurse closed the door, leaving me and Drew alone in the room. I wanted to hold her in my arms and console her but hesitated, too afraid I'd hurt her.

Instead, I sat on the edge of the bed and held her hand, my presence all I could offer her.

38

DREW

My head pounded, my ribs ached, and my arm throbbed. The rest of my body felt sore from head to toe. My throat was bone-dry.

"I'm sorry for my parents' behav..."

Logan took offense to my apology, jumping in before I could finish my thought.

"Are you kidding me? I'm sorry all of this happened. I don't give a shit if your parents don't approve of me. I don't need their say-so, and to tell you the truth, you don't either. I know I'm not one who should speak about family members sticking together, being I barely speak to my parents, but from what I gather, your father has you on a tight leash. When are you going to cut the cord? If money is the only thing holding you back, I'll help you out."

His words rang true. I closed my eyes. "I know. It was awful, Logan." I didn't touch his comment about helping me out financially.

"You don't have to talk about it now. Like the nurse and everyone else said, you should rest. But I'm here if you do want to talk about it."

Thoughts about the horrific experience consumed me. Whenever I closed my eyes, that evil woman's face appeared.

"After you left, I washed up. I ate and chilled in my room. My dad called to tell me he and my mom were going to stop and grab a bite to eat before coming home. I waited, knowing an argument would ensue when they arrived. Out of nowhere, glass shattered. I ran to the other side of the house to check it out, and the next thing I knew, something hit me on the head and I blacked out. I woke up on a stretcher with paramedics around me. A girl was screaming in the background, saying she was your girlfriend and that she loves you."

My throat felt so parched. "Can you please give me some water? It hurts too much to move."

He reached for my cup and put the straw to my lips. I drank some of the chilled liquid, feeling a cold sensation as it slid down my esophagus and entered my stomach.

"Was she the stalker?" I took slow, deep breaths, the pain in my head excruciating. Why couldn't the doctor give me something stronger for pain? I'd have to remember to ask when the nurse returned to check on me.

"Yes." He took a deep breath. "The cops arrested her. I agreed to press charges, and once you're feeling better, you can do the same for assault and battery as well as breaking and entering, since she broke into your parents' place."

"This is horrible. I can't believe she did this to me."

"Drew, I feel terrible. This is all my fault and I don't know how to help you." He swiped his hand through his hair, his eyes filled with the same amount of pain I'm sure mine revealed, if not worse.

"It's not your fault. And you being here helps me, in so many ways."

He smiled, tenderness filling his expression.

"Are you sure you don't want to sleep?"

"I don't think I can right now, my thoughts are too wired." I sighed.

"Fuck." He faced the cold white wall. "Maybe your parents are right. I've been nothing but trouble to you. At first I argued against your mother's claims that I was messing up your life but seeing you in such bad shape… I'm starting to think she's right."

He rose and walked to the foot of my bed.

"Logan, the only part of me that doesn't hurt right now is my heart. If you walk out that door, it'll shatter into a million pieces." He couldn't destroy me again. He just couldn't.

"Me looking at you in such pain has my heart shattered into a million pieces. Here you are lying in a bed with a broken arm, bruised ribs, a fucking mesh thing around your head, a concussion, and God knows what else. And it's all because of me. This is my fucking life!"

He threw his arms up in frustration.

"It'll be fine. We'll work it out." I'd beg him to stay if I had to.

"It won't be fine. It's not fair for me to bring you into the craziness of my world. It's fucking selfish, if I'm speaking honestly. And I can promise you, the apeshit behavior of this fan won't be a one-time episode. There will be more lunatic fans. Of that I can assure you. I'd never be able to live with myself if something were to happen to you because of me."

"You've hired security. We'll be more cautious." My heart ached more than the rest of my body now.

"Indefinitely? It's not fair for you to have to change your entire life because of mine."

"I want to, Logan. I love you." I reached my hand out for him.

"I love you too, more than you can ever imagine which is why I have to leave you right now. Please know I'm doing it to protect you. For once, I'm thinking of someone else's best interest instead of my own. I love you enough to make sure you never have to go through something so horrific ever again on my account. The only way to guarantee that is to make a clean break. I'll make sure Camilla takes good care of you and gets you the best deal she can for your songs."

"Don't do this…"

He shook his head, holding his hand up to cut me off. I had lost. He had already made up his mind. A tear slipped down my cheek.

"I was a fool to think I could have it all. I'm rarely in one place.

How's that going to work for us? I'm leaving in a week for several months. What will you do, sit idly by and wait for me to come home only for me to go right back on the road again? That's bullshit. And I don't want to have to constantly worry that some psychotic fan is going to chase after you again."

Tears fell from his eyes. "Please remember you'll always own my heart."

"Logan, please don't go." My voice gained strength. He wouldn't take hold of my extended hand.

"It's what's best."

He shuffled out of the room.

I closed my eyes and cried my heart out, the one now broken into a million pieces for the second time by Logan Trimble.

39

LOGAN

*L*ike a motherfucker, I left her alone. I could promise it hurt me a hell of a lot more than it hurt her for me to walk out of her hospital room. With each passing second the aching in my gut intensified until it blossomed into the most excruciating pain I had ever felt. I had tried everything in my power to keep Drew safe and make things good for her. But I failed.

More than anything else, I wanted her to be happy, but I came to believe I couldn't be the source of that joy, especially after witnessing her mental and physical condition. My God, one might think a Mack truck had driven over her.

Fuck! All I seemed to do was wreak havoc on her heart. I couldn't continue to do so.

Tyler and Steve drove me home. I told them they could take off, thanking them for their services. In all truth, I didn't want anyone in my house. All I wanted was to take every fragile tchotchke and throw it against a fucking wall.

Inside my studio, I grabbed my guitar and strummed it, playing it the only thing I knew of that would keep me sane. I ran through every song on our set list. I played until my fingers screamed in agony.

I played until I couldn't strum another chord. Then I played some more.

I pulled an all-nighter. Trevor and Joey showed up around eleven.

"What the fuck happened to you? You look like shit, man." Joey eyeballed me with concern.

I flipped him the bird and took off for the kitchen to help myself to a bottle of water from the fridge.

"Seriously, what's up?" he asked, the two of them following me.

I gave them the abridged version.

"You walked out on her *again*?" Joey puckered his lips, shaking his head. "Ooh, that's harsh."

"No, what's harsh is her parents blaming me for everything that went down as well as bringing her grief. What's harsh is the fact that we're leaving town in a week, and I don't know when I'll be able to spend quality time with her again. It's a no-win situation." I took a swig from my bottle.

"Why're you being so dramatic? Make it work." Trevor had a hint of pissed-offness to his tone.

"That's easy for you to say. Your girlfriend works with us. The same goes for you." I pointed to Joey.

"Then bring Drew along too. She can continue writing songs on the bus while we tour."

"What the fuck are you even talking about, Trevor?" I shook my head at his asinine suggestion.

"You heard me. I'd rather have a bus full of women than seeing you so beaten down. Honestly, dude, you need to take a look in the mirror."

"Trust me, if I look as bad as I feel, I'd rather not."

"Listen, you know I'm always straight up with you. I have to say you royally fucked-up this time, brother," Joey said bitterly.

"I can't hurt her any more than I already have. Her mother was right, Drew's been through enough."

Joey got in my face. "She's fucking been through enough because of you. And now you're hurting her and putting her through the wringer *again*. How could you leave her at her worst? Drew's the best thing that ever happened to you, and you know it. She's the reason you fucked anything with two legs and a pussy, tossing women aside, pretending or denying they even had feelings. All of it so you wouldn't develop any toward another woman and have to go through the pain you felt when you lost her. Fuck, man!"

"Who the fuck are you to judge me? You chased every piece of ass that presented itself to you before Teva came into the picture!"

"You're right but I wised up and realized what I had in front of me and did whatever the fuck I could to make things work with her. You forget I was with you the night all that shit went down years ago. All of us were. And all of us were there when you raged like a lunatic for months on end because of the mistake you'd made."

I charged to the living room and dropped down on the couch. My head pounded like Trevor beating on his fucking drums. I closed my eyes and rubbed my brow, hoping, praying it would relieve some of the tension building inside my head.

Joey's piece of shit rant followed me into the living room.

"I don't think you'll recover this time around."

"What the fuck does that mean?" I gave him a death stare.

"The guilt will continue to feed on you like a parasite."

"Ah! I'm so fucking stupid!" I got up and paced back and forth in front of the couch. Joey and Trevor watched.

"I'll second that." Trevor put in his two unwanted cents.

"Fuck you, Trevor. You had the hots for Dani for fucking ever and wouldn't man up enough to admit it. So I don't want to hear your bullshit."

"At least I made the right decision in the end. You can too." He sat on the loveseat.

"She'll never forgive me after how I left her."

"You won't know unless you try."

Well, seems Joey decided to get a PhD in Psychology overnight.

At least he gave good advice. Whether I chose to follow it was another story altogether.

40

DREW

The cops showed up at the hospital in the early morning to get my statement. Things were still hazy in my mind. I told them what I remembered.

One of the officers placed his laptop on the tray table and slid it next to me.

"Ms. Sanders, I'm going to show you pictures of six women. Please tell me if you recognize any of them."

My attempt at sitting up was futile.

As soon as I saw the girl's face on the small screen, I pointed to it. I would never forget her beady eyes and how she had screamed frantically when the police cuffed her, shouting she and Logan were lovers and that they should call him to help clear her name. She'd cried, yelling that she and Logan had engaged in a one-night stand that had turned into a passionate love affair. And when I came into the picture, I ruined everything. Therefore, I deserved to die. What a crazy and delusional woman.

Two separate charges were filed against her. The first, aggravated battery, which meant she had the intent of harming me with the use of a deadly weapon. The officer advised me it was generally classified as a second-degree felony. Her punishment would be up to fifteen years in prison or fifteen years of probation and up to ten thousand dollars in fines.

Gosh, the thought alone sent chills down my spine. I was so lucky my parents had come home when they did. I didn't want to think about the alternative.

The second offense, home invasion, was a first-degree felony. That would be my primary charge against her, since it carried more weight. In addition, she'd used a weapon on me, which upped her charges and would give her a minimum sentence of sixty-six months in prison. I never wished ill on others but my hope was that she rotted in jail, the evil bitch.

My mother picked me up a few hours later. I blamed my foul mood on the pain in my body, but my heart hurt so much worse. I couldn't tell her Logan walked out on me. I wouldn't let her delight in my suffering.

Whenever I pictured his face, I saw the hurt in his eyes before he left my hospital room. How could he have left me in such a battered state, especially when I chose him over my family to stay with me? Did that not prove to him how much he meant to me?

"I made an appointment for you with an orthopedist and a neurologist. The orthopedist will see you later this afternoon, so he can cast your arm. The neurologist will see you in a few days to check your head."

It hurt too much to talk, so I listened without responding.

"I know you don't want to hear it, but you offended me and your father last night when you asked Logan to stay when I specifically offered to take care of you."

"Not now, Mom, please."

"I'm surprised he didn't offer to bring you home from the hospital." She pulled out of the hospital parking lot.

Her selfishness knew no bounds. She only tried to dig the knife deeper into an already gaping wound.

"Why are you doing this?" I had my teeth clenched so tight my jaw ached.

"Doing what?"

"Trying to manipulate me. Whatever. What's done is done. I want you to know that Logan played one of my songs for his manager, who then brought it to a music executive. His label wants to buy my song. They asked for me to send others as well."

It didn't feel as exciting saying it now, knowing Logan wouldn't be celebrating the opportunity with me. In fact, it only brought tears to my eyes.

"Don't even tell me you're giving up school for an unstable career in songwriting. Ugh. I wish you'd never run into Logan at that ranch. It makes me so darn angry. I'll have you know your father and I are not going to support you forever. You need to get a career. Kate did. It took her a while, but she found her calling. You have to do the same, Drew."

"Oh my God, do you hear yourself? I work and pay my own bills. I barely ask for a thing. If Dad paid me more, maybe I could get my own place. It's not like I'm lying around in bed all day doing nothing. I work my ass off at the clinic and take classes. You know what? I'm done trying to please the two of you. As soon as I feel better, I'm out."

"Oh stop making threats. You know you're not going anywhere."

"No, this time I mean it. You can go ahead and put an ad in the paper to hire a front-desk person at the clinic. I'll help out until you find a replacement for me. I should've made this decision months ago. Logan was right. You and Dad try to keep me on a tight leash, close to home. In my heart of hearts, I don't think you want me to get ahead and move on because then you'd have to be alone with Dad."

"How dare you say something so cruel to me."

"It's the truth. You don't think I know how miserable you are with him? Be real. The two of you fight constantly. You immersed yourself in Kate's life and whatever chaos she would bring into the house, the perfect escape for you, so you wouldn't have to dwell on your own unhappiness. Then when she got involved with Joe and settled down, you tried to get overinvolved in my life. I can't take it anymore. I'm suffocating. I couldn't figure out what I wanted to do with my life, but deep down I always knew I wanted more, to see more, to do more. There's an entire world waiting for me to explore. In my current situation, I'll never have the opportunity to see what's out there for me. Logan was a blessing in disguise. If I can sell one song, I can sell another. That's my passion, writing. And I'm going to stop being afraid to follow my dreams. Can you say the same?"

"I'm warning you. Don't bring up my theater days."

"Why not? You wanted to be an actress. Dad considered it to be a pipe dream, similar to your view of Logan when you first found out he wanted to be a professional musician. You tried to brainwash me into believing the same thing, that he'd never succeed or amount to anything. Well, you know what? Logan followed his dreams and made it. You didn't."

She slammed on the breaks, causing me to be thrown forward. The seatbelt slammed against my ribs. I yelped in pain.

She pulled over to the side of the road.

"You deserve to be in pain. I can't believe you're trying to put all this on me. For once, take responsibility for yourself."

"Why don't you do the same, Mom? If you don't mind, please drop me off at Kate's."

"She's at work. Who's going to take you to your doctor appointment?"

"I'll take a car service."

"Stop acting like a child."

"I'm serious. Please drive me to Kate's. I have a key to her place."

"Don't do this, Drew. Some mistakes can't be forgiven."

"According to you, *no* mistakes can be forgiven."

"I'm going to pretend this little conversation between us never happened. I advise you to do the same. I'm taking you home. After you see the doctor, if you still want to go to Kate's, she can come and pick you up at the house."

My mother accelerated back onto to the road and drove home. Neither of us said another word during the trip there.

41

LOGAN

I kept postponing the inevitable out of fear Drew would push me away. Not that I blamed her. My behavior had been despicable to say the least.

Camilla called me and the guys together for a meeting. We were leaving in two days to head back on tour. She went over city details and time frames. We wouldn't have another extended break for about two months. She went on and on, discussing meet and greets and our new heightened security measures thanks to Liz Piper.

While she spoke, I zoned in and out. The pain in my heart overflowed to other areas of my body, causing my limbs to feel weak and my senses to be dulled. All in all, I felt like shit. Getting myself together had to be a top priority because touring became gruesome. I needed to have focus, stamina, and energy. Right now, I had none of it, no motivation to do anything whatsoever, a first for me.

"Logan... Logan..." I thought I heard a female voice say my name. "Logan!"

Yup, I had. I faced Camilla, devoid of any expression, too numb to show any emotion.

"What in the hell is going on with you?" She gave me a thorough inspection. "You look like something the cat dragged in."

My face had no desire to get involved either. Neither did my mouth. I didn't reply. Basically, my body sat in the meeting, but my mind drifted someplace else, wondering how Drew's head felt, if she had worked things out with her parents, if she hated me. That thought alone had me frowning. Guess my mouth worked after all.

"I'll tell you what's wrong with him." Joey spoke to Camilla, his eyes on mine.

"Don't get involved in my shit, Joey." This time my face showed some movement. Well, mostly my eyes; I glared at him.

"No, man, either shit or get off the pot. I already told you, I'm not going through this shit again with you. We've been down this road before, and I don't want you dragging us down the path of destruction with you."

Camilla put her hand out, clearly not understanding the happenings taking place around her. She studied me, waiting for a response. I didn't give her one. "Logan, does this have something to do with Drew?"

My focus drifted toward the table. Just hearing Drew's name caused searing pain to shoot through my entire body.

"Yes. The asshole left her in the hospital after that shit went down with his stalker, and he hasn't been in touch with her since. The dick somehow thinks she's better off without him. I think he made the right choice, don't you?" Joey sarcasm had me glowering at him.

"Fuck you, Joey!" I stormed out of the room, slamming the door behind me.

I raged down the hall and out the exit, desperate for air. I couldn't breathe, a feeling which had become quite familiar over the last several days.

"Hey."

Shit, Camilla headed toward me. I so didn't want to deal with her.

"Listen here, Logan. I know you've been under a lot of stress these last few weeks with the entire stalker situation and all. It's understandable. But my sense is this has more to do with Drew."

I put my hand up, not wanting to talk to her about this.

"Please, hear me out. I've known you guys for years. When you spend so much time with people, you learn a lot about their idiosyncrasies, their preferences, how they behave in public versus private. I've seen it all. But I've never seen you so despondent. I'm concerned as both your manager and your friend."

Friend?

I leered at her.

"Don't look at me with such disbelief. You know I care about you guys. I also know if you don't patch things up with this girl, that shit you're feeling inside won't disappear. It'll fester and build. As your friend, I don't revel in seeing you hurting. You were over-the-wall ecstatic when you were with her. Shit, you blew off Jessica Hauser at the video shoot. In my wildest dreams, I never would've thought I'd see that happen. But it did, which shows me you're committed to making this thing between you and Drew work. Now as your manager, I can't let you bring this negative energy with you on the bus. It'll affect the entire band. It'll affect your performances at shows. The label has a lot of money riding on you guys to perform well. In your present state, I don't see that happening. You have two days to sort this out before we take off."

"Thanks for the pep talk."

I took off for the parking lot. According to me, the meeting was adjourned.

"Logan!" Camilla called after me.

I ignored her, got in my car, and screeched out of the lot. I didn't know where to go. I had no desire to go to my empty house. I hit my fist on the steering well. "Fuck!"

Listening to tunes, I drove nowhere in particular. Yet somehow I ended up parked in front of Drew's house. I stared at the door for a few minutes, my stomach tied up in knots. I couldn't do this. I put the car in reverse, then noticed the garage door opening. I put the car in park again.

To my surprise, Kate walked outside carrying a few bags. She caught sight of me, set the bags down, and approached my car. I got out and greeted her.

"What're you doing here?" She sounded angry yet also somewhat hopeful.

"I came to see how Drew's doing." My voice disgusted me. It sounded pathetic and desperate.

"Drew's not here." She nodded to the bags sitting on the asphalt next to her car. "I just swung by to get some of her stuff."

"Where is she?" I shoved my hand into my empty pocket.

"I know she would have my head if she knew I told you this, but she's been staying at my place since she got out of the hospital. Things between her and my parents got extremely heated, and she asked if she could stay with me and Joe for a while. I'm on my lunch break, so I told her I'd drop by and pick up more of her things."

"I see. I have to talk to her. Please, Kate."

A fine line appeared between her brows. "I don't think that's such a good idea. She's in a bad place emotionally. You totally screwed her, and as her big sister, I can't let you do it again. It's not fair to her."

"That's why I'm here. I fucked up royally. Let me make things right. I'm leaving in two days, and I can't go with friction between me and Drew."

"Which is all the more reason to leave her alone. You'll go to my place, make your apologies, build up her hopes, and then leave town for who knows how long. You've got to let her move on."

"I can't. I'm in love with her."

"So you've said."

"No. These past few days without her made me realize how empty my life is without her. I'm begging you. I don't do the begging thing. Please let me see her. I can't get in touch with her because her number's been changed. You're my only hope right now."

She sighed heavily and grunted. "You're putting me in a bad position, Logan." She paused as if debating whether to agree or not.

"Fine." She slipped a key off her key ring and handed it to me. "This is the key to my apartment. You can let yourself in. I know if you knock, she won't open the door for you. Please leave my key on the kitchen counter, and whatever you do, *don't* fuck things up this time. I'm warning you. If you think that stalker girl caused harm, you haven't seen anything. I can be a real bitch when I want to be, one of my finer qualities. Now give me your phone number, and I'll text you the address."

The text with her address popped up on my cell a few seconds later.

She pointed a finger at me. "Listen here. She loves you. I know she's going to try to push you away, but don't let her. Don't give up."

"I won't. And thanks."

I gave her a peck on the cheek.

"Yeah, yeah. Go on."

I took Drew's clothing, figuring I might as well bring it with me, and left for Kate's apartment.

42

DREW

The advance from the label was nice, but not enough to pay my bills unless the song became an overnight sensation. Therefore, I searched for jobs on the Internet. Moving back in with my parents was a definite no. My mother thought I kidded when I gave my notice to hire someone else at the clinic.

After my orthopedist appointment, I sat with both of my parents and had a heart-to-heart. I informed them about Logan, because I had no reason to keep it from them. They'd find out sooner or later, especially since I cried nonstop. I could only use the stalker card for so long.

I told them I would stay with Kate temporarily until I found a place of my own. Kate agreed wholeheartedly, thinking I'd made the right decision to get out of their house. And if I had to take fewer classes because of my work schedule, so be it. I wasn't in a rush, especially since the classes I took got me nowhere in my career. Writing was all I wanted to do, and as long as I could incorporate it into my life, I didn't care what path lay ahead of me.

Camilla contacted me to say the label loved my second song as much as the first. I felt hopeful, and with my backbone fully intact, I had the confidence to move forward and leave my past behind me.

The front door unlocked, and I jumped, my lungs working at full capacity. Every unexpected noise startled me since the incident.

Oh yeah, Kate's bringing me more clothes.

It must have been her lunch hour. She told me she would drop more of my stuff off.

"Kate?" I went to the door. My jaw fell open when Logan entered rather than my sister. I didn't know whether to punch him or hug him. At the moment the urge to punch him felt stronger.

"Logan? What're you doing here? And more importantly, how did you get a key to Kate's place?" I didn't budge. I didn't want him to think he'd be staying.

He stood frozen, which made me feel self-conscious. I glanced down at myself. Nope, nothing had changed, the same old me with a few bruises and a cast on my arm.

"Hello?" I said it obnoxiously because he hadn't responded to anything I'd said.

He dropped some bags in the foyer. My clothes? How did he get them? What the hell was wrong with him? He looked out of it. He'd better not be on something. But I knew Logan well enough to know he didn't do drugs. Besides, his eyes were clear, not hazy or red. They were sad, but clear.

"I'm so sorry, Drew."

Sorry didn't cut it this time around. He could take a hike for all I cared.

Fine, I did care, but still, I'd cried my eyes out for the last several days and hadn't heard from him once. And now he showed up at my sister's apartment with a simple apology and bags of my clothes? Sorry, buddy, but actions spoke louder than words. His action of leaving me at the hospital in my shocked and physically harmed state said enough. And Kate would be getting an earful as soon as Logan left regarding the clothing she was supposed to bring me.

"I hope you feel better with that off your chest. But your apology isn't accepted. Now would you please mind leaving? And give me my sister's key. I don't know what you said to her to make her give it to you, but I'll deal with that later." I put my hand out. He didn't place the key in it. I clenched my jaw in frustration. Why wouldn't he listen to me? "The key." I shook my palm to reiterate my request.

"I'll give it to you after you hear me out."

"I don't owe you a damn thing. You got your message across quite effectively the other night."

"No, I didn't."

His gaze darted back and forth between me and the floor. All the color had drained from his face.

A small part of me wanted to hold him in my arms and tell him everything would be okay, but the bigger part said where the fuck was he when I'd needed someone to hold me and tell me everything would be okay?

"You had your chance. It has since passed."

He sighed heavily. "Please. Give me five minutes. If you still want me to leave after, I'll walk out and never bother you again."

Grrr! Stubborn man! I padded to the sofa but changed my mind at the last second and sat on a chair instead. I didn't want him too close to me. Whether I wanted to admit it or not, he still affected me.

I checked the time on the cable box. "Your five minutes starts now."

He sat on the couch, his butt half on, half off, and leaned forward. He stared at the coffee table between us.

"I fucked up again. I shouldn't have left you alone in the hospital. Whether you want to believe me or not, it killed me inside to walk out that door. I thought about all the pain I had caused you and what your parents had said to me about me screwing up your life. So much shit had gone down, and I took their words to heart. Your parents love you and want what's best for you. I do too, which is why I didn't think it was fair for you to have to suffer the consequences of my celebrity status. I wanted to protect you more than anything but my efforts were futile. To see you lying in that hospital bed ripped my heart into pieces. I blame myself for all of it, because if I had done a better job of keeping you safe, none of this would've happened. And if I can't keep you safe, someone I love with all my heart, what can I offer you?"

Trying to hold back my tears didn't work. The tsunami came with a flood to follow. He continued to stare at the table in front of him.

"I've spent the last three days holed up in my place, playing music until my fingers bled. That had always been a source of comfort for me, my go-to to help me collect my thoughts and get centered, but the more I played, the worse I felt. That's never happened to me before, and I realized why. It's because something was missing, and that something was you."

He finally made eye contact with me and saw my tears. I sensed his struggle to want to come and comfort me, but he refrained.

"Logan." I closed my eyes to gather my thoughts. "I can't do the back-and-forth thing anymore. One minute you tell me you love me and want to be with me, that we'll make it work when you're on the road. Then the next minute you tell me you're no good for me and leave. I can't live with your indecisiveness. My heart can only take so much, and you've truly done a number on it."

He stood and walked toward me. I leaned back defensively, watching him, not knowing what action he'd take. To my surprise, he got on his knees and rested his head on my lap. My hand went to his hair, stroking it, without my brain's permission.

Is he crying?

"Logan?" I asked in a soft tone.

He looked up at me, tears filling his eyes. If at all possible, the million shredded pieces of my heart fell apart even more.

"Please give me another chance. I need you in my life. I want you in my life. You belong in my life."

"I hear you, but you're leaving town in a few days. I just don't see how it can work." My tears continued to trail down my cheeks, and I sniffled. The pain in my head came back with a vengeance. It had actually started to feel better too.

"It'll work because I want you to join us on tour."

Say what?

"Joey's girlfriend, Teva, travels with us. She helps Dani with meet and greets and other backstage stuff. As an aside, Dani and Trevor are together. I'm not sure if I told you that, but it's neither here nor there. The bottom line is I want you to be with me. You can bring your guitar with you. You'll have plenty of time to work on your music. And if it's money you're worried about, I have enough for both of us to live very comfortably. If you don't feel content with that, I'll have Camilla put you on payroll, and you can work with Teva and Dani..."

He rambled on and on. With my good arm I managed to hoist him up enough so I could see into his eyes. "Are you serious about this?"

"As serious as a heart attack. I love you, Drew Sanders. You are my one and only. You always have been, and you always will be. Please say you'll at least consider joining me and the guys on tour." His eyes had such desperation in them.

"I don't have to think about it. My mind's already made up."

He swallowed hard, blinking rapidly.

"I'd love to join you on tour. I can't think of anything else I'd rather do."

"God, I love you so much, baby." He suffocated me in his arms, being ever so careful of my ribs.

"And I love you so much."

43

LOGAN

Packing for the road felt good. I couldn't wait to feel the energy from the crowd again and be with the guys, my brothers. I had them over for dinner along with Teva and Dani because I wanted Drew to reconnect with Dani and meet Teva prior to being locked up on a bus with them.

Dani lovingly embraced Drew, and the two of them spoke as if it had only been days since they'd last seen each other.

Teva, inevitably a doll baby, accepted Drew with open arms.

Drew's parents weren't too keen on the idea of her getting on a tour bus and traveling the country with me and the guys. I hoped with time they would change their mind about me. I loved Drew with all my heart and knew no other man would ever love her as much as I did.

Camilla officially took Drew on as a client, managing her career, and our entertainment lawyer did the same. I knew in my gut Drew's songs would take off. Camilla also informed me and the guys that the producer loved the song Joey and Dani penned for his movie project and wanted us to record it. I couldn't stop smiling. To think, one of our songs would close out a movie. What a fucking head rush.

Drew relished every place we visited, saying she had never been anywhere and wanted to see the world. Every chance we got, she wanted to sightsee, even if just to eat at a hometown restaurant. Her excitement was contagious. It became somewhat of a game between all of us. We would research different places we wanted to visit prior to arriving at our next destination. Drew brought a ton of creative and positive energy with her, and both the girls and guys alike loved having her around, especially me.

A few weeks into the tour, we had two shows booked in the same town. I surprised Drew by reserving us a hotel room. After the first show, I had Tyler, who now worked with the band round-the-clock along with Steve, drive us to the hotel.

"Where are we going?" She snuggled into my arms in the backseat of the Escalade.

"You'll see when we get there."

"How about a hint?"

"Nope." I wouldn't give her an inch.

Tyler pulled up to the valet. He informed the attendants we wouldn't be requiring their services. He

left us alone in the car to go inside and check us in. I snagged a baseball cap out of my backpack and covered my head. I couldn't chance a mob scene taking place in the lobby. Our popularity seemed to have doubled over the last few weeks, and day by day we became more recognized, which was why the label had agreed to hire more security. They didn't want another Liz Piper disaster taking place if they could prevent one.

"Are we staying here?" Drew checked out the grand hotel from inside the SUV.

"We sure are."

She bounced up and down in her seat. It thrilled me to see her so happy. I had always held back financially, but now with Drew in the picture, I spared no expense. I wanted to make her dream come true and show her the world. And I would, city by city, state by state, country by country, until the two of us saw it all.

"All set." Tyler assisted me and Drew out of the car.

He led us through the lobby. An attendant had an elevator waiting and didn't allow any other passengers to ride inside with us.

Tyler would be staying in the adjacent room, so I'd have to consciously try to keep my moans down to a minimum, not an easy task when buried inside Drew.

She and I entered our suite.

"Holy shit." She dropped her purse on the floor. I dropped my backpack next to me and took in the scene along with her: marble floors, plush leather sofas, a plasma television mounted on the wall, and granite countertops in the small kitchen. "Was all this truly necessary?"

"Are you happy?"

"Ecstatic!"

"Then yes, it's truly necessary."

She jumped into my arms. I stepped back a few feet because I almost lost my balance.

Since I already had her in my arms, I took her into the bedroom. I considered it to be the best place to start a tour in a hotel room, at least in my experience it had been.

The bedroom had the same amount of luxury as the rest of the place—plush carpet, stately mahogany wood furniture, large television mounted on the wall, definitely first class.

I placed her on the bed.

She scanned the room. "It's so beautiful."

"As are you."

She smiled, pink spread across her cheeks. I loved that I could still do that to her.

"So, Ms. Sanders, did you enjoy the show?"

"I did, especially the *hot* guitarist." She raised a brow and licked her lips.

"You're in luck then, because I'm extremely selective with the women I choose to bring into my bed."

"Really? And what is it that catches your eye?"

"That's a simple question for me to answer. First of all, I prefer women with small feet, like yours." I slipped off her canvas sneakers and tossed them aside.

"I'm glad I passed that test. What else?"

"I prefer my women to be naked, so these jeans have to go." I lifted her up and unsnapped her denims.

"I wouldn't want you to think ill of me." She spoke with faux innocence.

"Could have fooled me. Here you came on to me after a show, and you're worried about whether I'll respect you in the morning?"

She pressed her lips together. "If I can recall correctly, I believe you"—she pointed at me— "came on to me." She pointed at herself.

"Does it matter? I have you here in my bedroom, don't I?"

"You're just full of yourself, aren't you?"

"I'd prefer to fill you, babe."

"Wow, and crude too."

"I can be pretty cocky. Speaking of which." I pointed to the bulge in my jeans. "Care to help me out?"

"I'd love to."

She unfastened my denims. I assisted to expedite the process.

"As I was saying, I prefer women who have soft legs. Take your gams, for example. Gorgeous." I glided my hands up her freshly shaven skin, like silk.

I kissed her ankles, her knees, her inner thighs. She squirmed under my touch.

"This here is one of my favorite parts." I snuck my finger underneath her panties and swiped it between her folds. Her liquid heat fired me up to no end.

"Yeah?" She was already breathless. She raised her pelvis so I could get the barely there underwear off.

"Yes, ma'am." I inhaled deeply, her scent intoxicating me. "I have to say I've never smelled anything so tempting and inviting in all my life." I peered up at her to find her cheeks a deeper shade of red.

"Add blunt to your charming personality."

I grinned, leaning forward and tasting her. I closed my eyes. Every time I ate her out, the experience got better. I couldn't understand it but went with it.

She angled her pelvis toward my mouth. She loved when I went down on her. She wouldn't say it outwardly, too embarrassed, but I knew her truth. The woman became unhinged, ready to blow the minute my tongue flicked her clit, which it did right now.

She widened the space between her legs. I spread her lips and sucked on her, running my tongue down to her opening, probing her entrance.

"Mmm."

I could relate to her sentiment, my cock stirring in response.

No flesh remained untouched. I did a few laps around the area, consuming her, feasting on her as if I hadn't been fed in days. Hell, it hadn't even been twenty-four hours since we'd last fucked.

My pinky took a trip around back. She tensed.

With the flat of my tongue, I applied steady pressure to her clit.

Her body began to shake, my cue to slide my little finger in her ass.

"Oh my God, Logan!" She screamed at me and for me.

It didn't stop me from continuing. Her body writhed underneath me. I had discovered my sweet girl reveled in this new type of play. Yay for me.

After removing my mouth and releasing my finger, I climbed over her, keeping my hand a good distance from her. I didn't want to kill the mood by washing it just yet. It would have to wait.

Her lids remained partially closed, her gaze met mine.

"I guess the tabloids are right about you. You are the bad boy of Steam."

"That's right, babe, and you're the special woman who captured my heart and ruined it for all others."

She kissed me, winding her arms around my neck at the same time. Her tongue led mine, rolling over it, the two of them together having a party.

She pulled away.

"What is it?" I was unsure of why she broke our intense connection.

"Hand me my phone."

"What? You want me to get your phone?" Talk about ruining a moment.

She nodded.

"Okay." I sighed and got off the bed.

Since I was up, I cleaned my hands in the bathroom, then retrieved her phone from her purse in the foyer.

I handed her the device. She tapped the screen, and music started to play.

I recognized the song immediately, David Soul's "Don't Give Up On Us."

My heart softened, emotion overtaking me. This had been our song back in the day. Who would've thought the lyrics would turn out to be a metaphor for me and Drew?

I said my thanks every night that she hadn't given up on me—or us, for that matter.

A tear leaked out of her eye. I wiped it away. We stared at each other for a few seconds.

When I resumed kissing her, I took control of the tongue situation, using mine in a milder, less heated manner with hers. David's soulful voice chimed in the background.

It reminded me of the night when I had taken Drew's virginity. We were at my house. My parents were out for the evening. The two of us had been dating for several months. Drew had dragged it out for as long as possible until she gave me the go-ahead. I could still picture her naivety as the two of us undressed. I had my own chunk of nerves going on.

All awkwardness left when I held her in my arms. Nature took over, telling us both what to do. Not the greatest sexual encounter of my life but undoubtedly the most memorable. And all the love I felt for her then had grown by leaps and bounds.

She wrapped her legs around me, in the same manner she'd done the first time we made love. I closed my eyes. Tears now pooled in them. I didn't understand why I was crying. We'd had more than our fair share of bedroom fun over these past few weeks. I guess something about the moment, the music playing, the fact we were actually together all these years later when we should've never parted in the first place. Heady stuff.

But in a way, I felt grateful I had experienced so many other women. It made me appreciate Drew all the more. Like I had just told her, she was the one who'd captured my heart and ruined it for all others, permanently.

As I eased in and out of her in a steady rhythm, my eyes flicked open to find tears leaking out of hers as well. We gazed at each another, our bodies again letting nature take over and do its thing.

Pressure began to build, and I closed my eyes again, my body tensing over hers as I emptied myself into her, giving her all of me in the process.

She arched her back and moaned, her body freely giving in to her orgasm. I watched how beautifully she succumbed to the pleasure filling her. A sense of peace and contentment emanated from her. Her lips parted slightly and a soft breath escaped her.

She opened her eyes to find me staring. Her cheeks were again a pretty shade of pink, this time from the aftermath of lovemaking.

"Wait here a minute. I have something for you."

She gave me a questioning look. I pulled out of her and rolled off the bed. My backpack still sat on the floor in the foyer. I grabbed the box I'd hidden inside it when I'd packed my overnight bag and brought it to the bedroom.

She shifted onto her stomach, lying flat but resting on her elbows, her succulent naked body sprawled out on the bed. What a magnificent sight.

"What's that?" She nodded toward the gift in my hand.

I handed her the box and sat next to her on the bed.

"Open it and see."

"You bought me a present?"

She sat up hurriedly and placed her hand over her heart, her whole face lighting up. She took the box from me and opened it. Her jaw fell open when she saw the diamond bracelet with a white-gold heart charm hanging from it.

She flipped it over in her hand, reveling in its brilliance.

"It's beautiful, Logan." She smiled warmly.

"Did you read what's inscribed on the heart?"

She inspected the charm. I had the jeweler I'd purchased the bracelet from engrave the letters *L* and *D* and the word *forever* on it, just like I had engraved on the plank of wood at the cabin back at the ranch all those years ago.

"Oh my gosh. How thoughtful and wonderful. I love it. I love you!" She jumped on my lap, almost making me fall back, and hugged me.

I brushed her long hair off her face and cradled her cheek in my palm. "And I love you, *forever*."

The End

Sign up here for Faith's newsletter and receive **bonus** chapters of Hold Me, Promise To Fulfill, and Risk Worth Taking. Plus, get inside info, pre-sales of new releases, and follow the women from the Hilltops Series in their Heroines of Hilltops corner.

OTHER TITLES BY FAITH STARR

Faith Starr's books are all standalones but are best read in sequence

The HILLTOPS Series
Destiny
Purity
Diversity

The MUSIC FOR THE HEART Series
Hold Me
Promise to Fulfill
Risk Worth Taking
Remember Me
The Right Time
Holding Out
Jonas's story...

NOVELLAS
Sinful Agreement

Other Titles by Faith Starr

Sign up here for Faith's newsletter and receive bonus chapters of Hold Me, Promise To Fulfill, and Risk Worth Taking. Plus, get inside info, pre-sales of new releases, and follow the women from the Hilltops Series in their Heroines of Hilltops corner.

For more information about upcoming releases, please visit her website:
www.faithstarr.com

Follow Faith Starr on:
Pinterest (A true Pinterest junkie)
Instagram
Facebook

PLEASE REVIEW MY BOOK

Dear Reader,

Book reviews mean a lot to an author. If you have a minute or two, I'd appreciate it if you could please provide an honest, sincere review.

Thanks so much!
    Faith

MEET FAITH STARR

My outside world includes managing my husband's medical practice, being a mom to three wonderful kids and two dogs. My inside world is where I find inner fulfillment and purpose. It includes escaping to the confines of my home office to write romance fiction, my passion.

For me, there is absolutely nothing like creating fictional characters, getting into their minds, and giving them a life of their own with all the emotions that go along with it. I am swept away, head over heels in love, with each and every alpha male I create and the confident women who steal their hearts. These characters have become a part of me that will live on forever.

Being a romantic at heart, with a bit of a dirty mind, I relish in creating believable stories that touch upon readers' heartstrings, provoke thought, and hopefully provide a bit of insight into some heavy topics.

Being married since 1995—wow, how time flies—I am a firm believer in the concept of "Once Upon a Time" and "Happily Ever After"

Meet Faith Starr

because I have found mine. Aww, I know, so mushy. But that's me in a nutshell, a softie with a big heart, just like my characters! A bit of a nut too.

ACKNOWLEDGMENTS

Writing Logan and Drew's story took me on many highs and lows. The playlist combined with the characters deep love and affection for one another did my heart in repeatedly.

With that being said, I wouldn't have been able to get their story from idea, to script, to my readers, without the support of some special and important people who assisted me during the process.

Ann Curtis who originally gave me the chance of a lifetime. You will forever have my gratitude. You did me in on this one, that's for sure. I learned a ton. I may have complained about the overwhelming amount of revisions to my husband, but in the end, all the hard work paid off. Thank you.

Rebecca Fairfax. You have taught me more than you could ever imagine with your suggestions and feedback, giving me a sharper eye in the process. Thanks for all your support, both editing related and otherwise. I'm blessed to have the opportunity to work with you. Thank you.

Kelly Ann Martin for creating covers that rock, no pun intended. You are truly talented in your craft. I love your work, your enthusiasm, and your dedication. Here's to many more covers together!

Glow for your enthusiasm to continue reading my initial drafts, paying

Acknowledgments

special attention to details, providing genuine and straightforward feedback, for your encouragement, friendship, and trust. You're amazing.

The wonderful bloggers who give me their time and read my stories. I am truly grateful.

My mom for always believing in me and encouraging me to trudge along even when I complain how exhausted and burned-out I am. And for promoting my books to everyone you meet even though I won't let you read them. You have been, are, and always will be my biggest fan. I love you.

My dad, who may no longer be with me physically but who I know is watching over me, encouraging me to continue following my dream, just like Drew does in this story.

My three beautiful children for being patient, encouraging me to never give up and chase the dream, supportive, understanding of my endless hours sitting in front of my computer, and accepting (hopefully) my particular genre of writing. Still, like grandma, you guys aren't allowed to read my books. I love you all. You inspire me in ways you'll never know.

My loving husband for being patient, considerate, and understanding of the tireless hours spent in front of my computer. Thank you for giving me the space I need to let my creativity shine, for being a constant sounding board, and for providing wonderful ideas and feedback before, during, and after the writing process. Your input is fantastic and greatly appreciated. But most of all, thank you for affirming my belief that true love exists. You inspire my hero's in ways you can't even imagine. I love you with all my heart. Always and forever.

My higher power for giving me the inner strength to persevere even when I want to throw in the towel and give up; you are my eternal guiding light. I am forever grateful for your wisdom and guidance.

RISK WORTH TAKING MUSIC PLAYLIST

David Soul - "Don't Give Up On Us Baby" – Logan and Drew's song. Played it a million times during their final scenes and pretty much cried every time!
    Westlife
    Scorpions
    Def Leppard – "Love Bites", "Foolin'", "Bringin' On the Heartbreak"
    The Baby's
    Electric Light Orchestra
    Cliff Richard – "Devil Woman", "We Don't Talk Anymore"
    '70's Playlist on YouTube
    Toto – I Won't Hold You Back

Made in the USA
Middletown, DE
27 July 2025

11314969R00217